# A Founder for All

**Abraham Clark, signer of the Declaration of Independence**

BARB BALTRINIC

Knowing our past helps us protect our future!

Barb Baltrinic

*A Founder For All*
*Abraham Clark, Signer of the Declaration of Independance*


This is a work of historical fiction. While most names and places in the story are real, dialogue and much of the narative is a product of the author's imagination.

First Paperback Edition: December 2012

Cover and Interior Design by D. Robert Pease
www.walkingstickbooks.com

*Published in the United States of America*

*To Mike and Mark*

*Honor Your Roots*

# Table of Contents

Chapter 1: Just a Boy on the Farm .......... 1
Chapter 2: Education .......... 27
Chapter 3: The Surveyor and Counselor .......... 39
Chapter 4: Marriage and Family .......... 59
Chapter 5: Facing Personal Losses .......... 79
Chapter 6: Civil Unrest .......... 97
Chapter 7: Election to the New Jersey Provincial Congress .......... 113
Chapter 8: The Declaration is Conceived .......... 129
Chapter 9: Continental Congress .......... 147
Chapter 10: The Declaration is Finalized .......... 161
Chapter 11: The Signing .......... 177
Chapter 12: The War Intensifies in 1776 .......... 193
Chapter 13: 1777 .......... 213
Chapter 14: 1778 .......... 235
Chapter 15: 1779 .......... 257
Chapter 16: 1780 Brings Elizabethtown Down .......... 269
Chapter 17: The End of 1780 .......... 295
Chapter 18: 1781 .......... 313

Chapter 19: 1782....................................................................331
Chapter 20: 1783....................................................................343
Chapter 21: 1784-1786.............................................................353
Chapter 22: 1787-1788 The Constitution...................................373
Chapter 23: 1789....................................................................389
Chapter 24: 1791-1794.............................................................411
Chapter 25: The Death of Abraham Clark...............................425
Acknowledgments.....................................................................439
About the Author.......................................................................443
Historical Background..............................................................445

# Chapter 1
# Just a Boy on the Farm

**Abra walked at a healthy pace**, yet not so fast that it winded him. King's Highway was really just a lane and half wide, but it was the principal route from New York to Philadelphia. The occasional traffic on King's Highway was typically the only thing that disturbed the quiet of the Elizabethtown community. Abra looked around at the familiar landscape and relished the early morning air which hit his face.

It was 1739, and life was pretty simple in the New Jersey farmlands. Abra Clark knew the history of his small town in New Jersey and could easily point out the early landmarks, including the saw mill, corn mill, and the tan yard up the river. His great-great grandfather, Richard Clarke, had been one of the early settlers of the region, having been a shipbuilder who migrated from New York to settle in New Jersey in 1678. Richard had taken 300 acres of farm land, and had also secured land for three of his children when he moved to the area. That land remained in Clark hands, divided up among the many Clark relations in Elizabethtown, New Jersey. Richard had continued ship building, but eventually many of the Clarks enjoyed farming as their trade.

Abra shook his head to push the thought of farming from his head. He didn't know what he wanted to do when he was grown, but he knew that farming was not it. Not even the building of ships could interest him, although he heard many stories from his father and uncle about the various ships that their ancestor had built. Today small ships came to port along the wharfs by Ogden's Mills and trade flourished for the still small settlement located along the Elizabeth River, yet Abra never found the shipbuilding trade interesting.

Abra continued his brisk walk, nodding to a passerby as he passed one of the taverns along the way. Several taverns were on this main thoroughfare, including the Terrill Tavern where many travelers stayed the night during their travel. Despite the absence of much traffic on the King's Highway, people always waved or made friendly salutations when passing through this community. Abra had never known people to not be content. It was a time of peace in Elizabethtown.

Abra briefly glanced at the book he had just borrowed. He couldn't wait to begin reading. He wished that his school offered more books, but borrowing from neighbors had become Abra's habit. Abra knew his teacher and his parents thought highly of his academic abilities. He excelled in his studies and could repeat verbatim what he learned in school. He could readily recount the early origins of Elizabethtown as the first permanent English settlement in New Jersey. His teacher had carefully explained how a group of Englishmen of New York wanted to colonize New Jersey. Richard Nicolls, the Duke of York's deputy governor, gave permission to purchase a large expanse of land from the Lenni Lenape Indians. Chief Mattano had signed the deed and it became known as the *Elizabethtown Purchase*. The schoolmaster had told the students, which were mostly young boys, that Elizabethtown had been named after Sir George Carteret's wife. Carteret had been one of the Proprietors of Carolina while serving as Treasurer of the English Navy.

Abra chuckled to himself when he remembered the argument between several of the boys after church as to the naming of the settlement. Young Evans believed it was named after Queen Elizabeth of England, but he was quickly put to rights by one of the elders of the church. "Master Evans. Those who do not know the history of their land will certainly display a lack of commitment in protecting it when time demands it." Evans turned a deep shade of red when he was reprimanded. "It was Carteret who became involved in the evolving government of what we now call New Jersey. This very place was named after his wife in recognition for his work in securing our place among the colonies." The elder walked away, and Evans would have made a wry face had he not noticed his friends looked equally stunned that they had not known this tidbit of information.

Abra had thought himself lucky that he had paid attention in class the day this information had been shared.

Abra enjoyed school and especially enjoyed learning about the history. He practically memorized the lessons taught by his teacher and would return home and repeat them to his father and mother. “Father, did you know that Carteret borrowed the ideas from the Carolina Colony for the Concession and Agreement which provided freedom of religion for Christians in New Jersey back in 1665, a year after the colony was founded?”

Thomas Clark looked at his son’s face and pride swelled within him. Abra was becoming a young man capable of carrying on a meaningful conversation with adults. Thomas enjoyed hearing his son’s enthusiasm about history especially since he had not been afforded the opportunity to complete his schooling because of the large farm responsibilities of the Clark family. Thomas looked at his son who stood anxiously awaiting acknowledgement from his father. Abra often would repeat a piece of history to his father, and then wait to see how his father reacted. Thomas knew that his response would affect the way Abra would digest the history he was learning.

“Abra, once Carteret protected the right of religious freedom, we saw many new churches spring up around the area.” It was true. There were many churches within the limits of Elizabethtown and its surrounding communities. The Clarks belonged to the Presbyterian Church which was just a log building. His father and others of the church were pushing to build a more formal church as the population of the area was increasing. Abra was proud that Elizabethtown was one of the oldest settlements in New Jersey and the people, no matter what their version of religious practice, lived peacefully side by side. Elizabethtown was certainly an archetype of what the colonies had wished to establish in the new country.

As Abra pondered these memories, he was fast approaching the Clark farm. The family farm was in an area of Elizabethtown called Rahway. Abra's great grandfather, Richard, had owned all this area, and Abra's grandfather, Richard, had taken over this parcel of land to farm. It seemed that with each generation the land got divided and passed down to the next generation. Abra sighed as he thought that one day he, too, would be expected to take over the family farm duties.

Abra Clark turned into the dirt lane which led to his home. Abra searched the landscape to see if his father were anywhere near. Abra wanted to be rebellious by not returning home and jumping into the farm chores which he knew awaited him. His eyes searched for a tree which would shield him from the now burning sun. Abra found his spot and he relaxed when he did not see his father nearby. Abra stretched his tall, lean body out under the tree and pulled opened the book he had just borrowed from Mr. Ross. His book rested on his chest as his eyes greedily searched the pages. He enjoyed reading about ancient history and the changing tide of civilizations. It was not long before Abra was lost in the pages.

Thomas Clark had been working in the fields since early morning and was curious as to why his son had not joined him. He had walked back to the house and did not see Abra, so he walked toward the highway in search of him. Abra was so absorbed in his book he did not realize his father had stepped beside him and was looking down at him under his straw hat.

Thomas stood shaking his head and wondering why he had to ask his son to help with work on the farm. Although he was proud of his son's aptitude in learning, he was disappointed that Abra was not a willing assistant at his chores. Abra resisted the manual labor his father demanded. It wasn't that he was lazy; he just didn't care about the day-to-day chores of farm life. He also became flushed with the effort farming demanded and tired easily.

The Clark farm was a nice piece of property and the gentle rolling hills produced much food, albeit at the hand of Thomas and his few hired workers. It was not a large farm, but it was enough to produce necessities for his home and for trade. The largest part of the farm was corn, which was able to fend for itself once planted. The beans, however, required more assistance. Thomas looked down at his son who was oblivious to his father's presence. Abra's slender hand effortlessly turned the page of his book.

"Abra. I need your help today."

Abra was startled and looked up at his father who was looming above him, outlined by the sun at his back. Abra slowly dropped his book, and turning his head slightly away from his father, he rolled his eyes. "Help doing what?" asked Abra. Thomas looked at him with a look of exasperation. "Sorry, father. Where do you need my help?" Abra immediately felt remorse for feeling put out by his father's request.

"I want to break up the ground around the beans. We've not had enough rain this season, but word is rain is on the way." Thomas knew the soil needed to be broken so the water would soak in to nourish the roots of the plants. The ground had become so hard the rain would likely roll off and the much needed rain would be of little value.

Abra knew this work would be more than a day's labor. He preferred the quiet of apple and peach picking as he could stand and stretch as he worked rather than hunching over his back in the rows of carefully grown bean plants. Fruit picking was far less labor intensive than the summer crops Thomas planted. Abra wished his father would get more hired men to work the fields. The hired men were working at the neighboring farm this week, so Thomas only had his son to assist him. Abra plucked a piece of grass and carefully tucked it into the seam of the book to mark his spot in the book, then pushed himself up and headed toward the house. He found himself wishing he had a brother, a younger brother, one that he could delegate to work in his place, thus leaving more free time to read. It was hard being an only child. There were times Abra felt lonely on the farm. His father, Thomas, was typically a quiet man unless he got involved in a discussion with neighbors or his brother, Abraham. Abraham was not only Thomas' brother, but his best friend. Abra always admired the relationship his father and uncle had, and often wished he had a sibling who would be his confidant and friend. As Abra strode toward the house, Thomas looked after his son, then took his hoe in hand and walked toward the bean field.

The Clark house was white clapboard and it had a small porch on the front. It had been built in 1705 on the Clark farm halfway between Elizabethtown and the center of Rahway. It was built by Thomas Clark, Sr., just five years before he died. Thomas Sr. left his wife, Hannah Norris with four young sons to raise, Thomas Jr. being the oldest at age six. A family relation had come to help on the farm and Thomas consistently worked with him in the fields, learning from an early age the responsibilities of farm life. Thomas quickly gave up his childhood in order to help support his mother and brothers. His entire childhood was spent in the fields, and as he grew, his responsibilities increased. He often took his younger brothers into the field and had acted the paternal role in teaching them the workings of the farm. Thomas did not recall a childhood as his life had been a constant memory of hard work and sacrifice. Despite this, Thomas remained happy as farming as a natural vocation for him. He felt the soil was as close to him as any relative or friend could be. The soil responded well to Thomas' care and yielded an abundance of food for the young family.

Thomas was married to the land, until he met Hannah Winans. One look in her eyes and his heart was overtaken. Hannah was slight of frame, and Thomas imagined himself her caregiver, just as he was the caregiver of the farm. When he married, the house was given to him by his mother. It was in this house that Thomas and Hannah raised young Abraham, or Abra as he was called by family.

As Abra walked toward the house and could see his mother working over a large bowl. Hannah Winans Clark was a small woman with her hair tightly pulled back from around her well defined face. Abra loved to listen to the stories his mother would tell him about her family, the Winans and the Melyns, and their beginnings in the colonies when they were newly formed. It was Hannah's grandfather, John Winans, who had emigrated from Holland and became one of the eighty associates who founded Elizabethtown in 1664. His wife, Susanna Melyn, was the daughter of Cornelius Melyn who came from Amsterdam to the colonies where he had an order granting him most of Staten Island. Eventually Cornelius and his wife, Jannetie Adriaens, settled in New Haven, Connecticut. Their daughter, Susanna, married John Winans and they moved to Elizabethtown. It was Hannah's habit to carefully enter all the names in the family Bible, and

Abra would sometimes sit and try to remember how all these families were related. Neighbors and friends throughout the area were interconnected through the Winans, the Melyns, and the Clarks. Hannah's parents, Samuel and Zerviah, only had two children, Hannah and Samuel, however there seemed to Abra to be dozens of cousins and other relations, all confused by the use of the same names. Whenever his parents talked of family, Abra would pull out the Bible to reaffirm who was being discussed.

When Abra entered the kitchen his mother was mixing dough for bread. She looked up and brushed a stray hair away from her brow, and wiped her hands on her apron as she heard her son enter the house. "Abra, put on your old breeches so that you don't ruin that pair. You continue to outgrow your clothing faster than I can replace it."

Abra nodded to his mother and walked to his room, a small enclosure with a bed and a chest for his clothing. No one would call Abra lazy, but it was clear that he did not enjoy physical labor. He knew that being the only child meant that he had little choice but to be of service to his father. He was thankful that the farm was one of the smaller plots in the Elizabethtown area. Abra dropped his book on his bed and pulled out his old pants from the chest. There was a tear starting in the knee area, and he knew he would have to be careful not to rip it apart. He could not bear to make more work for his mother. She was fragile and small and Abra's heart softened whenever he was in her presence.

Hannah Winans was a firm Presbyterian and enjoyed singing the church hymns at home, but was never brave enough to join the church choir. Hannah's ability to read was limited to Bible passages and occasional letters she received from family. Her life on the Clark farm revolved around cleaning, cooking, and working the small vegetable garden near the back door of the house. She also had a small patch of wildflowers which she would occasionally clip and bring into the sparse house. She was soft spoken and when she spoke with her son, her fingers would comb through his hair as she gazed directly into his face. Abra enjoyed listening to his mother's soft voice when she would sing while working, thinking no one could hear her. Before leaving the house Abra leaned over his mother's shoulder and laughed aloud. "You are beating that bread dough as if you were trying to whip the devil out of it!"

Hannah chuckled and elbowed his son away from her. "You'd best remember that I can pack a mighty wallop when I need to, young man!" She smiled at her son who was already as tall as she and growing quite handsome.

Abra laughed and said, "I think the only thing that has ever seen your mighty wallops are the butter churn, bread and pie dough and the chickens that peck in your garden!" Abra gave his mother a quick kiss, pulled his hat down over his eyes, and stepped outside. He was not far from the house when he heard the sweet strains of his mother's voice singing.

Thomas was right about upcoming rain. The air was thick

and the sun hot. Abra picked up one of the hoes from the wagon and walked out toward the fields at a pace that was less than enthusiastic. Thomas' head was bent to the task and he did not look up as his son moved quietly into place across from him. Abra followed next to his father working the hoe between the plants, careful not to dig too closely as the plants looked dry at their base. In his mind Abra created races against his father to determine who would get to the end of the row most quickly. This seemed like a way to pass the time as the Clark men were not overly talkative when alone. Abra pretended that there was a prize awaiting the one who finished the row the fastest. This game was futile as Thomas was strong and exact in his movements. Abra had to work hard to keep up with his father. Thomas knew he son was putting forth effort to keep pace with him, so he slowed slightly in order to keep his son with him rather than moving forward and not working side by side. Thomas looked into his son's face from time to time and studied the intent look Abra wore. Abra was thirteen that summer and his frame was growing every day. His hat covered his eyes but Thomas could see his son's mouth was firmly set. Thomas smiled because he knew when his son put his mind to something, he was a hard worker.

Father and son worked silently and diligently throughout the late morning, stopping only to drink from the ladle in the bucket of water which Thomas moved to the end of the row they worked.

Thomas was a respected man in Elizabethtown, New Jersey, and was called upon to serve as a judge. The townsmen thought of him as being a fair and honest man. It was Thomas' brother, Abraham, who encouraged Thomas to take on the position, especially since farming was seasonal work.

Thomas' brother, Abraham Clark, was a military man and was knowledgeable about politics. He knew about all the recent taxes on non-British molasses the colonists were importing to be made into rum. There was much talk about how the colonists were not allowed to make decisions for themselves, and how they had no say about the increase in taxes for necessities, like molasses. Many colonists used the molasses in cooking, but they also used it to make rum and the added tax would increase that cost. Abraham was quite vocal about taxes and the rights of the colonists. When Abra overheard this conversation he ventured a comment of his own. "Perhaps the King is trying to tax us on sinning, after all too much rum is not good for the soul!" Both Thomas and Abraham laughed at Abra's wit.

Thomas so admired his brother that he and Hannah were in total agreement to name their only son after him. It was because Abraham lived so close and visited so often that Thomas and Hannah called their son, "Abra" in order to avoid the confusion in their conversations. Thomas hoped one day his son would live up to the name he had been given and be proud to be called "Abraham" by his peers.

Thomas continued breaking the dirt clods around the young plants. Thomas looked at his son and thought it was a good time to broach a topic he had been avoiding. "Your Uncle Abraham says that the King is raising taxes to offset his war. I will have to make the farm larger in order to pay the additional expenses. With you leaving for school, I will probably need to hire on some extra help."

Abra at first felt a twinge of guilt that his father was put into a position to do more work because he wanted an education for his son. Abra felt a twinge of panic as he considered that he might have to quit school and work the farm. He selfishly offered a quick alternative. "Father, I can cut back on some of the expenses and borrow more books for my classes," Abra offered.

"The cost of your books is meager by comparison to what the King is levying against us. First it was the Molasses Act back in '33, and it seems that expenses keep going up each year. King George needs more money to finance his latest war, and his first choice is to place his financing on the back of the colonies. I hate to see the colonists forced into cheating, yet they are smuggling molasses in order to avoid paying the taxes. That can only lead to more enforcement coming from Britain. Your education is important, Abra. Your mother and I will get by. We always do. Meanwhile, let's see if we can get through at least two more rows before we go in for dinner. Later we can come out and work the soil until dusk."

Abra nodded and felt ashamed that he had balked about

helping his father. Thomas never complained about costs. Other farmers had more children so there were extra hands to help on their family farms. With no siblings, it left Abra to be the only assistant his father had. The thought of slavery was not appealing to Thomas or any of his neighbors who had strong Quaker values which had remained in the area long after the Quakers left it. Often complaints among the men were voiced that the land owners of the southern states were able to accumulate wealth, but on the backs of owned men through slavery. Many of the northern land owners hired on indentured servants, mostly men from Ireland looking to get ahead in the new world but not being able to afford the costs of moving. Abra's uncle had told them that nearly half of the population was indentured servants in states like Virginia. Virginia had begun their indentured servant trade back in the early 1600's when England gave the landowner an additional fifty acres as a head right for buying indentured servants from England. The investment paid off as Virginia was able to build huge farms run mostly by these men. Since Virginia produced tobacco, a very labor intensive crop, the English provided them with many indentured servants as the majority of the Virginian crops were exported. There were also Negroes purchased and owned by some of the larger landowners, but around Elizabethtown, most of the farms only used indentured servants.

Abra heard that many land owners were cruel to their indentured men, but locally the farmers appeared to be fair to their workers. Abra had heard talk of many runaways who couldn't take the brutality of their masters. Although posters were made to look for the missing servant, they were rarely found. Uncle Abraham said many would leave for the frontier and face the savages rather than the brutality of their owners. Abra pondered that perhaps it was the influence of the church that kept the local farmers in line.

Thomas shared a contract of two men with Mr. Hendricks, a landowner near him. Hendricks had a larger farm, so he paid more of the contract. Thomas' farm was just less than three hundred acres along the Elizabeth River. There was no way Thomas and Abra could have done all the farming alone, so it was necessary to get help. The servants' papers were bought through a ship captain and the contracts lasted seven years. Thomas' men would travel between the two farms and help with the fields during planting season and other jobs on the farms during the winter months. Often they would do home repair and furniture making and repair the farm tools and equipment. Thomas' men had their own quarters located between the two farms. They were loud men with thick Irish accents. Abra enjoyed working alongside them because they, unlike his father, would talk the entire time sharing stories from back home and stories filled with morals that all children should learn. Even Thomas would laugh aloud at some of the tales told by Egan and Ronan. Egan's wife, Deirdre, would occasionally come to the Clark farm to help Hannah with preserves and pickling. Deirdre was an excellent cook and at times when Hannah was ill, Deirdre would fill the house with the aroma of pot pies filled with corn, tomatoes, peas and beans. Deirdre worked mostly at the other farm as their cook and housekeeper, so Thomas rarely had Deirdre come to the house unless Hannah was in need of additional help. The Hendricks family had many young children so Deirdre was needed to help with housework and the babies.

Some of Abra's friends saw their mothers working in the fields; however Thomas was resistant of such work and allowed Hannah to only work the small vegetable garden next to the house. Hannah had lost a lot of blood when Abra was born, and although she recovered, she was never as strong as she had been before. Thomas was very protective of her and did not want her working in the larger fields. Despite this, Hannah was never still. She was always working on something and always took the time to talk to both Thomas and her son. Unlike many women in town, Hannah seemed to truly listen when her men talked, and she was unafraid when it came to sharing her opinion.

Abra and his father finished off three more rows, and Thomas smiled as it was he who had to keep up with Abra's newfound energy. It was a bit later than usual when the two approached the house. Hannah met them at the front door wiping her hands on her apron. "Wash up you two, and please use the boot scraper before you drag the fields onto my clean floors. Dinner will be on the table shortly."

Thomas bent down and kissed his wife on the top of her head and returned to the porch to scrape the mud off his boots. Abra filled the bucket from the well so he and his father could wash up outside. When the two entered the house their meals were placed in front of them and Hannah quickly took her own seat. "Bless us for this food, oh Lord, and thank you for the many blessings you have afforded us," said Thomas. Abra had bowed his head, but he always looked up to watch his father. At the end of the blessing, Thomas always gave a special smile and a wink of his eye to Hannah. She would then give her head a little jiggle as a soft smile spread across her lips. Although Thomas was not a very demonstrative man, it was evident that he loved his wife.

"And thank you, God, for providing us with apples for the delicious pie we are going to enjoy!" said Abra.

Hannah laughed. "That pie was supposed to be a surprise."

"Mother, I could smell it as soon as we walked toward the house. I just wanted God to know that I appreciate all the apples I had to pick so we could enjoy a delicious treat."

Hannah laughed and Thomas shook his head. Hannah talked as she served food from the dishes. "We need to pick up the supplies for Abra's schooling. We also need to make arrangements for his room and board for the winter months when weather keeps him from traveling home."

Abra broke in, “Mother, I am going to borrow some of my books from the Marshes. Mr. Marsh said that I could borrow anything they had that complies with the reading list.”

“That would be most helpful,” said Thomas. “The Marshes are good people.”

“And as for room and board, I was thinking that maybe I could ask if they need someone to work the fireplaces at the school when the weather gets bad. I think one of the Woodruff boys did that one year and he was allowed to sleep in the school in one of the closets when the weather was bad. He is not returning to school this year.”

Thomas smiled at the newfound frugality which Abra had just adopted. He had always been careful not to discuss financial issues with his son in the past; however the latest taxation proposals would be cutting into their tight budget.

“Oh, I don’t know if I like the idea of you sleeping at the school, Abra,” Hannah quickly said.

“Mother, you fret too much. The boy is capable of starting to help out a bit. If he can get a job at the school, it would certainly save us money instead of hiring out room and board when he cannot come home because of the weather.”

“With the drought this year, perhaps we won’t have a bad winter,” suggested Hannah.

“We’ll see what the weather brings. Meanwhile, let’s think about what else we can plant next season to increase our crop.” Hannah quickly looked at Thomas, then back at Abra.

"Don't worry, Mother, I told him about the new expenses. He is old enough to know what is happening in the colonies."

"Children should not have to be worrying about such matters," sputtered Hannah as she sopped her piece of bread in the gravy.

"Abra is no longer a child. He is fast approaching manhood. He is already thirteen, and he has had more education than most of the boys in these parts. I am confident that when he returns to school he will certainly hear talk of the government and there will be lively debates because of the Loyalists attending that school."

Thomas knew that New Jersey had been at the forefront in supporting education. As far back as 1693 the state began levying taxes to support education, which was mostly organized by the Presbyterian Church. Elizabethtown families built the log house in 1728 which served as their church and their school. In the early days Thomas remembered having to carry a gun to church as protection against the Indians. Now it was a much safer trip to the church for everyone, and the church was being expanded by the second building.

Thomas looked at his son and knew that Abra was not inclined to follow farming. It would be necessary for him to be prepared for some other line of work. Abra was thirteen now, and Thomas was not certain what line of work would befit his son. Whatever it was, no doubt, schooling would have to be a part of that. Abra had already attended some classes at the

Presbyterian school in the past, but Thomas knew it was time for him to take advantage of additional classes. A thirteen year old would need to know a career path. Thomas thought surveying would be a good field. Many of the cases Thomas had to rule upon as judge involved land disputes and surveyors were needed to protect land deeds. There was certainly a need for honest and intelligent men in this field.

Abra listened to his father intently and watched his father's expressions, trying to determine if his own father objected to the King's taxes. Abra knew that his uncle and father often talked quietly about matters of politics, but would silence themselves when Abra entered the room. Thomas did not realize that this made his conversations with his brother all the more attractive to Abra. Abra would quietly sit and listen to the men talk while he helped his mother shuck corn or churn butter. Perhaps his father was in agreement with King George II, a German born king, who recently entered into a war with Spain. Such action meant rising costs to the British crown, and as costs rose, the colonists feared they would be expected to financially support the cause. Abra knew that the income from the farm produce had not fluctuated over the years; however the expenses, including taxes, kept increasing. Even though the colonists were paying less in taxes than those in Great Britain there was a general fear that they could easily become easy targets for the King's need of income. Much of the raw materials needed in Great Britain for their industrialization came from the colonies; however the export costs did not equal the import costs of the manufactured products. The colonies were facing many more increased costs and small farmers, like Thomas, had to increase their crops to maintain the status quo.

Abra pondered how he felt about the financial changes. Cutting back on his education would have made him angry, and if the taxes became too high, that just might happen. Most of the boys of Elizabethtown his age did not get much more education than simple reading and writing and some ciphering. He knew that the additional education he was getting was because of his father and mother's desire for Abra to better himself. Thomas' education was meager at best, although it was probably a step more than most of the local farmers.

Hannah broke the silence. "Abra, please gather more firewood and I need you to gather the afternoon eggs."

"Yes, Mother," Abra said. He took his dishes to the basin and picked up the basket sitting on the corner shelf. He knew that there was already a ready supply of cut wood which Egan had already chopped, and that his mother would have already collected the first batch of eggs in the early morning, so there wouldn't be as many at this time of day. He also knew that if he wanted to read more before going back into the fields with his father, he needed to finish these chores as quickly as possible. He knew that his mother would give him an insignificant chore so she would talk with his father. "I will take my leave so I can spend valuable time with the ladies of the hen yard so you and father can secretly talk about me," Abra said with a laugh.

After he left the kitchen, Hannah turned to her husband. "Thomas, do you think it wise that we talk about the changing politics in front of Abra?"

"Now, Hannah. That boy is thirteen years old. You cannot treat him like he is a little boy." He considered for a moment whether to continue. He knew Hannah did not grasp the depth of the politics of the time. He decided to carefully explain why he was so concerned. "Hannah, there is change brewing in the colonies. My brother says that George II fought with his own father for years, and he is greedy. When he took over the English throne in '27 he demanded an increased allowance of 800,000 pounds! Where do you think that money comes from, except the back of the English, the Irish, and the colonists when they have to pay heavy taxes on everything they put up for trade? If George II had such little regard for his own father, he certainly will have no loyalties to the English and Irish! And we need to keep an eye on Charles Stuart who has been gaining support in Scotland. He feels he is the rightful heir to the British crown, and that could mean a civil war within Great Britain. We very well could end up being drawn into a war right here in the colonies which would certainly rip up all family loyalties. Here in Elizabethtown we have English, Irish and Scots all living together, and there have been many families that have been united through marriage, unlike what you see back in Great Britain. Abra will soon be old enough to have to fight if war does break out."

Hannah's face fell and she bit her lip in concern. "Abra is in school and he is just a boy. There will be no talk of going off to war. Thomas, you know I don't like to talk about politics. I don't have a head for it. But what I do know is that people here are peaceful and friendly. I hardly believe that they would begin to fight against each other just because the King starts something in England."

"Hannah, we have been fortunate to live peaceful lives. Unfortunately there is change happening. We need to pray that it does not come to the colonies. So far our involvement has been limited to financial issues. It certainly has the potential to become worse than this. People here are already strained financially. Even King George has to realize that we are still building here, and that costs money. We are given governors who get appointed by the King and too often they feel they are royalty and we colonists are to support them in the same manner as the King. Instead of looking for ways to help us, the governors look for ways to help their own finances. Very little funding has found its way to help any of the colonies build themselves. It seems instead that we are left to our own accord to finance all the changes, so long as we follow the guidance of the appointed governors."

"Enough of this talk. I just want Abra to get his education.

We will have to economize as needed," said Hannah with a wave of her hand to indicate that the discussion was over. Thomas started to say something, but it was obvious Hannah wanted no more talk of taxes, wars and budgets.

Abra entered the house with the firewood as his mother was waving her hand at Thomas and turning away shaking her head. Abra wondered what had transpired in his absence. Hannah patted him on the cheek as he moved past her to the fireplace and her hand combed through his hair as he passed. His father strode to his chair and lowered himself stiffly into his seat. He looked at his son, then leaned back and closed his eyes for a short nap before they would set off for the fields again. Abra took this opportunity to go to his bed and pick up his book. He opened it, but his mind drifted instead to a time when he would go to school and the day to day chores of the farm would be behind him. As he thought this, the clouds opened and rain poured down. Abra relaxed his body as he knew chores were done for the day and he could enjoy reading without impending farm business.

# Chapter 2
# *Education*

**Nearly two and a half years had passed** since the decision for Abra to continue to attend school. He was now a tall lanky young man of nearly sixteen. By the time he took care of his duties at the school cleaning the fireplaces, cutting wood and cleaning the school rooms, the long ride home would leave him little time to even help out on the farm. Thomas agreed that Abra should stay at the school much of the time, returning home three days of the week when weather allowed. To compensate for the loss of Abra's help on the farm, Thomas and his neighbor bought yet another indentured servant contract and the three servants spent were allotted more time than in the past helping at the Clark farm.

Abra's visits home were filled with stories of lessons learned, as well as talk that was stirring among the young Presbyterian boys and instructors. Hannah would sit quietly by the fireside sewing or at the kitchen table preparing bread dough and watch her son with pride as he discussed with animated enthusiasm the political changes happening in England. Hannah often would stifle a cough and wave off the concern that her husband and son showed. She would never interrupt with talk of her weakened health. The pneumonia she had suffered the year before had left her very weak, and both Thomas and Abra would guard her against any chill. Abra was attentive to his mother's comfort often helping her with her kitchen work and settling her in her chair near the fire so she could be part of the discussion. Although Hannah seldom participated, the pride she had in her son who was becoming a well-spoken young man was evident in her eyes and the smile on her face. Abra often made her laugh with his witty commentary.

Uncle Abraham and other farmers and friends of the Clarks would often visit the Clark Farm. In the past, Thomas protected his son from the financial problems of the colonies; however Abra soon became part of the adult circle and protecting him from stories of the changing politics of Elizabethtown and the world was unthinkable. Often it was Abra who would bring news to the table which his father and uncle had not heard.

"Father, did you know that Robert Walpole is hated by King George II?"

"Yes, Walpole was appointed by George I, and anything George I supported, his son resisted."

"Then how was it that Walpole was allowed to serve as Prime Minister?"

Thomas remembered the conversation he had with his brother about this very matter. “It seems Caroline, George II’s wife, is the one who encouraged George to keep Walpole as Prime Minister, despite her husband’s revulsion of anything to which his father had placed a stamp of approval.”

“Walpole is supposed to be retiring this year” Abra stated.

“Where did you hear that?” Thomas said in a startled voice.

“It has been the talk of school. What do you think will happen when he does retire?”

Thomas considered this. “It was Walpole who had established the modern constitutional monarchy. He had organized a cabinet that answered to the Parliament who was then accountable to the wealthy landowners and merchants of the Whig party.”

Abra continued. “At school we have talked about the possibility of the Tories gaining control in England. It is also no secret that there is a strong movement for Charles Stuart to return to the throne. One of our teachers said that ‘Bonnie Prince Charlie’ has enough support in Scotland and is hoping to push his anti-Catholicism view which would cause civil unrest in England.”

Thomas again had not heard this tidbit of information and considered how that would affect the colonies. “We should be thankful for Walpole’s intercession during the past twelve years. Despite being called a liar, thief and rascal in the past by the King, he served England well over the past fifteen years even though he was unable to keep the king from declaring war on Spain. As for Charles, I don't know how that would fare for England or for us in the colonies if the Stuarts returned to the throne. You know it would come at a price when you have a war within all of Britain, and the colonists would be expected to not only pay for the war, but could even be called upon to fight in the war. Look at how many English, Irish and Scots we've got living here in the colonies now, even here in Elizabethtown. They live side by side. It would ruin us."

Thomas looked at his son. Abra had turned his attention back to his book when the conversation had stopped. Thomas' pride welled in his chest that his son was becoming aware of global issues. He regretted that he would now have to curtail that development. Thomas had been dreading the topic of discussion he knew he had to open with his son. Thomas took a deep breath. "Abra. We need to have a serious discussion." Abra looked up at his father and at first looked at his mother, thinking there was news about her health. Thomas shook his head. "No, the problem is the cost of your education." Abra felt a chill in his body. He closed his book and looked at his father intently. "It will be impossible to send you to college as we cannot afford it." Abra's chest tightened. He had always assumed his parents would want him to continue his education. This news was startling.

Thomas went on to explain. "William and Mary College is not something we can afford. I know this is a huge disappointment.

I have been trying to consider some alternatives. Abra, you have done well in your studies, and your mother and I could not be more proud of you. The problem is that the next step in your education would be college and there is no way we can stretch our budget that far. Even now we are stretched to the breaking point in trying to maintain the crops and making enough money through what we sell. Plus, Egan and Deirdre's contract will soon be expiring and I want to give them a little piece of land to call their own. They have been a great asset to me over the years. Ronan still has another three years and Ethan has five and a half years left on his contract. I will have to put out more money for yet another servant or two in order to maintain what we have now. These contracts are becoming more expensive as the need continues to rise in New Jersey." Thomas looked at his wife and knew there would also be more need of a female domestic's help as Hannah's health had not rallied. He decided not to mention this in front of Abra. "It is time to make some choices as to what you will do with your future. Do you have any idea of what field of study you would like to pursue? You are always welcome to share in the handling the farm."

Abra had an answer; however without college it was highly unlikely that he could pursue it. "Father, I would like to work with the law. I have watched you over the years and admired your work as a judge. I feel that there are people who have no protection against those who have money and can afford to defend themselves. I would like to practice law."

Thomas smiled at his son. It was quite evident that Abra had grown into a compassionate young man who cared about his fellow man. He also knew that there was the reoccurring theme of laws and trials in all their discussions. "You know that financially we cannot support college."

Abra's face dropped and he looked down at his hands to avoid looking into his father's eyes. His disappointment was obvious. He knew his father had thought about this for some time. He was thankful for the sacrifices his father made throughout the years to guarantee that his son could get an education. The welling disappointment, however, could not be hidden. He had always pictured himself in the courtroom. He enjoyed watching his father serve as judge and was proud that his father was a fair and honest man. Times had changed and rarely could anyone without a full education serve as a judge in a courtroom. Abra recognized that cases had to be presented well in order to get a fair decision. Sometimes his father felt that there was often considerable doubt in a decision he made, yet his hands were tied unless the facts and evidence were presented to overturn a decision. Abra would often consider what facts should have been presented in order to win the case. Many lawyers were looked at with disdain because of their dishonesty and their manipulation of facts. Abra knew he would never do that. Now he would never have the opportunity to do this work to help the people, like Egan and Ronan and others who were hoping to one day have their own property and be able to protect their rights, but not having the money to get proper representation. For a moment, Abra feared his father would expect him to become a farmer.

Hannah looked at her quieted son and said, "Have you thought of becoming a preacher? You care so strongly about people. I'm certain Reverend Caldwell would give you advice."

Abra looked startled. "No, mother. Although I believe than people should be led to live fair and just lives, I don't see myself living the life of a preacher."

Thomas broke in. "I have noticed that your mathematic skills are excellent and have considered hiring a tutor to teach you the surveying trade. There is money to be made in this field and this would be an excellent match for your skills. I have many cases brought before me with land disputes. There are not enough trained surveyors in the area and often we have to wait for decisions because of our lack of talent. With more land being distributed to the colonists, an honest division and identification of property lines is needed to protect those who put down their hard money on a piece of land. What would you think of this?"

Abra considered this, but it had not been something that he had ever pictured himself doing.

"Of course, there is the farm and we could section a piece off for you and look for additional land for you to purchase." Abra shifted uncomfortably. He knew this was not what he wanted to do. While he knew that farming would always keep food on his table, he also knew that he did not have the disposition to be a full time farmer.

Reluctantly he faced his father and admitted, “No, father, I am not interested in farming, at least not as a sole enterprise.” His father nodded knowingly at Abra’s admission. “While I have never considered the job of surveying, I would like to learn more about it. Do you believe it is something I could do?”

Thomas actually breathed a sigh of relief. He had been pondering for some time how he would approach this topic with Abra, and what kind of employment Abra could do. Thomas knew his son was dedicated and worked as hard as he could. In fact, with Abra being an only child, he bore a greater burden than most boys his age as other farmers had multiple children who helped with the farm. Thomas admired his son’s fervor in reading and learning, and it was because of this Thomas knew Abra would do what was necessary to learn the trade of surveying. The conversation had actually gone better than he thought. He knew Abra would prefer to continue his formal education, however financially that was not possible.

“You know, Abra, a proper surveyor would have eliminated all the land title and land tax disputes that have plagued Elizabethtown since the very beginning. While many people distrust lawyers, an honest surveyor is held in high esteem. It is a worthy profession.”

Abra nodded. “I just haven’t thought about this before.” Abra’s brain raced as he pondered what kind of life he would have if he followed this career path. He was fearful of not accepting it because it would mean taking another look at farming. He steadied his face and looked at his father. "I guess I wouldn't mind learning more about surveying," he said in a voice that was less than convincing.

Thomas ignored his son's facial feedback. Sometimes a parent has to do what is best for his child, he thought to himself. "Fine, I have someone in mind. I will make the arrangements, and after harvesting this year, we will begin your tutoring. I've talked to Mr. Johhanson about employment as a surveyor and he said that they are severely understaffed, however finding the right person with the right skills has kept him from hiring someone. If you were to get the tutoring you need, and serve as an apprentice for a short time, you could, no doubt, begin work in this field within a year or two."

Abra looked at his parents. It seemed the decision had already been made. Abra realized there was really nothing he could do in protest. It was either follow this line of work, or go into farming, and he knew he did not want to do that. For the first time, Abra was speechless. He had really never considered other employment other than law. Hannah was looking intently at him, seeking some sign of acceptance. Abra smiled at her. To Thomas he said, "Father, I hope that I won't be a disappointment. I know how hard you have worked to give me the education I have had so far. I will work hard to make you proud."

"You have already made us proud with your accomplishments at school, and that you helped finance your education through working. I really believe that this surveying work will suit you, and it will allow you to live the kind of life your mother and I hope you will have." Abra gave a weak smile to his father. He really had no idea how surveying was done, but he trusted his father would secure for him the best teacher possible.

"Father, wasn't James Alexander a surveyor?"

"Yes. Do you remember the talk your uncle repeated about the land disputes that lead to riots when James Alexander had to draw up the boundaries between New York and New Jersey in 1740? Whenever land is involved, tempers run hot. The surveyor must be careful and honest when writing up the surveyed border descriptions so that people are getting the land they think they are buying. This can upset the apple cart for those who have farmed a piece of land for years and think it is their own, when in reality, the real boundaries dispute their belief."

Abra thought about that and realized that even if he could not become a lawyer, certainly a surveyor was close to legal representation of those who needed representation. Abra stood tall as he pictured himself, uncompromising and honest in his duties as a surveyor. Perhaps he could do this!

Harvesting season came, and Abra's formal schooling came to an end. Abra worked hard with his father in the fields during the harvest. It was important to him that he pay respect to his father for all the sacrifices Thomas had made for him. He worked alongside his father and the hired men and tried to keep their pace. Although Thomas knew his son was working as hard as he could, he knew Abra could never match their pace. It was hard for Thomas to look at his son and know that he did not enjoy farming the same way he did. Thomas loved the cycle of planting, cultivating and harvesting. There was pride in watching the labor of his hands grow. There was a sense of power and sometimes helplessness in watching God's play in the successes and failures in the crops. Thomas found farming to be almost spiritual. He knew, however, that his son did not relish it the way he did. He was hopeful that his encouragement of Abra learning how to survey land would be successful and his son would find the same pleasure in it that Thomas felt in farming.

Abra spent that harvest season working harder than he ever did in a classroom. His mind would play with what his future held. He had never thought about surveying as a job. In fact, he knew very little about it. Abra always liked a challenge. In school he was a very successful student because he always enjoyed the challenges of learning. He had always thought he would practice law; however he could not ask his father to provide even more sacrifices in order for him to go to college. He had just never considered a second plan. Abra knew that if his father had suggested surveying as a career, he knew that meant that his father had researched it and wanted the best for him. Abra set his face hard and set himself off to work in the fields to show his father his appreciation.

In the evenings during the harvest, Abraham practiced his ciphering. He would make up problems and time himself when figuring the solutions. After the harvest, Thomas paid the surveyor, Johannson, to tutor his son in the trade and to allow Abra to follow along with surveyors in the field to learn the work.

# Chapter 3
# The Surveyor and Counselor

**Abra soon learned that surveying** was among the oldest professions in the world going back to ancient Egypt and Babylonia indicate. He had always enjoyed reading about these cultures, so now learning about a trade that dated back to these times was exciting to him. He quickly learned that it was not only land that was surveyed, but water rights which were so important to the New Jersey farmers. He was also required to learn to do mapping, which at first caused Abra problems as he was not very artistic, and the act of mapping required the surveyor to be exact in sketches outlining land boundaries. He was very adept at writing out the land descriptions, but he was challenged in the drawing of the maps. However, with a lot of patience and determination, he learned how to draw a map as well and indicate the topography of the land. As his studies continued he realized that a land surveyor also became a counselor who helped the farmers identify the best choices for crops based upon the water and drainage in an area. He learned that land surveyors were actually like engineers as they could predict the suitability of where buildings could best be built without damage to the foundations due to the land itself.

For Abra learning surveying had been very easy work. His mathematical skills made this training very easy and by the time Abra was nineteen years old, he had become quite proficient. As more people settled into the area, old farms were broken up into smaller holdings divided between siblings as parents passed on, or sold to other settlers to the area. In all cases, the land had to be exactly surveyed to guarantee legal rights to land. As Thomas continued to serve as a judge, he called upon his son to help with land dispute cases.

Whenever Abra was called as a surveyor to testify in court about land disputes, he was intrigued by the business in the courtroom. He witnessed repeatedly how poor people were often swindled out of their land by greedy landowners. There were many who were given land when they finished their indentured contract, however many would have these lands taken away because they were not verbal enough to fight against those who victimized them. Abra's yearning for practicing law increased as he spent more time in the courts representing poor clients. Although Abra was a very good surveyor, he did not find the spiritual feelings Thomas had with farming. While working as a surveyor was an economically good choice, Abra did not feel the satisfaction he felt when working in the court. Leaving his job and going to school was no longer an option as it was just too impractical. Abra felt that his destiny would be in surveying and representing poor clients in land disputes.

As Abra's expertise and reputation grew he found himself being called upon to testify in more court disputes over land boundaries. Abra's expert and honest findings were always appreciated. What excited him more than testifying was learning the outcome of the various disputes. Since several cases were in his father's court, Abra openly discussed the cases with his father and uncle.

"Father, do you think I could read over the reports from the disputes? I was certain the outcome of this last case would have been different."

His uncle said, "Abra, you know what the problem was? It wasn't boundaries of the land they were disputing. It was that McIntyre couldn't read and verify what was written in those deeds. He settled on one thing, and that Curry fellow knew it. McIntyre should have had someone read over what he signed his mark on to be certain it said what he thought he was buying."

"That's not fair," Abra sputtered.

"Don't matter. There is no law against being smart and manipulating a situation to your advantage if your opponent doesn't seek to help himself."

Thomas interjected, "Probably half of the disputes in my court are because of ignorance of reading. Many others are because of surveys not done correctly in the first place. Life is different from when the savages marked their boundaries based on a forest or a plain. The landscape keeps changing. What was a forest one day becomes a farm the next. The Lenape Indians who first settled here were content to live on the land as it was laid out to them. As our population grows and as we have more people wanting to buy their own little plot of land from England, everything has to follow the letter of the law."

"It's everyone's responsibility to learn to read in order to protect their property and family," Abra argued.

"Son, you got an education only because I could afford to hire on more men. Your mother was insistent that you learn to read and cipher so you would not become one of the men who are disadvantaged because you can't protect yourself against the written word," said Thomas.

"Your father is right," said Uncle Abraham. "Even though New Jersey has been pushing for education, many men just cannot afford to let their children stop working the land. They need their children as farmhands."

Abra looked at his uncle. "Uncle Abraham, the men should at least protect themselves by having a surveyor look over their land deeds to make certain everything is in order."

"Again, you propose that all men are honest. Many of the

larger landowners have surveyors in their pocket. The kick-backs at altering an agreement are worth their weight in gold."

"Such men should be arrested," an angered Abra said.

"And who do you suppose is going to file the lawsuit? It costs money to do that, and when you are living from hand to mouth, such luxuries are unheard of," his uncle said.

Thomas interjected, "Money does most of the talking in the colonies. Also, it is who you know. The local magistrates are appointed by the governor, who is appointed by the King. Rest assured that if you offer any protest to those in charge, you will find yourself at the short end of the stick."

"That's not fair either," said Abra.

"Maybe so," said his uncle. "But that is our reality. Relying on the old world way of giving a handshake in a gentleman's agreement is a thing of the past. A man's word is no longer to be trusted."

"That's pitiful," sighed Abra. Looking at his father he said, "Father, men here know you are honest, and I've watched you make trade without legal documents signed or witnesses present."

Thomas quickly replied, "That may be, however in things as important as land, you cannot sign away your rights without protecting yourself. If a man sold you a plot of land that he thought was pretty worthless to him, then he discovers that there was an artesian well beneath it that could provide much needed water to his crops, trust me, he will look at ways of adjusting those boundaries so you cannot have that particular parcel."

"That's theft!" Abra sputtered.

"Prove it. If you don't have the legal documents to protect you, you will always stand to lose. A potato in trade is just a potato. Someone cheats me in trade, I will be angry, but I can grow more next year. I would stand the wiser no longer trading with that man. But land...ah, land is forever. Once you sign it away, there is no next year. Once you buy it, you must protect it."

Abra recognized the truth in this as he had been called upon to testify in several land disputes during the past year. His passion about the rights of the poor intensified his desire to know more about the way the laws were written. Abra began his quest to teach himself about the law. He knew that he could not afford to go off to college with the luxury of just studying and not working. Those days were over for him. He could not ask his father to financially support such an endeavor, and although Abra was living comfortably, it was because he lived very frugally that he could do so on the modest income he made from surveying.

Abra's days were spent surveying or testifying in court about land boundaries. At night he buried himself in legal script studying cases where people were victimized and lost their land because of those whose greed of power and wealth pushed them to take what was not theirs. Even though Abra felt the colonies were the sole property of Great Britain, he wanted to know more about how the savages lost their rights. His father arranged for him to read the land deed contracts dating back to 1664.

*This Indenture made the 28th Day of October in the Sixteenth Year (1664) of the Reign of our Sovereign Lord Charles the Second, by the Grace of God of England, Scotland, France and Ireland, King, Defender of the Faith etc between Mattano Manamowaone, and Cowescomen, of Staten-Island, of the one Part, and John Baily, Daniel Denton, and Luke Watson of Jamaica, in Long-Island Husbandmen, on the other part. WITNESSETH, that the said Mattano Manmowaone and Cowescomen, , hath clearly bargained & sold unto the said John Bailey, Daniel Denton, and Luke Watson, their Associates, their Heirs and Executors, one Parcel of Land Bounded on the South by a River commonly called the Raritons River, and on the East by the River which Parts Staten-Island and the Main, and to run Northward up after Cull-Bay, till we come at the first River which sets Westwards up after Cull-Bay, aforesaid, and to run West into the Country twice the Length as it is broad from the North to the South of the aforemention'd Bounds; together with the Lands, Meadows, Woods, Waters, Fields, Fences, Fishing, Fowling, with all and singular the Appurtenances with all gains profits and Advantages arising upon the said Lands, and all other the Premises and Appurtenances to the said John Baily, Daniel Denbton, and Luke Watson, with their Associates, with their and every of their Heirs, Executors, Administrators or Assigns, for ever, to have and to hold the said Lands with the Appurtenances to the said John Baily, Daniel Denbton, and Luke Watson, with their Associates, their Executors, or Assigns. And the said Mattano Manamowaone, covenant, promise, grant and agree to and with the said John Baily, Daniel Denbton, and Luke Watson, and their Associates, their Heirs and Executors, to keep safe in the Enjoyments of the said Lands, from all expulsion and encumbrances whatsoever, may arise of the said Land, by any Person of Persons by reason of any Title had or growing before the Date of these Presents: For which bargain and sale, covenants, grants and agreements in the behalf of the said Mattano Manamowaone, and Cowescomen, to be performed observed and done the aforesaid Parties are at their entry upon the said Land, to pay to the said Mattano Manamowaone, and Cowescomen, Twenty Fathoms of Trading Cloth, two made Coats, two Guns, two Kettles, Ten Barrs of Lead, Twenty Handfuls of Powder. And, further the said John Baily, Daniel Denbton, and Luke Watson,, do covenant, promise grant, and agree to and with the said Mattano Manamowaone, and Cowescomen the aforesaid Indians, four Hundred Fathom of white Wampum after a Years Expiration from the Day of the said John Baily, Daniel Denbton, and Luke Watson's, entry upon the said Lands. In Witness whereof we have hereunto put our Hands and Seals the Day and Year aforesaid*

*The Mark of MATTANO*

*The Mark of SEUAKHENOS*

*The mark of WARINANCO*

*Sign'd, Seal'd and deliver'd in the Presence of us*

*CHARLES HORSLEY*

*The mark of RANDLE HOWETT*

Abra nearly retched when reading the land deed. He could see immediate problems with the surveyor work listed, but more importantly he saw that the savages had been grossly mistreated in the trade. He began to even wonder if they knew what they had signed. They sold that amass of land for 2400 feet of beads, a couple of coats, and eighty feet of cloth, a couple of kettles some black powder and two guns and some lead to make bullets. How could they have known what they signed away? Who protected their rights, not that anyone had ever considered Indians having rights. He knew that in order to keep the peace, King Charles had agreed to such trades in order to keep the savages away from lands where colonists were to settle. It was felt that the Indians had plenty of other land in the frontier where they could settle, even if it meant their battling against other tribes to secure their own place in the frontier. However, the severity of the injustice in trade and in victimizing the seller was evident. Abra had never considered that such inequity could come at such a price. For the first time he understood why so many of the savages became enraged and hostile toward the colonists when they realized what they had signed away for a few beads and trinkets. The two guns Mattano received could hardly save him from British militia now protecting what they determined was legally theirs.

Abra couldn't wait to talk to his father and uncle about the Indian issues. Uncle Abraham remained firm that the savages were just that, savages, and that they brought military action against them when they attacked the colonists. Thomas, however, spoke compassionately about how the Lenape Indians were much like the illiterate landowners who could do little to protect their rights. Abra knew that both his father and uncle recalled their childhood and riding in the wagon to church with his grandfather carrying a gun to protect them in case of attack. Abra had never witnessed such alarm, however he knew that whenever he left the safety of Elizabethtown to do survey work he carried a gun as a precaution. His father had drilled him in shooting a rifle as a young boy. Abra was not overly fond of hunting, but as he grew older he began to understand his father's need to train his son to protect himself.

Abra's love of history pushed him to further study his own birthplace and the many land disputes of the past. The

Westfield area had been part of Elizabethtown from 1664. The triangle of land was marked originally by the boundaries of the Rahway River on the west and the Watchung Mountains on the southeast had been the subject of much hot debate.

There was a long history of land disputes between the east Jersey Proprietors, who were British investors, and those of the Elizabethtown Associates. It seemed that the Clinker Lot Division started the majority of the conflicts when one hundred one acre lots were parceled out in a one hundred seventy one block of land back in 1699. Governor Gawen Lawrie had a land survey done by Captain John Baker on the western boundaries of Elizabethtown. Baker was an Indian interpreter. It appeared to Abra as he studied the land surveys that Baker had been less than honest, and when he was called before the court and questioned, he received only a slap on the wrist for the inconsistencies his survey presented. Baker cheated not only the Indians, but the governor as well.

The problems first began when the Proprietors had purchased their land. The land in question had been awarded by King Charles II to his brother, the Duke of York. The Duke later gave the land to Lord Berkeley and Sir George Cateret when the Duke left the colonies. The Elizabethtown Associates had purchased their tract of land west of Staten Island from the Dutch who had first settled in the area. Richard Nicoll, the English governor of the area, allowed the Elizabethtown Associates to purchase the land from three Leni Lenape Indian chieftains. What they did not know was that the Duke had given the bulk of New Jersey land to his royalist friends. The Elizabeth Associates had purchased land from someone who did not actually own the land! Legal struggles over the land broke out between the Proprietors represented by Berkely and Carteret, and the Elizabethtown Associates. Because the Associates had more people to defend their side of the legal battle, vs. the Proprietors who were fewer in number, the dispute finally ended in a compromise.

The early Associate settlers were listed as Acken, Badgley, Baker, Brooks, Bryant, Clark, Connet, Cory, Craig, Crane, Davis, Denman, Dunham, Frazee, Frost, Hendricks, Hetfield, High, Hinds (Haines), Hole, Jennings (Gennings), Lambert, Littell, Ludlum (Ludlow), Marsh, Meeker, Miller, Mills, Pierson, Robinson, Ross, Scudder, Spinnage (Spinning), Terry, Tucker, Willcox, Williams, Woodruff and Yeomans. These early settlers stood together and fought against the British land exchange. Despite the law being on the side of the Proprietors, they were outnumbered by the Associates. The dividing of the land became known as the Clinker Lot Division. Town lots had been laid out on both banks of the Elizabeth River for a two mile stretch. As there were already seven hundred people living in the settlement, the decision was made that there was sufficient population to make Elizabethtown a town, however there were enough people in the west fields of Elizabethtown to make additional settlements. These became boroughs of Elizabeth: Westfield, Rahway and Springfield.

As Abra read about the Clinker Lot Division, he recognized so many families who settled in the area were still there today. Many of these families worshiped at the Presbyterian Church and some of the more influential families had sons who went to school with him. The tug of war between those investors of England and those colonists who were trying to abide by the rules in a land that was unsettled and barely released from savage control was the basis for many of the stories Abra had heard from his father and his uncle. Angry Indian attacks followed due to the conniving trade by the English, which was certainly why Thomas demanded Abra learn how to shoot a gun.

Abra knew that those early settlers of the Associates who wanted to establish their settlement tried to follow the rules, yet their collective lack of literacy kept them from being able to research more thoroughly. One thought in Abra's mind kept bothering him. The Associates would never have won the legal battle. It was their sheer force in number that protected their rights. The fact that there were so many families standing up against the Proprietors, who were mere overseas investors, protected the Associates' interests. Abra considered what would have happened had the Proprietors lived in the colonies. He shook his head thinking how differently things would have turned out for their small community.

Thomas would supply his son with various case reports he had handled through the years, and Abra would study them and discuss with his father and uncle the various cases. He soon became proficient in identifying the flaws in the presentations. It became very clear to him that often the poorest farmers were the ones who lost cases.

It was Egan and Deidre, the former indentured servants who had once worked on the Clark farm, who came to Abra asking for advice when they were trying to protect a portion of their small farm they purchased from the neighboring landowner. It seemed that Egan was told the land boundary included a small stream which he needed to divert for crop irrigation, yet when he began digging, he was challenged as to his rights to that creek. Abra knew Egan could not afford a real lawyer so he agreed to represent him in court. It was the first time Abra stood before a judge acting as a counselor. He was nervous, yet confident that he had truth on his side. When the judge ruled in his favor, Abra patted Egan on the back and shook his hand.

"I promised you payment for representing me, Abra. You did me right fine," the Irishman beamed.

"Take your time, Egan. I know you are good for the money." Egan had promised Abra money that would come from this next crop.

As Egan turned to hug his wife, Abra caught sight of his uncle in the courtroom. Abra quickly said his goodbyes to Egan and Deirdre and walked swiftly to the back of the courtroom.

"Uncle Abraham. I didn't know you were in town today," said Abra as he reached out to shake his uncle's hand.

"You did fine work today, Abra. There is need of honest men like you in New Jersey." Abraham studied his nephew's face. Abra's once thin face was now matured and his shoulders were broader than the last time he had seen him. Abra was turning into a capable and reputable man, and Abraham smiled as he looked at him. "You will find that people will come to your door because you are honest and fair, Abra Clark. Remember to maintain that reputation. It will take you far!" Abra smiled at his uncle as the two left the courthouse.

Abra offered his uncle an opportunity to share a dinner together, and the two talked throughout their meal, often forgetting to eat the food which was cooling on their plates. The controversial topic of interest was England's problems. King George's War had lasted for five years. Abraham told Abra news about the third French and Indian War. Much of the fighting took place in the land north of the colonies, but that changed when in 1745 there were raids by the French and Indian forces on the English forts in Maine. Many of the colonists under William Peppercell joined with the British soldiers led by Sir Peter Warren. Saratoga, New York had perished in the attacks and the city had been burned by the invaders. It wasn't until the British persuaded the Iroquois league of Indians to join forces against the French that the fate of the war would change. The war had finally ended with the

Treaty of Aix-la-Chapelle on October 18, 1748 which ended not only the Austrian Succession abroad, but King George's War in the colonies. The treaty gave Fort Louisbourg to the French which angered the colonist who had fought so hard to gain control of it.

"There was much anger on the part of those colonists in Maine and New York and even New Jersey which had fought to gain control of Fort Louisbourg. The lack of regard from the King did not build bridges between England and us."

"Do you think this will be a lasting peace, Uncle Abraham?" asked Abra.

"I am sorry to say I don't. I do not trust the French. They will not be satisfied with only Fort Louisbourg. They will want more. They presently have control over the frontier lands out west, and as the colonies continue to grow and expand, I am afraid there will be yet more wars between the English and the French. In 1752 the Marquis Duquesne who was the new governor of New France bought the instructions for a line of forts. Word is that the French are presently building forts at Lake Champlain, and the Wabash, Ohio, Mississippi and Missouri Rivers. It seems King George and the French are civil to one another, but neither trusts the other."

Abra thought for awhile. "Uncle, what about the Indians? This land was all theirs at one time. There have been attacks in the past as they ignored the sale of rights to the land."

Abraham sighed. "While I do not understand the savages,

they are an illiterate people and they do not have law on their side. The white man is not going to stop wanting more land. Look at Elizabethtown. Look at how many of our people yearn for more land, and how many have gone into the frontier to settle so they can own their own piece of land."

"That is true," pondered Abra. He had witnessed many of the local indentured servants leaving when their contracts expired to move away to find their own piece of land.

Abraham looked at his nephew and wondered what awaited this new generation. He had seen such struggles among the colonists, and this latest war, although it was not fought on New Jersey land, had certainly pulled some of their young men into the military. Abraham was certain there would be more to do with the French.

"Well, Abra, enough of this talk of war and westward expansion. Your father tells me there is a young lady in your life."

Abra blushed slightly and knew that his father had shared this piece of information with his uncle. "Yes. Her name is Sarah Hatfield."

Abraham clapped his hand on Abra's back. "That is certainly good news, Abra. I'm certain Hannah would have been happy to have known this young lady and how your face lit up when you said her name!"

Abra thought with sadness about his mother's death. It had been a difficult time for Abra as he had not been by her side when she died. His mother had looked so pale and weak the last time he had seen her. Abra recalled how his father had written to him to tell him of Hannah's passing, however by the time Abra received the post, the burial had already been held. When he returned home his first stop was the small cemetery outside the Presbyterian Church. Abra had stood beside the fresh mound of soil for more than an hour when a hand gently touched his sleeve. It was Sarah Hatfield. Abra looked at her for a moment searching for words. Sarah looked into his eyes and Abra could see her eyes welling. "I'm so sorry, Abraham, about your mother. It was unfortunate you could not be here for her service."

Abra thanked her for her concern, and Sarah promptly turned and left the small cemetery. Abra's eyes followed her as she climbed into her father's wagon. Mr. Hatfield tipped his hat to Abra and clicked the reins. As the wagon moved away from the cemetery gate, Abra saw Sarah slowly turn her head to look back toward Abra, and then quickly look forward again as the wagon proceeded down the road. Abra watched as it disappeared. As he turned and focused again on the grave of his mother, he noticed a small white crocus which had pushed through the surface of the soil above the grave. "Strange," thought Abra. "I don't remember seeing that flower before." Abra mentally said his goodbyes to his mother, and as he passed through the cemetery gate, the fresh flower filled his thoughts.

Abra's father had been very lonely since Hannah's death. For nearly a year he had gone to church alone, eaten dinner alone, and spent his evenings alone with the exception of visits from his brother, or Abra. Thomas was lonely. It was Elizabeth Radsey of Rahway who finally found a way to make Thomas happy again. She had a bright smile and brought Thomas out of the depression he had felt throughout Hannah's illness and death. The marriage of Thomas and Elizabeth was welcomed by all the family, including Abra. While he missed his mother, he knew that Thomas was happy with Elizabeth and he gave the marriage his full approval. It was Elizabeth who formally introduced Abra to Sarah Hatfield. It had been two years since Abra had first seen Sarah at the cemetery, and he only remembered her as a young girl who giggled at the sight of him when she was a youngster. Now she had transformed into a beautiful young woman with a soft smile. It did not take long for Abra and Sarah to find common interests and the two often found a way to be in each other's company.

"Abra?" Abra had drifted off into his own thoughts and was somewhat startled at his uncle's voice bringing him back to reality.

"I'm sorry, Uncle. I was going to ask if you'd care to stay in my rooms in town until you plan on leaving."

"That is very kind," answered Uncle Abraham.

"Actually, not so kind. I have an important appointment tomorrow morning, so I have to leave in the early morning to ride out to Isaac and Sarah Hatfield's farm."

Abraham laughed. “Abra, if I were a fortune teller, I’d say you have a question that is burning to be asked tomorrow.”

Abra smiled and said, “Could be. Could be.” Abraham laughed heartily and clapped Abra on the shoulder. Abra smiled as he rehearsed in his head his speech for Isaac and Sarah Hatfield. He planned to ask for their daughter’s hand in marriage. Abra slept well that night. It had been a good day. Tomorrow would be even better.

## Chapter 4
# *Marriage and Family*

**Sarah Hatfield was the eldest daughter** of Isaac Hatfield and Sarah Price. The Hatfield were considered well off in Elizabethtown, and Sarah was considered a fine young woman by all of the local families. She had often been pursued by local boys, but it was Abra who caught her eye. A couple of years after Abra's mother's death Thomas remarried. His wife, Elizabeth, was the one who invited Sarah Hatfield to join the Clark family for dinner one evening. Elizabeth had noticed Sarah secretly looking at the Clark pew and studying Abra's strong features. After church service, Elizabeth stopped Sarah and began a discussion about embroidery and invited Sarah to come to the Clark farm the following week for dinner so she could share a pattern Elizabeth was stitching on a new quilt. Sarah quickly agreed, and looked shyly to see if Abra was aware of the invitation. Abra, however, was involved in a conversation with his father and uncle.

The following week, Elizabeth asked Abra to take the wagon to pick up Sarah Hatfield. At first, Abra looked startled, but he did not question Elizabeth's request. Abra was twenty-three years old and many men his age were already married. Abra never considered marriage as he was always busy with teaching himself about politics, law and traveling when his work called upon him.

When he arrived at the Hatfield farm, Isaac Hatfield was working the well in front of the house. He greeted Abra kindly, and Abra quickly took the pail of water and carried it into the kitchen. The Hatfield kitchen was warm and very spacious compared to most. Isaac's wife, Sarah Hatfield, was putting a pie into a basket and covering it with towels. "Sarah and I were busy trying to use up all the fruit before it went bad. We figured a fresh peach pie would taste fine this afternoon." Sarah entered the kitchen carrying a cloak over her arm. Abra turned and caught his breath. Sarah typically pulled her hair back and had a bonnet fastened over it when she came to church. Today her hair was loose and flowing. There was a hint of auburn in her hair and her milky white face was radiant. She smiled when she saw Abra and her face flushed slightly.

"Hello, Abra. Thank you so much for coming to fetch me." She turned to her mother and asked, "Mother, is the basket ready? Abra, Mother and I baked this morning and I insisted on bringing a pie for dinner. Elizabeth didn't bake, did she?"

Abra honestly couldn't remember if Elizabeth had baked or not. Think, think, he chided himself. Then he remembered that the Clark kitchen smelled of rich stew and bread, but he did not remember smelling fruit pies. "No, no. I don't think Elizabeth baked anything today. I am certain she will welcome the pie."

Sarah smiled and added a jar of strawberry preserves to the basket. Abra quickly offered to carry the basket with the pie and preserves, and Sarah gathered up the basket with her quilting materials. Abra offered her his arm and they left the Hatfield kitchen after the two said their goodbyes to Isaac and Sarah. Sarah stood in the doorway watching as Abra and her daughter pulled away and murmured to herself that the Clark boy had certainly turned into a fine young man. She smiled thinking that her daughter had waited long enough to pick a husband, and she certainly would be well set if Abra turned out to be a suitor. "A good match. Yes, a good match."

As Abra drove the wagon back toward the Clark farm, the silence seemed to overwhelm him. Funny, he had no problem starting conversations with his father, his uncle, or the many men he worked with. He had no problem at church conversing with the many women and girls. However today it seemed he had no clue as to how to start a conversation with the lovely Sarah Hatfield. Sarah sat with hands folded in her lap and her eyes studying the scenery. A rabbit skirted in front of the wagon, and Abra jerked the reins. Sarah grabbed onto his arm to steady herself, and the two looked at each other. Both burst out laughing. "For goodness sake! That rabbit was nearly suicidal!" Sarah laughed. Abra agreed. The two paused for a few seconds, and then both started talking at once of the weather. After another awkward silence, it was Sarah who started talking. "How silly that we are acting so awkwardly. It isn't like we don't know each other. Our families have been in the same town, we go to the same church, and we know the same group of people."

Abra laughed and agreed. "I don't know what came over me today. I have no trouble talking. In fact, I have a reputation of talking far too much and asking far too many questions."

"That's not a bad quality. What questions would you want to pose of me if you were meeting me for the very first time?" Sarah asked.

"Typically I'd ask about your family and about where you lived."

"That's a good start. Let's begin with that. My name is Sarah Hatfield. I am the oldest daughter of Isaac and Sarah Hatfield. My mother was a Price."

"I didn't know you came from the Price family? There are a lot of Prices in the Elizabethtown area. Are you related?"

Sarah laughed warmly. "I would imagine we are related to at least half, and if we all dug deep enough, we'd probably find we had some common ancestry among us. What about you, Abra?"

Abra was proud of his family ancestry and told Sarah about the Clarke's of England and their voyage to the colonies. He told her of his mother's family. The two traded questions and answers until they arrived at the Clark farm. Abra was surprised at how quickly they had arrived. Dinner conversation was lively at the Clark table that night. Abra found himself on more than one occasion watching Sarah as she talked animatedly to Elizabeth and Thomas about her family, town and an assortment of other topics.

After dinner Thomas and Abra excused themselves to sit on the front porch. Elizabeth and Sarah pulled out their quilts and quietly shared stitch and pattern ideas while the men talked of politics. At one point Thomas mentioned that Georgia was considering legalizing slavery. Sarah dropped her stitching. "I am so sorry to interrupt. I know women folk are not supposed to be involved in political talk, but honestly. How can man own man? It is indecent to believe you can own another human being. I know that many in our colony have indentured servants; however we do not own these people. They have the hope of a good future. Once their debts are paid they have their freedom and they can seek the hope and promise of a good life here in the colonies, just as our ancestors did when they traveled over the Atlantic. Slavery is barbaric. It is unconscionable for people to treat other people as property." Suddenly, Sarah stopped and looked from Thomas to Abra. Both were looking at her with startled stares. Sarah bit her lip for a moment then continued. "I am sorry for my outburst. I know it is considered improper for women to participate in such talk, but I just had to say what I was thinking."

Abra looked at Sarah, and for one awkward moment there was no sound. Thomas slapped his knee and laughed aloud claiming Sarah had the heart of a woman, but the soul of a politician! Conversation was not at a loss after that. It was at that exact moment Abra fell in love with this spitfire woman who was not afraid to stand up for what she believed. Sarah was beautiful and smart. Abra was certain his mother would have approved.

Abra and Sarah Hatfield married in the Presbyterian Church in 1749, and quickly began their own family. Thomas and Elizabeth built a smaller house on the opposite end of the property owned by Thomas so that Abra and Sarah could live in the house where Abra grew up. Thomas also deeded fifty of his acres to Abra with the house. The year following their marriage found Sarah heavy with child. Abra's time was divided between his surveying work and occasional representation of local farmers in court matters, typically with land disputes as well as making land deeds and wills. Abra soon had a clientele who came to him asking him to defend them. Often times his payment was bartered in food and household goods. It wasn't long before Abra was known as a Poor Man's Counselor. Because of his limited time at home to tend the small farm he owned, Abra made contracts for Hagan, and Hagan's wife, Abigail, as indentured servants to help with the small farm. The Irish couple also had two small children and an infant.

"Why are you taking on a woman servant, Abra? Plus her

with children." asked Thomas. "Seems that you'd be better having two men help you with the farming. Your time away from home is increasing."

"Father, I want someone to help Sarah with the birthing." Thomas said nothing. He suspected that Abra didn't want the same thing to happen to Sarah as what had happened to Hannah when Abra was born. Not only had Hannah bled severely after giving birth to Abra, she lost two more babies well before her time was due. Each time she had lost more blood which frightened Thomas. He remembered being helpless in sending for help and he stood by awkwardly trying to calm Hannah as she bravely fought her terror. He remembered making a commitment to care for his wife and protect her from the strenuous chores of work on the farm. Hannah would insist on wanting to help, but Thomas had remained stern in his decision. Having an experienced woman to help Sarah with the birthing of his grandchild would make things easier for Sarah, plus there would be extra hands to help with raising children. Thomas looked at his son and nodded his head in understanding. He still missed Hannah, but Elizabeth was a fine woman and eager to help. She was a much stronger woman than Hannah, though much plainer in face. She never bore him children, but she was a good partner to him. Thomas knew that Elizabeth would make a good grandmother for Abra and Sarah's children and she would treat them like her own blood. Thomas recalled a conversation with his son when

Abra confided he was lonely as an only child. He hoped Abra and Sarah would fill their home with children.

Sarah was a good partner to Abra. She, like Abra's mother, was a church going woman with a sweet disposition. Her trim figure was always on the move as she worked in the house cooking, cleaning, and planting her gardens. She was very supportive of Abra's work and encouraged him in his work and studies. Abra still spent time in the evening reading over various documents, searching for inequities and points which could be debated. Sarah, unlike Abra's mother, was more understanding of the politics of the area, although she couldn't grasp all the subtleties of the laws. She did, however, allow Abra to sit at night and talk about the things he saw happening in their community, in New Jersey, the colonies, and occasionally in England. Sarah would sit attentively with her sewing in her lap and listen to Abra and interject words of support or understanding. As she looked at her young husband she saw a man who was respected among the people of Elizabethtown. He was already called upon by so many of their neighbors and area servants. Her eyes welled as she watched Abra reading by the fireplace in the evenings, and often she would join in lively discussions about the topics he would discuss.

"Abra, what is troubling you?" asked Sarah one evening when she sat across from Abra whose face was easily read.

"Sarah, a case was settled today over distribution of land. The defendant hired a lawyer to represent him in court. The trial kept being postponed, and more paperwork was required. The man was not wealthy and only had one servant helping him on a 150 acre farm, but he was spending all his time in the courtroom instead of his fields."

"Did he end up losing the suit?" asked Sarah, sincerely interested.

"Well, he won all right, but the fee the lawyer took erased any of the gain the defendant had. It is no wonder that lawyers are looked at as snakes."

"That's not fair, Abra. What is to be done about such things?"

"If it is not nipped, it will be lawyers and crooked politicians who will own all the property in the colonies."

"Abra, you are one of the finest men I know. Surely you can use what influence you have to make changes here in Elizabethtown and the neighboring boroughs. If we want to live peacefully in our own communities, we have to protect ourselves from those of influence."

"I know, Sarah, but I don't know what can be done."

Sarah sat quietly sewing, and watched her husband's face twist and he thought about this agitation. She knew he could not tolerate mistreatment of those who could least afford swindling. Abra got up and moved to his desk and began writing. Sarah continued her sewing until it was time to retire. Abra remained at his desk with the lamp burning beside him. Sarah did not disturb him, but went to bed. When Abra entered the room hours later she heard him sigh a deep breath and roll to his side. Sarah listened to hear his rhythmic breathing, but knew he was not sleeping, but thinking. She drifted off to sleep and in the morning, Abra was already out of bed. She found him back at his desk.

"Abra, did you not sleep at all?" Sarah asked as she approached him. She looked at the desk and saw a neat stack of penned paper and a larger stack of paper with visible markings scratching out lines.

Abra looked up at Sarah and smiled. "I think I have something here. You got me to thinking that I need to take a step forward to protect those needing protecting. If I am going to be a father, I need to protect my son, and all men of his generation from the mistakes taking place now."

"What is this?" Sarah asked pointing to the papers.

"I'm just drafting some ideas I may use at some time to promote equality among the common man. I have no idea what I'll do with it at this time, especially since England does not care about the rights of colonists, let alone the rights of the common man."

Sarah knew her husband's ideas were the ideas of an idealist, which was why she fell in love with him. Abra worked until he fell asleep in his chair and Sarah quietly gathered his papers and stacked them neatly on his desk. She nudged Abra to go to bed, and she walked him to their room.

Sarah had awakened early that morning and busied herself with her morning chores. She first felt the contractions after bending down putting away dishes in the cupboard. At first she ignored the pains thinking she had just overworked and strained herself. She could feel the baby move so she was not concerned. As the morning progressed, the pains became tighter and Sarah could feel her belly harden as the pain spread. Abra was working at his desk in the parlor when Sarah walked in, one hand holding the small of her back. He thought Sarah was coming to tell him their meal was prepared. "Abra. I think it is time." Abra jumped from his chair, knocking it backwards to the floor.

"Sit down right now, Sarah!" Abra said as he picked up the chair and reached for his wife's arm.

"I will go to my room, but you will need to get Abigail and my mother. Elizabeth is out of town until next week. My mother told me that the first baby tends to take longer so we have plenty of time," Sarah said calmly. Abra carefully walked Sarah to their bed. He helped her step out of her dress and slipped her nightgown over her head. He was alarmed as he watched Sarah bravely bite down on her lip and grip his arm when a contraction hit. He pulled back the sheets and helped ease his wife down to the bed.

"What can I do?" Abra asked as he tried to adjust the pillow to make Sarah more comfortable.

"Just go. I will be fine. It is early. This baby may not come until sometime tomorrow."

Abra looked closely at his wife's face. There were drops of

perspiration on her brow and upper lip. He went to the chest and pulled out a towel and dabbed her face. “Sarah, are you all right?”

“Yes, Abra. I just got a little over heated. I was baking earlier and the stove just made me hot. I am perfectly fine. Just go and get Abigail. It is early so there will be lots of time before this baby will arrive.” Abra pulled the sheet up over his wife’s swollen belly, bent and kissed her on the forehead, then quickly strode out of the room. Sarah could hear the door swing shut with a bang as he left. She didn’t hear the wagon moving, but soon realized he had taken the horse instead. Sarah was indeed nervous. She had never witnessed or helped birth a child. Her mother had told her what to expect, and shared what advice she could give her, but no one thought the baby would come right now. Although her belly had grown in size, she was still not as large as she saw other women. Sarah lay on the bed waiting for the pains to come. They seemed to be coming faster each time.

Sarah pulled the sheet off her and moved back to the edge of the bed. Her back hurt and she couldn’t be comfortable lying on the bed. She pushed herself up. As she stepped toward the bottom of the bed another contraction overpowered her. She gripped the bedpost and bent her head down as her belly strained. When the pain was over, Sarah went to the chest and pulled out the blankets she had knitted and the soft linen gown her mother had given her for the new baby. She laid them carefully at the bottom of the bed. Another contraction began, and suddenly water drained down her legs. "God help me," said Sarah as a feeling of panic began to overtake her. "Calm yourself down," she said aloud. She reached for a towel and dropped it to the floor and moved it around with her foot to dry the floor. The exertion seemed to start another contraction. She held on to the bed post and once again grit her teeth. "It is early. It is certainly too early," she said aloud again, as if to assure herself after the pain had stopped. She went to the kitchen and picked up the basin of water she had poured earlier for washing. She began to walk back to her room when another contraction hit. "Ahhhhh," she said as she struggled to put the basin down on a chair halfway back to her room. She was becoming increasingly alarmed at how often the contractions were coming. When the pain stopped she picked up the basin and continued to walk back to her room. She had barely gotten through the doorway when another contraction hit. Her hands shaking, she placed the basin down on the chest and she braced her hands against the chest waiting for the pain to pass.

Sarah pulled out several sheets and laid them across the top of her bed. At first she thought she would lay down on the bed, however she felt that if she laid down she would be unable to get back up. Another contraction hit as she stood aside her bed. She had put the towel to her mouth and bit into it as she screamed. Sarah climbed up on the bed, pulled up her gown, threw the pillow aside and knelt facing the headboard. She gripped the headboard and held the towel in her hand. She could feel pressure building inside her. Once again she put the towel to her mouth and bit it, screaming as the contraction hit.

Abra's horse galloped toward the servants' house. He could see Hagan and Abigail in the distance working in their own garden as they did every afternoon after eating a quick meal and before returning to Abra's fields. Abra bent down over the horse and kicked in his heels. The sound of the approaching horse made the two Irish indentured servants stand upright and they shielded their eyes with their hands.

"Why, it's Mr. Clark," said Abigail. "Do you suppose the Mrs. is ready? Seems a mite bit early. "

Abigail picked the basket with her own baby sleeping inside and began walking back to the house. Her husband followed behind carrying the tools. As Abra came within shouting distance they could hear him calling, his voice carrying softly in the spring breeze. "Abigail. It is time."

Abigail smiled and continued to walk to the house. By the time Abra arrived she was just approaching the doorway. "Mr. Clark, first babies take their good old time making their appearances. The Mrs. may not even be ready. Are your certain it is time?"

"I saw her have one contraction before I left, but Sarah feels it is time."

"Ah, don't be alarmed, Mr. Clark. Wee ones, especially the first, tend to make their parents wait for them," assured

Hagan as he clapped Abra on the back. “Why don’t you go on ahead and get Mrs. Hatfield from town. I will load up the baby and Abigail and we will head to the house. Trust me; you will have plenty of time. You know Mrs. Clark will want her mother there at her side.”

Abra wanted to go back to the house, but he knew Abigail and Hagan were probably right. “Fine. Just tell Sarah I will be back immediately.” Abra turned the horse and headed up the road toward town. The Hatfield farm was on the other side of the city limits. It would take three quarters of an hour to get to their farm and about an hour to get back. “Are you certain this baby won’t come for several hours?” Abra asked before he kicked in his heels.

“You’ve got a nice long wait ahead of you, Mr. Clark,” assured Abigail. “Now you go ahead and get Mrs. Hatfield. She will want to be there to attend Mrs. Clark and welcome that precious grandbaby into the world.”

Abra smiled a bit in relief, and moved quickly down the road. Abigail and Hagan laughed at the thought of first time parenthood. Abigail had given birth to three babies. Timothy was age five and Patrick was three. The baby, Alyson, was only a few months old. “I will take the wagon, Hagan, and I will take Alyson with me as she needs nursing. You keep the boys with you.” Hagan smiled at his wife. She was a hearty woman from a large family. Abigail had helped midwife many times back in Ireland. Hagan knew this was why Mr.

Clark had bought their contract. He knew Mrs. Clark was in good hands.

It had taken Mrs. Hatfield a small amount of time to pack her bag. She had not expected to be called upon so soon. She scooped up a pie which she had just baked and packed it into a basket, and she wrapped a small roast that had been cooked for dinner. Her husband, Isaac Hatfield, sat rocking in his chair waiting for the eventual calm he knew would arrive. His wife, Sarah Price, was a proud woman and very loving. She had been an excellent wife and mother to their two daughters and she was looking forward to assisting her daughter. Once Mrs. Hatfield had finished her packing, Mr. Hatfield helped her into the wagon. Abra tied his horse to the back of the wagon and took the reins. "I will come by in a week to meet my new grandchild, Abra. I will wrap up things on the farm here, and then be out to pick up the Mrs."

Abra was anxious to get back to his farm. "Thank you, Sir. We will be looking forward to having you visit. I am just now realizing I will be a father within the next day."

"Your work is just beginning, Abra," said Isaac.

"I suppose, but it is Sarah who is doing all the work right now, and I feel like I need to be helping her," sputtered Abra.

"Trust me; the women will handle all that. Men can run a farm and run the country, but it is nothing by comparison to a woman bringing a child into this world. That's the real work," laughed Isaac. "Now get on with you. I know Mrs. Hatfield will not be happy until she is in charge of your house!"

"Oh, go on with you," laughed Mrs. Hatfield. "I will see you in a week, Isaac." She waved at her husband as Abra clicked the reins.

When Abra returned home with Mrs. Hatfield he expected to hear the sound of Sarah's labor. Instead the house was peaceful and calm. Mrs. Hatfield had already bustled in ahead of him while he tied the wagon to the post and pulled out Mrs. Hatfield's bags and the prepared food. As he entered the kitchen there was the aroma of food cooking, and the house was still. Alarmed, Abra dropped the food on the table and quickly strode to the bedroom. As he pushed open the door he saw a pile of sheets and towels on the floor soiled and bloodstained. His heart was in his throat, and he turned his head toward the bed. There sat his wife propped up by pillows and holding a small bundle next to her chest. At first he thought it was another pillow, until he looked around and saw both Mrs. Hatfield and Abigail smiling next to the bed.

"Abra, meet your son," said Sarah softly. Abra looked into his wife's eyes. Her hair had fallen loose and was lying across the pillow, and her face was radiant.

"Are you all right," asked Abra? "Is the baby all right? How did this happen so fast?"

Sarah smiled and said, "I am fine and so is your son." Mrs.

Hatfield quietly left the room to allow father and son a moment to meet.

"Thank you, Abigail," said Abra as he turned to look at her as she picked up the bundle of soiled linens.

"Don't thank me, Mr. Clark. It was your own Mrs. who birthed that baby alone. When I got here she had already done the hard work," laughed Abigail.

"What? How did it happen so fast?"

"Seems to me this young man has a lot to do in this world and he had a mind to get started without any 'by your leave' from the rest of you," said Abigail. "He is healthy, and has all the fingers and toes, although he and his mum are a bit tired for all their efforts."

Abra looked at Sarah as she gently pulled the baby from her breast. "Here, Abra, hold your son."

Abra took the small bundle into his arms. He had never held a baby before and he was nervous. "Why, hello, little man," said Abra. As he cradled the baby in one arm, his finger traced the baby's face. A little fist appeared and the fingers wrapped themselves around Abra's own finger. "He's so little, but his grip is strong. He is a handsome young man."

Sarah smiled and yawned. "It seems as though I have been the only one working today, and I am exhausted," she said. Mrs. Hatfield came into the room and quickly took command of the room. She arranged the pillows and sheets around her daughter, and took the baby into her arms. "Now you go and get yourself some dinner, and I will get acquainted with my grandson." Abra nodded and bent down to kiss his wife.

"Does my grandson have a name?" asked Mrs. Hatfield.

Sarah looked at Abra and said, "Aaron."

Abra smiled and looked at his son. "That is a good, strong Christian name. Welcome, Aaron Clark," he said as he gently traced his son's face. Aaron waved his little fist for a moment, and then settled into sleep.

"You go now, Abra. Get some dinner. Abigail is heating up some food for you. And, Sarah, get some sleep. You have worked hard today."

Sarah smiled into Abra's face and closed her eyes. She had indeed worked hard but she was satisfied that Aaron was healthy and strong and would make a fine young man one day. Abra watched her as she slept and love welled in his heart. She was indeed a strong woman. With Sarah by his side, he was certain he could conquer all the problems of the world.

# Chapter 5
# *Facing Personal Losses*

**Abra Clark's fear of being lonely** was erased when he began his family with Sarah. Sarah had given birth to eight children over a fifteen year period. Aaron was already a young man of fourteen by 1764. He was followed by the births of Thomas (1753,) Abraham Jr. (1755,) Hannah (1757,) Andrew (1759,) Sarah (1761,) Cavalier (1763,) and Elizabeth (1765.) Sarah was a strong woman and brave woman. Even when young Abraham Jr. died in 1758, and Cavalier in 1764, Sarah maintained her strong attitude, never displaying her grief in front of her family.

Abraham Jr. was only three years old when he died of scarlet fever. At first the young boy complained of a sore throat, and Sarah gave him warm tea with honey in it to soothe the discomfort. At this same time the child of the Clark's indentured servant was suffering the same symptoms. The children had played together in the yard while Molly was working in the gardens. Molly's son lost his appetite and complained of his ears hurting. A fever then took over and the boy lost his life after suffering several days. Sarah and Abra were alarmed and began a vigil over their son, watching for any changes. Abraham Jr. soon became lethargic and lost his appetite. No amount of coaxing on Sarah's part could get the child to eat. Sarah noticed the boy's tongue and the roof of his mouth developed red bumps and told Abra to fetch the doctor. "He has strawberry tongue," said Dr. Lampe after examining the boy. "And, look here. There is a red rash developing on his chest."

"What does it mean," asked Abra, although he knew the answer already.

"It is scarlet fever. Seems there are many cases of this in the area. You need to isolate the boy from the other children and keep him cool and comfortable. Encourage him to eat. If a fever spikes, bathe him in tepid water. There is not a lot we can do. Just watch for fever and treat that. If the rash doesn't spread within the next day, he should be fine."

Sarah moved Abraham Jr. to her room and kept the doorway covered so the other children would not enter the room. She tried to encourage Abraham to eat, but he refused. By nightfall a fever began to overtake him, and the rash spread from his chest to his abdomen, then eventually his entire body. Sarah refused to cry in front of him, but continued to talk calmly and encouragingly to him. The fever lasted two days, and the skin began to chafe where the rash had appeared. Sarah could feel the swelling in Abraham's neck and she tried to keep him comfortable. Sarah had only slept a few hours each night throughout her vigil. On July 26th, on a hot summer morning, young Abraham drew his last breath. His mother and father were at his side and Sarah draped herself over his lifeless body sobbing. Once the tears escaped her, Sarah stood and began to prepare her son for burial. Abra looked toward the ceiling and took strength from his wife. He went to the barn and began the task of making a coffin for his three year old son. When young Aaron came outdoors beside his father he asked, “What can I do, father?”

Abra looked at his son who was only seven years old, yet was already willing to help in a crisis. “I need you to go to the servants’ quarters. I need you to tell them to fetch your grandfather and let him know that young Abraham has left this earth. Your grandfather will know what to do. Have him contact the preacher.” Aaron took off immediately, relieved he had a mission which would let him escape the obvious pain he saw in his parents’ faces. It would also allow him to let loose his own grief for his brother. This was the first time Aaron knew the person who died. He had never experienced firsthand grief and how to grieve. Other young children had died from other farms; however Aaron did not know them personally.

The following day the family placed the small coffin holding young Abraham in the back of their wagon, and they traveled to Rahway to the churchyard. The grandparents,

Uncle Abraham, the servants, and several neighbors were all in attendance as they lowered the little coffin into the ground in the churchyard. Sarah's courage and strength were not overlooked. Her children cried, but she held back her tears and tended to her children's grief. It was the first loss Sarah had ever had, but she held firm to her faith that her son was now in God's hands.

It was only six years later that Cavalier died in infancy and the family again mourned their loss, yet Sarah remained positive and supportive of her husband, never allowing her grief to show. At night when the children were put to bed, Sarah would say her prayers and soft tears were shed over little Cavalier who only lived a couple months. His body had been wracked with fever during February when he was only a month old, and Sarah was unable to break his fever. After a night of holding him and rocking him softly in her chair, Abra found little Cavalier dead in Sarah's arms in the morning. Sarah looked at Abra with a tear soaked face and said, "I couldn't save him, Abra. I tried. I really tried, but he was so weak. He just breathed slower and slower until there were no more breaths in him." Abra took the child from her arms and carefully laid him in the small crib. He lifted his wife from the chair and wrapped his arms around her. Sarah sobbed uncontrollably until her oldest children awakened and entered the room. Sarah quickly mopped her face, bit her lip, and gathered her children around her.

"It's all right, Sarah. You did everything you could. He was just too little," said Abra. It was Aaron and Thomas who helped their father build a small coffin of pine wood. Sarah lined it with the soft blankets she had made for her babies. She carefully laid the infant in the box, and stood beside Abra as the lid was fastened. The other Clark children stood in a circle around the small coffin and Sarah softly sang a hymn. Even later that day when the small box was lowered into the snow covered grave in the Rahway cemetery, Sarah had remained strong, holding the hands of her youngest children and telling them that Cavalier was already at Jesus' side. Shortly after Sarah found she was again with child. Elizabeth was born at the end of the same year, clearly several months early. Sarah made certain the tiny infant stayed out of every draft as if it had been her fault that Cavalier had taken the chill which caused his death. Despite Abra's assurance that Cavalier's death was not her fault, Sarah became even more protective of her children.

With so many mouths to feed, Sarah's life was always a whirlwind of activity. Abra had bought more indentured servant contracts in order to keep the farm and to help Sarah with the raising of the children. Sarah initially had resisted the extra hands as she was fiercely independent; however she soon accepted Abra's decision. Because so much of the day-to-day chores were done by the servant, Sarah was able to begin teaching her children their letters and how to read Bible passages. Sarah's education was limited, but she wanted her children to have some advantages. Abra, meanwhile, had a small addition built on the back of the house in order to house his growing family.

The Clark house was always filled with men from the town and neighboring boroughs. Abra worked out of his house offering legal advice and counsel. He was nicknamed the "poor man's counselor," often taking produce in trade for his services. His clients would often fill the small farmhouse with talk of politics, law and farming. Abra's father and uncle were often at the house and continued to share opinions on the changing politics of the colonies. Discussions had been more frequent since 1760 when King George III took the throne. Although he had been the first King George to actually be born in England, and to speak English as his native tongue, there were still questions to his loyalties. Unlike his father and grandfather, George III never went back to Germany; however he had enemies throughout Europe.

George III had overturned the power of the Whig party, replacing them with a Tory, who ended up resigning after one year. George then focused his attention on trying to force the colonists to settle land disputes with the Indians so that the costly endeavor of protecting the frontier could come to an end. The colonists were not paying the same taxes as the British, and the British did not want to burden the cost of protecting the colonists from the Indian attacks.

There was much debate in England about this issue, along with all the other political and war problems George was facing.

One evening in particular there was great rejoicing in the Clark house when Thomas and Abraham arrived with news that the war on the frontier with the French was over.

"I'm telling you, the biggest problems occurred when the French started building all those forts in the frontier lands. That Virginian Lieutenant Governor, Robert Dinwiddie, was issuing out land deeds to citizens of Virginia to move out to the frontier and settle. When they got out there, the French were set up for attack. They had built forts all over; including taking over a British fort they were calling Fort Prince George on the Ohio River. The French showed up, forced the British out and finished building the fort that's now called Fort Duquesne. That young Virginian officer, George Washington, was sent out demanding that the French leave," Abraham shared with his brother and nephew in an excited voice. Abra's sons, Aaron and Thomas sat attentively listening to the adults.

"Why did the French think they had a right to the land," asked Aaron timidly.

"Well, Aaron, the British and the French have been disputing the territories since 1750 when the French were directed to take possession of the Ohio Valley and kill off all the British in the area. They then tried to take over all the lands in Pennsylvania setting up forts as settlements."

“Was the land actually theirs?” asked Aaron as he sat on the floor in front of his grandfather.

“Well, that’s the thing. How could anyone protect what’s his if no one is there to protect it? The British could call land theirs, but until they have troops out there protecting it, and people there settling it, the land is up for the taking,” answered Abraham.

“And the French were only too willing to take,” added Thomas as he ruffled Aaron’s hair. Thomas was overtaken with a coughing spell and the boys waited politely until their grandfather caught his breath.

“Why didn’t the British just send troops and protect the land?” asked Aaron.

Abra answered, “Well, they did. That young Virginian, George Washington, was sent out to protect the British rights. He heard tell that the French were going to attack, so he made a preemptive strike.”

“Was that the start of a war?” Aaron asked.

“Not just yet. Washington won that first battle, but was soon defeated in the next. There were just more French troops there. Can’t win a battle when you can’t have equal numbers,” said Thomas.

“So what happened next,” asked Thomas, eager to hear the rest of the story from his grandfather and great-uncle.

“The British sent out Major General Edward Braddock as commander-in-chief. He sets up troops from Virginia to march out to the frontier, but ends up getting defeated and Braddock gets himself killed" said Abraham.

"So was this war?" asked Aaron.

Abra responded. "You would think so, but it wasn't until sometime in 1756 that war was actually declared. For two years the British were losing, but finally their luck changed when they planned a three part attack on three different French forts."

"Is this what they called the French Indian War?" asked Aaron. "The boys at school talked about that."

"Well, it wasn't called that until recently, and it is only called that here in the colonies," said Abra.

"So, who won?" asked Thomas as his attention shifted from one speaker to the next.

His twelve year old mind was trying to picture all the players involved in this war.

"Well, there was a tug-of-war between the British and the French fighting all the way into Quebec. The British knew they had to capture Quebec to really win, so they had an army of 9,000 soldiers and twenty ships and fought for fifty-two days in 1759."

Young Thomas said, "Stop. Where did they get all those 9,000 soldiers?"

Abraham looked at young Thomas and said, "Many were from Britain. But many were young men who were taken into service. They even took young boys your age to carry supplies."

Thomas looked startled for a moment, and then imagined himself acting bravely on the battlefront. "I wouldn't be carrying any old supplies. I'd take my rifle and shoot down the enemies."

Aaron looked at his brother and shook his head. "Easy to say that, but at school they talked about a lot of boys, especially from Virginia, who died in those fights. The French didn't care who they were aiming at. Man or boy, you could be a target. Uncle, what eventually happened?"

Abraham continued. "The British finally won that battle, and as a result they controlled most of North America. They signed the Treaty of Paris last year giving all of North America east of the Mississippi, except for a place called New Orleans, to the British. But, the French ended up giving up New Orleans and the lands west of the Mississippi to Spain" explained Abraham.

"Wait a minute. If they called it the French and Indian War, where do the Indians come in?" asked Aaron, looking very puzzled.

"The Indians were also fighting the British at the same time the French were fighting them. And there were some tribes which were actually helping the British fight the French because they didn't want the French taking over their lands. Darn confusing. In fact, even though we settled things with the French, we are still fighting the Indians right now," said Abra.

"We don't see many Indians around here," said young Thomas.

"No, but there was a time when your grandfather was your age that he carried a gun with him everywhere he went," said Abra.

"Maybe I should carry a gun all the time like Grandfather did," stated young Thomas.

Abra laughed. "I don't think so, Thomas. We are living in a much more civilized area. It is pretty peaceful in these parts. In fact, other than the last of the Indian wars going on out west, we are living in peace here in New Jersey." Abra stood and looked at his sons. He was proud of their interest and their ability to follow the politics that grown men often had difficulty following.

Thomas was again overtaken with a coughing fit. When he gained his composure, he looked at his grandsons. "Funny thing is in Britain they called the war the *Seven Years War*. Only problem is it took nine years here in the colonies. In some of the papers coming from Europe they are calling it the *Fourth Intercolonial War*, as well as the *Great War for the Empire*. It will be interesting how this will be penned one day in the history books. There are so many inconsistencies because of the expanse of land and the time it takes to report what happens. It will take years to sort everything out to get one clear concise accounting of what actually happened."

Young Thomas laughed. "That's right, Grandfather. Maybe this will be the Great Fourth Intercolonial Seven to Nine Year French and the Indian Wars for the Empire!" The men chuckled, and even Aaron laughed at his brother's cleverness. Thomas ruffled his grandson's hair.

"Could be, Thomas! Could be. Can't be any more confusing than what we hear in the news that comes to us."

"The two of you need to go help your mother with chores. I have some business I need to discuss with your grandfather and great-uncle," broke in Abra. The boys obediently stood and moved to the chicken coop where Sarah was collecting eggs.

"Father, I wanted your advice. I have been asked by the Royal Governor, William Franklin, to take a position as a commissioner to survey and divide the common lands of Bergen Township between Newark and Trenton. I would also lay out a road and oversee its building."

Thomas stood up and clapped his son on the shoulder. "Why, that's wonderful, Abra. You've built quite the reputation among these parts as a fair man."

Abraham pointed out, "You probably would have gotten an appointment before this time, but you really burned some of the people who had their hands in everyone's purses. I heard talk that some of them worked hard to keep you out of the political scene."

Abra had also known this. In many disputes families with "old money" felt they should already win any dispute. Their position did not dissuade Abra from a fair outcome. "Didn't matter. I still stand for my beliefs. The common man has got to be protected; otherwise we will suffer the same as our forefathers did in England. Elizabethtown is growing. So many of the indentured servants are finishing their obligations, and many move out west, but just as many stay here to get their own piece of land. Who will protect them? They were scorned in Ireland, and they came here just a step above slavery. We've been lucky that the local landowners treat their servants well. Just look at what has happened in Virginia. No one has protected the common man there and they've got servants on the run and court disputes over non-fulfilled contracts."

Abraham added, "Well, until the King understands that the colonies need to be unified, things will never change. Seems they are too divided. It's like ancient Rome. The Empire fell because the interest groups divided them. It was every man for himself and no one thought of the greater good of Rome. The colonists have got to learn to stand together so they can protect their rights here in the colonies."

"That's right. If people stopped looking at their own needs and realized we could get things done if we stood up together, we'd get things accomplished. There has always been strength in numbers," said Thomas who leaned back with his chair and chewed on a piece of straw as he talked.

Abra thought about the truth in that. He remembered back to the stories he had heard at his father's knee as a child about the Associates and the Proprietors and the early development of Elizabethtown. Even though the Proprietors had the legal rights, they were unable to overpower the decision favoring the Associates. They had won the right to own the land where Elizabethtown now stands because of their strength in numbers.

Again Thomas broke into a coughing fit. "Father, are you all right?"

"Yes, it is just a little congestion. It will pass. And as for taking the appointment as Commissioner, I say do it. There can be no more fair a man than you, son,"

Abra smiled at his father. "Thank you, father. Of course, this means I will be away from home even more than I am now.

"Your uncle and I will look in on Sarah and the children. This is a good move for you, Abra. Have you talked it over with Sarah?"

"Yes, and Sarah says I should do this. She is certain she can handle things on the farm."

"She's a good woman, Abra. I have to say she has stood beside you through good and bad times. She knows you have so much to offer your fellow man, and this appointment will no doubt be the first of many." Thomas thought about how Sarah never questioned Abra accepting produce and food in payment for services. She knew they could make more money through farming, or from Abra working for those with strong ties and financial ties with England. Her husband insisted on helping those who had no other avenue of help, and Sarah supported his choice.

Abra watched as his father and uncle walked together to their wagon and waved as they pulled out of the yard. Abra was proud that he had such mentors as them.

Abra took the appointment and as expected, he traveled much of the time. The job took him away for weeks. In September, 1765 he was traveling home when he was waved down by a neighboring farmer. “Abra! Abra! Whoa!”

“What is wrong?” asked Abra.

“Your father has been sickly. My wife has been staying with your children. Sarah has taken the baby with her but she went to stay with Elizabeth to help with your father.”

Abra turned his wagon around and headed back up the road to his father’s home. He tied off the wagon and entered the house. Sarah was in the kitchen fixing a tray of food. “Oh, Abra! There was no way to contact you. Your father took ill two weeks ago and today he has taken a bad turn. He had severe fever which wracked his body. The doctor came by, but gave us no real hope.”

Abra’s chest ached and his throat constricted as he walked back to the small bedroom. His father lay propped with pillows and Elizabeth was dutifully sitting beside him holding his hand, and mopping his forehead with a wet cloth. Abra had always felt his father was a strong and big man, but now he looked small and weak. “Father. It’s me, Abra.”

Thomas’ mouth moved and his eyes fluttered open. His voice came out small, “Abra, son. Glad to see you. Sit here beside me and tell me about Bergen.” Thomas’ voice struggled and was only above a whisper.

Elizabeth stood and Abra took her place. He mopped his father's forehead and he told him about his encounters in Bergen and the work he was doing. His father would drift to sleep from time to time, but Abra and Elizabeth took turns sitting beside him. Two days passed and there was no change in Thomas' condition. Early on the morning of September 11$^{th}$, Abra heard a horse approaching the house. He remained with his father when he heard Sarah's alarmed voice. Sarah swiftly came to the bedroom and looked directly at Abra. "Oh, Abra" she whispered. "We just got word that your Uncle Abraham died this morning of a heart attack." Abra gasped, and at that same moment, his father's eyes opened wide. Thomas tried to speak, but no sound came from him. He strained forward, and then fell back into the pillow. He was dead.

Elizabeth smoothed Thomas' hair off his face, as Abra sat looking into his father's face. A look of peacefulness had settled across it, but there was no peacefulness in Abra's heart. Abra stood and walked out into the yard. He looked up at the sky and wanted to scream. His father and his uncle were his mentors. He had always looked to them for advice and encouragement. Both gone. Both gone in one day. It was too much. Even when his three year old son, Abraham, and infant son, Cavalier, had died, Abra stood bravely beside his wife and children and did not cry. Abra was not a man of tears, but now they streamed down his face.

Abra had the brothers buried side by side in the churchyard of the Presbyterian Church in Rahway. They had been brothers, best friends, confidants, and mentors. Abra vowed he would make them proud of him and do the work they had encouraged him to do. Little did he know a change was coming to the colonies; a change that not even Abraham or Thomas could have predicted.

# Chapter 6
# Civil Unrest

**Two years had passed** since Abra's father and uncle had passed. All of Thomas' land was deeded to Abra, so his land holdings tripled in size. Thomas' indentured servants continued to work the farm, and Elizabeth, Thomas' wife, continued to live in the small home they had built. Abra's commitment to the farm was renewed as he saw in it security for his young and growing family. His two oldest sons, Aaron and Thomas, had the same passion for farming that their grandfather had, and Abra knew they would oversee the farm crews.

Surveying work continued to keep Abra busy and away from home. Abra had done such a fine job with the surveying and dividing of land in Bergen Township, that government leaders took notice of him. In 1766 Abra was appointed High Sheriff of Essex by the British appointed governor. Abra took this job seriously, as he did everything he undertook. He often wished he could talk about it with his father; however he soon found that his two oldest sons, Aaron and Thomas, were always anxious to hear of their father's work. The two boys had quickly taken over the reins of the farm in their father's absence, and they scheduled all the work needing done. They readily worked alongside the servants in preparing the fields, planting, and harvesting. They marketed their crops and made careful choices in purchases for the farm. They enjoyed returning home in the evenings and taking their places at the crowded Clark table and sharing with their mother the business transactions they had handled. Sarah knew her sons were sacrificing further education in order to take on the additional tasks on the farm. She arranged for a neighbor to visit once a week in the evening to work with the boys on their reading, writing and ciphering since leaving for school was now impossible. She knew that her husband was doing meaningful work for Elizabethtown, and there had been talk of his moving into other positions. Whenever Abra argued that he was needed at home, Sarah insisted that his work for the colonists was far more important, and she was more than capable of keeping the family in good order on the home front. Her stubbornness on the subject put an end to any debate Abra may have ventured.

When Abra would return home after several days or weeks from home, he would talk to his sons about not only his job, but of news he had heard in his travels. One evening as Abra and his sons were walking back from checking the fields they engaged in discussion about his job as Sheriff.

"Father, are you paid for this position?" asked Aaron.

"No. It is more of a duty to the crown. Typically a man who has proven himself as honest and moral is asked to serve, knowing that man has an income which is self-sustaining."

"Shouldn't the King pay such people," asked Thomas.

"As it stands in the colonies, such positions are not paid."

"Why would you agree to do it, father, if it does not pay you, and actually costs you," Aaron asked.

"Son, men are often called out of a sense of duty to do what is right for his fellow man. If no one would take on this job, imagine how the colonies would be when no one was held accountable to follow the laws and the rules. In Europe the common man often goes without representation and all laws are made in favor of the rich. My work here helps keep the laws fair for everyone, including the poor."

"Father, the King has an income coming from the colonists from the Sugar Act of '64 and Stamp Act that was passed last year. Why can't this money be used to pay for proper leadership in the colonies," asked Aaron.

Abra looked at his son. "The Sugar Act was designed to raise money for the Crown through levying duties on anything imported into the colonies that wasn't from Great Britain. It was strictly a way to control what was happening in the colonies, as well as a way for the King to secure more money for England. The money was never meant to be allocated to colonists. The colonists were angry that they were being taxed and had no say about the amount or the use of the taxes."

Thomas said, "We should print our own money in the colonies. That way we can pay England what it wants, and have money to use here."

"It doesn't work that way, Thomas. The colonies actually had started printing their own money and the King put a stop to that with the Currency Act. All money printing was to be done by Great Britain, this way the colonies couldn't manipulate finances in their favor. Then to show the colonists that they meant business, the King sent more soldiers to the colonies to oversee the laws were followed. Adding to the insult, the King then issued a Quartering Act in 1765 that told colonists they had to provide lodging and supplies for British soldiers. The threat of sending more soldiers to make the colonists adhere to the rules, and then force the colonists to pay for the upkeep of those soldiers put salt into the wounds of trust. This was also a way to show the colonists that they belonged to the Crown and their job was to support the Crown. All it did was anger the colonists. Great Britain believes that the colonies exist for the benefit of the mother country."

Aaron asked, "They had to let soldiers live in their houses?"

"No, the Act just made the colonists pay for barracks, food and supplies. Some loyalists surrendered their homes and property for a price, but typically the colonists didn't have to let troops live in their houses."

"Well, that was a good thing. I've heard some of the men in

town talking about a new tax. Something about stamps," said Aaron.

"That would be the Stamp Act," answered Abra.

"So what was the purpose of the Stamp Act, Father?" asked Thomas.

"The Stamp Act levied a tax on every official seal or stamp placed on documents in the colonies and in Canada. All official documents had to have a stamp sealed upon it to declare its authenticity. The Act was very unpopular and the colonist protested this expense. The idea was it would offset the cost of handling the ever expanding legislative issues developing in the colonies and Canada."

Aaron said thoughtfully, "Haven't there been protests to this act, too?"

Abra stopped walking and took a seat under the tree near the road where they were walking. He was glad that his sons wanted to know more about policies which would one day affect them directly. "William Pitt the Elder and Lord Rockingham fought to repeal the Stamp Act. The unrest seen in the protests of the colonists was obvious. Shouts of 'Taxation without Representation' were heard in Massachusetts, and that quickly became the battle cry throughout the colonies. Add to this that groups like the Sons of Liberty started forming and planned attacks on those who were to collect the taxes."

"Sons of Liberty? Who are they"" asked Thomas.

"If you were to ask the King, he would say they were traitors to the Crown," answered Abra.

"How did they protest?" Thomas asked.

"As most groups of secrecy, their protests were done under the cover of darkness. They started a grass roots campaign of informing the colonists of what was going on, making the political issues topics of discussions in all homes rather than just the homes of the policy-makers. It wasn't long before all the stamp agents resigned out of fear for their lives. The Massachusetts Assembly called a meeting of all the colonies. All but four colonies attended and passed a *Declaration of Rights and Grievances* where they let it be known that colonists were British citizens and until the Crown allowed representation in Parliament, they could not levy taxes against them."

"How did the King react?" asked Thomas.

"Well, he soon heard that statues were built in Pitt and Rockingham's honor in New York City. It became obvious to King George that there was civil unrest brewing in the colonies. To hold control over the colonists the King also began enforcing the Navigation Acts."

"What are those?" asked Thomas.

"They hold restrictions on the colonies from trading with anyone other than England. The King is fearful that the colonists are getting too powerful for their own britches. If the colonies were allowed to make trades with other nations, they could build their own treasury and begin making political changes on their own."

"Father, were there always all these taxes and laws passed onto the colonists?" asked Aaron.

"Actually, no. We always had regulations, but the Crown was happy that people were actually here, developing and protecting the Crown's property.

Aaron sat quiet for a moment and began to fidget with the hem of his pants. Abra looked at his oldest son, knowing he was mentally debating something in his head. "Out with it, Aaron. What is bothering you?"

"There has been talk of men wishing to break free of the King," said Aaron.

"Breaking free from England?" said Thomas with an astonished look.

Abra was surprised his son had heard this piece of talk. "Aaron, I need us to be very careful in our discussions of such things. Yes, there is talk beginning, however to speak such things aloud is to be a traitor to the King."

Aaron sat quietly for a few moments, and Thomas looked from father to brother. "Father, do you think the colonies should revolt against the King?"

Abra was silent for some time. He carefully chose his words. "Boys, you must remain quiet about what I share. It is not for public knowledge."

Both boys nodded their heads to their father and sat

waiting to hear what he said. "I have begun attending meetings which discuss revolt. The colonies are disorganized and it is hard to determine who would stand beside you and who would be an enemy. If such a plan were to take effect, it would be a Civil War here in the colonies as men would be loyal to the crown and others patriotic to the colonies. We are very much disjointed in our beliefs. Some want to remain loyal to the Crown. Others want total separation from the Crown."

"Where do you stand father" asked Aaron cautiously.

"I feel we should have equal rights as Englishmen and get Parliamentary representation. As the colonies have begun to gain financial and economic stability many believe we have become a threat to the Crown. In protest to increased demands by Great Britain, many are supporting economic opposition and boycotts which will not be met with any sense of acceptance. I believe if things progress we will have a standoff and there will be a decision as to whether we strike for independence. While I would prefer the equality of an Englishman, if that were not offered, then I believe I would strike for independence."

Both boys stared at their father. They admired their father and knew that such a statement took much consideration. Abra continued. "If such a revolt were to take place, you need to understand that you will both be of age to fight. The British are well armed and will not tolerate any such revolt. The colonists know this and will not lightly make such a decision. Even our pastor, Reverend James Caldwell, has been attending these meetings. He feels strongly that the colonies should be free from Great Britain." Abra paused, allowing this information to settle on his sons. "Know this, however. Many of our neighbors wish to remain loyal to the Crown, so any open discussion of this topic places all of us in a dangerous position." Abra stood up and both of his sons stood as well, looking into their father's face.

They all walked in silence. It was Aaron who broke the silence. "I agree, Father. You are right. It is like we are being asked to serve as slaves to England. That's not right." Thomas nodded his agreement with his brother.

Abra continued. "I have been asked to serve on the New Jersey Council of Safety, and it is a position I believe I will take. I must discuss it with your mother, but she has been supportive of all decisions I have made in the past."

"What will this job entail?" asked Aaron.

"Well, those leaders of New Jersey are already seeing the writing on the wall. They can see what has been happening in other colonies, and if problems are on the rise there, it will not take long for the same to happen here in New Jersey. They know that we need to have plans ready to protect the landowners and people of New Jersey, especially if a revolt were to happen. I do not anticipate such a revolt happening anywhere in the near future, but be advised that such talk has already begun. I need you to promise not to discuss this outside of our home. To do so could have dire consequences for me and for others, and our home could be in jeopardy of retaliation."

Both boys agreed that the conversation would not leave their circle. Aaron's chest appeared to swell with pride that his father had confided such information in him. He was nearly sixteen, but he understood he was old enough to fight should a war ever break out. He also knew that whatever side his father took, he, too, would take that same stand.

Abra and his sons walked back to the house, and the boys quietly asked their father which of the local landowners were likely to want a revolt. Each name mentioned, Abra would ponder a moment and say, "Loyalist," or "Patriot." Both Aaron and Thomas understood the significance as it was clear that many of the families of Elizabethtown were divided and if such a revolt occurred any time soon, there would, indeed be civil unrest in their peaceful Elizabethtown. They also noted that at this time, most of the families were identified by Abra as Loyalists; thus Aaron and Thomas knew that outside discussions of this topic needed to avoided.

As weeks progressed the Clark boys became more aware that the issue of taking sides was becoming the most significant choice for all men in quiet Elizabethtown. The unrest was not only evident in conversations, but even in church. Reverend Caldwell of the Presbyterian Church's feelings were becoming evident each service as he began to make political references in his sermons. Several Loyalist families had begun to miss services. Their absence spoke volumes to the congregation, but Reverend Caldwell did not stray from his commitment. Elizabethtown was not troubled with all the bigger concerns caused by the Navigation Act as they were not a major shipping port, however they had certainly been affected by the Stamp Act and Sugar Act, although many of the landowners had merely accepted these decisions. Abra knew that as more Acts were levied against the colonists, eventually, even Elizabethtown would be pulled into the political debates. For now, it was understandable that so many were still loyal, but once the locals began to have their purses squeezed he knew loyalties would change.

He was right because in late 1767 Great Britain imposed the Townshend Acts in an effort to finance the rising cost of governing the colonies. Parliament passed the Townshend Acts and taxes were imposed on glass, lead, paint, paper and tea. This raised more ire among the colonists because nearly everyone was affected by the newly initiated taxes. The climate in the colonies was markedly anxious, even in Elizabethtown which had not been faced with the political clamor seen along the coastal cities of Virginia, New York and Massachusetts.

Despite the fluctuating political climate, Abra's home life continued to flourish. Late October of 1767 brought the birth of Abra and Sarah's ninth child. When naming him, Abra was concerned. "Sarah, I should like to name this child after my Uncle Abraham, however I do not want to disrespect our young Abraham who died nearly ten years ago. Is it wrong to want to name this son that same name?

Sarah smiled. "Abra. Your uncle, and yourself, and our young son all shared an honorable name. It is said that when a child takes on a name, he lives to the reputation of that name. I can think of no better name than that of your uncle, and yourself to bestow on our son." Abra smiled at his wife. He knew that of all the women in Elizabethtown, he had married a soul mate. He hugged her, and looked into the face of his newborn son.

"Well, Young Abraham. You have big shoes to fill. Your great uncle was a wonderful man."

"As are you, Abra!" added Sarah. "As are you!" Sarah looked into her husband's beaming face and saw before her a man who had already made a difference in Elizabethtown as well as New Jersey. She also knew that his present activities would lead him to dangerous decisions, but she was confident Abra would be a voice of reason in any group he represented.

Five years had passed and in 1772 Sarah and Abra had their tenth and last child, Abigail. Abra was already forty-seven years old, and the small Clark home now housed ten people. Many changes had happened in the colonies. Abra was spending a lot of time away from home and attended various meetings. His sons, Aaron and Thomas, were both young men of their early twenties, and they went to meetings with their father when the duties of running the farm allowed. The political changes caused an ebb and flow of change among the

Elizabethtown landowners. Many who had once been strong Loyalists were now attending meetings discussing revolt against the crown. Others, who at first felt they would benefit from independence from the Crown, were skeptical about retaliation and consequences for turning from the King. It seemed that every month loyalties were changing.

"Father, what do you think will happen if the colonists actually band together to revolt against the King?" asked Aaron.

"Well, there has been a temporary calm because of Prime Minister Lord North's work to withdraw the custom duties. However the King demanded the tea duty remain in order to 'keep up the right,' as he put it, to tax the colonists. There is presently talk in Massachusetts of rebelling against that tax."

"If Massachusetts rebels alone, they will fail," said Thomas.

"I am afraid you are right, son. They have already shown their hand when they protested the Quartering Act. Massachusetts said they would take arms against the British if they tried to enforce the Quartering Act, yet when the troops settled in Boston, nothing happened. Even Virginia tried to go alone against the Crown. The Virginia House of Burgess declared only the Virginia governor had the right to tax its citizens, and yet, they too folded. There needs to be a joining of the colonies so that we can be organized in how we deal with King George and Great Britain."

Aaron said, "Some of the locals are calling the protest in March of '70 the "Boston Massacre" when British soldiers openly attacked protestors."

"That's right," said Abra. "The British soldiers were surrounded by protestors, and they opened fire on the citizens killing five men. When they were tried for murder, they got off. The colonists of Boston were livid. Later there was an attack in Rhode Island against British troops, and instead of letting the colonists stand trial here, they shipped them off to Great Britain for trial."

"That's not fair. You know they won't get a fair trial there. They will be alone in England with no support to rally them or to hear their side of the story," said Thomas.

"That's why we need to organize the colonies so we have a united front. We cannot stage any kind of protest individually. It will take all of us joining together in a unified front to push British control out of the colonies," said Abra to his sons.

Abra's sons knew their father had abandoned his loyalist feelings and was already working behind the scenes to secure independence from England. They also knew that their father would provide calm and researched guidance to the protest plans. When Abra announced to them, "I have been asked to run for Provincial Assembly next year," neither of his sons was surprised, although they began to fear for their father's safety.

"How can you be certain you will not be betrayed by the Loyalists who are only too willing to serve as informants to the British for profit?" asked Aaron.

"There are no guarantees in these times, Aaron," said Abra. "If I am to stand for what I believe in, then I need to make the sacrifices necessary. I will be serving on the Committee of Observation and Correspondence for New Jersey, and I have been elected secretary of that committee."

"What is the purpose of this, Father?" asked Thomas.

"They started this in Massachusetts, and New Jersey had determined it makes sense to follow suit. Part of our problem in the colonies is that we have a lack of communication. Every colony is making up the rules on its own. We must stand united if we expect to survive what awaits us. This committee will guarantee that we are sharing what we not only observe, but organize protests in a united front. I cannot do this unless I have your support. I have already discussed this with Mother, and she, as always, is very supportive of my going."

"We support you in this, father. You don't need to worry about the farm, or Mother. We will stay here and make certain the family is safe." The boys knew that their father was making important choices which would affect the future of the colonies. They also knew that they may have to defend themselves against the scorn of local Loyalists. Despite their father's hard work to protect the rights of the colonists, there were those, even in Elizabethtown, who could not imagine life without the monarchy reigning over them. They viewed those who opposed the King as rebels, and the boys knew that their father was traveling among the circle of rebels against the monarchy.

## Chapter 7
# Election to the New Jersey Provincial Congress

**Abra Clark already recognized** that the British rule intended to squash the rights of the colonists. He had always been loyal to the Crown, but his passion for protecting the rights of the common man overruled his desire to please King George. At first he was careful not to proclaim his feelings aloud, knowing that there was strong local Loyalist sentiment, however Abra began to attend secret meetings where the local men discussed their growing concern over their role under the British rule. Abra would meet in secret with other local men, and occasionally with others who were brought to the Clark farm, or met in the upstairs apartment of the Wheatsheaf Tavern, and occasionally at the local farms of others. The local men all felt that Abra was honest and of pure intent when he declared that it was time for the colonies to form their own government. It was not a surprise to many when Abra was elected in 1775 to the Provincial Congress of New Jersey, thus labeling him as a Patriot. Abra's outspoken views quickly identified him as a Patriot spokesperson in New Jersey.

News traveled to New Jersey that the British had already begun fighting in Massachusetts. The December, 1773 Tea Party had set off retaliation by the Crown and their first attack was in April, 1775 in Concord and Lexington. The British passed the Coercive Acts to force the colonists in Massachusetts to pay for the tea destroyed by the Patriots dressed as Indians. As a result, the colonists resisted the Acts and they began to stockpile weapons and ammunition. The British learned about this and went after the munitions. Abra repeated to Aaron and Thomas the stories he had heard. "Seems the British wanted to retaliate against the Colonists for their Tea Party protest. Colonists were watching the ports and the troops which were stationed in Boston in an effort to protect themselves against any retaliation. Well, the Redcoats picked up and started their march out of Boston heading for Concord where it was expected they wanted to capture the arms depot the colonists had stockpiled in Concord, Massachusetts. A William Dawes of Boston rode out from Boston to Lexington to warn them that the British were coming. Paul Revere and Samuel Prescott joined Dawes along the way, but they were surprised by a British patrol. Revere was captured by the British, and Dawes turned back, but Prescott managed to escape and got to Concord and warned them that the British troops were on the move."

"What happened when the troops got to Concord?" asked Thomas.

"The militia was waiting for them on April 19th. When the British troops moved from Boston toward Concord, they passed through Lexington. Shots were fired in Lexington and the colonists had to withdraw but they sent a serious message to the Redcoats that they were not going to sit back."

"Who started the firing?" asked Aaron.

Abra shook his head. "No one seems to know who fired that first shot, but once there was an exchange, the British were not going to back down."

"What happened when the Redcoats marched into Concord?" asked Thomas.

"The British wanted to capture those weapons so the colonists would be unprotected. Instead of the easy fight they had in Lexington, the colonists of Concord were ready for the Redcoats and were able to protect the arms depot. The British had to retreat while the militia men inflicted 273 casualities on a force of 700."

"So do you think that is the end of the fighting for now?" asked Aaron.

"We'd like to believe it, but there is no way the Crown will allow their troops to be ridiculed by the colonists, who they are now treating like property. There was retaliation, but this time it was in Vermont."

Thomas added, "Was that Ethan Allen? I heard about that."

Abra nodded. "Yes. Ethan Allen and the Green Mountain Boys, as they are being called, seized Fort Ticonderoga where the British were storing weapons."

"I heard that Ethan Allen was captured," said Aaron.

"True. This just occurred on the tenth of this month, so we are still awaiting word on what happened."

"So are we at war, Father?" asked Aaron as the three walked quietly along the road together.

"Aaron, the colonies are not organized enough at this point to declare war. There are these pockets of discontent, but we are not even unified in any way. There are militias, but even they are disorganized and scattered. If we are to protect ourselves from any British retaliation, we need to be organized."

"Isn't that what the First Continental Congress was designed to do?" asked Thomas.

Abra answered. "Yes. They met for a little more than a month back in the fall of '74 with the idea they'd organized things for the Second Continental Congress which was to meet in '75. Only twelve colonies were represented as Georgia refused to be part of it. They met in Philadelphia in secret and their main focus was on how they would respond to the Intolerable Acts levied on us by Britain."

"Father, we are proud that you were elected to be a delegate for the New Jersey Provincial Congress," said Thomas. "You know that we will work doubly hard in your absence on the farm."

"I appreciate that. I will be leaving next week and I am

counting on you both to take care of business in my absence. And Thomas, I know that a certain young lady has caught your eye, but I am hoping that you will still be committed to helping at home."

Thomas laughed. "Father, Elizabeth Dixon has not confirmed that she has any designs to marry me at this time. But I must admit, I am taken with her."

"Your mother and I like her and her family, Thomas. I am certain that if you decide to take a wife, you would find no objections from your mother or me."

"Now if only Aaron here would respond to some of the looks he's given at church..." started Thomas.

Aaron playfully pushed his brother. "Thomas, there are enough 'looks' going on between you and Elizabeth. I'm surprised you even hear the Pastor Caldwell's sermon in church!"

Abra sighed, "I am concerned that Pastor Caldwell be careful of his sermons as there are many loyalists in these parts, although there are many changing over to the Patriots point-of-view. One of the townsmen overheard one of the British soldiers calling Pastor Caldwell the 'Rebel Priest.' He is a passionate man whose calling to the church can only be seconded by his calling to patriotism for the colonies."

"He's a good man, father, and I am certain he knows when to turn off his rebellion," said Aaron. Abra was not so confident.

Abra traveled to New Brunswick where he met with the other eighty-six delegates from the thirteen counties of New Jersey. They began their work on May 23, 1775. At first, delegates proclaimed their loyalty to the Crown and insisted that they would remain loyal to Great Britain. As the Congress continued their work to design self-governance, it was Abra Clark who stood firm in his belief that each delegate needed to use his one vote to proclaim his conviction in loyalty to the Crown, or his belief that they needed to protect New Jersey against the tyranny of Britain. Days were filled with tension and finger pointing as the delegates debated among themselves. The term "traitor" was heard often, and Abra knew that he would be considered such for his involvement.

Abra wrote letters home to his sons and Sarah, sharing with them the highlights of his work in New Brunswick. Transporting letters had become dangerous business. An act of secrecy was always considered by Abra as he knew any interception of his letters would provide the British the ammunition needed to charge him with treason. Letters being delivered home were always hidden among baskets of produce and baked goods being delivered to the Clark farm as "payment" for some legal assistance Abra had provided. Sarah never openly removed the letter until she was safely inside the house and she had drawn the curtains. Four letters were delivered today; one to Sarah and one to Aaron and another to Thomas. A fourth letter addressed to Reverend Caldwell was also in the bundle. Sarah took her letter to her room to read alone.

*My dearest wife,*

*My time away from you and our family weighs heavily on my heart, however the work I am doing will do more to protect the common man than any other action I could do at home. My esteemed colleagues and I have worked tirelessly to pen a State Constitution which maps a self-governance of New Jersey. The work takes us late into the evenings and I have been diligent in my protection of each citizen of our state and his rights. It would be too easy for us to design a government which would mirror the very government from which we are seeking to break free.*

*My nightly prayers are to hold you and our children safe. I understand that Thomas' plans of marriage to Miss Elizabeth Dixon have been planned, and I will welcome her properly into our family upon my next visit home.*

*I fear that Aaron has postponed any plans of marriage as he has taken the responsibility of head of the family seriously and has discouraged any thoughts of marriage. It is unfortunate that his adult years have been plagued with the present governmental crisis which could indeed pull him into potential war.*

*Yes, my dear Sarah, I must confess that discussions of potential war have been voiced. We know that by planning self-governance for New Jersey is in direct opposition to the wishes of the British Crown, however if we are to live with the freedoms we were promised were ours, then such freedoms cannot be enjoyed while under the tyranny of the Crown.*

*Please kiss each of our children and pray for me each day, as I do for you. My love for you and for your support in my causes grows daily.*

*Your loving husband,*
*Abra*

Sarah held the letter to her heart and wiped the tears streaming down her cheeks. She knew she must compose herself before sharing news with the children. She also knew that both Thomas and Aaron received correspondence, and she worried about the information Abra would have shared with them in an effort to protect her.

Sarah was right in her thoughts of Abra's letters to Aaron and Thomas. Both boys were quietly talking with their letters spread on the table before them as Sarah entered the room. As she entered the room, both boys carefully folded their letters and placed their hands upon them. "What news does your father share with you?" asked Sarah. At first her sons sat silently and tried to dissuade their mother from this topic. "Boys, your father wrote me that war may break out. I am not ignorant of what is happening. I would expect the two of you to share with me what news your father has sent."

Aaron looked at Thomas, and Thomas nodded to his brother. "Mother, father wrote that New Jersey is to create its own militia in an effort to protect ourselves should war break out. Our concern is that the British have set up camp on Staten Island, and that is only twenty miles from the New Jersey shore. I have been talking to Thomas, and I feel very strongly that I am called upon to help in this cause. I want to travel to New Brunswick and offer my help. Thomas will stay on the farm and help oversee the crops. Andrew is old enough to be of great help here on the farm and we have enough servants to do the work."

"Elizabeth and I plan to marry in September, and she will move here with us and we will both be here to help," added Thomas.

"I like Elizabeth, and I would welcome her in this home and I would feel secure in knowing you were here to protect the children and myself. Aaron, I know you feel you need to join the militia, and while I am hopeful that this talk is unnecessary, I also know that your father wants New Jersey to be able to protect itself should the British retaliate. We also have our servants who will be here to help us."

"Mother, I know that some of the servants will request breaking their contracts if they join the militia. Father has agreed that if war does break he would welcome our servants in protecting our rights; however he fears that the farm will be left unprotected. Mother, you know that father would be targeted because of his identity as a Patriot. I want to secure more servants so we have a surplus to help us until this business comes to an end," said Aaron.

Sarah had not thought of the servants leaving the farm, but it made sense. She also knew Abra was fighting not only for their rights, but for the rights of all men, including those who would one day complete their contracts and become citizens of New Jersey. "When would you leave, Aaron?"

"Mother, I would like to leave immediately. Father has indicated that they are already mustering troops into the State Militia."

Sarah had not expected this. She sat silently for a moment staring into Aaron's face as if memorizing it, while at the same time forcing back her tears. She stood and Aaron jumped to his feet and faced his mother. She reached up to his face and pulled it toward her and kissed him on both cheeks. "Aaron Clark. You are your father's son. I know this is work you must do. I pray that God will protect you and all of us. You must do what you feel you must do. Go with my blessing." Aaron hugged his mother and as he did he felt her shoulders shudder. Sarah turned, squared her shoulders, and walked away from her boys before they could see the tears streaming down her face.

Aaron left early the next morning after a quick goodbye to his mother and his family. He and Thomas shook hands and said some quiet words to one another. He had packed extra shirts, wool socks, britches, as well as cartridges into his saddlebags. Sarah had wrapped bread and meat into a cloth which he put into another saddlebag. Aaron gracefully mounted his horse and Thomas handed him his flintlock rifle. Aaron's youngest siblings bid goodbyes and Abigail and Elizabeth cried as their brother pulled back the reigns of the horse. Aaron pulled his tricorn hat down over her eyes, turned his horse and galloped away. Sarah stood watching his disappearing figure until he vanished from her sight. She hurried the younger children back into the house and began issuing chores for them, mostly to distract them and keep them occupied while she considered the changes happening in her life. Thomas immediately left to work in the fields making certain his mother did not see the emotion in his face.

Sarah now watched for correspondence daily from Abra and from Aaron, although she was disappointed in not hearing from Aaron at all for several months. When she did, his letters were terse and shared very little information. He briefly stated the training he was receiving and that his company was always on the move. Sarah at first was angered that he never revealed where he was, then Thomas told her that in a state of war, correspondence had to be limited, especially by the military as it could fall into British or Loyalists' hands. Sarah took a strange comfort in this as she preferred to know her son was safe and hidden from British guns, although she still felt anxious that she had no idea where her son was or if he was eating right, or if he were healthy. Aaron had spent his life on the Clark farm and Sarah had seen him every day of his life, and now suddenly she had no idea where he was. When her mind drifted in this direction, she shook it off and busied herself with the many jobs on the farm. Sarah had now taken on some of the work in the fields as several of the men asked to sign off to join the militia just as Aaron had predicted. Sarah couldn't deny the servant's desire to join the militia as she knew Abra's feelings on this matter. She also felt that if there were enough men fighting, the British might give up and just go home. She laughed at the thought of the British troops traveling back to King George, shrugging when questioned as to why they had returned. There was certainly little to laugh about these days.

Sarah was hanging laundry on the line to dry when a letter from Abra arrived. She slid it into her pocket and acted like the deliverer had just stopped by to visit. Sarah continued to hang the laundry, although her first impulse was to rip open the sealed letter and read it immediately. Sarah had adapted this cautious charade in order to keep Abra's messages safe. Once she had finished the laundry and had thrown some grain to the chickens, Sarah went into the house and drew the curtains. In her room she removed the letter and lovingly touched the address. As her eyes peeled the letter, a feeling of optimism quickly overtook her. Abra sounded so positive that his enthusiasm nearly leaped from the page.

*My darling Sarah,*

*As you know from past correspondence, when I first arrived here there was little unity, let alone uniformity in thought among the New Jersey delegates. I rather thought we were inventing governments as we went along.*

*Our labors to write a New Jersey Constitution have been successful and presently we are debating the fine points of it before ratifying it. I am confident it will pass and I am proud to have been a part of its conception.*

*Also, I am proud that we have formed a strong New Jersey Militia, of which our Aaron has been part. He is already training to be an officer as his age and strength make him a fine leader of the young men who have joined the militia.*

*We have been communicating with the other colonies and it appears most are following our lead. The Second Continental Congress is already working on organizing a Continental Army and in June named George Washington as commander-in-chief. Washington had done such a fine job with the French-Indian War; he is a seasoned soldier and excellent leader, not to mention Patriot. I feel a kinship with him as he began his career as a surveyor before he served in the Army. Washington has a fine record with leadership and we are content that we have selected the appropriate commander.*

*We have recently heard of a one day battle at Breed's Hill in Charlestown where they tried to protect a Boston shipyard. When the British attacked, our militia fought bravely. They had so little ammunition that in order to conserve it they cried, 'Don't fire until you see the whites of their eyes.' They fought until they ran out of ammunition, and then retreated, allowing the British to take the hill, although many of the British died in the battle.*

*Sarah, you know that throughout my life I have fought for the rights of the common man. Well, the common man is now fighting for himself. The stories that come to us about the battles have been heartwarming as the colonists are finally fighting for themselves and their rights.*

*The Continental Congress has been most complimentary to the work we are doing in New Jersey. They have encouraged the other colonies to imitate the work done here and in New York and Massachusetts. Our provincial congress took over executive authority. We have made appointments for various governmental posts as well as military and judicial appointments, totally ignoring the authority of both Royal Governor William Franklin and the New Jersey colonial Legislative Council or upper house. Such a bold move has forced Britain to recognize that we are striking to be self-governing. Other colonies are following our lead.*

*I plan to return home in time for the marriage of Thomas and Elizabeth, however my stay will be limited as the work here is fierce.*

*Affectionately yours,*
*Abra*

Sarah read the letter several times. It was obvious that Abra had heard from Aaron, and the news was good. For that she was thankful. Abra's letter also made her proud that her husband was such a vital part of the changing government. She always knew he was fair and just, and now he was able to put his passion to work. That night she shared her letter with Thomas, and the two speculated late into the night what the future might hold for the colonies.

## Chapter 8
# The Declaration is Conceived

**That September, 1775**, Abra and Sarah stood proudly watching as Thomas and Elizabeth were married. The celebration was cut short when Abra had to leave immediately to return to the state legislature.

Letters sent home from Abra were picked up in Elizabethtown. There were always letters to Sarah and letters to both Thomas and Andrew. Sarah would read her letters aloud to the children at the dinner table. Thomas and Andrew's letters were shared only in part with their mother. Nine year old Abraham would follow his brothers and try to find out what their father had written about the strike for independence. The Clark family tried to maintain as much normalcy as possible. The younger children were aware that their father was doing important work, however conversation was restricted. Thomas and Andrew would occasionally go to the Wheatsheaf Tavern to talk to the other men of Elizabethtown and Rahway. The tavern stood on the St. George Highway and was at the far limit of the Clark farm. Thomas and Andrew would share the contents of their father's letters with the men they knew were Patriots; however they were careful not to share when strangers were in the tavern. Their father had warned them that times were changing and it was their duty to protect the family and the farm and to talk with strangers could jeopardize not only them, but their mother and younger siblings.

Sarah was not comfortable sending any of the children off the farm for school as she was fearful there would be repercussions because of Abra's involvement in Congress. There were still Loyalist families in Elizabethtown, although more had changed sides as the restriction of colonist rights began to take its toll on the residents of New Jersey. Instead of school, Sarah tutored the younger children herself. Although Sarah would have liked to hire a tutor for Andrew, to economize Andrew's education was limited to what she could provide, and additional tutoring from Thomas as time allowed. The boys were typically in the fields all day working with the remaining servants, and Thomas and Andrew would take turns going to town to handle purchases and sales, always making certain one of the two were always on the farm.

In one of Abra's letters, Thomas shared with Sarah that Massachusetts' militia was calling themselves the "Minute Men" because they would need to be ready at a minute's notice to fight. Massachusetts had already had their ammunitions seized by the British and had already had battle in their colony. As much as Sarah prayed, she knew that it was only a matter of time before the British began making their presence known even here in Elizabethtown. Sarah told her sons of her fears after reading Abra's letter to them. The boys made little comment about her anxieties. After Sarah left the room Thomas looked at his brother and said, "Andrew, I am considering joining the Militia. Don't tell Mother just yet. We needn't worry her more than she is already with Aaron and Father away. I will want Elizabeth staying here on the farm while I am gone. She will be of help with the younger children."

Andrew was shocked. "I can understand why Massachusetts needs to be ready. They have had outright protests and are on the shoreline and the British fleets would land there, but do you think New Jersey will have the same kind of action?" asked Andrew.

"The majority of New Jersey is right on the shoreline so the British fleet will find easy access. Elizabethtown is tucked away into its own little bay, but it will be easy for ships to come into our port. Look at how many ships come in to Elizabethtown's port already. If war were to break out, we would be right at the forefront."

It was not long before both Thomas and Andrew began practicing with the local militia. Young Abraham would practice as well. He already owned his own gun, and he would practice shooting targets in the open fields. Sarah never made comment about these activities. She just fervently prayed that all this practice would be unnecessary.

Thomas entered the kitchen early November. "Mother, I need to speak with you." Elizabeth was at his side. At first Sarah thought the two were going to announce that they were going to leave the farm and move closer to the Dixon farm where Elizabeth's parents lived. She was not prepared for what Thomas had to say. "Mother, I have enlisted. I will be leaving immediately. I would like Elizabeth to stay on here at our farm."

"But, Thomas, is it necessary to join up now? It will be going into the winter season. Surely with the winter months looming near there will be no fighting," Sarah argued.

"Mother, there have been more and more instances of skirmishes with the British troops already stationed in the colonies, and some problems right here in New Jersey. There have been much retaliation to the Greenwich Tea Burning last year, and more British troops have been stationed in New Jersey. Wherever there are British troops, there are fights. Although no one is really calling it a war, there are enough battle lines already being drawn."

"But the British are on foreign ground. They are not home. I am certain they are being quartered for the upcoming winter and the fighting will stop."

"Mother, fighting may or may not stop during the storms of winter, but the reality is that we need to be prepared to fight against them when the British move. Presently we are not organized enough to stand up against Great Britain, but we need to get ready. You know the work Father is doing. The British have to know that each of the colonies is moving in the same direction and they will not tolerate it. We have to be ready to protect what we have built otherwise we will become little more than slaves to England."

Sarah knew Thomas was right, just as Aaron and Abra had been. She had heard stories repeated at church, and Rev. Caldwell made it no secret that things were not going to be peaceful for some time.

Thomas said his goodbyes in the early morning and rode off toward Trenton to join the state troops. Elizabeth stayed at the Clark farm, but was often heard crying. Thomas had promised he would visit when he could. Winter months were actually peaceful months for the most part. Thomas and Aaron were able to return home for a short visit during the holiday season with news that both were being trained as officers. The Clark men sat around the table talking in hushed voices about the news Andrew had heard locally at church and at the Tavern, and what Aaron and Thomas heard in the fields, and what Abra heard in the legislature. Several nights other men from the area joined them to discuss the political news. Reverend Caldwell would also visit on occasion. The holiday season had not even come to a close and both Aaron and Thomas left again to go back to their troops. Abra left to return to Trenton, and Andrew remained on the farm to protect the Clark homestead.

The winter months were lonely and quiet on the Clark farm with very little communications. Sarah comforted herself saying that it was good there was no news as that meant the troops were not fighting. She took great strength from her Sunday meetings at the church where she was able to talk to other mothers and wives to learn any news. Rev. Caldwell always made comment in his sermon about the efforts of the colonists and strengthened his congregations through their prayers and positive thoughts about the work being done. It was in March when a letter arrived for Elizabeth from Thomas.

*My darling Wife,*

*I have been named First Lieutenant of the Eastern Company of Artillery for our State Troops. I have been working very hard with our men drilling and preparing for any reprisals from the British once the weather breaks. We have already moved troops to areas where we expect problems. Forgive me, but I am unable to share the exact nature of our work and location. Just know that I think of you and my family every day and I pray that all of you are safe. Give my love to my mother and the family.*

*Your devoted husband,*
*Thomas*

Elizabeth held the letter close to her heart and tears streamed down her cheeks. Sarah sat quietly near her and reached over to hold Elizabeth's hand. "Is everything all right?"

"Oh, yes. I am sorry. Thomas is safe. He sends his regards and love to you. He has already been named First Lieutenant, but I cannot help but fear for his position. I have nightmares about fighting and wake up with a start fearing that a shot has been heard and Thomas is there."

"Now, now, Elizabeth. You need to pray for courage while we wait to see what will happen. Thomas is a smart young man. He will not take unnecessary risks. He loves you and will want to come home to you," assured Sarah.

"I am fearful that he will not see his firstborn if fighting breaks out."

"Firstborn? Elizabeth?" Sarah looked at her daughter-in-law.

"Yes, I figure the baby will come this autumn. If fighting starts this spring, I am fearful that Thomas will be targeted and he will never come home to see his child."

Sarah stood up and pulled Elizabeth to her feet. "Elizabeth Dixon Clark, you listen to me and listen clearly. You must not think negative thoughts. You are just scared since this is your first child. You are to pull yourself together and take to your Bible if you are feeling low. Thomas will be coming home. He needs to come home to a wife who will be strong and support him in the sacrifices he is making for not only us, but all the colonists, especially those of Elizabethtown and New

Jersey. Now dry your eyes, and let's go look at some of the baby clothes I have in the chest. That should get your mind on thinking about the future and good things to come." Elizabeth looked at Sarah and found strength in her eyes and demeanor. Sarah Clark always kept a calm and sincere face in front of family, neighbors and friends. Elizabeth knew Sarah would cry in her room sometimes, but she always kept her composure in front of others. Elizabeth knew that was probably why Thomas wanted her to stay with Sarah. Sarah would not allow self-pity or sorrow.

The Congressional debates perservered between Patriots and Loyalists. It was Thomas Paine who published in his pamphlet, *Common Sense*, the idea that a declaration for separation from Britain needed to be made. The pamphlets were widely distributed and soon copies reached every colony where locals posted them for public readings. Abra knew his sons had read the *Common Sense* pamphlets and heartily agreed with Paine's views. Abra wrote Andrew letters about the work of the Congress; however he knew how dangerous it was to have such information delivered from Philadelphia to Elizabethtown. He also corresponded when he could with Aaron and Thomas, whose location was never the same because of the training of the various militia troops. Abra carefully guarded the information in his correspondence in order to protect the work of Congress, as well as his family. He knew they were embarking on work which could only be considered Treason to the Crown. He recognized that even in Congress there were still Loyalists among them, although each colony tended to replace their delegates as the decision to strike for independence became more real. The Virginian delegates formally presented their resolution on May 27 and the entire focus of the Congress was focused on debating the resolution. Despite all the debate, no formal resolution had been presented to Congress and until such happened, the debates would continue.

Finally on June 7th Richard Henry Lee of Virginia presented a motion to the floor. Lee read for his carefully penned parchment in a steady voice to a silent Congress, "*Resolved, that these United Colonies are, and of right ought to be, free and independent States, that they are absolved from all allegiance to the British Crown, and that all political connection between them and the State of Great Britain is, and ought to be, totally dissolved. That it is expedient forthwith to take the most effectual measures for forming foreign Alliances. That a plan of confederation be prepared and transmitted to the respective Colonies for their consideration and approbation.*"

A hush fell to the floor, and it appeared as if everyone froze in place for a single moment after Lee voiced the formal resolution. Then as if the spell was broken, a voice broke the silence. "I second that motion," shouted John Adams of Massachusetts. At once the air was filled with voices, finger pointing and some delegates shouting. The meeting was called to an abrupt halt and was to resume the next day. The delegates left the meeting hall quietly grouping with fellow delegates, each group trying to analyze how the motion should be handled. That night meetings were held in hushed voices throughout Philadelphia and all delegates were careful not to meet in public places for fear of being overheard.

Only Maryland, New York and New Jersey had not authorized their delegates to commit to Independence. From New Jersey John De Hart, Richard Smith and Jonathan Dickinson Sergeant had resigned their seats in Congress because they remained loyal to the Crown. John Cooper refused to attend the sessions. That only left William Livingston as a delegate.

On June 8$^{th}$, Congress resumed their work however the debates were loud and strong. Various Patriots stood on several occasions to argue against the points made by Loyalists and lobbied for rationale and thought on the issue of independence. He reviewed the many injustices brought on by the Crown. The main focus, however, was on what the future would hold if the colonies declared their independence. The debates continued on June 10$^{th}$ until it became evident that the moderates of Congress were reluctant to declare independence. They submitted a motion to postpone Congress for three weeks in order for each colony to reevaluate the motion of independence. A vote was taken in favor of a recess; however it was obvious to all the delegates that the resolution would pass. Congress therefore appointed a Committee of Five to prepare the formal document and on June 11th they announced the committee. Thomas Jefferson of Virginia, John Adams of Massachusetts, Benjamin Franklin of Pennsylvania, Robert R. Livingston of New York and Roger Sherman of Connecticut were assigned the task to meet and create the document after a seven to five vote was taken to take a three week break from Congress. It became obvious that some of the Loyalists would not be returning when Congress reconvened. It was known by the delegates that the colonies would send replacements that would stand behind the motion to declare independence.

Abra had an opportunity to travel home for a short break from work on the New Jersey Provisional Congress. News had already traveled back to the New Jersey Provisional Congress about the proposal now on the floor in Congress. Abra immediately met not only with his son, Andrew, but neighboring land owners and men, careful that he was only speaking to fellow Patriots for the cause. “Men, it is weighty work being done in Philadelphia. Word has come back to us that when Congress reconvenes they should have the formal document which we will present to King George declaring our independence.”

“Who is doing the writing, Father,” asked Andrew.

“A thirty-three year old from Virginia named Thomas Jefferson has been given the task of penning the declaration of freedom. He had been a member of the Virginia House of Burgesses and wrote some political pamphlets in the past, so he has a bent for such writing. He also composed the draft of a proposed constitution for Virginia. His work was excellent. We know he will use some of the wordage of Richard Henry Lee's resolution as well as George Mason's Declaration of Rights for Virginia which I saw in draft form printed in the Pennsylvania Evening Post. He will no doubt borrow some of those well penned ideas as they now apply to what we all desire: our freedom and our rights."

"What do you suppose the Crown will do when this document is presented," asked one of the neighbor farmers.

"What do you think they will do? Sit back and accept it? Don't be ignorant. They will declare outright war against the colonies, that's what they will do," replied another man.

"Abra, do you think we would be prepared to fight if the Redcoats are turned loose on us?"

"If you had asked me that question a year ago I would have responded negatively. However, our boys in each of the colonies have been signing the muster rolls and going off for training. Every colony now actively musters troops. I can't say that we have all the fancy trappings the Redcoats have, and money is scarce for supplies, but I know that we would be ready to stand up for what we believe in. Our George Washington is now General-in-Chief and he has taken this job seriously. He has been meeting with militia leaders in all the colonies and organizing troops and various forts. My Aaron and Thomas have already been training to serve as officers and in their correspondence they say the men are preparing seriously. Any man who joined thinking it was just for folly has quickly learned that the work of the militia is serious. Aaron's main concern is that if a full outright war takes place, more men will be needed than just those who have volunteered. The other issue is funding to support the troops. We have no organized Treasury and supplying our boys with food, weapons and gear will certainly be problematic. Those are issues which Congress would have to address before we turn over this document. The reality is that although we are much stronger now than we were even a year ago, we are still nowhere near where we need to be if we are attacked in a full war."

"The British are strong. Look what they did to the French." Other men nodded and mumbled stories they had heard.

Abra broke in again, "True. But I believe with all my heart that the colonists are much stronger in their desire to take our freedoms and protect them. Our families came to the colonies and were promised freedoms which have been grossly ignored by the Crown in recent times. If we do nothing we stand to serve as slaves to Britain. This war will be fought on our land, in our colonies, in our backyards. We must protect what is ours."

"In our backyards? Wouldn't the war stay in Philadelphia, Massachusetts, and Virginia?" asked one man. Several nodded in agreement.

Abra's face was serious as he shook his head and spoke. "You would be kidding yourself if you believed that. Elizabethtown is nearly next door to Staten Island in New York, and there will certainly be activity there as British troops are already stationed there. Our ports will be easy access for British ships, especially if they want to spread out. No, gentlemen. If war breaks out, I can practically guarantee that Elizabethtown will see more than her share of misery." Immediately the men became animated in their discussions determining how they could protect their farms and families.

"If we join up and muster, who is left to defend our wives and children," asked a landowner who had five little children under age seven. "I'd want to fight, but my wife certainly can't aim a gun."

"Maybe she needs to learn," said another man.

"Sacrifices will be made by everyone," said Abra. "I, too, am left with that problem as my son Aaron has already left. Thomas has left also, and his wife remains with us on our farm and she is with child. I will be unable to be here to protect my family and farm as I will be working out of town. My family knows this is the sacrifice we will pay in order to get freedom for all of us."

The men nodded and after several other testimonies, the men parted to go to their own homes. Many had the seed placed about the seriousness of what was happening and the knowledge that Elizabethtown would face battle. Fathers looked at their sons in a different light that night, knowing that their boys would soon turn to men when fighting came to Elizabethtown.

Aaron surprised his family with a short visit, but what was more surprising was his announcement. "Mother and Father, I have asked Susanna Winans to be my wife. It is our intention to marry immediately as I must return to my post."

Sarah was delighted with the news. She had secretly hoped Aaron would marry one day. He was always so serious and never allowed himself time to socialize. Susanna was a distant cousin to Hannah Winans, Abra's mother. Susanna was a strong young woman who took great pride in her work at the church, educating the younger children of the Presbyterian congregation. Sarah knew she would make a good wife for her son.

"Son, where will Susanna stay when you leave?" asked Abra.

"She will remain with her family for the time being. Father, I have asked her father to look in on the farm and on Mother while I am away."

"That gives me a sense of peace," said Abra, "although we have Andrew here on the farm to watch over things. I must admit I am fearful that our peaceful Elizabethtown may see fighting right here. I also fear that troops may demand to be housed in town, or even on our farm. Without someone watching over Sarah, Elizabeth and the children, I would rest uneasy."

Aaron and Susanna married the next week. Reverend

James Caldwell performed the ceremony. His service welcomed the joining of both Aaron and Susanna into holy matrimony, but he added his own commentary about the state of the colonies. “A marriage is a union and that union can only be as strong as what each partner puts into it. If husband and wife unify, there is no enemy who can penetrate their united front. Presently we are seeing our thirteen colonies torn apart because they are not unified against a common enemy. If our colonies worked as hard as a husband and wife do to maintain their marriage and unity, no enemy could ever harm them. May we pray for our colonies to join together through the efforts of the Continental Congress and form an ever binding marriage which will stand firm against the tyrannies which are attempting to tear them apart.”

After the service Abra clapped James on the shoulder. “Interesting sermon, there, James. You would best serve on the pulpit of the Congress alongside Patrick Henry!”

The Reverend replied, “Abra, so affirmed I am in this business that I will be leaving at the end of this month to serve as chaplain to our New Jersey Continental Line under Colonel Dayton. I can better serve and inspire our boys in battle to win what needs to be won. My parsoning here is limited as people are fearful to even leave their homes because of British patrols. God will understand that the present strife we face will lead us to a more unified country as well as a more God fearing country. I can lead more men to His eyes by serving alongside them.”

Abra looked at Caldwell for a long time. "You've thought this out, have you? I know my Aaron and Thomas would feel more secure knowing you were at their side to give them strength, courage and faith. It would also give me a measure of relief to know someone was pulling some extra help from on high and looking out for my boys and the sons of all the other men and women from these parts." After a short pause, Abra asked, "Aren't you fearful that you are mixing politics in your sermons?"

Caldwell chuckled. "Recently Nicholas Cresswell from England was touring the colonies and visited many of our Presbyterian churches. He was heard saying that the Presbyterians were hoping that if the leaders of the church supported the cause of liberty, the Presbyterians would be named a national religion should the colonies achieve freedom from England."

Abra responded, "Do you believe that?"

"No, although it is true that the Presbyterian churches are unilaterally supporting independence. While there are ulterior motives by some to see a greater role for Presbyterians as a national religion, I do not believe the colonists would tolerate it. The lessons of our early forefathers bear witness that in securing freedom of religion when settling the colonies, it is doubtful they will swiftly accept one national religion, regardless of the support for independence."

Abra nodded. "You are no doubt correct in that. I suppose

our first battle needs to be securing freedom from Great Britain. Once that's achieved, our other freedoms will need to be established and protected. There is so much work yet to be done."

The two men shook hands, and Abra promised to stay in touch with Caldwell.

# Chapter 9
# Continental Congress

"**Abra, we need you** in the Continental Congress," said John Hart.

"John, you know that I support this action, but I am fearful to leave my family unprotected. Traveling to Philadelphia means leaving my family in the hands of my sons. They are just young men and times are changing. It was one thing to be in Trenton with the Provincial Congress, it is another to be in Philadelphia, which is further away from family. Already I am fearful that the British are on Staten Island and my farm is in jeopardy of being a battleground."

John paused and looked at Abra for a long time before saying, "Abra. Times are changing. We need you in Philadelphia at the Continental Congress. What you contributed here in New Jersey in making our state's Constitution, and organizing the militia has been a model for the other colonies. Everyone knows you are fair and reasonable. You are always first to protect the rights of the common man. Those rights will continue to be challenged unless we have the right people in Congress to guarantee we take the right steps to protect ourselves. If change is going to happen, we need every level-headed representative we can get."

Abra asked, "Who else has been selected?"

"Richard Stockton, Francis Hopkinson, Dr. John Witherspoon, and myself. There would be five of us, Abra. All of us are of the same thinking that we need to break free of the Crown, not just as a colony, but all thirteen colonies in one unified effort."

Abra looked out toward his fields. It was June 21$^{st}$, 1776 and the crops were already planted and growing. He knew if he left, not only would his farm be left without his input, all work in the New Jersey Provincial Congress would end. They would have to find another representative. He also knew that despite the changes happening in the colonies, there were still some Loyalists in Elizabethtown, and although he had always been a fair man to all, there was no accounting to what could happen in his absence. Abra looked at Hart and said, "I fear not only the British, but our own homegrown tyranny. There are those who have already exhibited greed of local power here in the colonies and they would be every bit as dangerous as the British troops. Such a decision is huge as I put my own family and home in harm's way. I have to talk to Sarah before I commit."

"We need to make a decision soon, Abra. All the colonies are sending representatives, unlike the First Continental

Congress where Georgia refused. New Jersey wants to replace the representatives who are remaining loyal to the Crown at this point. New Jersey leaders want to replace the congressional delegates there who are against independence. Your name was immediately mentioned and I said I would ride out to your place to discuss this."

"John, I am right proud that people respect me that much. It is a big decision. I have never really left New Jersey for any extended period of time. This would certainly pull me away for some time, especially if it is decided to seek independence. I know that they have been considering a legal document to declare freedom from Britain, and full outright war is likely. King George is certainly not going to give up the colonies without a fight, and New Jersey has sat on the fence for some time, but the Provincial Congress has taken a stand. There are still plenty of Loyalists locally," said Abra.

"You know, Abra, the fact that you are taking a stand will give some of those men the courage to stand beside you. They haven't been affected until recently by the changes in the taxes. If they see a man like you standing up for independence, they will re-examine their own consciences."

"I'll send Andrew out tomorrow with my answer. I need to think this through, John. It is serious business, indeed." The two shook hands and Abra stood watching as John Hart rode away. Abra turned and walked slowly back to the house. He could see Sarah standing in the doorway waiting for him.

"Well, Abra, what did Mr. Hart want? His riding out here directly means there is some matter of importance."

"Sarah, there has been an outcry in New Jersey as our representatives have been Loyalists and the tide is changing. I have been asked to serve in the Continental Congress."

"Isn't that in Maryland?" asked Sarah.

"No, in Philadelphia."

"How long would you be away, Abra?" asked Sarah, looking directly into her husband's face.

"Sarah. The other four men they have selected are all Patriots. They all want independence. They know that I have had those same feelings. This will not be a quick answer. All thirteen colonies have to meet and agree, and if it is decided to strike out for independence, you know there will be a full war."

Abra watched his wife as she turned and busied herself with the food she was preparing. She kept her face turned from Abra for a time, and Abra stood quietly waiting. He watched her pull her apron up toward her face for a moment. Her shoulders squared and she turned toward Abra and stood directly before him. "Abraham Clark. There is no finer man in these parts. I have been proud to call you my husband, but in these days I am proud to call you a representative of our people. You have always been honest and fair to everyone with whom you dealt. People have come to you for counsel over the years and you have never been a self-serving man. Is this something you feel you need to do?"

"Sarah, I believe it has to be done. To pull back would make us slaves to the Crown. Already we are being taxed with no opportunity to have a voice in England. Troops have already been sent here to monitor us and then we are charged for that aggravation and there have already been outbreaks of attacks and counter-attacks, mostly in Massachusetts. It really got started after that tea dumping."

"Wasn't that when Indians dumped the tea sent into the Boston Harbor?"

Abra sat down at the table and pulled Sarah to a chair facing him. "Sarah, those were not Indians. They were Patriots who were looking for yet another cause to raise attention to the inequities the colonists were dealt by England. It was just like the Greenwich Tea Burning here in New Jersey. The Patriots dressed up like Indians and dumped 342 chests of tea into the Boston harbor and we know the King is planning more retaliation. The mutiny has been set and the colonies recognize that we must work together to fight whatever King George sends out for punishment. The King has passed the Boston Port Bill which cut us off from England. There are many colonists who have cried out that this is wrong. Severing the ties to England meant cutting communications with family still in Great Britain. Of course, King George knew this and counted on the Loyalists being outraged by the acts of the colonial rebels. But more to the point, the Act declared an end to any rights of the colonists, especially those of Massachusetts. Some felt England was reducing the colonists to slaves."

Sarah nodded as she listened. Some of this talk she had gathered from conversations she had overheard when the men would come to visit Abra on the farm. "How dangerous is this, Abra?" Sarah asked, her eyes showing the concern she had not only for her husband, but for her children. She knew that if there was war, her sons would become involved. Aaron was already twenty-six and part of the militia, and Thomas twenty-four and recently married and his wife was with child. Andrew was seventeen, and he was already announcing he would follow his two older brothers wherever they went.

"I cannot lie to you. It is dangerous. Outwardly stating we want independence is treason to the Crown and would be treated as such. I also know that should war break out, the war would spread to New Jersey. We certainly don't have ships to take the war to England; however King George's fleet is extensive. Our Continental Army is young and inexperienced. I am also not convinced that our state militias are strong enough to fight against the English troops. I feel if I were to go to Philadelphia it would be my job to make certain that these things are considered before the representatives are swept by passion to take on more than we can support. I also know that if we move forward and fail, I would be tried as a criminal and we stand to lose our property, not to mention face penalties for being a traitor. That would spell ruin for our children."

Sarah's eyes welled and she looked down at her hands in

her lap. Her husband could be killed. Her sons could be killed in battle. She and her younger children could be turned away from the farm and left to fend for themselves. She was also not foolish. She had heard stories of women who had been molested while their men folk were away from their farms. She had her daughter-in-law Elizabeth, and her younger daughters, Hannah, Sarah and Elizabeth to worry over, as well as Aaron's wife, Susannah. Her chest felt heavy as she tried to breathe calmly. She looked up into Abra's face and saw that he was intently studying her face. They sat for several moments across from one another in silence. Finally Sarah broke the silence. "Abra. I have trusted you with my life. You are a sound and reasonable man. My womanly wish is that this business with the King would just disappear and life would go on as before. Our lives have not been overly vexed. But if what you say is true, we will no longer have the freedoms we have enjoyed in the past. I have heard stories told of slaves in the southern states on the plantations. Some of them are mistreated so badly and children are sold off from their parents like heads of cattle. I do not want a life of slavery for my children. I give my leave, Abra, for you to do what you think is best. Andrew will be here to watch over the farm and keep us safe. If war does break out, I know that our sons will follow your lead and act as men to protect us." Tears were streaming down her face.

Both turned abruptly at a sound from the kitchen doorway. Andrew was standing there listening.

"How much have you heard?" asked Abra.

"Enough to know you are being called to service, Father," said Andrew. "If you go, I will be here to take care of things. We have done it in the past and we can do it again."

"Son, it will be more cumbersome than in the past as I would be in Philadelphia and would not come home for weeks or even months at a time. It will be dangerous for me to travel."

Andrew responded, "Father, I am a man now. We have been listening to talk for some time and knew there would be changes. I am old enough to be helping more on the farm and we have workers to keep it running." Abra was now glad that his work locally had forced his hand in buying more servant contracts, despite those who had already joined the New Jersey militia. It would indeed make this transition smoother.

"Well, Abra, what is your plan?" asked Sarah.

Abra looked at his wife and sons and replied, "I feel it is my duty. If I meet with others in council and discuss such political changes, then I need to stand by that talk and put action behind my words. I will admit, I am concerned about the time spent away from the family, but I know that this is important work."

"Then you have my blessings, Abra," said Sarah and wrapped her arms around him.

The next morning Andrew rode out to tell Mr. Hart that his father would be joining him in Philadelphia. Sarah busied herself washing and pressing clothing and packing trunks for Abra to take with him.

A post arrived in late June from the state legislature. Abra carefully opened the parcel at his desk and read,

*22nd June, 1776.*

*To Richard Stockton, Abraham Clark, John Hart, Francis Hopkinson, Esquires, and the Rev. Dr. John Witherspoon, Delegates appointed to represent the Colony of New Jersey in Continental Congress.*

*The Congress empower and direct you, in the name of this Colony, to join with the Delegates of the other Colonies in Continental Congress, in the most vigorous measures for supporting the just rights and liberties of America. And, if you shall judge it necessary and expedient for this purpose, we empower you to join with them in declaring the United Colonies independent of Great Britain, entering into a confederacy for union and common defense, making treaties with foreign nations for commerce and assistance, and to take such other measures as to them and you may appear necessary for these great ends, promising to support them with the whole force of this Province; always observing that, whatever plan of confederacy you enter into, the regulating the internal police of this Province is to be reserved to the Colony Legislature.*

Abra knew that this letter would arrive as the former delegates had already received oral confirmation of this on

June 7[th]; however the written affirmation now made his work clear. His mind filled with the work ahead of them. They must keep their eye fixed upon their goal of becoming independent and joining the colonies into a confederacy. Abra wondered what the new government design would resemble. He knew there would be no monarchy; however the discussions which he had been party to range from monarchy to dictatorship. It was now that Abra's love of history would benefit him as he could look at the ancient civilizations and contribute ideas of the best from history. There would be so much to do, but first, they must win this battle against Great Britain, and Abra knew it would not be easy.

When the time came for Abra to return to Philadelphia, Andrew approached him.

"Father, we need to be ready to fight to protect what is ours. You were right when you told the local men war would come to New Jersey and directly to Elizabethtown. Mother and Elizabeth will be safe as will the children. I cannot sit idly and not support you when you are sacrificing for all of us and all of New Jersey and the colonies. I am my father's son after all. I have watched you risk your own life and safety to protect all of New Jersey as well as all the colonists. How can I not do the same?"

Abra looked deeply into Andrew's eyes. He knew nothing he could say could persuade Andrew from his stance, yet he expected nothing less. How could he ask his own son not to do the same he was asking other men to do? If the colonies were to become independent, it would take sacrifice of everyone, every family, including his own. He shook his son's hand, and pulled him into a hug. "I am proud of you, Andrew. I am proud that your mother and I have raised you to be a man of honor."

Abra finished all the paperwork and business he was handling and selling a small parcel of land which had been left unseeded. This money would be used for his extra expenses living in Philadelphia. When all was in readiness, Abra's trunk was loaded into the wagon. Abra said goodbye to all his younger children, and Sarah and Andrew joined him in the wagon to take him to town to catch the stagecoach. Sarah remained unusually quiet throughout the trip to town, fearful that she would lose control and cry. Abra and Andrew talked about the latest news. When they reached Elizabethtown, they were joined by John Hart. The families shared a meal at the local tavern as they awaited the coach. Goodbyes and promises of letters passed between family members and Sarah stood in the street waving her handkerchief as the coach pulled out of sight. She climbed back in the wagon and didn't talk all the way home. They arrived back on the farm late into the evening, and as Andrew unhitched the horse from the wagon, Sarah went into the house. Andrew could see his mother moving things around in the kitchen. When he entered the house, Sarah had already retired to her room. He was about to enter when he heard her muffled cries. He quietly went to his bed and thought about the changes that were forecasted for the colonies. He knew that he was now the man of the house until his father could return safely home.

Abra arrived in Philadelphia on June 28, 1776. Abraham Clark quickly took his stand for independence, vocally reaffirming in each small group of delegates the need for freedom to protect the common man in the colonies. "The common man will forever be enslaved to the Crown if we do not unify and demand our independence," he said. When several delegates challenged him as to protecting themselves against the British troops who would certainly retaliate, Abraham Clark again stood firm that sacrifices had to be made. "Our own personal comforts must be put aside for the better good of all our fellow colonists. The promise of becoming independent would make us all free citizens of united colonies."

"But, Abraham, you are forgetting that there are those among us who would stand to lose so much in this war. My family has large land holdings and we cannot be expected to ignore our property and fight against the British who are our countrymen," said a delegate from a southern colony whose wealth came at the backs of his many slaves.

"Be aware, Sir, that if we do not fight for independence you will forever be enslaved to Britain. You mistakenly believe that if we continue with the status quo Britain will stop issuing levies against us. History has taught us that is not true. We have stood by and watched unfair taxing and restriction of our rights. When protest was done in Boston harbor, retaliation was swift and severe. We cannot view ourselves as one class over another. We are fellow countrymen who are fighting for the same thing. We demand our freedoms and rights to vote, which has been denied us whether of the upper echelon, as you describe, or the common man. Besides, we will most certainly be punished for the protests and actions done up to this point," replied Abra.

"Mr. Clark, what sacrifices are you to make? Your farm is reputably small and you have far less to lose should the British declare outright war on us," said another delegate.

"Because I have less property does not mean my sacrifice would be any less worthy than yours. The fact that I have so little means I have everything to lose whereas you have so much, some loss would still leave you with property. I have sons of an age who would readily fight. My sons Aaron and Thomas felt it their duty to join. I stand to lose my sons, and in their absence, the very safety of my wife, daughters-in-law, and my six younger children as well as a new grandchild soon to be born. Already my passage home is dangerous because of British patrols and Loyalists too willing to earn ease with the Crown by turning on their fellow countrymen," replied Abra passionately. His words put a sting on several of the Southern delegates' attitudes. Several Patriots standing nearby nodded their heads in understanding as they listened to Abra's arguments. "Sacrifice? Everyone will need to sacrifice in order to make our colonies united and independent and free for our children and their children. Anyone who has been within these walls knows each of us has already sacrificed because of our dedication to this cause. Alas, this is only the beginning of sacrifices to be made. The men of Massachusetts and Breed's Hill have already sacrificed, and as we stand here, they are preparing to sacrifice again. It will be on the backs of the common men of the colonies, their sacrifices that lead us to independence. Their bravery will be the greatest sacrifice in order that all of us, whether rich man or poor man, can be free in our own independent country." Abraham had spoken boldly, however in his heart he feared the safety of his family back home, and for his sons and friends who were already enlisted.

No sound was heard as Abra looked about the room, and then slowly took his seat. Suddenly a thunderous applause started and the delegate who had challenged Abra sat quietly, considering what he had heard.

# Chapter 10
# *The Declaration is Finalized*

**During the three week break** from Congress, Jefferson had penned a draft, then made modifications as proposed by John Adams and Ben Franklin. A copy of the draft had been sent to George Wythe, a fellow Virginian who had served as mentor to Jefferson; however Wythe had made no significant changes to the draft. Another copy was sent to Richard Henry Lee, who had made the formal resolution to break free from Britain. Lee also made no significant changes. A third, but not complete draft was sent to Edmund Pendleton, who was serving as President of the Fifth Virginia Convention. Again no significant changes were made by Pendleton. Jefferson felt the document was now fit to present. When Congress reconvened on June 28$^{th}$, a copy of Jefferson's draft, copied in John Adams' hand, was presented to Congress.

Members of Congress examined the copy of the declaration and debated the points made. Abra carefully examined the wording making certain that it expressed clearly and concisely what they intended. He knew copies would be made and distributed to all the colonies and it would be read in every public place. The document had to be so clear that every man of the colonies would know exactly what was being sent to Britain.

Only minor changes had been made by Franklin and Adams on the original draft. The title of the resolution was, "A Declaration by the Representatives of the United States Of America in General Congress assembled." For three days Congress altered Jefferson's document. Their most significant change was to eliminate a paragraph restricting slave trade and statements denouncing the people of England for their participation in a war against the colonies.

"Why should we not include restriction of slave trade," asked a northern colony delegate.

Abra quickly responded, "Sir, there are colonies here who utilize slaves and our purpose here is to seek independence, not finger point over the moral issues of slavery. We need to stay focused on what we desire and that is independence. The document will be read throughout the colonies and if we include passages which point blame on practices of our own colonies, it will be lost in debate and our intentions will not be supported. We must stay true to what we intend and that is to break free from Britain and the Crown."

Several more debates stemmed from this, but in the end the delegates agreed to remove that passage. However, there was even more debate over removing the passage denouncing the English for their part in fighting the colonies. Again Abra was vocal about this passage needing to be eliminated. "My good gentlemen. We need all the colonists to be in support of our declaration to become free of Britain whether they are Patriots or Loyalists. Not all the English believe we should be treated as we are. Not all the English are declaring war against us. Denouncing the English would have further damage in our own colonies to those with close ties to family and friends still in Britain. If we pen that, we are asking the colonists to turn their backs on their families and friends still in Great Britain. That is not our intent. Our intent is to be free of the government, not sever ties to family. If we ask our colonists to do that it may be too great a sacrifice. If we want to rally support, we must stick directly to our cause in this document. It needs to be clean and direct. We want independence from Britain and we want to become our own nation."

Again, many agreed with Abra's opinion, and after several more hours of debate, it was agreed that the passage be removed. In all their effort to modify Jefferson's document, a point of order had been ignored. "Gentlemen, please, remember we still have a motion on the floor which has not been voted upon. Before we can do anything else, we must vote on Lee's resolution.

The Congressmen quickly took their seats and a vote was called on July 2$^{nd}$. Abra quickly responded, "Aye" when called upon to vote. In the end, Lee's resolution to declare independence of the colonies from England passed. Once this resolution was passed, the next order of business was to formally vote on the Declaration. Abra and others expressed their enthusiastic approval of the document, however he cautioned the Congress to consider what the future would hold once the document was delivered. “Understand, there will be retaliation, and we must be prepared to fight the British troops. Presently our troops are organizing and training, however we are not near enough organized to beat the British. How will we support our troops so they can fight for our freedom? Declaring freedom is one thing, getting it will be quite another.” Abra sat down and several other men stood and made suggestions as to how each state could work toward financially supporting their own militia. Warehouses of supplies needed to be organized and the delegates discussed at length how that would happen.

On July 4th, Abra took the time to write his friend, Elias Dayton, a letter. Elias, a merchant from Elizabethtown, was a veteran from the New Jersey Blues in the French and Indian War, and was presently with the Third Battalion of NJ operating in upper New York. Abra had heard about the battles in Quebec in December of 1775, and the battle in Fort Ticonderoga. Communications were difficult to receive, and Abra wanted to share what knowledge he had heard with his friend. He openly shared his fears for his family as well as his fears for the colonies should they not win this war. Abra was worried that Howe's troops could move into New Jersey and he knew that the New Jersey militia would be there to fight, or to move into New York should Howe move there, but he also knew that had Howe landed his troops immediately, he would have caught the colonists unawares and the fight for independence would be over before it began.

*Philadelphia*
*July 4 1776*
*My dear Friend*

*Our seemingly bad success in Canada, I dare say, gives you great uneasiness. In times of danger, and under misfortune, true courage and magnanimity can only be ascertained. In the course of such a war we must expect some losses. We are told a panic seized the army. If so, it hath not reached the Senate. At the time our forces in Canada were retreating before a victorious Army, General Howe with a large armament is advancing towards New York.*

*Our Congress resolved to declare the United Colonies Free and Independent States. A Declaration for this purpose, I expect, will this day pass Congress. It is nearly gone through, after which it will be proclaimed with all the state and solemnity circumstances will admit. It is gone so far that we must now be a free independent state, or a conquered country.*

*I can readily guess at your feelings upon hearing that*

*General Howe with 130 transports is between New York and the Hook. This was our last account; no express hath come in this morning. All seems uncertainty where they will land. I assure you I don't feel quite reconciled at being here and the enemy at my door at home. All reports agree that New Jersey is all in motion to meet the enemy in case they pay our province a visit, or to assist New York as occasion may require. Had General Howe landed his forces as soon as he arrived, he might have carried all before him. Possibly while I am writing this, he may be reaping the fruits of a victory. This seems now to be a trying season, but that indulgent Father who hath hitherto preserved us will, I trust, appear for our help, and prevent our being crushed; if otherwise His will be done.*

*I have no particular news more to communicate. No news from your family to send. I wrote you the day before I left home. I am among a "Consistory of Kings," as our enemy says. I assure you Sir, our Congress is an august assembly, and can they support the Declaration now on the anvil, they will be the greatest assembly on earth.*

*As I am not able to communicate to you anything but what the public papers will announce, you will readily perceive I mean to let you know you are not forgot by me. Tho' I address myself to you, Sir, yet I mean to include my much esteemed friend, Mr. Caldwell in it.*

*We are now Sir, embarked on a most tempestuous sea;*

*life very uncertain. Seeming dangers scattered thick around us. Plots against the military, and it is whispered, against the Senate. Let us prepare for the worst. We can die here but once. May all our business, all our proposes and pursuits tend to fit us for that important event.*

*I am Dr. Sir,*
*Yours & Mr. Caldwell's most Obedient & Humble Servant*
*Abra Clark**

Abra signed and sealed his letter, then after giving it over for delivery, he moved the floor for the vote on independence. Each man entering the hall walked solemnly and talked in hushed but animated tones.

"Gentlemen, please. We have a point of order. A motion has been placed on the floor whether to accept the Declaration."

Again the delegates took their seats. A silence fell upon the room as each delegate was called; he clearly stated his name, state and vote. When it came time for Abra to vote, he stood. "Gentlemen. I am Abraham Clark of New Jersey. I vote aye." It was July $4^{th}$, 1776, and Congress approved the Declaration. It was formally adopted by unanimous vote of all the colonies represented.

The delegates knew that now it would be essential that they follow every proper protocol and be certain that there was no question that all of Congress supported this action.

*actual letter

A vote was immediately taken to authenticate and print the document with all the changes. John Hancock, President of Congress, signed the document which made it authentic. Congress then agreed that copies of the declaration were to be sent to the several assemblies, conventions and committees or councils of safety. Abra reminded them that it would be necessary to send the documents to commanding officers of the continental troops and head of the army. This too was agreed upon and all the delegates agreed that from henceforth they would no longer be the colonies, but hereafter known as the "United States."

John Hancock carefully took the signed document to the Philadelphia shop of John Dunlap. About 200 broadsides copies of the Declaration were made between the evening of July 4$^{th}$ and the morning of July 5$^{th}$. The updated copy read as follows:

*When in the Course of human events, it becomes necessary for one people to dissolve the political bands which have connected them with another, and to assume among the powers of the earth, the separate and equal station to which the Laws of Nature and of Nature's God entitle them, a decent respect to the opinions of mankind requires that they should declare the causes which impel them to the separation.*

*We hold these truths to be self-evident, that all men are created equal, that they are endowed by their Creator with certain unalienable Rights, that among these are Life, Liberty and the pursuit of Happiness.—That to secure these rights, Governments are instituted among Men, deriving their just powers from the consent of the governed, —That whenever any Form of Government becomes destructive of these ends, it is the Right of the People to alter or to abolish it, and to institute new Government, laying its foundation on such principles and organizing its powers in such form, as to them shall seem most likely to effect their Safety and Happiness. Prudence, indeed, will dictate that Governments long established should not be changed for light and transient causes; and accordingly all experience hath shown, that mankind are more disposed to suffer, while evils are sufferable, than to right themselves by abolishing the forms to which they are accustomed. But when a long train of abuses and usurpations, pursuing invariably the same Object evinces a design to reduce them under absolute Despotism, it is their right, it is their duty, to throw off such Government, and to provide new Guards for their future security.—Such has been the patient sufferance of these Colonies; and such is now the necessity which constrains them to alter their former Systems of Government. The history of the present King of Great Britain is a history of repeated injuries and usurpations, all having in direct object the establishment of an absolute Tyranny over these States. To prove this, let Facts be submitted to a candid world.*

*He has refused his Assent to Laws, the most wholesome and necessary for the public good.*

*He has forbidden his Governors to pass Laws of immediate and pressing importance, unless suspended in their operation till his Assent should be obtained; and when so suspended, he has utterly neglected to attend to them.*

*He has refused to pass other Laws for the accommodation of large districts of people, unless those people would relinquish the right of Representation in the Legislature, a right inestimable to them and formidable to tyrants only.*

*He has called together legislative bodies at places unusual, uncomfortable, and distant from the depository of their public Records, for the sole purpose of fatiguing them into compliance with his measures.*

*He has dissolved Representative Houses repeatedly, for opposing with manly firmness his invasions on the rights of the people.*

*He has refused for a long time, after such dissolutions, to cause others to be elected; whereby the Legislative powers, incapable of Annihilation, have returned to the People at large for their exercise; the State remaining in the meantime exposed to all the dangers of invasion from without, and convulsions within.*

*He has endeavored to prevent the population of these States; for that purpose obstructing the Laws for Naturalization of Foreigners; refusing to pass others to encourage their migrations hither, and raising the conditions of new Appropriations of Lands.*

*He has obstructed the Administration of Justice, by refusing his Assent to Laws for establishing Judiciary powers. He has made Judges dependent on his Will alone, for the tenure of their offices, and the amount and payment of their salaries.*

*He has erected a multitude of New Offices, and sent hither swarms of Officers to harass our people, and eat out their substance. He has kept among us, in times of peace, Standing Armies without the Consent of our legislatures.*

*He has affected to render the Military independent of and superior to the Civil power.*

*He has combined with others to subject us to a jurisdiction foreign to our constitution, and unacknowledged by our laws; giving his Assent to their Acts of pretended Legislation:*

*For Quartering large bodies of armed troops among us:*

*For protecting them, by a mock Trial, from punishment for any Murders which they should commit on the Inhabitants of these States:*

*For cutting off our Trade with all parts of the world:*

*For imposing Taxes on us without our Consent:*

*For depriving us in many cases, of the benefits of Trial by Jury:*

*For transporting us beyond Seas to be tried for pretended offences*

*For abolishing the free System of English Laws in a neighboring Province, establishing therein an Arbitrary government, and enlarging its Boundaries so as to render it at once an example and fit instrument for introducing the same absolute rule into these Colonies:*

*For taking away our Charters, abolishing our most valuable Laws, and altering fundamentally the Forms of our Governments:*

*For suspending our own Legislatures, and declaring themselves invested with power to legislate for us in all cases whatsoever.*

*He has abdicated Government here, by declaring us out of his Protection and waging War against us.*

*He has plundered our seas, ravaged our Coasts, burnt our towns, and destroyed the lives of our people.*

*He is at this time transporting large Armies of foreign Mercenaries to complete the works of death, desolation and tyranny, already begun with circumstances of Cruelty & perfidy scarcely paralleled in the most barbarous ages, and totally unworthy the Head of a civilized nation.*

*He has constrained our fellow Citizens taken Captive on the high Seas to bear Arms against their Country, to become the executioners of their friends and Brethren, or to fall themselves by their Hands.*

*He has excited domestic insurrections amongst us, and has endeavored to bring on the inhabitants of our frontiers, the merciless Indian Savages, whose known rule of warfare, is an undistinguished destruction of all ages, sexes and conditions.*

*In every stage of these Oppressions We have Petitioned*

*for Redress in the most humble terms: Our repeated Petitions have been answered only by repeated injury. A Prince whose character is thus marked by every act which may define a Tyrant, is unfit to be the ruler of a free people.*

*Nor have We been wanting in attentions to our British brethren. We have warned them from time to time of attempts by their legislature to extend an unwarrantable jurisdiction over us. We have reminded them of the circumstances of our emigration and settlement here. We have appealed to their native justice and magnanimity, and we have conjured them by the ties of our common kindred to disavow these usurpations, which would inevitably interrupt our connections and correspondence. They too have been deaf to the voice of justice and of consanguinity. We must, therefore, acquiesce in the necessity, which denounces our Separation, and hold them, as we hold the rest of mankind, Enemies in War, in Peace Friends.*

*We, therefore, the Representatives of the united States of America, in General Congress, Assembled, appealing to the Supreme Judge of the world for the rectitude of our intentions, do, in the Name, and by Authority of the good People of these Colonies, solemnly publish and declare, That these United Colonies are, and of Right ought to be Free and Independent States; that they are Absolved from all Allegiance to the British Crown, and that all political connection between them and the State of Great Britain, is and ought to be totally dissolved; and that as Free and Independent States, they have full Power to levy War, conclude Peace, contract Alliances, establish Commerce, and to do all other Acts and Things which Independent States may of right do. And for the support of this Declaration, with a firm reliance on the protection of divine Providence, we mutually pledge to each other our Lives, our Fortunes and our sacred Honor.*

On July 5th, copies of the Dunlap broadside were sent by messenger to the various state assemblies, conventions, and committees of safety and to the commanding officers of the continental troops. There were also additional printings of the Declaration of Independence from New Hampshire to Virginia. The Declaration of Independence's first appearance in a newspaper was in *The Pennsylvania Evening Post* on July 6$^{th}$.

On July 8, 1776, Colonel John Nixon read the Declaration of Independence in the State House yard to an audience of Philadelphians who knew important work was happening within Congress. Cheers went up from most, but there were those who hung in the background, still uncommitted to change, and fearing the retaliations which would certainly follow.

Twenty-three other newspapers published the Declaration throughout the colonies before it was ordered to be written as a final copy in a clear hand on July 19$^{th}$. News spread quickly throughout the colonies that Congress had declared independence, and the former colonists braced themselves for what would surely follow.

On July 19, the Declaration of Independence was ordered to be hand written on parchment paper and the title changed from *A Declaration by the Representatives of the United States of America in General Congress Assembled* to *The Unanimous Declaration of the Thirteen United States of America*. The parchment copy of the Declaration was to be signed by every member of Congress. The document was copied by Timothy Matlack, a Pennsylvanian who had been an assistant to Charles Thomson, the Secretary of Congress.

Vice Admiral Lord Richard Howe sent correspondence to England on July 28th, and again on August 11th with a copy of the Declaration. This was the formal announcement to Great Britain that the United States had declared independence. For Abra, he knew there was no turning back. There would be war. There would be bloodshed. And he knew he was now a political enemy of England who could be punished as a traitor.

# Chapter 11
# *The Signing*

**While Abra was still in Philadelphia**, he continued to worry about elections within New Jersey. He took every opportunity he could to share his worries with others who shared his insights. Being a traitor and placing his family and himself in harm's way was always on his mind. He communicated often with Reverend James Caldwell, and often several others from Elizabethtown in whom he felt he could confide. He heard in church service the story of the four lepers who could either remain at the gates of the city and die of their disease, or enter the city which had been stricken by famine and die of starvation. Abra was feeling he, too, was in a place where there was no happy ending. Like the leper he realized his fate had been to remain a victim of Britain's brutality and live a life of indignity, or sign the Declaration of Independence and face the possibility that he was now a traitor to Britain and either he or his family, or both could perish from punishments. There appeared to be no silver lining to either choice although he fully intended to carry through and sign the document.

Work in Philadelphia continued to be hectic. A formal war effort would be needed. A government would need to be established. Leaders would have to be selected. Abra's days began early each morning with committee meetings, drafting materials, and reading correspondence. Mail from home was limited, although when he received any mail it was a welcome relief. His friend, Elias Dayton, of New York, was one of the men with whom Abra felt he could share his concerns. Although Abra knew he was respected among the people of Elizabethtown, he was also aware there were still Loyalists living there, and they could, at any time, turn on his family. During a short visit home after the formal reading of the Declaration, Abra wrote to his good friend.

*July 14, 1776*
*from Elizabethtown, to Colonel Elias Dayton;*
*stationed at German Flats, New York:*

*My dear friend:*

*I continued at Philadelphia till Thursday last when I returned home . . . Our Declaration of Independence I dare say you have seen — a few weeks will probably determine our fate — perfect freedom, or Absolute Slavery — to some of us freedom, or a halter.*

*Soon after going to Congress at Philadelphia we had news of General Howe's arrival at Sandy-hook, and a few days after of his landing on Staten Island, and surrounding it with his forces — From your feeling for your town and family when you first received this news, you can form some judgment of mine, tho' I was much nearer to them — I expected nothing less from this event than Eliza'Town, long obnoxious to the Enemy, would be laid in Ashes, and indeed, had they come over they would have met with no Opposition, as our Militia a few days before had marched to New York by request of the General.*

*Most affectionately Yours,*
*Abra Clark**

Abra's fear for his family filled his mind every free moment. Howe's men were now stationed on Staten Island, and New Jersey did not have a large enough militia to help with the cause and protect its own territory. While home he visited many local farmers to ask for their support and protection of his family while he continued his work in Philadelphia. Everyone was preparing for the probability that war would happen and New Jersey would be in the front lines.

By August, Abra moved back to Philadelphia. He had little time at home with Sarah and the children; however the work that the Congress had undertaken demanded his speedy re-

*actual letter

turn. Upon returning to Philadelphia, additional news from the battle fronts was reported. Maps were laid across every available space and groups of men gathered around the various displays as news leaked about the movement of troops. Abra was constantly pulled to the map of New Jersey to keep informed of what was happening.

Abra's work was not limited to Philadelphia. He remained actively involved in the governmental decisions of New Jersey. Posts would arrive asking his advice. Because of New Jersey's location, they stood to lose the most when war started. He also knew the British not only had their trained troops, but their hired men, and they were well equipped and well fed in comparison to the meager provisions provided the colonial rebels.

Abra and the other delegates were greeted with news that Washington had 10,000 men now under his command; however there were 130 British ships with 42,000 sailors and soldiers sitting in anchor awaiting orders to join those forces already on land. The meager army of the colonies would certainly face the mightiest military force in the world. This the delegates discussed as they awaited the formal signing of the Declaration. Despite the great odds against them, and the fact that word had arrived that anyone signing the Declaration would be considered a traitor and would be hanged as such, the delegates remained firm in their conviction that signing the Declaration was necessary.

On August 2, 1776, the members of the Continental

Congress assembled and it was recorded in the Journal that the Declaration of Independence had been engrossed and was signed. The general public did not know the names of the individuals who signed the Declaration until some months later. John Hancock, who was the President of the Congress, was first to sign. He signed with a bold signature, and laughingly told the others that he did so in order to allow King George to see the name without the use of his spectacles. After signing Hancock stood and addressed the other delegates. "Gentlemen, we must be unanimous. There must be no pulling different ways. We must all hang together." For a moment all was quiet. It was Ben Franklin who broke the mood. "Yes, we must indeed all hang together or most assuredly we shall "hang" separately!" The gallows humor was greeted with some much needed laughter, but when each delegate came forward to sign, he did so with complete seriousness. There were fifty-six signatures of delegates from thirteen states who signed the historic document.

Georgia:

Button Gwinnett

Lyman Hall

George Walton

North Carolina:

William Hooper

Joseph Hewes

John Penn

South Carolina:

Edward Rutledge

Thomas Heyward, Jr.

Thomas Lynch, Jr.

Arthur Middleton

Massachusetts:

John Hancock

Maryland:

Samuel Chase

William Paca

Thomas Stone

Charles Carroll of Carrollton

Virginia:

George Wythe

Richard Henry Lee

Thomas Jefferson

Benjamin Harrison

Thomas Nelson, Jr.

Francis Lightfoot Lee

Carter Braxton

Pennsylvania:

Robert Morris

Benjamin Rush

Benjamin Franklin

John Morton

George Clymer

James Smith
George Taylor
James Wilson
George Ross

Delaware:

Caesar Rodney
George Read
Thomas McKean

New York:

William Floyd
Philip Livingston
Francis Lewis
Lewis Morris

New Jersey:

Richard Stockton
John Witherspoon
Francis Hopkinson
John Hart
Abra Clark

New Hampshire:

Josiah Bartlett
William Whipple

Massachusetts:

Samuel Adams
John Adams
Robert Treat Paine

Elbridge Gerry

Rhode Island:

Stephen Hopkins

William Ellery

Connecticut:

Roger Sherman

Samuel Huntington

William Williams

Oliver Wolcott

New Hampshire:

Matthew Thornton

As Abraham Clark stepped to the table to attach his name to a document that would change the course of history, a momentary sensation of excitement filled his body. A serious smile broke over his face. "Gentlemen, today we let it be known to all of mankind that we are willing to make the sacrifices necessary to start our own government. I proudly affix my name to this sacred document knowing I am ready to face the consequences of this dangerous action. I sign with the resolution of becoming a free born citizen of America." He bent and signed the Declaration of Independence. Among the signers, three were only in their twenties; eighteen were in their thirties. Abra was 50 years old. Ben Franklin was the oldest signer. All had long lives ahead of them, however each knew that his signature placed himself and his family in jeopardy.

Abra's friend, Elias, sent a post congratulating Abra for his appointment in Philadelphia. How Abra wished he had the leisure to talk directly to his friends. Instead, late in the evenings in his meager rooms, Abra would pen letters with hopes that they would be delivered without interference.

*Philadelphia August 6th, 1776*

*My Dear Friend:*

*Our Election for Council and Assembly Sheriffs, etc. come on next Tuesday in all the Counties of New Jersey. I now feel the want of you in Elizabethtown. I sat down to consider to whom I might venture to write on politics and have none that I dare speak plainly to; had you or my much esteems friend, Mr. Caldwell been there, I should have been at no loss. I have none like-minded. I have friends, it is true, but none there now that I dare speak with freedom to. I have written to several, and desire they will not keep my letters secret, so that I hope I shall not be charged with secret practices.*

*As to my "title," I know not yet whether it will be honorable or dishonorable, the issue of the war must settle it. Perhaps our Congress will be exalted on a high gallows. We were truly brought to the case of the three leapers. If we continued in the state we were in, it was evident we must perish; if we declared Independence we might be saved, we could but perish. I assure you Sir, I see, I feel the danger we are in. I am far from exulting in our imaginary happiness. Nothing short of the Almighty Power of God can save us. It is not in our numbers, our Union, or our valor that I dare trust. I think an interposing Providence hath been evident in all the events that necessarily led us to what we are. I mean Independent States—but for what purpose, whether to make us a great Empire, or to make our ruin more complete, the issue only can determine.*

*I am my dear friend,*
*Your sincere Friend and Humble Servant*
*Abraham Clark**

Abra signed and sealed the letter and sent it by post to his friend. His mind weighed heavily as the fear he felt for the safety of his family, and the families of all the signers, continued to grow within him.

After the signing of the Declaration of Independence, Congress recessed until December in order for the delegates to meet within their own states to ensure the militias were organized and supplies were being stockpiled for the troops. During their absence, Great Britain's retaliation was swift. 10,000 troops first arrived in New York harbor with Generals William Howe and Charles Cornwallis in August, and stood unopposed. Soon there were 32,000 troops in New York. At first the Americans thought the troops were all British, but

*actual letter

it was learned that 18,000 of the troops were hired out as auxiliaries to Great Britain. They were subjects of King George III of Britain. There were troops from Hesse-Kassel, Hesse-Hanau, Brunswick-Luneburg, Waldeck, Ansbach-Bayreuth and Anhalt-Zerbst. Many of the lot were debtors, petty criminals, or conscripted to service for very low pay. Although these Hessian troops were well disciplined and excellent soldiers, the bulk of their payment went to the German royalty who had hired them out to the British. A regiment was typically 500 men at the start of the war. Howe and Cornwallis certainly had plenty of regiments to protect the British rights in comparison to the meager Continental Army and state militias.

During Abra's time home he was able to oversee the harvesting and storing supplies for his family. He made arrangements with several older servants to work directly at the house in order to help Sarah, but also to protect them. Abra knew that he needed guaranteed help at home and with the war looming in their front yard, Abra had to guarantee Sarah had enough help. Although it was against his beliefs, Abra purchased two young Negro boys and their mother. Sarah was angered at this decision, but Abra was insistent.

"Abra, I am not happy about owning people. You have never supported slavery in the past. What reason would you think this was acceptable?" said Sarah after Abra returned home with the slaves.

"You know how I feel about slavery, but with all the indentured servants joining the musters, there just are not enough men on the home front to protect our families. I am not the only one going this route, Sarah. Believe me, if there were another way I would certainly do it. As it is, these two young boys are good workers, and their mother will help with the gardening and the children. With Thomas's son, Jonathan, just being an infant and living here with you, there was even more need for protection on the farm. I only have Andrew here to run everything and protect you."

Sarah knew that there was no discouraging Abra. He had already made the decision and made the purchase. "Abra, I don't even know how to treat slaves. I am telling you right now I will not treat them any differently than I did our servants."

Abra smiled. "I would expect nothing less of you, Sarah. The servants will be freed at the end of their contracts. I promise these boys will not die in slavery. Please just understand that I cannot do my work in Congress without knowing my family is protected." Sarah nodded knowing that there was no alternative; however her face did not show happiness in this fact. In December as Abra was on the road to Philadelphia, a post was delivered to him that the Continental Congress was fleeing from Philadelphia and was moving to Baltimore. Abra had to change course and was on the lookout for interference on the road. Throughout his trip to Baltimore, Abra continued to worry about the safety of his family and how he would arrange for posts to be delivered home. Upon arriving in Baltimore and securing a meager room, Abra was quickly apprised of many of the hardships various fellow signers had faced. William Ellery's house and property were destroyed in Rhode Island. Abra shared news of Richard Stockton. These stories worried Abra and the others, however not one delegate mentioned abandoning their choice.

The war was officially started when the British troops marched into New York and tried to capture the Americans. General George Washington moved his troops into battle and for three days in late August the soldiers battled. Washington ended up retreating under cover of darkness and the British celebrated their winning the Battle of Brooklyn. By September 15, the British occupied New York City. The following day, the British won another battle at Harlem Heights. The British then faced off against the American in White Plains, New York, and the American troops retreated on October 28th. By November 16 the British had captured Fort Washington, in New York, as well as 2,818 Americans and one hundred cannons, muskets and cartridges. Shortly after that Fort Lee in New Jersey was captured. On December 6th the British took control of a naval base in Rhode Island and on December 12th the British captured Major General Charles Lee. The colonists were losing every battle.

Abra was torn with each report of loss. The signers had all agreed this was the right thing to do, yet it did not make it easy to hear of the many losses the Americans were facing.

The maps appeared red with blood where they marked in red the British occupancy. Abra also knew that New Jersey would be easily taken if the British turned their attention there.

Abra and several other delegates spoke of needing something to charge the American Army with the strength it needed to continue what seemed to be a helpless battle. It was in December, 1776 that Thomas Paine wrote another essay called, "The Crisis."

*"These are the times that try men's souls, the summer soldier and the sunshine patriot will, in this crisis, shrink from the service of his country; but he that stands now, deserves the love and thanks of man and woman. Tyranny, like hell, is not easily conquered; yet we have this consolation with us, that the harder the conflict, the more glorious the triumph. What we obtain too cheap, we esteem too lightly. 'tis dearness only that gives everything its value. Heaven knows how to put a proper price on goods; and it would be strange indeed if so celestial an article as Freedom would not be highly rated."*

Abra read the words and his heart swelled with pride and hope. Freedom. That would be the battle cry which would either move the troops to gaining liberty, or crush them into slavery.

Copies were made and distributed and Washington was so inspired by Paine's words, he made his troops listen to the essay being read. The essay had done its work, and the Continental Army was reaffirmed in their work.

# Chapter 12
# *The War Intensifies in 1776*

**Word came that there were British troops** moving into Trenton and Princeton. So far there were no troops in Elizabethtown, and Abra prayed that none came. The state militia was further north, but there was no word of battles near Elizabethtown. Abra studied the maps on display on the Congress floor. There were always delegates near the maps discussing the latest moves and reports. Each delegate would first question the safety of their own state and sounds of relief or despair would be heard in their voices. Congress continued to meet in Baltimore, Maryland rather than Philadelphia in an effort to protect themselves from retaliation of the British.

The delegates were not pleased at the progress of the American troops as they had lost every major battle since August of 1776, yet Congress remained committed to their cause. Abra rallied fellow delegates by saying, "It is only the beginning. Our troops have to learn how to fight against an organized army like the British. We voted confidence in George

Washington. Certainly he will lead our men to victory." Other delegates full heartedly agreed with Abra. If there were those who doubted, they were careful not to voice it at this juncture. Some of the delegates who had signed the Declaration of Independence had not returned as their family commitments, or their state's leadership needed them. None of the signers indicated they no longer supported their decision; however some felt they were more useful in their home states, and still others had business to handle in their own homes in order to keep their families safe.

In November, 1776, Richard Stockton, a fellow New Jersey delegate and signer of the Declaration, was returning from a fact finding mission when he was captured. Although he had arranged safety measures for his own family moving them to Monmouth County, Stockton was taken prisoner after a Loyalist leaked information to the British about Stockton's whereabouts. When Congress learned that Stockton was not only captured, but was being mistreated by his captors, their concern grew as each of them faced the same potential fate. Abra and his fellow delegates discussed the real possibility that they could all have the same fate as Stockton. Abra was especially concerned as this happened at Princeton, which was not far from the Clark homestead. He knew Sarah and the boys would have heard of this turn of events which would make any travel home more dangerous for Abra and safety for his family even more important.

Christmas of 1776 was quietly celebrated by the delegates in Baltimore. The delegates worked daily in the Henry Fite House where they held Congress. They worked on communications and drafting ideas for a government once they won the war. This optimistic thinking was led by men such as Abra who cheered the delegates into optimistic thoughts of the outcome. Humble meals were shared among small groupings of the delegates, each group worked on different committees when a shout could be heard throughout the hall as a messenger ran into the Congressional floor. "What is this outburst," questioned the President of the Congress.

"I beg your pardon, Sirs, but I knew you would want word immediately. George Washington's troops have crossed the Delaware during the night and surprised the British troops in Trenton. He won the battle! We won our first major battle!"

All the delegates jumped to their feet and shouted. Whoops and hollers were heard throughout the room and there was much clapping on the back and hand shaking. Those delegates who had returned to Congress reserved and uncertain were now caught up with the celebration.

"How in Heaven's name could he have crossed the Delaware River? Isn't it frozen?" asked one of the delegates.

Another responded, "Not completely frozen, just parts were frozen."

"I thought Washington was in Pennsylvania," said one delegate.

"He was, but they pulled off a surprise attack during Christmas night. Some crossed in boats, some walked across the ice on the Delaware River and surprised the Hessians encamped just outside of Trenton, New Jersey."

Abra said, "Trenton? My God, that is not far from my home! And my Thomas is an officer stationed near there."

"Seems the Hessians had celebrated Christmas a little too much. They awakened to Washington's troops surrounding them. The battle only lasted forty-five minutes and Washington ended up taking 900 prisoners!"

"Wait, if they captured 900 men, that means they can take their weapons!" declared one delegate.

"That's right!" said another. "That is going to help our militia in fighting. This news will certainly spread and boost the egos of our men, and the added artillery will certainly help our cause! This will help with the morale of the men, and increase recruitments!"

There was much celebration in Congress that day. Their somber Christmas was forgotten, and now they rejoiced in their George Washington's victory. Only days later word came that Washington had again won a battle in early January at Princeton, New Jersey. Abra was alarmed as he knew both battles were near Elizabethtown. He feared for his family, and his boys. It seems he had just left the farm a few weeks before and in his absence there had already been two major battles near his town.

Another delegate asked, “What is the matter, Abra. Are you concerned about your family?”

“Of course I am. But, I stood before and said that we all had to make sacrifices. I pray that God is protecting my family. My two oldest boys and my son-in-law are already mustered in the army. Aaron is an officer, and I haven’t heard from Thomas as to where he is. My son Andrew is home protecting the family and I pray he is keeping them safe.”

John Hart was standing nearby and overheard the conversation. He placed his hand on Abra’s shoulder. “Abra. I received a letter from my wife and she wrote news of families of Elizabethtown. She wrote that your Andrew joined up. He’s not at home. He left a letter to his mother and left during the night without any goodbyes.”

Abra was surprised, but he did not let his voice falter. “I should have known once fighting broke out, Andrew would leave. He’s seventeen. He’d feel it was his duty if battles were happening right in our own backyard. I am proud that he believes in the cause.” Abra attempted to keep the alarm out of his face as he felt it was his duty to keep positive thoughts about goals Congress had voiced, but his fears for Sarah and the children gripped his stomach. That night Abra’s prayers were intense as he worried for his family’s safety, and he wasn’t certain who would be watching out for them. The Hessians were rough, and knowing they were in the proximity of his home did not allow peace of mind to Abra. He reread a recent letter he had received from Aaron.

*Dear Father,*

*I am hoping this letter finds its way to your hands. Suffice it to say our General is working very hard to rally our men against what appears to be insurmountable odds. Our General has done much to encourage our men. My men are loyal to the cause, but shoes, proper clothing, and food are needed. Many men joined up during summer months and they did not bring the proper clothing to see them through harsh elements. Our state militias have not provided enough for our men to keep them satisfied. Food is also a problem. I am afraid some of my men have stolen from local farmers to satiate their hunger. It seems cruel to punish them for such actions as I myself have felt the pangs of hunger at times.*

*The purpose of this letter is to give you warning of news we received about the Hessian troops located in New Jersey. To put it delicately, we have received word that some of these men have behaved in a reprehensible manner. Under permission of British Lord Francis Rawdon to take what they need from the colonists, the Hessians have been known to steal from citizen's barns and crops. They have burned fences and some houses. One captured Hessian told officers his philosophy of war was whatever is portable is stolen, and whatever is fixed is burned down, and if a woman is not willing, ravaging her was acceptable. Father, I fear for our women. Mother, Thomas's wife, Elizabeth, and our Hannah, Sarah, Elizabeth and Abigail are defenseless against these men. My darling Susanna is with her parents and family, but I fear for her safety as well. Mr. Winans has agreed to travel from Rahway to look in on mother and the family from time to time, however travel is dangerous these days, as you well know. Thomas also said that Andrew has mustered, so there is only little Abraham at home as the man of the house. I do not share this to break you from your work, but for you to encourage the delegates to supplying what we need so we can win this war. This war must be won so we can keep our families safe.*

*Your obedient son,*
*Aaron Clark*

Abra had heard about the attacks on women, but he thought they were just isolated events. This communications made him believe it was more common than he had believed. He had shared this information with other delegates. Some had already heard stories of these attacks. "We must do something about this," said Abra.

"What can be done? We cannot just leave our work to return home to protect our own families. Our task is set before us and we must protect the rights of all Americans, not just our own families."

"I agree. But we must come up with a way of paying our troops and giving them the supplies and food they need so they can protect not only our families, but all the families, especially those where battles are being fought." Abra shared the letter from Aaron with several delegates.

"It's the same all over, Abra. Our state militia is struggling to keep the men from returning home. Stories like what Aaron wrote you would send them right back to their houses to protect their women."

Abra paused for a moment. "Washington has been doing an excellent job recently. The few victories gave our troops a taste of how success feels. We need to give him the support he needs. If his troops feel they have the support of those of us declaring independence, they will fight for the cause. God bless Thomas Paine. His "Crisis" paper did wonders on building troop morale, but those were only words. We need to give proof we appreciate their work and will financially support them. We have got to get more weapons, clothing and food in their hands."

Another delegate quickly pointed out, "That's all well and good, Abra, but we have no treasury. The price of victory is dependent upon each state which is to provide for its own state militias."

Abra nodded. "True, however not every state has organized a state constitution which outlines funding for the militia and the Continental Army. There are also those who feel that they have been paying to Britain all these taxes, and now they are being forced to also pay for state militias. There is resistance among the people in being open handed. As the war escalates, people want to hoard their money and supplies in order to provide for emergencies with their own families and further retaliation from the British. Some feel having stockpiled reserves will give them leverage in buying their safety if personally attacked by the British. This makes sense, however at this juncture we cannot force people to pay. We can only count on those like Paine who rally not only the troops, but our citizens to support the cause. This war must come to a speedy and successful conclusion if we are to protect our women and children from the barbaric attacks being reported."

The other delegates agreed that financing would continue to be their biggest hurdle in winning the war against the British, who had not only sent their own men, but had hired out troops to assist them in squelching the American rebels. It certainly appeared that the British had the upper hand in numbers of troops, and their attacks on women and property. Those who had pushed for independence now desperately wanted to obtain it in order to put to an end the suffering of defenseless citizens who were in harm's way, as well as their troops which were underfed, under clothed, and under supplied.

As busy as Abra was with the business in Baltimore, and the fear that he carried over his family being attacked, he never anticipated the letter he received from home from Sarah.

Upon reading it, Abra sank into his chair and clasped his head in his hands. He slowly picked up the letter and reread the words again in disbelief.

*My dearest husband,*

*I am overcome with grief and I have been unable to stop the flow of my tears. Our Elizabeth was taken over by fever. Her illness came suddenly and her bouts of coughing would not cease. She was taken from us within just a week's time. This happened soon after your departure for Congress. She was buried in the churchyard near our first Abraham and Cavalier. Elizabeth was a mere fourteen years, far too young to have left this earth. Only last week she was helping me in the kitchen. Pardon my brevity. I am so burdened with sorrow. I will give the children extra caresses from you in your absence.*

*I know your work keeps you in Congress. This will be difficult for you knowing you will never see her smiling face again. I whispered to her just before she ceased to breathe that you would always remember and love her, as would I. I think of how many of our young men in the colonies who lost their lives in the early battles. I know we are blessed that Elizabeth died in her bed, and not at the hands of war. My grief is nothing in comparison to the mothers who lost their sons in the battles, yet I feel heartbroken. I must regain my strength so I can comfort little Abraham and Abigail.*

*We have seen an increased number of British soldiers in Elizabethtown. We have taken to remaining on the farm and not leaving the house except for necessity. Mr. Winans has graciously stopped by repeatedly and brings supplies. We have heard word that troops are entering New Jersey, and it makes us fearful for our safety. I have practiced with the children and hired help hiding in the root cellar in case strangers come to our door. Our two Negroes and their mother have been very helpful and the two young men have taken to not only protecting our farm, but watching out for the children. I wanted to give them guns to learn to shoot, but I was told not to do so by Mr. Winans and others. I promise to keep the children safe. Please remain safe. I long for your safe return to us and a speedy end to the battles that occupy our minds every minute of the day.*

*Your loving wife,*
*Sarah*

When Abra read the words of Elizabeth's death, he stopped and his hand clasped his mouth. Tears rolled quietly from his eyes as he reread the words of his daughter's death. Abra knew it was impossible to travel home, especially with the increased number of British troops entering Elizabethtown. Abra was now considered a traitor, and he knew he needed to remain away from public view. Abra thought of his young daughter, and grieved privately in his rooms. So many young men were dying in the battlefields. He felt akin to their fathers and mothers who sacrificed their children for this cause which he had taken a part in creating. His loss, albeit horrific, was nothing in comparison to the recognition that mothers and fathers were lying awake at night thinking of how their sons died alone and afraid in the field, without benefit of their parent at their side. Abra only told a few of his colleagues of his loss, and he bolstered himself up with the commitment that they must win this battle so that all the sons could return to their homes, as free men.

A letter arrived for Abra from Thomas mid-January, 1777. Abra sat down to read the words his son had written without benefit of desk or proper stationary.

*My dearest Father,*

*As you know I was promoted in the Eastern Company of Artillery for the New Jersey state troops. My detachments of the company have been stationed at the Blazing Star in Woodbridge from July to November; however we moved to assist in the battle at Trenton on December 26$^{th}$ with General Washington. Our work was easily done as the troops did not anticipate an attack. Typically the Hessians are well equipped and well-guarded; however our surprise attack caught them unawares. The morale of our men was greatly* *enhanced with our victory, which buoyed our efforts when we marched on Princeton on January 3rd. Father, these battles were only miles from our own quiet Elizabethtown. It worried me that such battles were so close to home, but that was the reason I enlisted. I feel that I have done more to protect my family by fighting our enemies directly.*

*Father, it was during the battle at Princeton that Captain Neil was killed. Our men were greatly distraught at this loss and we each in our minds considered how our families would react should the same fate befall us. I have been appointed Captain of Artillery for the Continental Army under the leadership of Col. John Lamb. We will be leaving for Brandywine.*

*I have not received word from my wife, Elizabeth, which is not surprising as we have been on the move and our mail is difficult to connect. I have sent letters to her; however I fear she may not be getting my letters. Could you please let her know that I am well and thinking of her and our son, Jonathan and I pray for them daily? Send my regards to Mother and the children, and to Aaron.*

*Your son,*
*Thomas Clark*

Abraham was astonished that his son had been in face to face battle against the British troops. He could only imagine that Aaron and Andrew were also in battles. That night Abra couldn't sleep. His thoughts kept envisioning his children fighting for their lives, and bravely protecting those who were unable to serve. He knew that Thomas had not heard about his sister, and he would have to write to him and send him news of her death, although he felt certain it was unlikely his post would be received. Abra feared for his sons' safety and their health. He was even more fearful for Sarah and his children as now they were unprotected except by servants. When Abra would drift to sleep he would jerk awake in a scene of terror of his wife and children being attacked by Hessians. Although he wanted to be there with his family, Abra knew that the work he was doing in Congress was of utmost importance. When others questioned his personal sacrifice he could never share the terrors of his dreams and fiendish fears of his defenseless family being attacked.

The battle-weary rebel troops moved to Morristown, New Jersey to set up camp for the winter. Washington made the Arnold Tavern his headquarters. This three story building had a wide center hallway. Washington made his bedroom a room on the second floor over the bar area. This way he could hear any noise being made if he had retired, and the front windows allotted him a chance to see what was happening on Western Avenue. The troops respected Washington, and Abra reminded delegates of this fact whenever they grumbled about Washington and his lack of successes in the battlefield. "Washington has been doing the best he can with what we have given him to use in this war. We are fortunate and should thank God each and every day that the men do respect him, for the respected man is able to lead men who lack food and shelter into winning a cause," Abra would tell those who complained. "My sons find him to be a supreme commander and count it their blessing that Washington has chosen to lead them in this war. We could not find better."

Col. Jacob Ford had built a powder mill in Morristown for ammunition to be used by the rebel troops, making it an ideal place for Washington and his 3,000-4,000 troops to winter and to plan for the upcoming spring. Washington's men spread out on the nearby farms. Washington would attend service in the Morristown church which had a bronze bell in the 125 foot steeple. The bell had been a gift of King George. Washington would smile that he worshiped in a house that had been adorned by the King from who Washington was praying to be severed. During the winter a smallpox epidemic spread among Washington's men. The church was made into a medical facility and Reverend Thomas Lewis cared for the men. Washington demanded a radical and controversial inoculation be given his men. In the end twenty-seven men died along with Reverend Lewis who treated the men, then caught the disease and died with them. They were all buried in the churchyard. Washington was convinced the inoculation had saved the majority of his men. Once again, the troops rallied behind their leader as they considered him a caring and resourceful leader.

The Morristown location was perfect for Washington as it allowed him to have the food and support necessary for his army although blankets, shoes and socks were sorely needed. Sawmills, gristmills, forges, tan yards, stills, taverns and a fulling mill were part of Morristown. Messages were delivered throughout the winter months between Washington and Congress, both working on plans which would give the small rebel army any advantage over the larger British Army. Washington spread out his troops to the neighboring farms of the Kembles, Wicks, Guerins, Fords and Arnolds. Washington had information leaked that he had 12,000 men in Morristown, rather than the meager 3,000-4,000 men in his army. While Abra congratulated the brilliance of Washington to spread advantageous propaganda, he remained concerned that so many New Jersey farmers and citizens were giving up their own homes to quarter troops. Congress had no means to compensate them and Abra felt New Jersey was paying a bigger price in supplies, disposition of homes when quartering troops, and emptying of their stocks to feed and clothe the troops. While Abra felt the cause was necessary, he feared the economic drain on New Jersey would destroy the small state after the war was over. In the quiet of his room, Abra penned notes to himself about changes in the laws which would need to be enacted after this war was over. One such law would be the right for private citizens to refuse quartering of troops unless they were rightfully reimbursed.

During the winter camp, the American troops had prepared for battle under the direction of Washington. Washington was no fool. He knew that the majority of the British troops were hired mercenaries, Hessians, who really had no personal stake in this war. A plan of propaganda and espionage was devised. Congress devised a three-man committee to make a plan for encouraging the Hessians troops to quit their service to the Crown. Thomas Jefferson devised an offer of land grants to Hessian deserters. It was Ben Franklin who joined the committee and arranged for the leaflets to look like tobacco packets, thus guaranteeing they would land in the common soldiers' hands.

Washington also sent a friend, Christopher Ludwick into the enemy camps, pretending to be a deserter. Ludwick was born in Germany and had traveled to the colonies where he became a baker, best known in Philadelphia for his gingerbread. When the Revolution began, Ludwick was too old to serve as a soldier, but he was commissioned by Congress to be the Superintendent of Bakers. It was his honesty that set him apart from others. Other bakers would make 100 pounds of bread for every 100 pound of flour supplied. Ludwick quickly pointed out that those bakers were making money off the government as the water and yeast added weight to the dough, so he demanded bakers he trained to make 135 pounds of bread for every 100 pounds of supplied flour. Washington loved Ludwick's honesty and devotion to gaining Independence. Pretending to be a deserter, Ludwick would talk in German to the Hesseins and tell them about free land grants which were being offered to any Hessian deserter. As a result hundreds of Hessians deserted their posts.

Benjamin Franklin also falsified a letter supposedly sent by a German prince to the commander of the Hessian mercenaries. In the letter it listed a high number of Hessians supposedly killed, thus a greater amount of blood money, which was to be paid for each lost Hessian soldier, was to be paid to the prince. The letter also encouraged the officer to allow wounded to die, thus more money would come back to the purported "prince." As copies of the letter were circulated among the Hessian troops they became angry that their prince really didn't need or want them, that they were just a way of making more income. When word spread among the Hessians, it was no surprise that many lost their desire to support a prince who was only collecting money for their services, and that they were worth more dead than alive to their prince. Thousands of Hessians deserted their duties to the British Crown. Instead they joined the large German-American population of the colonies. Abra and his colleagues were pleased that the plans were working. Every little bit would bring the war to a closer end.

Meanwhile, the work of Congress continued. Mary Katharine Goddard used the original hand written copy of the Declaration to set the type in her shop. A copy of the Goddard printing was ordered to be sent to each state on January 18, 1777. The publication had its desired effect and suddenly increased support was found in each state as the citizens demanded they support their leaders' efforts. What the delegates could not have expected was that copies of the signed Declaration landed almost immediately into the hands of the British. Now the families of the signers were targets for retaliation both from the British and potentially disgruntled Americans unhappy with becoming targets of the British and hired troops who treated all the Americans with the same disdain.

Congress continued their work until March 4, 1777. Congress planned to move back to Philadelphia and continue their work there. Abra and his fellow delegates packed trunks with important papers and prepared them for shipment via various carriers in order to protect and secure shipment from possible interception.

Washington's troops would return to battle May 28th after a harsh winter with few supplies and food. The morale of the troops was constantly a challenge. The fact that the

Americans had won two major battles before wintering had helped, however the long break had also allowed the British troops to reorganize and plan their attacks, including retaliation against the traitors who had signed the Declaration. Abra looked forward to returning home to be with his family for at least a short time and prayed it would be a safe journey.

# Chapter 13
## *1777*

**Abra's visit home was short**, but it allowed him time to visit the grave of Elizabeth, and time to comfort Sarah and the children. He visited his neighbors and asked them to continue looking in on Sarah and his family. The men talked of the most recent battle which had happened in January. At the Battle of Princeton, New Jersey, General Washington had a victory over three British regiments under General Cornwallis in January of 1777. The battle was very close to his home and Abra had feared for Sarah and the children. Fortunately, with the win at Princeton, many of the British troops were no longer in the immediate area. Abra prayed that the British would focus their efforts elsewhere now that they lost the battles in New Jersey. Abra's few short days with family ended, and Abra left again for Philadelphia in the crisp air of March.

There was never a shortage of stories which came to Congress through a wide variety of sources. Abra always listened most intently to those which centered in New Jersey.

Congress had finally been able to arrange a prisoner exchange for Richard Stockton, a New Jersey Declaration signer. However the celebration of his release was short lived when it was learned that Stockton had suffered ill health in the hands of the British, and upon returning home he found his home, library, writings, and considerable inherited wealth gone. He returned home an invalid and a reminder to the delegates of Congress of the fate that could await them. Regardless, Congress continued to hold strong to their cause.

In late May, 1777, it was George Washington who sought a plan to sew a flag which would rally the men. Washington was joined by Robert Morris and George Ross to plan a unique flag for the troops. Flags were important symbols in battle for identification of troops or ships. Such a flag would provide for the rebel troops a representation of what they wanted to achieve: their own nation. Washington had suggested thirteen six-pointed stars, one star for each colony. Washington's Commander in Chief flag had a six pointed star on a blue background. The plan was changed to a five pointed star. A group of women began sewing and distributing the flags throughout the colonies. It was in June of 1777 that Congress passed the Flag Resolution. "Resolved. That the flag of the United States be 13 stripes alternate red and white, that the Union be 13 stars white in a blue field representing a new constellation." Congress knew that to rally the rebel troops through a much needed symbol was a small price to keep the men fighting for the cause. Abra was excited about the creation of a flag. "It is no small thing that we give the men something to protect in battle. The flag bearer will not allow the flag to falter, and the men will fight all the harder to keep the flag moving toward victory. It will build troop morale and give the men a focus in battle," said Abra to a colleague. "It also reinforces that all thirteen colonies are working together, on a united front, to obtain their goal, not individually, as I feared would happen." Abra knew that other flags had been used at the start of the war, but they indicated specific towns or states. If the men were not unified for the same cause, Abra felt that they would want to form governments separately after the war. The work the Congress was doing provided for a government for all of the states and a united front. This flag was a means of symbolically unifying all of them now.

Just when Abra thought the colonists were finally pulling together for a common goal, he learned that many from New Jersey had renounced their support of Washington and taken oaths of loyalty to the Crown. Abra was devastated. Many New Jersey Loyalists moved to British-occupied New York. Among them were families Abra had lived with as neighbors and worshiped with at church. He was at least thankful that they had not turned on his family, but had quietly left New Jersey to show their support to Great Britain. Despite this loss of support, the two victories at Trenton and Princeton caused thousands to rally to the cause of independence. It was this attitude that Abra knew he had to embrace and put aside the pain of losing former neighbors and friends who did not share his beliefs.

New Jersey stood in the center of the conflict and Abra was saddened to hear that there was within New Jersey civil unrest which stretched from the Ramapo Mountains to Cape May because of the split between Patriots and Loyalists. Many lost their lives and their properties. Theft, rape and vandalism was being reported. Abra would talk for hours with his fellow New Jersey delegates who were also torn over the future of New Jersey because of the split in allegiances. Some delegates felt that they may have to leave Congress in order to protect their families from potential repercussions. Abra said he would stay to the end. While his colleagues admired him, many could not separate themselves from the hardships at home or the potential of losing everything they had.

It was on July 5$^{th}$ that the American suffered their first devastating loss of 1777. After witnessing the British, under the lead of General John Burgoyne, moving cannons up Mount Defiance, the 2,000-man American garrison at Fort Ticonderoga on Lake Champlain abandoned the fort. Two days later Burgoyne easily defeated the Continental Army at Hubbarton, Vermont. This was shattering news as the Congress learned that Burgoyne brought 7,000 British regulars and Hessian mercenaries with the mission of sealing off New England so the rebellion would end. 400

Iroquois Indians had helped Burgoyne maneuver through the forest to the Hudson River.

Abra and the rest of Congress were stunned when they learned of the new twist of events. Congress feared that the increased support garnered by the British would halt the push for independence, and their small army would be annihilated. Unfortunately for the British, a turn of events changed the course of attitudes. David Jones, lieutenant of Burgoyne's troops, had been courting a 22-year-old orphaned daughter of a Presbyterian minister. The girl had been living with her oldest brother at Fort Edward, on the Hudson south of Fort Ticonderoga. Her brother had begged her to flee, yet she remained thinking she would be safe because of her relationship with Jones. She stayed with a friend, Mrs. McNeil. On July 27, a band of Iroquois arrived at the McNeil house. Mrs. McNeil was turned over to the British, but Jane McCrea's body was later found naked on a hill not far away. She had been scalped. Her long beautiful blonde scalp was later presented to the British by the Iroquois. Jane had been shot four times and stabbed numerous times.

When the story of Jane's brutal attack spread throughout New England, the colonists wanted revenge against the British for allowing such a thing to happen to an innocent girl. They were outraged that the British had employed the help of the savage Iroquois. The news had an unexpected outcome. Thousands of Loyalists, as well as those uncertain of which side to support, now supported the rebels in the cause of the Revolution. Stories circulated that the colonists' wives and daughters might suffer the fate of Jane McCrea, which caused men who had tried to remain neutral to join the rebel troops. First, colonists cut down trees to block the roadways which slowed the British troops' advancement. The Iroquois, accustomed to moving within the forests, quickly deserted Burgoyne. What started as a tragedy turned into the very battle cry the Patriots needed to rally the colonists to action. Abra celebrated this turn of events, although he could not help but fear for his own wife and children who were in Elizabethtown unprotected. Vivid nightmares of brutal attacks would awaken Abra from his sleep, yet he never disclosed his fears aloud as he was committed to seeing the revolution's success.

On July 31$^{st}$, the Second Continental Congress accepted the services of French captain of dragoons, Marie Joseph Paul Yves Roch Gilbert du Motier, marquis de Lafayette. Louis XIV had forbidden the nineteen year old Lafayette to join the rebel cause, however Lafayette escaped from custody, learned enough English to help him communicate, and went immediately to Philadelphia where he was given the rank of major general. Abra and other members of Congress felt this was an important advantage to the rebel cause. Lafayette had funding and political pull. Abra was quickly becoming known as a foreign diplomat in the Congress, and seeking foreign assistance was part of his duties. Abra was convinced Lafayette would be able to garner help from the French in fighting the British troops. The meager Continental Army needed the help of the French to battle the well trained and well equipped British.

It was at this time that Abra received news from home that his daughter, Hannah, planned to marry Captain Melyn Miller, a local New Jersey man who was in the Continental Army. Abra knew that he should be there for the ceremony, but travel at this time was risky, and there was too much to do in Congress. Abra sat in his room that night and wrote Hannah, a heartfelt letter. He apologized that he could not promise being in Elizabethtown for the August 11th ceremony. Although he knew that Sarah would intervene on his behalf, he felt that his role as legislator was continually interfering with his role as husband and father. He also knew that Melyn would be leaving for service, so Hannah would remain on the farm with her mother. This war was causing so many interferences with the life that Abra had envisioned when he first married Sarah. Hannah should be happily married and safe in her own home with her husband. Instead she would sit awaiting letters might or might not not arrive because of the difficulty in delivering posts. Not only that, but her marriage could easily leave her a widow. So many young women were losing their young husbands in this war. Mothers and fathers were losing their sons. Brothers and sisters were saying good-bye to their brothers and fathers, not knowing if they would ever see them again. Fathers were on the battlefield, not home to see their newly born infants. The thought of Jane McCrea entered Abra's mind, but he quickly put an end to thinking of this as it set him into a feeling of panic. Abra's mood was somber, but he knew that everyone was sacrificing. The only way this could turn out well was for the colonists to gain freedom. They must win. To not win was not an option. Loss would guarantee persecution for every man who fought in the war, and every legislator who allowed the colonies to fight for independence. No, they must win. Abra left his rooms with a stout heart and eager to continue his work and commitment for the cause.

It was early August when Congress received word of a major battle victory at Fort Stanwix in New York. Congress was told how the rebel militiamen under General Nicholas Herkimer stopped the British on their way to Albany. It appeared that the British were trying to join forces with General Burgoyne on Lake Ontario. Burgoyne had an army of 340 British regulars, 650 Canadians and Loyalists and more than 1000 Indians led by Joseph Brant, a Mohawk chief. On August 3rd the American rebels raised their flag inside the fort. Word came that Burgoyne was in route, so General Herkimer began gathering 800 men and boys from nearby farms. The skies had opened and a downpour of rain made battle, let alone movement, difficult. The Indians did not want to fight in the heavy rain and refused to fight. Benedict Arnold and the Continental Army arrived carrying the newly sewn flag, and the Loyalists withdrew from

Fort Stanwix. This news carried great tidings to Congress as it showed that the flag was having the desired effect in getting more men to stand up and fight against the British and their allies. The Congress cautiously congratulated themselves on winning the recent battles, despite being undermanned. "Best thing we did was get that flag finalized. It has been doing the trick in keeping our men focused and fighting for the cause," said Abra to a small group at dinner that night.

"That and our ability to leak potent information falsifying the numbers of troops," said one of the delegates.

"I'm not certain how our Reverend Caldwell would feel about our bearing false witness, but judging by his rebel sermons, I'd believe he would feel free to leak even more falsehoods if it meant our winning our cause," Abra laughed. There was little for the delegates to celebrate, so any opportunity to share good news and humor was quickly seized.

News quickly followed the win at Fort Stanwix that the British troops under General Burgoyne were not going to give up so easily. A troop of 700 mounted Hessian soldiers were sent by Burgoyne to Bennington to gather fresh horses. On August 16th when they arrived the Hessians were greeted by 1800 Americans under the command of Captain John Stark. The leader of the Hessians was shot, and his men were killed or captured. When word reached Burgoyne of this defeat, he quickly withdrew from trying to recapture Fort Stanwix. This news sent Congress into great celebration. It was looking like the tide had begun to turn for the Americans.

The celebration was short lived, however, when word arrived that the Continental Army had marched back to Fort Ticonderoga in September, and even though the American army outnumbered the British five to one, they could not get the British to surrender. This constant tug of war between celebration and heartache kept Congress in constant turmoil. Delegates would try to put a value on battles won and lost, to help them identify if they were winning or losing the war, however every battle was different, and communications were never exact. Congress had to rely on the messages they did receive and hope that the information was accurate. However a value system as to the importance of one battle over another was something no one could agree upon. Delegates from the areas where battles happened placed far more value on battles when their own statesmen were slain, despite the amount of land involved or the numbers of troops involved in the battle. Regardless, each report was listed on a tally sheet as to a win or loss, with hopes that far more wins would be listed as the war went on. Many delegates would excuse themselves to return home to handle safety issues in their home states when battles arose near their own homes. Fortunately, if they could not return, a new delegate was quickly put in place which kept Congress active and committed.

Abra was always on the lookout for posts from home. He gloried in any posts he received from his sons and son-in-law, or from his friend, Reverend Caldwell. A post from Thomas indicated he was heading toward Brandywine, Pennsylvania. Shortly afterward word came that there had been a battle at Brandywine, Pennsylvania, on September 11th. When Abra heard that the British won that conflict, Abra searched for news of his son as to whether he survived. News was difficult to procure, so the fate of Thomas was remained unknown to Abra. Although Abra was wrought with anguish worrying about his son's survival, he knew that if Thomas had survived, he would eventually receive word. Until he learned otherwise, Abra would hold on to the idea that Thomas was alive and well. It was the only way he could continue working on Congressional tasks. Abra had to put his faith in God and believe his family members were safe. It was during sleepless nights that Abra's mind would drift to family safety. He often knelt praying for protection of his family. When he would eventually fall asleep he would be awakened by nightmarish dreams.

Congress knew that the battles were increasing in number and in various places. News from the battle grounds sometimes took weeks to arrive. Waiting to hear the outcome of battles left each man of Congress anxious. Many men identified family members who lived where the battles were being fought, or they had brothers, sons, or nephews fighting in the battles. Abra gathered strength from the courage of his fellow delegates. Despite the problems their families were facing, the men of Congress continued on with the important work of designing a government and treasury plan which would be put in place once they won freedom. Being among men of this stature gave Abra the courage to continue with his work.

On September 19th the First Battle of Saratoga took place. The British marched into a clearing on Freeman's Farm but were met by 7,000 American troops of the Continental Army. Many American marksmen were able to kill the British who marched in straight line formation. When American reinforcements arrived, General Burgoyne sent messengers to General Howe at New York to send help. General Howe, however, loaded his 18,000 man army onto ships in New York and moved them to Delaware Bay. The Battle at Freeman's Farm was a rebel victory. It could not be determined if Howe received the plea for help, or if he had ignored the request as Howe outranked Burgoyne and was not subject to his plans or requests. When word of this came to Congress, celebration of the victory was cut short by debates as to why Howe did not send troops. Was Howe becoming nervous about the rebel Army's ability to outwit the fighting machine of the British?

Any positive rejoicing soon came to an end when on September 20th; General Washington rushed troops to defend Philadelphia. Congress had moved back to Philadelphia from Baltimore once the immediate threat diminished in Philadelphia. Now Congress was told to immediately pack up and move as the British were advancing on Philadelphia. Members of Congress scrambled to gather all the paperwork and necessities, and they were escorted out of Philadelphia to York, Pennsylvania. Paperwork on the Articles of Confederation which was near completion was everywhere, as well as all the maps and correspondence Congress maintained. Everyone worked in unison to pack all documentation into chests and get the chests loaded on various wagons. Abra worked on the area of finance and foreign policy, as this was his expertise. He quickly gathered all of his documents and sorted them into two different chests. The chests were separated so that if captured, all would not be lost. Congress had been debating the Articles of Confederation document for nearly a year and had spent the summer months writing it and fine-tuning it. They were anxious to complete their work. Once the members of Congress were securely placed in York, they quickly went back to work, knowing that messages from Washington would be more difficult to procure because of the increased movement of troops and the British now actively in search of the "ringleaders" of the revolt. Most delegates didn't even leave to seek rooms. Instead many stayed and slept in the same rooms where they worked. Abra and the others knew that if and when the war was over, a system of government needed to be in place. Their work was necessary and important and the distraction of the move was momentary. On September 26th, General Howe and his troops took over Philadelphia. News of this shocked Congress, but they felt that the momentum of American support was rising and that the Americans would ban together and see this war to a successful end.

1777 had seen the British make several errors in judgment, which many of Congress determined quelled the British chances of stopping the Revolution. The British had tried to cut New England off from the rest of the colonies by posting troops throughout the Hudson River Valley. It was learned that General William Howe was to drive north from New York City while General John Burgoyne was to drive south out of Canada. British General Barry St. Leger would drive down the Mohawk Valley in upstate New York. The plan probably would have worked, but General Howe decided to instead attack Philadelphia in an attempt to capture Congress, leaving Burgoyne and St. Leger to unsuccessfully try to control the Hudson River Valley on their own. Howe had hoped the Loyalists of Pennsylvania would aid in his efforts in capturing Philadelphia. Washington had foiled Howe's plans by intercepting the British at Brandywine Creek and Germantown.

Howe did have a plan. He hoped that by seizing Philadelphia, he would rally the Pennsylvania Loyalists, discourage the rebels by capturing their capital, and bring the war to a speedy conclusion. General Howe believed that if they could capture Philadelphia, which was the largest city in the colonies, the rebellion would come to an immediate end. Howe brought in 15,000 troops in an armada from New York City to the Chesapeake Bay, and then marched into

Philadelphia. Washington tried to block the advancement of Howe on the banks of Brandywine, but was outnumbered on September 22nd. General Lafayette was wounded in that encounter. Howe then entered Philadelphia unopposed.

General Howe's troops camped at Germantown, and General Washington planned a surprise attack on October 6th, however the plan was too complex. Washington's men had marched thirty-five miles, and then fought a four hour battle, and the British again won. Washington stood firm that his troops had fought well and would prevail in the end.

When word came to Congress of the failed attempts at stopping Howe, Abra supported Washington's leadership. "Only God knows what the outcome will be, but I believe that Washington has been blessed. He is a deeply religious man, and his faith in God will set him to leading our men to freedom," Abra said. He had to believe this as three of his own sons were on the battle front.

On October 7th the second battle of Saratoga saw an American army victory. General Burgoyne, and his 5,800 Convention Army of mostly Hessians were outnumbered at least two to one. General Gates refused to leave his tent when the battle began. Brigadier General Simon Fraser was leading the Hessian troops toward Saratoga. It was Benedict Arnold who went against Gate's orders and told a New Jersey sharpshooter, Timothy Murphy, to "Get Fraser," from a distance of 300 feet. The mortal shot, and Benedict Arnold's leadership, rallied the American troops who went on to beat the British. General Burgoyne and his entire force surrendered to General Gates on October 17th. The British troops marched to Boston, and left for England. Many of the Hessians were marched to Charlottesville, Virginia, and imprisoned in the Albemarle Barracks.

On October 27, 1777, John Hancock resigned as President of Congress. His health had been bad for some time, but he continued his diligent work. Fellow delegates, especially those who had signed the Declaration of Independence talked of how boldly John had signed the document, a testimony to his defiance against England. His signature followed his retaliatory comment about the British placing bounties on the heads of the leading rebels. “The British ministry can read that name without spectacles; let them double their reward,” he replied, referring to his signature which stood out large and clear among all the signatures of the document. Hancock stood to lose the most in the Revolution as he was the wealthiest of the colonists, yet he had served as the most outspoken in Congress. Hancock planned to return to Massachusetts where he intended to work on his state’s constitution. Upon Hancock’s farewell, Abra shook his hand and said, “John, it has been an honor and privilege to serve with you.”

Hancock forcibly shook Abra’s hand and placed his other hand on Abra’s shoulder. “Abra, Congress needs your steady leadership. I will pray daily for the work you and the others do toward securing our freedom.”

On November 15, 1777, Congress passed and sent to the states for ratification the Articles of Confederation, the country's first written constitution. Debates over the document raged between the larger states having a larger say in the government, and the smaller states fearing they would have no say. Abra was unsettled with this issue because New Jersey was small, and they would stand to be overpowered by the larger states. Jefferson proposed the idea of a Senate which would represent the states and a House to represent the people. This idea was immediately rejected by the larger states. After much debate a vote was taken. Each state would have one vote. Abra had worked hard to convince as many delegates as he could that they had to provide equal representation. "After all," he reasoned, "that is why we are fighting the war. We did not have equal representation with England. Let us not repeat the mistakes of the past."

The Articles of Confederation provided that at least nine states must consent to all important measures; required unanimous consent for any changes in the articles; provided no way for the central government to force states into compliance with congressional decisions; and denied Congress any power to tax or to regulate trade. The document was certainly a good attempt at organizing government for a country which was not really independent yet, but there were many things which left the delegates unsettled. Although Congress urged each state to pass the Articles as quickly as possible, that did not happen. With the war on, and travel risky, delegates had to travel to their states to get ratification before signing off. Abra knew it could take years before the document ever got ratified by all the states.

Meanwhile, Congress made the first of several requisitions of funds, to be paid by the states in paper money, and authorized confiscation of Loyalists' estates in order to fund the treasury. While Congress was trying to move forward in organizing government, the Americans were dealing with losses caused by the war. Having to provide money to the government added additional tension to an already strained population. The confiscation of Loyalists' estates also caused controversy as many of those families had been long established in America. Abra's concern over the financing of the new government was overshadowed by the lack of fairness in taking money from families long established in the colonies simply because they disagreed in the politics of those in Congress. He felt that it was not fair to fund a war and government off the backs of those who had lived side by side with those wanting freedom, yet the sacrifices being made by the common people for this cause was overwhelming. Many were not only sending their family members to fight, many had lost their property, and many knew that if independence was gained, they would be forever estranged from their families still in Great Britain. Abra would listen to the many arguments for and against taking the Loyalist properties to finance the war. It was hard for his conscience to support the mistreatment of some, yet the fruits of war were that the losers were made to pay the price. He knew that if the Patriots lost, Great Britain would make them pay the cost of the war. Abra knew the Loyalists would be made to support the costs of the war if the Patriots won.

News arrived that the British secured control of the Delaware River in November. This bleak news did little to encourage Congress. They knew that soon the troops would stop for the winter, and by ending on a negative note, the troops would have little cause for hope and celebration during the long winter months. Abra was one of those in charge of the treasury, and as such, felt the need to secure supplies to the troops. If they could provide food, shelter and supplies to the men, perhaps they would stay and continue to fight the cause. If they ended the year on a negative note in the war, then were made to suffer through the winter with even their basic needs unmet, Abra feared they would leave their posts and return to their homes in hopes of salvaging whatever was left to them. Abra immediately contacted his friend, Reverend Caldwell and awarded him an appointment as Assistant Commissary General. Caldwell was responsible for obtaining food and supplies for the Continental Army. Caldwell opened offices in Springfield and Chatham where he searched for both food and supplies which were in short supply. In trying to make payment for supplies he could procure, it was difficult to get the funds from Congress, although Abra worked hard to make the transaction. This did not impede Caldwell as he borrowed money in his own name in order to get the food and supplies needed. He was most proud of his ability to get shoes and boots from local tradesmen and these were happily delivered to the troops. It was never enough, but it was a start and Caldwell felt proud of his ability to help in the cause.

After the American army pushed back the British at Whitemarsh, Pennsylvania, George Washington led his 11,000 troops into Valley Forge which was just outside the British-held Philadelphia. For eight days the men struggled to move the mere thirteen mile distance. They were met with a snowstorm and several days of icy rain. The Congress had declared that everyone needed to observe a day of "thanksgiving." The troops had no food for the previous two days other than what they could find in the forests and fields. Their thanksgiving feast consisted of a half gill (half cup) of rice with a tablespoon of vinegar. Although it was not much, the men congratulated each other for what they had accomplished and set about building lodging to protect them from the upcoming winter.

It was December 19 and the war was at a standstill during the winter. The condition of the 11,000 troops was horrible. Valley Forge was ideally situated for protection with the river on one side and two small creeks which would stop advancing troops, and that the camp was located uphill which would make it difficult for any advancing troops. None of this offset the horrors about to settle on Washington's men. The British had already raided the two iron-making operations in the small adjoining village. The few military stores that had been hidden at Valley Forge had also been raided by the British, who not only took the supplies, but burned down the houses. Washington's men found nothing at Valley Forge but the trees in the area. 2,000 men had no shoes, and 1,000 were injured. Washington was heard to say, "You might have tracked the army from White Marsh to Valley Forge by the blood of their feet." Washington would ride his horse throughout the camps taking stock of his men and their needs. "No meat! No meat!" was the response he would hear as he rode his horse through the settlement. He used barns and churches for hospitals and provided shelter for his army which had celebrated victories, but had seen more defeats. His fear was that the men witnessed too much loss, and their present state of hunger, lack of clothing and shelter, and their long absence from home, would send many of his men to desertion. Fire cakes and cold water was the diet of the men. Christmas, a day which should have greeted the men with positive thoughts, instead filled the men with more despair as four additional inches of snow fell.

Washington immediately had his men begin making shelters. Each team of twelve men would build a 16x14 foot log hut which was six and a half feet high. A stone fireplace was built in each, and the roof was a wood board. Many of the teams would dig a two foot pit into the ground, which tended to give them a wind break within the hut when sleeping. The men would hang a piece of cloth to form a door in order to keep out the drafts, although the huts remained damp and smoky. The huts were aligned to form streets, and officers built their huts behind the troops' cabins. Although the building of the huts kept the men busy, it certainly did not erase their need for clothing and food and supplies. Washington knew he had to get Congress to spend money to support the army, otherwise they would watch their efforts fall from within.

# Chapter 14
## *1778*

**Abra listened compassionately** to the reports from Washington during the winter at Valley Forge about his needs for supplies. Abra's job was finances and he quickly learned that the Continental money was worthless as no one wanted to trade goods or services for the printed money they were producing. Abra took this position seriously as he now had three sons on the battlefield and there were countless other sons of common men who had sacrificed everything to fight for this cause. He knew he must rectify the problem Washington was having in supplying his men with food and supplies. Abra would fight with Congress to get the funding, then take those funds and try to find suppliers who would take the funds in honest exchange for the supplies Washington needed for his men. Most businessmen did not want to trade for the money, but Congress had nothing to offer except the printed money which many thought was worth nothing other than the paper it was printed upon. Nothing distracted Abra from this cause and it added much stress on him in trying to remedy the problem which seemed insurmountable.

Finding and securing supplies was easy by comparison to the task Abra had in finding wagons to ship the supplies. Many Pennsylvanian farmers hid their horses and wagons as they did not want to jeopardize their property in a potential loss to the British, nor did they want their wagons destroyed along the rutted roads leading to Valley Forge. There was also the very real possibility that the horses would be killed for food by the starving troops. Congress knew they needed someone to handle these problems of transportation so General Thomas Mifflin was given these responsibilities; however it was soon learned that he hated this job. Mifflin was loyal to the cause and wanted to be on the battlefield, not handling transportation and shipments, so he would often ignore his job. Thus, Washington's men suffered even more because the commissioned food and supplies could not be delivered. When posts arrived to Washington that supplies were not able to be transported, Washington discussed this with his men and General Nathanael Greene took over the responsibilities. Unfortunately, the troops had spent a horrible winter in Valley Forge without benefit of the long awaited supplies, despite the best intentions of Congress.

That winter temperatures remained cold and there were constant battles with rain and snow. Lack of privies and the habit of human filth being left everywhere added to the poor sanitation and continued health problems. Horses were slaughtered and the carcasses were left out in the open. Washington tried to issue rules to the men about these conditions, but they mostly ignored them because of their own weakness and anger at their situation. In order to force improvement, Washington issued a rule stating that any man who relieved himself anywhere but in the proper privies would receive five lashes. Men also would go upstream to get water, but would relieve themselves in the water which then contaminated the drinking water. Men became ill with dysentery and typhus and many died in the makeshift hospitals which also had few supplies. It was Dr. Bodo Otto, a German physician and his two sons, who turned over their spa at Yellow Springs, to be used as an Army hospital. Washington's fear was that the troops would break out in smallpox and that would wipe out the majority of his men. He again forced inoculations among the 3,000-4,000 men who had never had vaccinations for smallpox in the past. Washington was advised that the ill were laying in their own filth and the lack of air circulation in the huts was causing the spread of the illnesses. Washington demanded that windows be cut out in order to circulate air in the huts, or he encouraged men to move into tents. Instead of being seen as intervention for illness, many men felt Washington was being cruel to put them into more drafts and cold conditions.

The Congress had debated who would serve as allies to their cause. The Americans had solicited help from the French who had a long hatred of the English. Seven thousand French soldiers and nineteen thousand French seamen assisted the United States. With all the losses in battle, the French Foreign Minister put a halt on shipping ammunition to the Americans, and stopped sending seamen to assist the Americans. News of this reached Congress and a groan was heard throughout the hall. Reports came in that even George Washington was becoming discouraged by the odds they faced. Washington looked on hopelessly as the American forts along the Hudson River were easily captured by the British troops. "I think the game is about up," said Washington as he looked over his army of only 6,000 men. These men had volunteered and many of their terms of enlistment would expire by January 1st. Howe and Cornwallis looked at the American troops as a skeletal military and knew they had little to fear. Washington's men were hungry, poorly fed, ill, poorly armed, and it appeared no one was helping them.

Nathanael Greene assumed the duties of Quartermaster General on March 23rd and there was some improvement, however over 2,500 died during the winter, as did many of the horses. Nathanael Greene wrote to Washington, "God grant we may never be brought to such a wretched condition again." Even though the army suffered more than anyone could imagine, there was still a hopeful attitude among the men that they would beat the odds, and many even displayed a sense of humor at the odds they faced. The men ranged in age from 12 to 60, mostly white, but there were also Negroes and American Indians among the troops. As the men lived in the cramped huts, there were ample complaints of their living conditions. Albigence Waldo wrote, “my Skin & eyes are almost spoil’d with continual smoke.” Putrid fever, the itch, diarrhea, dysentery and rheumatism were some of the other afflictions suffered by the Continental troops. Supplies were difficult to procure as there was a shortage of wagons and the horses were starving. The troops needed 34,577 pounds of meat and 168 barrels of flour each day to feed the men, however such supplies were not available. Local farmers received handbills outlining the needs of the troops with offers to purchase said supplies. “Fresh Pork, Fat Turkey, Goose, Rough skinned Potatoes, Turnips, Indian Meal, Sour-Crout, Leaf Tobacco, New Milk, Cider, and Small Beer” were listed as the needs of the men. Meanwhile in problem filled camps, the men tried to maintain their spirits by singing and even putting on plays.

By spring the weather broke. General Nathanael Greene as quartermaster had troops begin improving the bridges and roads between Valley Forge and Lancaster so supplies could be delivered. Finally, after a long and hard winter where nearly 3,000 men lost their lives, supplies began to filter into Valley Forge. Additionally a company of seventy men arrived led by a German born patriot and baker named Christopher Ludwig. He had previously helped Washington's plans to get Hessians to dessert the British army. Ludwig refused payment, but he baked bread daily for the men, providing each man one pound of bread each day. To add to the good news, thousands of shad were spawning in the Schuylkill River. The men netted, salted and stored the fish in barrels for future use. The men gorged themselves on the fish, and it was said that for a whole month the entire camp and every man's hands smelled of fish. As word of these changes came back to Congress, Abra felt relief. His sons were on the front lines and he knew that their fates were held in the hands of Washington and he thanked God for sending people like Christopher Ludwig to rescue their troops from starvation.

Now that the men had relief from the horrors of the winter in Valley Forge, Washington started concentrating on turning his troops into a military front. One of his generals, John Sullivan, told Washington that, "This is not an Army. It is a mob!" Washington had to agree. He knew that the men had no self-discipline. They gambled. They fought. They wandered off camp and were caught selling their army equipment to non-soldiers for things not related to war survival. They did not know how to use their equipment properly. This must change.

It was at this time that Friedrich Wilhelm Ludolf Gerhard Augustin Stuebe, who called himself Baron von Steuben, was sent to Washington by Ben Franklin. Franklin had received an impressive recommendation of Baron von Steuben and sent him to speak with Congress. Although Steuben could not speak English, interpreters would help deliver his message. He told Congress he would serve without a salary so long as his expenses were paid. Abra was impressed with the man. Economically, this was affordable. It was also a great plan to have someone with military expertise help General Washington turn the struggling army from an angry mob into an organized force.

Debates throughout the evening among the delegates included caution as to Steuben's inability to directly communicate with the men, and Steuben's being a foreigner. Some felt Washington would not appreciate intervention from Congress in the handling of the troops. Abra continued to remind his fellow delegates that the price was right, and that Ben Franklin had recommended him and Ben had not made many mistakes thus far! As to Washington being upset, Abra reminded them that Washington had stayed focused throughout the rough winter months at Valley Forge by continually supporting his men and their needs. Who else knew better than Washington that his men needed help in becoming an organized force. In the morning Congress voted, and it was agreed that Steuben be sent to assist Washington at Valley Forge.

Upon arriving Steuben quickly recognized that the troops were in need of immediate training. Washington named him Acting Inspector General of the Army. Because Steuben could not speak English, Washington had two French-speaking aids serve as interpreters. Steuben immediately started drilling the men and would curse in broken English. He served as a model of the behavior he expected the men to follow. The men liked him and quickly worked to please him. The men also viewed Steuben as fair because he quickly cut out many of the officer's servants, and made the officers drill with their men. The men liked his fairness. Steuben would train one hundred sergeants, and when they passed inspection, they went on to train their men. Bayonet training was essential. Prior to this the men had used their bayonets for cooking over fires. They quickly learned the correct use of the bayonets which Steuben was convinced would turn the tide of the war to their favor. As Steuben worked with the drills, he wrote instructions into a manual which was then translated into English and titled, "Regulation for the Order of Discipline of the Troops of the United States." Every officer was to copy it and learn it. The overall attitude and morale of the Army was changing. When Washington's post to Congress gave updates as to Steuben's successful work with the men, Abra beamed. Finally they were doing something to really help this cause.

The winds of change were certainly happening for both the British and the Americans. General Howe was replaced by Henry Clinton on March 7, 1778. The British army had been demoralized after several defeats. Clinton, a junior officer, would continually pester Howe with plans on how to crush the American Continental Army. Now he would have his chance as the new commander.

For the Americans, things were changing as well. In March each man in the military received an additional month pay as a bonus for having survived the winter, and Washington added a ration of rum for each soldier. The men were certainly more encouraged by these changes in events. Then Congress announced to the troops on May 5th that the French had entered the war as their allies. Every man in camp enjoyed a gill of rum that night during the celebrations. The French quickly had uniforms and military gear sent to America. Once word began to spread of the positive changes in the war, the farmers began sharing more of their crops with the soldiers and more men joined the military.

Things were certainly looking up, and when word of this came to Congress, Abra and the others were encouraged that they would begin to see positive changes on the battlefields. Unfortunately there were those in Congress who felt that Washington's usefulness to their efforts had peaked and a new leader was needed. It was an Irish born; French raised solder named Thomas Conway who was a brigadier general began boasting of his abilities and leadership. Washington and the other American officers were not impressed. Conway began a grassroots campaign among the men that he and English army veterans Lee and Gates would be far better commanders as they all had more experience than Washington. After all, they reminded the men, Washington had lost nearly every battle except those at Trenton and Princeton. Congress began to hear other vocal critics of Washington including Thomas Mifflin, who had bungled his job as quartermaster for Valley Forge. Other prominent men like Dr. Benjamin Rush, John and Sam Adams and Elbridge Gerry agreed that it was time to change leadership. A letter was sent from Conway to Gates criticizing Washington. When word leaked to Washington that Conway had written, “Heaven has been determined to save your country; or a weak general and bad counselors would have ruined it,” Washington confronted Gates. Washington wanted the matter to be brought before Congress.

Debates raged between the Congressmen about whether to replace Washington as their Commander in Chief with General Gates. Abra was convinced that Washington was still the best choice as their commander as he had remained sensible even in the face of adversity. He also knew that the men respected Washington. “Yes, but will the troops continue to support a commander who is leading them into death?” asked one of the delegates.

Despite Gates’ refusal to leave his tent when the battle began, his supporters continued to sing praises of Gates securing the surrender of Burgoyne, and they petitioned Congress members to have Gates replace Washington as Commander in Chief. These debates distracted the serious work of Congress as they struggled to complete the Articles of Confederation. The battle lines within Congress between those who rallied behind Washington and those who supported Gates filled spare moments in Congress. Between finalizing the Articles and debating the Army's leadership, and following the war posts, the delegates had little time to worry about their own personal sacrifices.

Washington demanded that Congress address the issue of his leadership and determine whether he continue to be Commander in chief. There were those in Congress who wanted change, especially after the support of John and Sam Adams, two much respected men, in changing leadership to Lee or Gates. Again, the floor of Congress was filled with debates and arguments as to Washington's ability. Abra remained a constant supporter of Washington, and used the infrequent correspondence from his sons and from his friend, Reverend Caldwell, as support for Washington's leadership. He quoted passages from meager letters that not only his sons and Caldwell supported Washington, but there were passages with stories of Washington's leadership and the men's support and love of their leader. "Why would we take away a leader who the men on the front lines admire and respect?" asked Abra. "We can debate among ourselves, but in the end it is the men who will fight this battle and if they are happy following Washington, who are we to interfere with this? Just look at what happened this past winter. Men had no shoes or food and their clothing was in tatters, yet they remained loyal to Washington. If he were not a good leader, these troops would have deserted him and this war would be at a complete end and we would be facing certain death for our disloyalty to the Crown." Others nodded in agreement, yet there were still those who supported a change in leadership. Finally after a vote, Congress agreed that Washington should remain their Commander-in-chief.

When Washington returned to his men, he was warmly greeted by his men who told him that it was his leadership that kept their hope and belief alive. Washington thanked his men, and then informed them it was time to move. He had the men clean up the camp and bury the garbage and fill in the latrines. He headed his newly trained Army out on June 9th in an effort to go after the British troops who were on the move to New York.

The British believed they would have difficulty defending Philadelphia, especially now that the French had entered into the war. The British finalized their evacuation of Philadelphia on June 18th and returned to New York City led by General Clinton. The British soldiers dressed in red uniforms and wearing bearskin caps, or tricorn or leather caps. The Germans who accompanied them were wearing blue uniforms with the Prussian front brass plate. They looked impressive in their uniforms, but the Americans were not impressed. In only a few hours the American troops arrived and reclaimed Philadelphia. Along the path to New York, the British troops were harassed by the Americans who burned bridges, ruined wells, and blocked roads with fallen trees. The British were only able to advance forty miles in a week's time. Many Hessians deserted.

Meanwhile, Washington had his men in New Jersey waiting for the British troops, led by General Clinton, to move through on the way to New York. John Hart, one of the signers of the Declaration of Independence, lived in Hopewell. Washington quartered his troops on the Hart farm. In their strategy session most of the American officers voted not to attack the British while they were on the move and vulnerable. Lee informed the officers that the American troops could not beat the British army. When General Lee refused the job of leading the attack, Lafayette was named to lead the mission. Lee then changed his mind and stated that a mission this large should be his to lead.

Washington told Lee to attack on the 28th. The rest of the army would be ready to support them. Lee returned to his troops but did nothing to prepare for the battle. He did not check on maps or on correspondence from those in the field. Instead, Lee led his men to attack the rear of the marching British troops, but that made Clinton think they were trying to steal the supply train which was following his troops. Clinton turned his men back to protect their supplies, and Lee panicked in what looked like a full attack by the British on his part of the army. The army dressed in blue uniforms were joined by militia men in their hunting clothing. Together they were ready for battle. After the initial contact, General Lee ordered a retreat of his men, sending them to Monmouth Courthouse. Washington received word of this and galloped out to the retreating men and turned them around leading them back to attack. When Washington asked Lee for the meaning of this retreat, Lee offered excuses about his orders not being followed, and again said that Americans are not able to stand against the British. Enraged, Washington said, “Sir, they *are* able, and by God they *shall* do it!”

Washington led the troops into battle, and the men used the maneuvers learned from Steuben. The British continued their attack. Despite Lee’s problems on the battlefield, the Americans held their line. This time it was the British who retreated. The British, and General Clinton who once believed the Continental Army could be easily defeated, were surprised by the changed American troops who were far more ready for battle this time.

When Congress received word of the battle at Monmouth, it was evident that Lee needed to be court-martialed. Lee was found guilty, and was removed from the Army. Those who had encouraged the change of leadership naming Lee as the Commander were now contrite about their former attitudes. Abra congratulated his colleagues saying, “Thank

God we made the final choice we did. Otherwise this would have been the end of the war and the beginning of our hangings!" Congress was pleased with the changes in Washington's troops. Their soldiership and morale had much improved, and they were committed to following Washington.

While Abra celebrated with the news of the Monmouth confrontation, his knowing that the battle had happened on New Jersey soil made his worries of his wife and children again rise to the forefront of his concerns. He had not any recent correspondence from Sarah, or from Aaron, Thomas or Andrew. The little news he had received was through letters sent through other sources. Abra had to hold onto these to calm his fears about his family's safety. With the French allies, Abra hoped that this war would soon come to an end.

Stories of American heroism would boost the spirits of the delegates. The story of Mary Ludwig, a Trenton, New Jersey girl, who had married John Hays, a barber from Pennsylvania, was a story repeated often throughout the halls of Congress. When war had broken out, Hays signed on, and Mary followed him to battle serving the soldiers through nursing, cooking and washing clothing. In the camp she had earned the nickname of Molly Pitcher because she carried water from the spring to the men on the battle lines during the Battle of Monmouth. In the severe heat of the June 28th battle, her husband collapsed next to his cannon, and "Molly" took over her husband's position, and continued firing the cannon until the battle was over. Mary was granted a sergeant's commission, given by General Greene, and supposedly approved by George Washington himself. A song was sung often at dinner of Molly Pitcher and her bravery.

"Moll Pitcher she stood by her gun
And rammed the charges home, sir;
And thus on Monmouth bloody field
A sergeant did become, sir."

Abra smiled at the thought of this New Jersey girl fighting on the battle field, but his smiles soon turned to fear when in his dreams it was not Molly Pitcher, but Sarah standing on the battle fields, which were the familiar fields of the Clark farm. Abra jerked awake at the sound of the cannon blast which Sarah shot in his dreams.

As the summer of 1778 progressed, news of the French fleets coming in to help the Americans filled the Congressional floor with high hopes and discussions. First the British were pushed out of Rhode Island, which allowed the American and French forces to control the Narragansett Bay area. The struggle for control over Rhode Island continued throughout the summer, and although the Americans fought hard, the British appeared to have held control.

By the end of 1778 the focus of the war turned to the south. The British attacked and took control of Savannah, and

Augusta, Georgia. Only 50,000 Americans lived in Georgia, and of that number, half were slaves. Up until 1778, Georgia had not been involved in the business of the Revolution. Their delegates did sign the Declaration of Independence despite much of their population being Loyalists. The Georgians had not contributed money or soldiers to the Congressional cause. It came to a shock to those of Georgia that British General George Clinton would move his ships from New York to the South to claim control over them. 35,000 British, Tory and Hessian soldiers invaded Georgia. Meanwhile British Lieutenant Colonel Campbell took control of Savannah with no resistance. Continental General Robert Howe of North Carolina moved his regiment of 1000 men to try to protect the area against the thousands of British troops.

News of this turn of events reached Congress and at first there were those among the delegates who felt the Georgians were getting what they deserved, but this talk quickly changed when they realized that the focus of the war was now in the South, and there was little support in the south for the move for independence. The South was filled with large farms and relatively little population. The South also had a lot of money, and if the British captured the south, they would also capture the crops, the farms, and control the waterways of the south. General Clinton was already bragging that he had now complete control the first of the 13 American colonies. Abra and the other delegates quickly worked on strategies to help the southern states.

As 1778 came to an end Washington used the Middlebrook, New Jersey grounds for winter encampment for the main portion of the army. The New Jersey Brigade stationed themselves closer to Elizabethtown so that they could guard the coast. Abra was thrilled to know there were American troops near his home area. Another force was stationed at Danbury, Connecticut where they could move to defend the Highlands, or move into Manhattan Island if needed. The army was now between 8,000-10,000 men. There were only 10,000 citizens in Somerset County, and they were worried about being able to have the resources to handle that additional population of the Continental Army. New Jersey's state legislature worried that the additional costs of housing would further place the state in financial duress.

The soldiers once again built themselves log cabins covered with clay for their winter shelter. To assist the soldiers in their building needs a request from Deputy Quartermaster Jacob Weiss to the New Jersey legislature to provide the following items was sent: "Broad Axes, Adzes Claw or Carpenter's Hammers, 12 or 15 Cross cut Saws with cross cut and Hand Saw Files and also Saw Setts, 10 or 12 Saddles with the prices or distinguishing whose Merchandize, About 2 Ton Barr Iron as wrote for including that for Mr. How, 10 or 12 Bars Steel suitable for new Steeling Axes &c.-And a good Stove with pipes agreeable to dimensions."

In a letter Dr. James Thatcher, described the Middlebrook encampment.

*February 3rd.*

*Having continued to live under cover of canvas-tents most of the winter, we have suffered extremely from exposure to cold and storms. Our soldiers have been employed six or eight weeks in constructing log huts, which at length are completed, and both officers and soldiers are now under comfortable covering for the remainder of the winter. Log houses are constructed with the trunks of trees cut into various lengths, according to the size intended, and are firmly connected by notches cut at their extremities in the manner of dovetailing. The vacancies between the logs are filled in with plastering consisting of mud and clay. The roof is formed of similar pieces of timber, and covered with hewn slabs. The chimney, situated at one end of the house, is made of similar but smaller timber, and both the inner and the outer side are covered with clay plaster, to defend the wood against the fire. The door and windows are formed by sawing away a part of the logs of a proper size, and move on wooden hinges. In this manner have our soldiers, without nails, and almost without tools, except the axe and saw, provided for their officers and for themselves comfortable and convenient quarters, with little or no expense to the public. The huts are arranged in strait lines, forming a regular, uniform, compact village. The officers' huts are situated in front of the line, according to their rank, the kitchens in the rear, and the whole is similar in form to a tent encampment. The ground for a considerable distance in front of the soldiers' line of huts is cleared of wood, stumps and rubbish, and is every morning swept clean for the purpose of a parade-ground and roll-call for the respective regiments. Line officers' huts are in general divided into two apartments, and are occupied by three or four officers, who compose one mess. Those for the soldiers have but one room, and contain ten or twelve men, with their cabins placed one above another against the walls, and fitted with straw and one blanket for each man."*

The winter of 1788 was a mild one. Temperatures typically remained above freezing and spring arrived early. Quarter Master General, Nathanael Greene, was able to arrange for food and clothing for the troops that winter and the troops certainly faired better than they had the year before at Valley Forge. Even new uniforms were supplied by the French allies, which greatly increased the morale of the troops.

Abra sighed and hoped that the new year would finally bring a successful end to the war. His evening prayers lasted late into the night as he thought of each member of his family and the personal battles each was facing through this war. He counted himself blessed as he was indoors and could sleep at night knowing that he was relatively safe in his room with the safety of military men within his city protecting them. Sarah, his younger children, and his older sons, however, were not as safe. Abra lay awake for many hours praying 1779 would bring the end to the war and allow him to sleep more soundly knowing his family was safe.

# Chapter 15
## *1779*

**Abra left Congress** to work in the New Jersey legislature in 1779. Although Abra felt his work in Congress was important, his continual fear of his family's safety played havoc with his nerves. Abra was relieved to be home among his own people in New Jersey, which he had not been able to do while working in Congress. Too often he was unable to return home because of threats to his own personal safety. Abra's 300 acre farm had seen action during the past three years. Each time he heard of fighting in New Jersey he would fear the worst. His new appointment in the state legislature also afforded him time to spend more time with his family, something which gave him a sense of peace, especially when the war had been played so often on New Jersey soil. Sarah, too, was relieved to have Abra home with her. The years spent witnessing the war, the constant waiting for word of well-being for her husband and sons had taken its toll on her. Her once radiant face was now softly lined and the worry lines across her brow seemed fixed. Her hair, once thick and full of soft waves, now was pinned back into a tight bun which might be thought to pull away the many worries which crossed her mind daily. Having her husband near her again was comforting even though he was often away from the Clark farm, but near enough he could return in a day's journey.

Upon Abra's return to the state legislature he found the first order of business was to complete the design of the New Jersey state flag. It was Washington's idea that every outfit would carry two flags: their state's and the union's. Not only would this serve as identification, but it would build pride in the men as they fought for independence. The buff color was chosen by General George Washington when he was directed by the Continental Congress to prescribe the uniform for the regiments of the New Jersey Continental Line. He directed that the coats of the soldiers should be dark blue faced with buff. These colors were chosen by Washington to honor the original Dutch settlers of New Jersey. Dark Blue, or Jersey Blue as it was known, and Buff were the colors of Holland or the Netherlands. Abra found this decision making to be enjoyable compared to the hard tasks he typically faced while in Congress. For once he was pleased to be able to share his work with Sarah as much of his work in Congress was secretive and sharing such information stood in constant jeopardy of being intercepted.

Abra was a much respected member of the state legislature. Many of those who had signed the Declaration had dropped out of public service. Abra was one of the few who remained steadfast in his desire to serve and build the new country. Most of Abra's work both in Congress and now in the New Jersey legislature concentrated on financing and determining how New Jersey would fund their fair share of the war effort. The Continental Congress was borrowing heavily from individuals of some wealth who supported independence. Many had accepted chits handed to various farmers for livestock, timber, and grain needed by the troops. Each state was being asked to prepare a way and means to assist in repayment of these loans and chits once the war was over. When it was discovered that the British had been counterfeiting the Continental dollars, Abra's concerns grew. The British knew that by glutting the market with the counterfeit currency, the value of the American dollar would decline, thus keeping the colonies from being able to get supplies or pay their troops. He also knew that a faulty economy would destroy everything they had fought to achieve. That would be unacceptable. Abra worked long hours looking for ways to budget New Jersey's finances so they could pay their fair share and help keep the new government financial solvent once this war came to an end.

As spring arrived, Washington planned and gathered supplies for the march against the Iroquois in New York State. Abra knew there were men from New Jersey who joined in this campaign. He considered if his own son, Andrew, may be part of this contingent. The march led by General Sullivan in June, and included the New Jersey Brigade. Congress had approved of the attack as the Iroquois tribes had decided to side with the British in order to protect their own lands against the colonists should they win the war for independence. The Seneca, Cayuga, Mohawk, and Onondaga tribes, therefore, together with Loyalists forces, ravaged colonial settlements on the Pennsylvania and New York frontiers. The Sullivan Campaign, as it was known, was meant to subdue the Indians and reduce the chance of Indian attacks. Additionally, by destroying the food supplies of the Iroquois, the Americans believed the British would have more difficulty providing food for their troops during the following winter.

General John Sullivan and General James Clinton with 4,400 Continental troops arrived to burn Indian villages and crops. Washington's specific instructions to Sullivan described the mission objective as "total destruction and devastation" of the Iroquois villages. Prisoners were to be taken as hostages so as to guarantee any later peace settlement. Washington also included a warning not to accept any offer of peace before "the total ruin of their settlement was affected."

After winning the August, 1779 battle at Newtown, Sullivan was unopposed. From Newtown, Sullivan's forces moved to Canadasaga moving north of Seneca Lake. General Sullivan met with a group of American supporting Oneida Indians. They asked Sullivan to spare their Cayuga brothers. Sullivan told the Oneidas that the Cayugas had participated in frontier attacks, and the Cayugas would not be spared. Sullivan's men moved toward Kendaia, which was taken without a fight on September 5. A white captive left in Kendaia reported there were one thousand Indian warriors at Canadasaga, at the head of Seneca Lake. Sullivan found the village empty when the troops arrived. Sullivan divided his men with half moving west and destroying Canandaigua and Honeoye, and the other half led by Colonel Peter Ganesvoort moving eastward from Canadasaga to the Mohawk Valley. Forty towns were razed and crops destroyed. This left the remaining Indians unable to face the upcoming winter which dropped five feet of snow. The Indian population dropped dramatically from the devastation from the Sullivan campaign. It also left the British without a supplier for their food in this region. Those Americans on the Campaign trail recognized that this area of land was rich with water resources and farming resources. Many veterans vowed to return after the war to settle in this area which would no longer have the threat of Indians.

Abra often received news from friends still working in Congress, although messages were delivered carefully in order to not draw attention from the remaining Loyalists in the area. News of battles being fought across the colonies was constant. There was even news of skirmishes outside the thirteen colonies. Loyalists continued to undermine the Patriots. The Loyalists and Indians recaptured Vincennes, Indiana, but George Rogers Clark had forced them to retreat. The rebel forces went on to destroy many of the Native American villages. When such reports reached the New Jersey legislature Abra felt a sense of despair. The war was all consuming. Even the western territories were in the tug-of-war battle for control. Abra began to wonder if they would ever see peace, or if they would just move from one war to another in a constant quest for freedom. So many countries of Europe lived in constant war. Abra hoped that America would not have this same way of life.

Meanwhile, in the south, Washington was positioning a defense force between Augusta and Savannah, blocking the movement of supplies between the two cities. General Clinton thought that since the taking of Savannah had proven so easy, it would be just as easy to conquer Augusta. Commander Archibold Campbell led the British troops toward Augusta, but quickly met resistance and retreated back to Savannah. When word came to the New Jersey legislature about the retreat of the British, shouts of celebration could be heard throughout the hall. Each victory by the Americans was celebrated. When news was not good for days on end, any small victory was cause for immediate celebration, no matter how small a victory. Abra felt these small victories would give them the strength and encouragement to continue their fight.

Abra and several of his friends sat at dinner discussing the recent involvement of Spain in their war. The war was gathering interest throughout Europe. Spain saw it as an opportunity to benefit them. They offered to help the British if England would give them Gibraltar. When refused, the Spanish joined the French efforts in defeating the British. To many it appeared that this war was becoming a world war. Abra was not certain how having the Spanish join the fray would benefit them. The Spanish had a long history of wanting to settle in the Americas and Abra feared that should they become too active in this war, they may have to pay a steep price to Spain. An animated and heated discussion among the friends ended with no real answer as to how beneficial Spain's involvement would be for the Americans. As in many discussions, Abra found there was no set answer. They would just have to wait and see what turn of events awaited them as more European influence was seen in the war.

Abra was always concerned about the involvement of Indians in this war. When a message arrived that there had been two massacres on Americans by New York Iroquois and Seneca Indians, forces were sent in to eliminate the Indian villages. Their villages were burned to the ground, but the Indians scattered and remained hostile toward the Americans. He worried about the Indian reprisals and the fight extending in the western territories. It was like the once peaceful world of the colonies had gone mad. Abra sighed and shook his head. "At least there is little action happening directly in New Jersey at this moment," he thought. Abra stood before the tally sheet listing the various battles recorded thus far for 1779. It appeared that the British were still winning this war, despite the battles which the Americans called their victories.

As Abra stood looking over the list, several younger men joined him. They enthusiastically declared that the tide was turning toward the Americans. "Such optimism," thought Abra, as he listened to their interpretations of the weight of the battles. Clearly their youth viewed any achievement as a turnaround. Perhaps that was the outlook that was needed by everyone. Discounting the losses and only fixating on the achievements would keep spirits high and bring the promise of a successful end to this war. Abra smiled and for the first time in weeks, returned to his room with a smile on his face.

January 6-9 Sunbury, Georgia British victory
January 25 Briar Creek, Georgia British Victory
January 26 Burke County, Georgia British victory
January 29 Augusta, Georgia British Victory
January 30 Fort Henderson, Georgia British Victory
February 1 Royal Island, South Carolina British Victory
February 6 Kiokee Creek, Georgia **American Victory**
February 8-10 Wilkes County, Georgia Draw
February 9 Middleton's Ferry, Georgia **American Victory**
February 9, Brownsborough, Georgia British Victory
February 10 Vann's Creek, Georgia British Victory
February 14 Cherokee Ford, South Carolina **American Victory**
February 18 Herbert's Store, Georgia **American Victory**
February 26 Horseneck Landing, Connecticut British Victory

March Fort Morgan, Georgia British Victory

March 21 Beech Island, Georgia **American Victory**

March 22 Rocky Comfort Creek, Georgia **American Victory**

April 21 Onondaga Castle, New York **American Victory**

May 4 Coosawhatchie River, South Carolina British Victory

May 9-11 Hampton Roads, Virginia British Victory

May 20 Stono River, South Carolina British Victory

May 23 Stono Ferry South Carolina **American Victory**

June 1 Stony Point, New York British Victory

June 1 Verplanck's Point, New York British Victory

June 27 Liberty County, Georgia **American Victory**

June 28 Hickory Hill in Liberty County, Georgia **American Victory**

July 1 Wilkes County, Georgia **American Victory**

July 2 Poundridge, New York **American Victory**

July 5 New Haven, Connecticut British Victory

July 8 Fairfield, Connecticut British Victory

July 8 Green Farms, Connecticut British Victory

July 11 Norwalk, Connecticut British Victory

August 5 Morrisania, New York **American Victory**

Three days later Abra was alerted that a messenger had arrived with news of another battle in New Jersey. Abra moved quickly to hear the messenger tell of the battle at Paulus Hook. Abra questioned the messenger about the outcome of the battle. "Our army attacked at night after a fourteen mile march, but had to withdraw with the break of day. We took 159 prisoners, officers and men." Everyone broke out in a cheer, and the recorder moved to add the latest victory to the ongoing list. Although the news was great, it did not eliminate the fear in Abra that battles continued in the north and on their New Jersey soil. "It may be a win," he thought, "but at what price for New Jersey?"

As the months of 1779 rolled on, new battles were added to the ongoing list posted on the wall outside the meeting room. Representatives of the New Jersey legislature would congregate around the list and discuss their predictions and congratulate the wins, and would only talk in hushed tones about the British victories listed which were in their own state. Even if it had been a small battle, every battle which could be listed as American victory gave the men a stronger feeling of achieving their goal. Certainly the end of 1779 saw more victories and this was a good sign.

August 11-September 14 Allegheny River, Indian Territory, **American Victory**
August 14 Lockhart's Plantation, Georgia **American Victory**
September 5 Lloyd's Neck, New York **American Victory**
September 16 Ogeechee Ferry, Georgia **American Victory**
October 1 Savage Point, Georgia **American Victory**
October 17 Somerset Court House, New Jersey British Victory

For Abra, the end of 1779 was filled with anguish and despair whenever he thought of his sons off fighting the war and sleeping in fields and not knowing when they would be attacked. Although Abra could visit his home more often than when he was in Congress, he still spent most of his time in his rented room in Trenton. His anxiety of his unprotected wife, children, daughter-in-law, and grandson housed on the Clark farm weighed heavy on his mind. Abra spent hours in his room every night praying and lying awake until sleep overtook him.

## Chapter 16

# *1780 Brings Elizabethtown Down*

**Congress felt that what the army suffered** during their 1777-1778 winter at Valley Forge was horrible, however weather-wise, it was an average winter. The following year was a mild winter. But, the winter of 1779-1780 was the worst winter of the 18th century. Valley Forge had been the first winter camp for most of the army, and their inexperience led to the many problems they had. By 1779 troops were more accustomed to harsh military life and they had better survival skills, despite the weather conditions. Washington knew the Morristown area had a natural defensive location, thus they could not be overtaken by surprise attacks. It was also a great location for bringing food, supplies and clothing into the camp. There were many local resources such as water and trees for building huts and providing firewood. There were also many homes which could quarter officers. The home of Jacob Ford, Jr. was occupied by his widowed wife and children. Mrs. Ford rented Washington her home for the winter encampment. The four young Ford children and their mother and servants moved into two rooms, and the rest of the mansion was turned over to Washington's headquarters. Despite the seemingly good setting, the army suffered throughout that harsh winter, many resorting to theft for food, and many deserting because of conditions. Despite all of this, only one hundred men perished compared to the nearly 2500 who perished at Valley Forge.

When troops arrived in Morristown in early December, they selected Jockey Hollow to build their log-house city. The troops cut down 600 acres of trees and built 1000 log huts. Each hut was about 14x15 feet. Each had a doorway cut at one end and a fireplace built at the other. The huts were laid out in precise sections, each eight rows with three or four huts deep. Each hut held twelve men. The huts were not finished before the first of twenty-eight major storms hit Jockey Hollow between December and April. The Great blizzard of January 3 1780 dropped six feet of snow making roads impassible and burying some of the soldiers. The Hudson River froze solid and crossing the river was easily done on foot. The British even moved cannon to Staten Island over the ice. Food was limited and the men often starved. Pet dogs and tree bark were often eaten by the men. On January 14th, three thousand men raided Staten Island and stole supplies and blankets from the British. Ten days later the British did the same to Newark and Elizabethtown.

Abra was still home from the winter break from Congress. He had been re-elected to Congress and was to return to Philadelphia early in 1780. At the end of January Sarah was startled when the young Negro boy ran into the house to tell them that British soldiers were approaching. Sarah immediately went into action. Abra took a basket and put as much food into it that could be easily carried. Sarah ran through the house pulling blankets off beds and spare clothing. Sarah had rehearsed with her family escape plans in order to be better prepared should they be attacked. The family quickly moved outdoors and ran to the back of the house. They followed one after another in a single file and the young Negro boy followed last, brushing their path with a tree limb to hide their path. Once they got into the woods, they quickly ran to the area where they had built a windbreak against a rock outcrop to serve as a cover when they needed to hide. Abra looked at Sarah's serious face and the worried look of the children and servants. No one had said a word. They moved into their hide-out and huddled closely together to stave off the cold. It was several hours before Abra moved back toward the house to see if it was safe to return. When the family returned they found the British had taken some of the livestock and much of the food stored in the barn. They had also stolen the few articles of Abra's clothing and several older and threadbare blankets which had been left behind. Sarah was relieved that she had the children take the blankets from the beds and wrap them around themselves as they ran to hide. Sarah had long gotten into the habit to bury food in an outdoor root cellar. She was now thankful that the fresh snow had covered over the footprints she had made when going there to get food the day before. Had the British seen the footprints, they would have taken the supplies she needed to keep her family fed during the winter months. Whether they saw the brushing of the tree limb was not known. Perhaps they were more interested in looking for food and supplies rather than chasing after helpless women and children, thought Sarah. She just thanked God that they had not suffered injury. She was also thankful that they had not followed them into the woods as Abra was a traitor of the British. When Sarah considered what would have happened had they found Abra and knew his identity, she shuddered. Abra drew his arm about her as he knew what she was thinking. He, too, had considered the consequences. "Sarah, the men who came here were looking for supplies. They are just as desperate as our own soldiers are with this horrific winter we are experiencing. Had they actually seen me I doubt they would have known who I was."

"Perhaps," said Sarah. "But I am certain I am not comfortable thinking of the danger you are in when the British troops are near. You are probably safer when you are not home." She looked at Abra's face and could see that he agreed with what she was saying.

Several nights later, after Abra and Sarah had already

retired to bed, the sound of a horse galloping up the lane toward the Clark house was followed by a voice calling out for Abra. Sarah had already jumped out of bed and was quickly dressing, thinking a repeat of their trip to the woods would be necessary. By the time Abra got to the door, the rider was dismounting. It was one of their neighbors. "Abra, we need you to come to the parsonage. It's in flames!"

"An act of war or an accident?" asked Abra.

The rider said, "British soldiers, but they seemed to have moved away after they started the fire. We are trying to save what we can." He quickly mounted and left to gather more help.

Abra moved quickly to dress. Sarah went to the kitchen and began packing food and blankets to put into the wagon. Abra loaded shovels and tools. He then walked out of the house with his gun.

"Abra, what on earth is that for?" asked Sarah looking at the rifle.

"Somebody did this, and you can rest assured it was someone unhappy about Reverend Caldwell's church service," said Abra. He pulled Sarah close to him and kissed her on the cheek. "I want you to get the children together and go to our hiding spot until I return. If I am not back by tomorrow night, follow our plan for escape." He looked into Sarah's eyes and could see she had fear in them, but her jaw was set firmly.

"I am certain all will be well," Sarah answered, although in her mind she was already planning what she needed to pack in case they had to take flight. “When will this wretched war come to an end,” she thought as she pulled her hair back to pin it up so she could begin packing.

Abra left and drove his wagon to the parsonage. When he got there he found his friends and neighbors all working to try to save the building. As Abra jumped out of the wagon and grabbed his shovel he joined in the shouts of questions and answers as the men worked side by side trying to salvage what they could. Abra learned that Caldwell had returned home to find his offices ransacked and the parsonage set ablaze. The flames then jumped to the school house and it, too, had begun to burn. The men of Rahway and Elizabethtown worked side by side, but the flames were too high. Despite working into the early morning hours, the buildings were totally destroyed. Caldwell and his wife stood silently looking at the smoldering remains.

“What now?” asked Abra.

Caldwell shook his head. “I need to get my family out to Chatham to hide out. I’d suggest you take Sarah and the children and move as well.”

“We have our plan worked out,” answered Abra, “but we thought the British were moving their focus to the southern states and our Jersey land would be able to rest momentarily.”

“Apparently not,” said Caldwell. Both men pondered the stories they had heard about the British and Hessian troops and their treatment of the locals.

“Sarah’s packed up food and blankets. Take them and use

them. Take my wagon and use it to get to Chatham," Abra said as he continued to look at the smoky remains of their church.

"No, I stashed our wagon in the woods just in case patrols, ours or theirs, thought it would make good firewood," smiled Caldwell. "Seems they had enough firewood this time!" said James, nodding toward the smoldering remains. Abra always appreciated the way his friend could find humor to deal with the most tragic news. The two men talked briefly about their plans, and Abra left.

Abra saw that the two Negro boys were on patrol watching for any suspicious activity along the Clark border. They waved in acknowledgement to Abra as he passed, and Abra stopped the wagon to speak with them about a potential move for protection. The boys nodded in understanding and Abra knew that they were just as anxious about their mother's safety as Abra was about his family's. Sarah was waiting for Abra in the kitchen. She had already packed up food and clothing and was ready to leave if necessary. The younger Clark children were sitting quietly in the kitchen eating breakfast.

"I think it is necessary for you to move with the children and servants. I have to get to Philadelphia soon, and would feel better knowing you were with your family while we wait out this latest turn of events. Things have to improve soon." He held his wife in his arms and felt her strong shoulders go limp when she was embraced. Abra knew she was as strong emotionally as any man he worked with in Congress, but it was good to know she could let go for a moment while Abra was there to comfort her. For more than three years Sarah had handled everything on the Clark farm, and helped others in the area. She had gathered the children and servants and directed them to safety when British or Hessian patrols were seen in the area. Now it was Abra's turn to comfort his wife.

Abra helped pack the wagon with all the supplies and waved as his wife, children and servants all left for the protection of the Hatfield family. Abra then packed his things and left for Philadelphia after preparing letters to friends and the boys which he intended to send later that day. He looked at his home as he rode down the lane toward the highway and hoped that it would still be standing when he returned.

Work began immediately upon his return to Philadelphia. There was little time for visiting and sharing family stories with his fellow delegates. All seemed pleased to see Abra return to Congress, but they knew that the upcoming year could determine whether their work was in vain or the very foundation for which they had worked so hard to achieve. Abra was constantly in search of news from New Jersey. He learned that in January not only the Presbyterian Church had been burned to the ground but the courthouse was burned soon afterward. This was Abra's church, and the courthouse was where he had begun his life in politics, representing the poor farmers. It was the Hetfield boys who had led the British to the site. Cornelius, Job and Smith Hetfield were the sons of the patriot, Cornelious

Hetfield, Sr. who was fighting so hard for American independence. It saddened Abra to think of how the Hetfield boys had betrayed the work of their father. When the British met with the patriot forces near the courthouse, the British were able to capture forty seven privates and five officers. The records in the church and courthouse were completely destroyed. This war was certainly dividing families. Abra was further saddened knowing that all the family records and all his papers and records had been destroyed in that fire. It was almost as if the British wanted to erase from history the memory of those who lived, worked and now fought in this area. Abra thought about Sarah and the family having to go into hiding during these cold winter months, and hoped they would not have to do this again. He had felt guilty about having to leave so soon after the church attack, but he was also committed to the work in Congress. February could be fierce weather and to think of Sarah and the children all hiding in the woods was nearly more than he could take. He hoped they would be safe at her parents' farm. Abra then considered that he, very well, could have been captured during the attack. The church and courthouse were the places Abra typically met with other patriots to discuss the war. Had Abra been there, he had no doubts he would have been taken captive. The British had won that battle, but patrols moved on, taking with them their prisoners.

Work at Congress continued without a break. It was in the early spring when Abra received a letter from Sarah that she had returned to the Clark farm. She was determined to salvage what she could and to maintain their home during Abra's absence. Too many farms were pillaged during the war when left abandoned by fleeing families. Abra hoped that future battles would not be fought on New Jersey soil. Already New Jersey had seen many battles. Abra kept a neat list of the battles fought in his state which he referred to, especially when debating the costs of war and how some states were paying a higher price. He looked at the list, and it saddened him.

18th November, 1776, Fort Lee, N. J.
1st December, 1776, Brunswick, N. J.
17th December, 1776, Springfield, N. J.
26th December, 1776, Trenton, N. J.
2nd January, 1777, Assumpsick Bridge, Trenton, N. J.
3rd January, 1777, Princeton, N. J.
20th January, 1777, Somerset Court House (Millstone), N. J.
8th March, 1777, Amboy (Punk Hill), N. J.
13th April, 1777, Boundbrook, N. J.
19th April, 1777, Woodbridge, N. J.
8th May, 1777, Piscataway, N. J.
17th June, 1777, Millstone, N. J.
26th June, 1777, Short Hills, N. J.
22nd October, 1777, Fort Mercer (Red Bank), N. J.
18th March, 1778, Quintan's Bridge, N. J.
21st March, 1778, Hancock's Bridge, N. J.

8th May, 1778, Bordentown, N. J.

28th June, 1778, Monmouth (Freehold Court House), N. J.

6th October, 1778, Chestnut Creek, N. J.

15th October, 1778, Mincock Island (Egg Harbor), N. J.

27th April, 1779, Middletown, N. J.

18th July, 1779, Jersey City, N. J.

19th August, 1779, Paulus Hook (Weehawken), N. J.

26th October, 1779, Brunswick, N. J.

25th Janaury, 1780, Elizabethtown, N. J.

25th January, 1780, Newark, N. J.

He knew how he felt when his city was attacked, and knew that people throughout his state, and other states, felt the same when their city was attacked. They needed this war to end in their favor so their lives could be reclaimed and they could rebuild for their families and for the future.

Near July, a post was delivered to Congress and handed to Abra as he entered the room. "This came to us through some rather strange circumstances, Abra. It appears the deliverer had been a prisoner aboard one of the prison ships. Because he carried money hidden on his person, he was able to buy his freedom in exchange for his money and the promise to carry this post. It came through directly from the hands of the British, and it is addressed to you. He also told us that your son, Andrew, was on the prison ship, however his identity as to being your son is yet unknown to the British commander onboard." Abra took the letter and looked at it curiously. It was written in his son's handwriting. He broke the seal and began to read.

*My most Honorable Father,*

*I have been forced to write this letter from the bowels of the British Prison Ship, the Jersey. I was taken prisoner and delivered to this overcrowded Hell where many of our men are chained and mistreated because of the rebellious acts against King George. The suffering is severe. Within a week of my incarceration, it was revealed that I was the son of the American traitor who signed the rebellious document demanding independence. I was removed to a separate quarter where I am being beaten and starved. I was demanded to write this letter asking you to renege on your traitorous act.*

*I am your most obedient son,*
*Thomas Clark*

There were postscripts written by other rebel officers who identified Thomas and acknowledged the torture being given him with pleas that Abra act immediately for fear that Thomas would die as a result of the treatment he was receiving.

Abra sank into a chair and his complexion turned an ashen color. Those closest to him handed him a glass of water and offered help. Abra sat staring at the letter in disbelief. When asked if he was at liberty to share the contents, Abra silently handed over the letter. It was quickly consumed by those surrounding him, and very quickly the room became crowded and voices in hushed tones excitedly and angrily discussed the contents of the letter. “We need to act upon this immediately. We need to contact Washington and have his troops free those on this hell-hole ship,” one of the men said putting his hand on Abra’s shoulder. Abra drew himself up and looked about him. Another delegate said, “We know that the British mean business. Look what they did to Stockton. Word is his health will never recover after the treatment he received.”

“Gentlemen. I thank you for your concern. This doom is something I have feared all along. I am heartsick at the thought of what my sons are experiencing on that ship, and I fear that they will discover Andrew’s identity and do the same to him. However, I cannot ask Congress or Washington to stop our mission to rescue my sons. There are mothers and fathers at home feeling the same anxiety I am, and yet they have no connections to assist and eliminate their fears. I am no different from them. In fact, some of them bear a greater weight as their children died for this cause. We are committed to this purpose, and our children and the children of others joined into this fray because of their belief in our work. I must put my faith in my God and our soldiers to put an end to this war and to ease the pain my children and others’ children are living each day. If you will excuse me, I must send word to my wife as she is my partner and deserves to know the truth of what has happened."

Abra slowly stepped forward, and the group of men parted to allow him to pass. He had left the letter behind and the post was passed around the room. Abra was right that their focus had to be on the greater good, yet it was difficult learning what one of their own was suffering because of their stance. The men talked of Richard Stockton, another New Jersey delegate and signer of the Declaration who had been captured by the British, and the suffering he endured as a prisoner of war, and how after his release he went home penniless and an invalid. The men also talked of how the prisons of New York had filled in the early stages of the war in 1776, and then the British began the practice of turning aged maritime vessels into floating prisons. It was well known that these ships caused more young men to die than the battlefields. Tales of dysentery and typhus were reported, and many had reported watching the dead being either thrown overboard into the bay, or brought to shore and buried in mass graves on the shore. The Jersey was rumored to be the worst of the prison ships, and now their friend and colleague's sons were on the ship. Many men sat that evening and wrote letters about this latest turn of events and how the British were becoming barbaric in their treatment of the Americans. The letters streamed out to families in New Jersey, as well as throughout the colonies, as a warning of how barbaric the British were behaving.

Sarah had moved back home and was caring for her two youngest children, Abraham who was now thirteen and called himself the "man of the house," and Abigail, the youngest was eight. Abra and Sarah's daughter, Sarah, remained home helping her mother with the care of the children and the running of the farm. Often Sarah would look at her daughter with sadness as her daughter was now nineteen years old, and all the young men were off to war and her prospects for marriage were erased. This war had lasted too many years, and so many sacrifices had been made, but Sarah knew that the work her husband was doing was necessary. She smiled when she thought of Abra's dedication and passion, but she missed having him home to talk about their family and the farm. She longed for the normalcy of life without war and patrols and hiding. She would daydream of days when Abra would sit by the fire reading or talking politics with the local men, while the children played carefree after evening chores were done. As she looked at her son Abraham she recognized his growth into such a serious young man was due to his growing up only hearing talk of war. To think that he might one day also leave to fight frightened her.

Thomas's wife, Elizabeth was still living in the Clark house with their three year old son, Jonathan.  It was Sarah who comforted Elizabeth during Thomas' imprisonment. Sarah worried for both of her sons on the prison ship, but the torturing of Thomas was revealed to her through members of the church who had heard about it. Abra had not written about the torture because he did not want Sarah and Elizabeth to have to deal with the worries. He should have known better. Elizabeth would sit beside Jonathan when he would finally drift off to sleep, and she would touch his soft cheeks and think of Thomas and pray for his safe return. Jonathan was an innocent and a sweet child who played with pots and spoons on the kitchen floor, or would chase the chickens around the yard. One day when Elizabeth walked into the yard she saw little Jonathan running with a large stick, holding it out from his shoulder like a rifle. Elizabeth heard him calling out, “Bang. Bang bang bang.” Elizabeth was a soft spoken girl, but her voice was piercing sharp and she scolded Jonathan to stop. She sharply grabbed the stick from Jonathan and flung it away from her. Startled, Jonathan sat and sobbed. Sarah looked out at Elizabeth cradling Jonathan in her arms and rocking him as the little boy continued to sob uncontrollably. “Did he get hurt?” asked Sarah, wiping her hands on her apron.

“No. I spoke too sharply at him. He was pretending that stick was a rifle. It is my problem. He was just playing, but I read into everything any more. I just can’t bear to think of this war and all the young men going off to it. This war had been the only world this child has known. We scoop him up and go into hiding when patrols come near. We warn him not to make a sound and to sit still and not move. Children were meant to investigate and explore. They grow up soon enough, but it seems the only life Jonathan has known has been hearing the sound of rifles in the distance, and..."at that Elizabeth began sobbing. Sarah moved quickly to comfort her. "And I worry every day about Thomas and his brothers, and Hannah's husband, and my own brothers and cousins. They face uncertainty every day, every day. They have to look over their shoulders in fear that the next breath they take may be their last."

Sarah lifted mother and child up and led them back to the house. Jonathan was rubbing his eyes and had his head on Elizabeth's shoulder while still shuddering from his crying. "Elizabeth, you have to stay strong. You have to be positive and you have to think about how wonderful life will be after the war is over and we have our freedom."

"But what if we don't win...."

"No, Elizabeth. We will not have negative thoughts in this house. Abra is working so hard to help with the building of a new and independent country. The women have to remain strong and hold family and farm together. That's our war effort. We raise our children, we keep the farms going, and we keep the madness of fear at bay. Now, put Jonathan down for a nap and help me pack up some clothing to take to Susanna. She is already heavy with her second child, and she will have her hands full with Winans who is already two. I can't believe I'll have a third grandbaby in a short spell. These grandchildren will know freedom. That will be the memory they will hold." Elizabeth obediently squared her shoulders and walked into the house. Sarah shook her head. It was easy to tell Elizabeth to be strong when she herself spent most of her day worrying about the men folk of the family.

Although Abra had not sent word to Congress about the treatment Thomas was receiving on the prison ship, Jersey, another delegate of New Jersey shared the story through a post to Washington. It was not long afterward that Abra was greeted with the story of how Washington had responded when hearing about Thomas' torture. Washington already knew about the terrible conditions on the prison ships. He had written a letter in early 1777 to General Lord William Howe stating, *"You may call us rebels, and say that we deserve no better treatment, but remember, my Lord, that supposing us rebels, we still have feelings as keen and sensible as loyalists, and will, if forced to it, most assuredly retaliate upon those upon whom we look as the unjust invaders of our rights, liberties and properties."**

Stories continued to be told of several who escaped the ships and the treatment they witnessed. Each morning the dead would be placed on the forecastle, and then dropped down the side to be buried in a common shallow grave. Others had given testimony that to be in the hold of the ships was like the damned souls collected at the entrance of Hell in the *Inferno*, they were heard blaspheming God and their own births, and fretting and pacing with pallid faces and sunken eyes. Thousands had died on these ships and certainly thousands more would die

*actual letter

if this war did not come to an end. Discussions as to whether they should notify Washington raged between the delegates, however they agreed with Abra that others were also suffering and there was no one to wager for their safekeeping. In the end, someone copied the contents of the letter Abra had received and sent it to Washington who promptly captured a British officer and wrote a threatening letter that should the mistreatment of Thomas Clark not come to an immediate end, this officer should suffer the same fate. The individualized torture of Thomas Clark came to an abrupt end.

Abra was relieved with the news when it arrived that Thomas was no longer being tortured. It destroyed him when he heard that the only thing that was keeping Thomas alive was that his son Andrew and others prisoners were pushing bites of bread through a keyhole. Abra quickly sent a post off to Sarah and Elizabeth so they would know that Thomas was no longer being tortured and he was alive, yet still a prisoner, as was Andrew. Although Abra had only notified them of Thomas and Andrew's capture, he learned that others shared that information of Thomas's torture with Sarah. Later when he received a letter from Sarah thanking God that Thomas was alive he noted tear stains on the stationary. He didn't know if they were Sarah's or Elizabeth's, but he was certain they were tears of relief.

Abra's work in Congress focused mostly on treasury issues. It was apparent that with the war effort, many delegates would have to leave to handle problems at home. Attendance was a constant problem because the war kept interfering. There was also great frustration among many of the states in not knowing exactly what was happening in the war. Abra encouraged fellow delegates to write regularly to their state legislatures so that they would know what was happening and keep the rumors and speculations from being thought of as truths. For many the news from these letters was the only way anyone knew what the war effort was doing. Abra kept in contact with his family, friends, and with the New Jersey Governor, William Livingston. Letters were typically short, succinct and informative. Once written, delegates had to hope that they would be delivered without interference from the British. One evening Abra sat down to write to the Governor.

*Philadelphia, May 30, 1780*

*Sir,*

*Last evening and this morning we were amused in the town by a report from Charlestown that the enemy, having made two assaults on the 8$^{th}$ and 9$^{th}$, had been repulsed with the loss of about two thousand killed and wounded. A French fleet was off the bar and had taken possession of Stono and the shipping there. These flattering accounts upon enquiry appear to have but little foundation. I can find no intelligence to be relied upon more than contained in the enclosed* *extracts which were taken from Mr. Lawrence's letters from Wilmington in North Carolina.*

*Mr. Houston, being absent to visit his family, and Mr. Fell, confined with a fever, our state is unrepresented, though it is probable Mr. Fell will soon be able to attend as he appears to be on the mending hand.*

*We have officially from New Hampshire, Massachusetts, and Connecticut that they have passed the Laws on Finance Agreeable to the Resolutions of the 18th of March.*

*I have the honor to be with due respects,*
*Your Excellency's Obedient Humble Servant,*
*Abra. Clark**

Abra wanted his state to be aware of the serious work they were doing in Philadelphia. He took his job in finance seriously as there were constant struggles in getting the states to agree upon how to fund the war and the new government. There were also the problems of each state having their own laws which did not coordinate with the laws of other states. One such problem occurred when Abra learned that banished populations were being exiled from their states, and they planned to move into New Jersey. Correspondence was necessary to safeguard each state from the rules of another. Abra wrote a letter to Governor Livingston warning him of the upcoming problem.

*actual letter

*Philadelphia, June 10, 1780*

*Sir,*

*By a law of this state lately passed, the wives and children of all such who have joined the enemy are to depart this state in a short time. They are accordingly preparing for their departure, and I am informed they intend to remove into Jersey, where they say our laws will give them security and a safe refuge.*

*As I do not recollect any law in Jersey which prevents persons of that character from residing among us and by which they are removable, I think it necessary to inform your Excellency of their intention that the Legislature may, if they think proper, take measures for preventing our state's becoming a receptacle for the banished of other states.*

*I have the honor to be with due respects,*
*your Excellency's obedient and humble servant.*

*Abra. Clark**

Once Governor Livingston received Abra's letter, he immediately contacted the New Jersey legislature to write laws protecting New Jersey from incoming families of those who joined the British. Abra was satisfied that his work in Congress allowed him the opportunity to safeguard his own state through

*actual letter

his correspondence. There was a small part of Abra that felt he needed to protect the families of other Patriots when he recalled how the Hetfield boys had led the British to the church as an act to destroy those who followed the Revolutionary cause. Increased population of angered and displaced Loyalist families could potentially bring harm to the innocent family members of the Patriots who were fighting in this war, or like him, were working in legislature. Abra was relieved that the Governor had acted immediately upon his letter.

Abra worked diligently on the issues facing Congress. In June they were informed by letter from General Greene, the quartermaster general, that "The Congress have lost their influence. I have for a long time seen the necessity of some new plan of civil constitution. Unless there is some control over the States by the Congress, we shall soon be like a broken band." Abra knew he was right. There needed to be a civil constitution which would outline a new, and much improved governmental structure which would please all the states and guarantee unity among them. Arguments broke out on the Congressional floor when the topic was discussed. John Adams of Virginia said that each state should have its own government. "Congress is not a legislative assembly, nor a representative assembly, but a diplomatic assembly," stated Adams. Again, debates raged as to what type of government they would have if each state were to have their own government. Abra insisted that the common people wanted a national government. Groups of delegates worked together to propose ideas of how a government should be organized. It was decided that in August a convention of delegates would propose the idea for a governmental structure: one of state supremacy, or national government. All of the delegates weighed the pros and cons of each.

At the beginning of July word came to Philadelphia through the Secret Committee, which was in charge of military intelligence, about a long battle in Elizabethtown. Colonel Dayton, Abra's good friend, had the New Jersey militia settled near Elizabethtown when they were attacked. On June 6th, the British entered Elizabethtown and took control. What happened next stunned Abra to his very core. The messenger was sharing events of the story and holding documents he was to deliver to Congress. The messenger's face was filled with anguish as he shared the events of the past few weeks. When the British troops invaded, the women of Elizabethtown fled to their hiding areas, but Reverend Caldwell's wife, Hannah, refused to leave. She was certain that providence would protect her. Her husband was away and fighting in the war. She gathered her children about her and hid in an inside room of the house and she sat nursing her newborn baby. The house was surrounded by troops and one of the British soldiers peered through a window and saw mother and children inside. He raised his gun through a window and took aim. Two bullets shot into the room and into Mrs. Caldwell who fell to the floor dead with her infant still in her arms. A nurse grabbed the infant and scurried the other children out a back door as the house was set aflame. The neighboring houses were also set on fire. Hannah Caldwell's body was dragged out of the burning house and left laying in the yard for hours until the British finally gave permission for the residents of Elizabethtown to bury her.

Abra fell into a chair, stunned. His mind was overloaded with the words being said, the papers being read, and those around him who spoke sympathetic words to him. James' wife, shot to death as she nursed her baby? The men of Elizabethtown were off to war. How could the British be so barbaric? Abra weakly stood up and asked if there was any word of his wife and family, and he was reassured that although his house had been deserted, it had not been burned, although all the outbuildings were destroyed and the crops destroyed. Sarah and his family had escaped. Thank God, Abra thought, while at the same time shaking his head in disbelief at the thought of what James would do when he heard word of what happened to Hannah.

## Chapter 17
# *The End of 1780*

**By July a new problem arose** in Congress. Abra was contacted by Moore Furman, a wealthy New Jersey merchant, who had been appointed Deputy Quartermaster, with the task of delivering supplies to the soldiers. Furman was frustrated with the lack of monies given by Congress to pay for the supplies the troops needed. As Abra worked on finance issues, he was left to address Furman's requisition.

*Philadelphia, July 11, 1780*

*Sir,*

*Your application for a draft of money on the Treasury of New Jersey was referred to the Continental Treasury, who gave me encouragement that a draft should be issued to the amount of all the money due from the State to the Continental Army, which I supposed would have been a great advantage to the state as most of the taxes would have been discounted with creditors of the public. It would have given relief to the holders of assigned certificates, but this has not taken place further than to satisfy Mr. Marsh's disbursements.*

*I wrote to the Assembly to know their opinion on this subject, but they never favored me with an answer, which left me uncertain how to act. Some suggested that our legislature intended to pay the debt of the state by charging provisions furnished the Army the last part of last winter, but I thought it in their interest to consider these supplies as part of the specific supplies to be furnished this year. This I acquainted the legislature of and requested their directions, which I have not obtained, and little was said on the subject.*

*Our wounded officers and soldiers at Baskenridge are suffering for want of bandages and lint for dressings, on which subject by the order of the medical committee, I have taken the liberty to address the enclosed letter to your lady.*

*I am, Sir, your obedient and humble servant,*

*Abra.Clark**

Abra quickly learned that the problem with the state treasuries was that supplies had been sent to the troops by some states, and they felt this should discount the amount owed to the Continental Treasury. The accounting of these transactions was difficult to secure. There was also the issue of fair

*actual letter

contributions to be paid. Abra found himself swallowed by hot debates on this issue as state's argued as to what a fair share should be. They rebelled against England for unfair taxes so Congress needed to be careful to make their taxing fair to all. Meanwhile, Moore Furman became so frustrated with the lack of financial support; he resigned his post as Deputy Quartermaster. Such resignations were not taken lightly as people like Furman were influential and Congress needed them to support the work of Congress. While Abra tried to be compassionate about the problems Furman was facing, he could not guarantee payment for transactions until the states hammered out their record keeping. Britain was allocating a lot of money into this war, thinking it would be short and easily won. They now found themselves with the French helping the Americans, and Holland threatening to aid the Americans which was making the war longer than anticipated.

There never seemed to be a moment of rest in Philadelphia. Not only was Abra trying to work on the money issues of Congress, the debate continued over a civic constitution declaring the type of government they would have once the war was won. Finally in August the convention of delegates from three states met and proposed their decision on the state supremacy or national government issue. It was resolved that there should be "under the superintendancy and direction of one supreme head," and they said Congress should hold this power. It was young Alexander Hamilton, a secretary for

George Washington, who was most stirred by this decision. He encouraged a representative of New York to propose that a general plan for a national government be designed. Congress considered such and it was suggested that they have a plan mapped out by November. Congress had adopted the Articles of Confederation however it was not yet ratified by several states as they were still awaiting signatures. With delegates continually leaving to deal with issues in their state or in their homes, Congress' ability to move forward was often halted by the absence of those who needed to vote. The Articles were declared by many as, "not fit for war or peace." Abra agreed. The idea of state supremacy would "defeat the powers given to Congress, and make our union feeble and precarious," as many were heard to say.

Within the same discussion another issue was brought forward to the floor of Congress. Washington had written of a concern he had in finding a permanent military force. "We have lived upon expedients till we can live no longer. The history of this war is a history of temporary devices instead of a system." Blunt words, but the Congress agreed that the status quo for the way they have been doing business would no longer suffice. A new plan of action was needed. Abra knew that Washington was right. He knew New Jersey had sent all the men it could into the war as so many battles were fought on their own properties. Because so many men fought, his state had picked up the expenses and supplied the troops as they fought, and as they wintered. Many states had not contributed as much, yet by property and population they were much larger than New Jersey. Would the government be equal in power for each state? What about the common man? Would the common man's rights be protected by a national government? Abra posed these questions among his colleagues and encouraged them to consider what was needed for a future government. Not once did anyone suggest that all of this work, planning, debating, contracting, and organizing would be for nothing. Abra could never believe for a moment that their efforts were in vain. The war had to be won and a government that protected all men, both those of wealth and those with nothing, and states with large populations and land resources and those which were small, needed to be in place once liberty was achieved.

Such weighty matters as a national government and a constitution and figuring out a treasury plan kept Abra busy from morning to night. One of his main focuses was on how to pay for this war. Some states had borrowed. Some states had not paid their share. Some states had no means to pay, or the ability to borrow to pay their share. What money the government had purchased very little. These problems continually plagued Abra.

As if the very important issues of Congress were not enough, Abra found himself often in the center of decisions to be made about appointments and jobs to be given through

New Jersey's legislature. He was often asked his opinion as he was so respected. Abra sometimes found it hard to not be persuaded by his own friendships and prejudices. Instead he tried to provide positive feedback and keep his own personal feelings out of the decision making process. His motto was always to be fair and just. One such decision was in August when he had been involved in a discussion about an important appointment. Abra was not happy with the decision that was made among the delegates, so he quickly drafted a letter to Governor William Livingston of New Jersey.

*Philadelphia, August 19, 1780*

*Sir,*

*Colonel Pickering, Quarter Master General, will call upon your Excellency on the appointing his Deputy for the State. The appointment is to be by the approbation of the Executive Authority. He requested Mr. Houston, Mr. Fell and myself to name such as we thought proper. We accordingly named Mr. Condict, Mr. Furman and Mr. Caldwell, either of which we supposed might answer, which of these he will prefer I cannot say. Perhaps he will leave it to you to take either. We named Mr. Condict in consequence of your Excellency's recommendation last winter, but for my part I wish he may not be the person for this one single reason: I think he will do his country more service in the station he now fills, in which*

*I fear his place will be but poorly supplied and we ought not to take from the legislature one of its firmest and most useful members at a time such characters are of so much importance there.*

*As to Mr. Furman, the settlement of his accounts for past expenditures will perhaps induce him to decline it. Upon a persuasion he cannot properly attend to both.*

*Mr. Caldwell is acquainted with the business, can endure fatigue and is capable of great dispatch, but I am wholly at a loss whether such an appointment would be acceptable to him or not. If he will accept and I had the appointment, I should not long hesitate in my choice. I do not mean to say anything to Mr. Condict's prejudice, as I believe he would execute the office with great fidelity, but must nevertheless think he ought to decline it unless there is a clear prospect that his present place will be supplied equally advantageous to the public, which is a matter I something more than doubt will be the case.*

*I am, Sir, your Excellency's most obedient*
*and humble servant.*

*Abra.Clark*

*P.S. By Capt. Dennis the bearer of this, I send forward*
*a letter and two sealed bundles from Mrs. Jay.**

*actual letter

Abra knew that Condict would execute the office well; however he feared that New Jersey's legislature would suffer at the loss of his expertise if Condict were to change jobs. Abra was always focused on what would be the best choice for his state and people. Pushing for his good friend, Reverend Caldwell, however was not just because of his friendship. Abra knew Caldwell to be passionate about the outcome of the war. Abra's influence was taken, and James Caldwell was named Assistant Commissary General. It was a great choice because not only did Caldwell help raise supplies, but he worked out an alarm system between various locations of New Jersey in order to protect them against advancing British troops. Abra was delighted that his influence had not been mistaken.

Abra's days were always the same. He would awaken in the morning and prepare himself for the day. His room and keep provided him a meager breakfast. He would quickly walk to the hall and the first order of business was to check the ongoing list of battles. As posts came in, the information was listed for all to inspect. Because communications were often delayed, the lists were rewritten carefully to keep the battles in as close to chronological order as possible. As Abra would review the list for the year, his eyes would always seek mention of New Jersey. Although most of the focus of the war during 1780 had been in the South, the militia of New Jersey remained active. New Jersey provided iron and worked iron, muskets, and shot, and gunpowder, as well as salt and cloth. The ports of New Jersey were essential in the war effort especially since Long Island was controlled by the British. There were plenty of sea battles off the New Jersey shore. There were constant reports of many hundreds of small skirmishes and raids in the New Jersey ocean water. The New Jersey militia used whaleboats to raid the British ships and camps along Long Island and off Sandy Hook. These skirmishes never made it to the list of big battles posted on the wall, but word would always come back to Philadelphia. What concerned Abra the most was that New Jersey was fighting a civil war as families were divided as Patriots and Loyalists. Many boys of the same family were fighting against each other. The constant raids on farms between the warring factions also concerned Abra as he worried how his neighbors would return to living peaceful lives among each other once the war was over. Such deep hatred and passions would not end easily. Abra sighed and returned his focus to the list.

January 14 Staten Island, NY **American Victory**
January 25 Elizabethtown, NJ British Victory
February 3 Young's House, NY British Victory
February 26-March 2 Fort Johnson, SC British Victory
March 5 Mathew's Ferry SC British Victory
March 6-7 Charlestown SC **American Victory**
March 8 McPhersonville SC British Victory
March 14 Mobile, West Florida **Spanish Victory**
March 17-18 Salkehatchie River SC British Victory

March 22 St. Andrew's Creek, SC Draw

March 23 Colleton County, SC British Victory

March 25 Savannah GA **American Victory**

March 26 Charleston County SC **American Victory**

March 28 Sunbury GA **American Victory**

March 29-30 Charleston County SC **American Victory**

April 2 Harperfield NY British Victory

April 5 Ogeechee River, GA **American Victory**

April 8 Fort Moultrie, SC **American Victory**

May 2 Haddrell's Point SC British Victory

May 7 Fort Moultrie SC British Victory

May 22 Caughnawaga NY British Victory

May 29 Winnsboro SC **American Victory**

June 7-23 Elizabethtown NJ British Victory

Here, Abra paused as he remembered the horrific events of that battle and how his good friend, Rev. Caldwell's wife was slain by the British and how his own family had narrowly escaped. The battle of June 7th at Connecticut Farms had caused all of the houses to be burned. Although the Clark house had remained standing, all Abra's out buildings were destroyed by the Hessian led troops. If it weren't for the New Jersey militia taking a stand at Springfield along the Rahway River, the tide of the war could have changed. Abra had sent word to his friend, Reverend James Caldwell, but his letter did not get delivered. Abra sought information about Caldwell.

A week later Abra had been approached by a messenger who had returned from New Jersey with news. “Mr. Clark, I know that you have been asking about the Reverend Caldwell and I have been directed to tell you about a battle fought at Connecticut Farms.”

“Is Caldwell all right?” asked Abra, immediately fearing the worse.

“Right as ever, Mr. Clark. The Reverend has been serving as chaplain for Dayton’s regiment. All was well until they saw the British advancing. The men had a serious lack of wadding for their rifles and the fear was that they would not be able to fire at the British. The Reverend gathers up all the Watts hymnals he had on hand and began tearing out the pages to use as wadding in their rifles to guarantee better shots at the British. Dayton kept yelling at Caldwell to stand back, but the Reverend was having no part of that. He kept running up and down the line yelling to the boys firing, ‘Give ‘em Watts, boys!’”

Abra recalled laughing aloud at the image of James doing this. He could picture James running back and forth behind the men, passing out his prized hymnals to be used in what he was certain James would say was “God’s work!”

“How did the battle fare?” asked Abra.

“Not well, Mr. Clark. Even though the troops did an admirable job of holding off the enemy, the British still laid claim to the battle. Good news is that the British have left the area and right now reports say there are no British troops advancing in New Jersey."

"That is certainly a relief," said Abra. Poor James, thought Abra. He had not known of Hannah's fate. Abra recalled the letter he wrote to his friend, asking the messenger to get it into Reverend Caldwell's hands.

Abra shook off the memory and remembered the other detail of the Battle of Elizabethtown. In other messages, Congress learned that the British had 6000 men under General Knyphausen who came to Elizabethtown from Staten Island. His goal was to seize control of the Watchung Mountains and reach Morristown where Washington had both supplies and weapons. The Americans had 2000 Continental and militia soldiers. Although the Americans fought bravely, they were vastly overpowered by the shear force of the British army. The British pushed on toward their goal but were stopped again by the Continental and militia army. Again, the British won. The British went on to burn down all the houses except four, then pushed onward toward Morristown. Abra thanked God his house was left standing and none of his family was injured. Abra bowed his head in prayer for a moment, and then returned to the list.

June 8 Catawba River, SC **American Victory**
June 18 Hill's Iron Works SC British Victory
July 20 Lawson's Fork SC **American Victory**

July 13 Cedar Springs SC **American Victory**

July 13 Gowen's Old Fort, SC **American Victory**

July 15 Earle's Ford SC **American Victory**

July 15 Prince's Fort SC **American Victory**

July 16 Fishere Summit PA British Victory

July 20-21 Bull's Ferry, NJ British Victory

July 21 Colson NC **American Victory**

July 25 Mars Bluff SC **American Victory**

July 30 Thickety Fort and Fort Anderson, SC **American Victory**

July 30 Hanging Rock SC **American Victory**

August 1 Green Springs SC **American Victory**

August 15 Port's Ferry SC **American Victory**

August 27 Kings Tree, Williamsburge County SC **American Victory**

September 10 Mask's Ferry NC **American Victory**

September 21 Wahab's Plantation, Lancaster County SC **American Victory**

Abra again paused. He remembered the feeling in Congress when it was learned that Benedict Arnold had betrayed West Point, New York, giving information to the British in exchange for what he thought would be financial rewards and success. Abra thought, Arnold? A man who was such a solid Patriot and now a traitor made Abra shudder. Abra shook his head. Benedict was not the only traitor. There were others who had tired of this war, and thought the Americans just could not win and it was better to make alliances with the British rather than face the consequences. Those who betrayed the cause felt that the financial stability of the war effort was ineffective. States fighting about how much they were being asked to finance the war effort and those who were in the know were aware that it was an uphill battle. Abra wondered which was the greater enemy: the British, or their own inability to financially fight this war and compensate those who had contributed so much. Many were disgusted with the Congress and its apparent lack of ability to unify all the states. Abra knew that they would have to remain firm and work harder to get the funding and supplies necessary to win. Winning was the first step. After that, having a government in place which would grant fair treatment to all would be the next hurdle. Abra knew he would continue to fight to make their new government one that was fair to all people, unlike the government they had been given by the British. Men like Arnold sold out in an effort to secure his own wealth. Abra and others had given everything they had to guarantee a fresh start for America. Abra shook his head and breathed deeply at the thought of how people like Arnold could desert their cause. Abra returned to the list.

October 8 Richmond Town NC British Victory
October 9 Polk's Mill NC British Victory
October 16 Schoharie Valley NY British Victory

October 18 Caughnawaga NY British Victory

October 25 Tearcoat Swamp SC **American Victory**

November 3 Great Swamp NC **American Victory**

November 15 White's Bridge and Alston's Plantation SC British Victory

November 18 Brierley's Ferry SC British Victory

November 21-23 Fort George NY **American Victory**

December 1-2 Clermont SC **American Victory**

Dec 11 McCormick SC British Victory

December 14 Nelson's Ferry SC **American Victory**

Abra looked at the list again trying to determine if the Americans were winning. It was hard to say, but he knew his fellow delegates felt there were more American victories now than in the past. Even when plagued with money issues, traitorous acts, and personal tragedies, the Americans were fighting. They were fighting because they wanted freedom.

Abra joined several other men in the meeting room. There was an excited discussion about the British declaring war against Holland. Abra had not heard this report. He knew that their former President of Congress, Henry Laurens, was headed with a treaty to Holland, with a request of borrowing ten million dollars for the war effort. Abra knew that by 1780 the British government was spending more and more money on the war and now had France fighting against them, and the Americans were not as easily conquered as they had thought.

When Holland indicated they would give aid to America, the British gave sanction for the British minister to announce that the British ships may plunder the Dutch ships. One of the delegates shared that an official of England had said, "The British cruisers might know where to go for the richest prizes." Britain went on to attack a ship on which Henry Laurens was headed to Holland. When attacked, Laurens threw his papers overboard, but they were quickly recovered by the British. Laurens was taken prisoner and held captive in the Tower of London.

All of the delegates talked with animated fury. "You know that the rest of Europe will be watching this and England is setting themselves up as the bully," said one of the men. "King George is making enemies of all of Continental Europe," said another. England was looked at as an unjust realm looking for opportunity to overtake the weak.

Abra had followed the capture of Laurens, and had a special empathy when thinking of his own sons who were in captivity. He had worked on the treaty wording and felt that Holland certainly knew what it was like to feel subservient to Britain. Forming a treaty with them was good business, but now Holland was facing the wrath of King George. On December 20th, King George declared war against Holland. As he made his announcement, British ships captured two hundred Dutch merchantmen with cargoes of more than five million dollars. This and the taking of St. Eustatius Island by the British set all of Congress and Europe into a frenzy.

Abra knew that Congress was counting on the financial support and supplies from Holland. He also knew that the rest of Europe would be waiting to see what Britain had in store for them. Perhaps this would be a turning point in the war. Perhaps with the new year they would finally see a positive change in this war.

As Abra headed back to his room he was stopped and handed a letter. He tore open the seal and the words made him stop. The letter was from his friend, James Caldwell, notifying him that Abra's oldest son, Aaron, was being held prisoner in the Sugar House in Brunswick, New York.

# Chapter 18
## *1781*

**Abra had been working** in Congress nearly constantly, with only brief visits home during the past year. He had withstood the news of his son, Thomas, being tortured on the prison ship, Jersey, where his third son, Andrew, was also held captive. Now his oldest son, Aaron, was being held prisoner in Brunswick, NY. The memory of Hannah Caldwell's brutal death, and the fear that Abra had for his own wife and children were constant. Abra slept very little as the work of Congress was never-ending. He was on the finance committee, and the foreign policy committee. His opinions on the writing of a new governmental plan were always sought, and his firm conviction that the common man needed protection was always voiced in every meeting he attended. The constant messages of the Secret Committee which brought correspondence from the front lines of war always caused Abra to catch his breath as he waited word of confrontations in New Jersey. Abra continued to support decision making in the New Jersey legislature despite being away in Philadelphia at Congress. So many delegates were constantly called away to their home states for state or family business, leaving Congress to wait until it had a majority vote on any given decision. There were three delegates from New Jersey, however often Abra stood alone representing his state. The toll of the war was wearing on Abra, and he was often suffering from pains within his chest from the stresses he felt.

After a brief visit home, Abra returned to Philadelphia to learn that a matter of importance had been presented to Congress. England had refused to allow Bibles printed in England to be shipped and allowed to fall into the hands of rebels. Washington had indicated that his men wanted Bibles to carry with them. Attempts at importing Bibles from other countries proved to be difficult. Washington felt such comfort as having a personal bible would certainly keep his men comforted as well as serve as a continued reminder that non moral behavior was frowned upon by not only the officers, but God. The King James Bible was the first fully translated Bible in English, however a bible was needed that would be small enough for a soldier to carry in his pocket was not available.

"It hardly seems necessary that we stop our work to concern ourselves with reading material for men who are in the battlefield," said one delegate quietly within Abra's hearing.

Abra quickly turned and asked, "And Sir, do you suggest that we, who are separated from our families during these stressful times, do not find comfort in reading our Bibles within the safe harbor of our rooms? Should we not grant those men who are on the battlefields, sleeping in open fields without benefit of an evening fire and a warm dinner the same comfort we ourselves find? It seems to be so little for the very sacrifices they are making to ensure our work meets fruition." Others nearby agreed. That day Congress issued an act for the printing of a bible which their soldiers could easily transport.

On January 21st, it was Robert Aitken who answered the call of Congress. Aitken's petition was studied to determine if he were qualified to take such an important task. Aitkin's credentials were impressive as he had published the Journals of the Congress and Thomas Paine's essays which were instrumental in gathering the initial strength and support to wage war against Britain. A committee was formed to determine if Aitken's proposed Bible would be acceptable.

At the start of the war, the troops had wintered well into March before starting back onto the battlefields. That was no longer the case. The first major battle of 1781 was reported after the January 17th battle at Cowpens. The British had won major battles in South Carolina by fighting en masse at Savannah, Charleston, and Camden. It appeared that the British would gain complete control of the South. The southern Loyalists quickly joined forces with the British. There was a strong possibility that the British would win perhaps the entire war, or at least the southern states. Such an outcome would divide the Americans, thus the Patriots were pushed to fight harder. There were two wars going on, and Congress knew this. There was the obvious war of the British and Americans, but there was also a civil war between the Patriots and the Loyalists. Neighbor fought neighbor and old hurts were remembered and turned into the causes for rebellion. Congress knew that the Americans needed to turn the tide of this rebellion and win. Stronger strategies were necessary to guarantee success. Such messages were sent to Washington.

General George Washington sent Nathanael Greene to South Carolina to face off with the British. Greene split his men into two forces; one was led by General Daniel Morgan. Morgan knew a victory was necessary, but his men were talking of defeat. Morgan had to prevent that his men would not run when attacked. To avoid this, Morgan placed his men with their backs against the river so that they could not retreat when attacked. Morgan was a presence on the battlefield, encouraging his troops by riding up and down the lines cheering his men on. When attacked, Morgan's men moved with precision, using the woods as their cover, and a third line of cavalry led by William Washington, a nephew of George Washington, came galloping upon the British troops and overwhelming them. In the confusion, the British thought they had won the battle, however Morgan rallied his troops and they turned and made a bayonet charge on the British. After an hour, the battle was over and the British had 110 men killed, 200 wounded, and 500 captured. Morgan lost only twelve men and had sixty wounded. It was a clear Patriot victory. Morgan's men were surprised at their own success, and their confidence increased.

When word of this reached Congress a shout was heard that made it seem the war was over. As the details of the battle were shared with the delegates, hearty congratulations were heard throughout the hall. It certainly appeared that the Continental Army was gaining strength and the much needed experience in fighting the well trained British troops. Soon afterward news arrived that the Patriots had captured Georgetown, South Carolina after a two day battle. It was only January and already Congress felt that the war was taking a positive turn.

Very late in February Abra was in the hall when word came from North Carolina of a critical battle. Indeed, new strategies were being tried by the Americans, strategies which were unpracticed. "Can you believe it? Henry Lee really butchered those Loyalists at Haw River in North Carolina," said one of the delegates.

"What happened?" asked Abra, as a group of men gathered to hear the story.

"The Loyalists were all gathered together and the Secret Committee had sent false communications which led them to believe that Tarleton was coming to review the troops. Along comes Lee's men wearing green jackets, just like Tarleton's men wore. They were totally unsuspecting of the attack!"

"It serves them right for what Tarleton did at Tarrant's Tavern in butchering our men," added other.

"A real Trojan Horse mentality," said Abra as he joined the men in celebration. "It seems this is what we need to get the Loyalists to reconsider their actions. I hate to see us fighting with our own Americans, but until we win this war, we have no alternative. I fear that even after we win, there will be long-standing bitterness to those who chose to fight against us." Others agreed, and stories of family and friends who stood opposed to the work being done in Congress were shared with doubts that relations could ever return to their pre-war status.

On March 1, 1781, Congress became the Congress of the Confederation. The Articles of Confederation had final ratification, although Abra had not been in attendance for the signing. Abra had worked on the language and design and was in full support of the Articles although he knew that this was a temporary fix for their need of government. These Articles of the Confederation set the rules for operations of the "United States" confederation. It was "a plan of confederacy for securing the freedom, sovereignty, and independence of the United States." The rules allowed for the making of war, negotiating diplomatic agreements, and resolving decisions about the western territories. They could mint coins and conduct financing loans from inside and outside the United States. One particular line of the Articles was much debated upon and that was Article XIII which stated that "the Union shall be perpetual" and that their laws would be "inviolably observed by every state." Abra felt strongly that this article be included, however there were states which debated that a federal government have control over the states. "Once this war is over," said Abra," we need to stand firm as one country. To not include such language at this important juncture in time would be the very cause for future rebellion within this country."

Abra was known among his colleagues as a federalist as he feared the Articles lacked the provisions for an effective government. Abra's stand was based upon his knowledge that the government through the Articles, though faulty, was the necessary step they take in order to further organize a proper working government. Abra knew that the Articles lacked taxing authority and must rely on the states to grant funds. He also wanted the government to resolve the issue of unpaid war debts from the various states. Abra's main contention was the lack of balance between the large and small states in decision making. Presently there was a policy of one state, one vote, which was not fair to the larger states that had to pay more, but only received one vote. Abra feared that if they did not address this issue, larger states might later have cause to pull from the union. Although the "one state-one vote" mentality benefited small states, like New Jersey, Abra saw that there could be a problem in the future. It seemed to Abra that their work was never done.

By the end of March Congress heard of the Battle of

Guilford Court House in North Carolina where Major General Nathanael Greene fought against Lord Cornwallis. Although Greene's men retreated from the field, and Cornwallis claimed a victory, Cornwallis had suffered a great loss of men. It was estimated that over one fourth of Cornwallis' men were killed in that battle, which seriously affected his troop morale and military strength. Again, Congress celebrated, although they listed the battle as an American loss.

Congress was often frustrated with the lack of complete information. They would often receive partial information or conflicting information, and would need to rely on duplicate reports in order to get a clear picture of what was happening. Such was the case in late March when word was received that there was a naval battle, yet Congress could not ascertain who was involved. It appeared to be too early in the year for French ships to be arriving for the cause, yet the individual movement of various ships already in the American waters were difficult to identify and follow. Messages from the ships as to their strategies and battles were nearly impossible to transmit to Congress. One particular day caused great stress when conflicting reports arose over a three hour battle which had occurred as was reported through multiple sources; however no one could confidently identify what ships were involved and what the outcome was. Abra sat in his room that evening and penned a letter to his friend, posing his fears that two of their ships, the Confederacy and the Saratoga, may have been hit in battle.

*Philadelphia, April 1st. 1781*

*Dear Sir:*

*I yesterday was favored with your letter, but know not when or from whence it was written as it was without a date.*

*The night before last we received an official account of General Greene's engagement with Cornwallis on the 15$^{th}$ of March. It differs but little from the accounts before received. The victory was on the side of Cornwallis as General Greene retired from the field with nearly 300 killed and wounded, and four field pieces lost and near 900 militia and come Continentals missing who mostly ran away in the beginning of the action. His order of battle was three lines—the North Carolina militia composed the first in front with the field pieces, most of those run away without firing a gun throwing away their arms, some few of them fired once, some twice, but none more. Of those about 550 are missing. The Virginia militia principally composed the second line. They made some short stand, of these about 260 are missing but not supposed to be taken. The third line was Continentals. The engagement was very severe and obstinate, and the victory dearly purchased owing whole to superior discipline. One or two more such victories would ruin his Lordship as he must be greatly encumbered with his wounded. Cornwallis was 160 miles from Camden and near that distance from Wilmington, the nearer seaport. My greatest fears are that* *the detachments from New York are gone to his relief and may join him before General Greene can be in condition to renew the fight, though in case Cornwallis attempts to move, he will probably meet with a constant annoyance from our troops, who, it is said, are in high spirits and wish for another engagement.*

*You must have heard before this a full account of the naval engagement on the 16th between the French and British fleets. The former's bending their course for Rhode Island, and the latter's going into the Chesapeake, which by a letter from the Marquis had put to sea again on the 24th. One part of the Marquis' letter informs that soon after the British fleet had gotten out of the bay he heard a very severe cannonade for three hours without interruption. As he had not heard of the French fleet's returning for Rhode Island, he thought the engagement was between them and the British and appeared extremely anxious to hear how it ended. It is certain the French fleet was on their way to Rhode Island on the 19th when the Hermoine left them and came into this river. With whom this engagement could be is only conjecture. If any such battle really happened it must be either the fleet bound to Rhode Island meeting with one or more French ships which had returned, or the second division bound to Rhode Island from France, which is the most general opinion. But how that fleet should happen to be at the mouth of the Chesapeake is a question not easily answered. Besides, it seems rather too early in the year for their arrival. I think it might be our frigates the Confederacy and Saratoga bound here from the Cape at whom they might fire three hours on a chase at long shot. This however is my fear, but I am alone in it.*

*As to politics, I never mention any in a letter unless I am certain of a safe conveyance. The letter you mention to have sent me some time since I received and to the best of my recollection answered.*

*I am, Dr. Sir, Your Humble Servant,*

*Abra. Clark**

In the next month reports of battles and battle strategies that defied former practices surprised Congress. In Fort Watson, South Carolina, General Henry Lee had a tall log tower built with a platform on top of it. On the platform he stationed riflemen who overlooked the fort. The British, fearful of being hit by the rifleman, ended up surrendering and the American counted another victory. At Fort Motte, South Carolina, Lee and Francis Marion forced the British to surrender the fort by setting the fort on fire. The Americans were finding some victories easy, like when they attacked the British at Fort Granby in South Carolina and the British troops quickly surrendered. Perhaps, Congress hoped, the British troops were weary of the battles and being on foreign

*actual letter

soil. Whatever the reason, Congress celebrated each victory.

Abra continually tried to maintain his communications with his friends and those of the New Jersey legislature, as well as his wife. He wanted to communicate with his sons, but he feared to do so. Even if he would have guaranteed safety of delivery, he feared would cause potential harm to them if found by their captors. Abra was constantly under stress and strain, and finally decided it was time to leave Congress for a short time so he could go home and be with his family. He had been on constant duty nearly sixteen months and he was tired. He left for a visit home, and while there he decided he needed to ask forgiveness in needing time away. The constant stress had taken its toll on him, and his inability to get any rest in Philadelphia left him exhausted both mentally and physically. For the past sixteen months he was often the only delegate from New Jersey in attendance, and if he left, he feared New Jersey would be without any representation. After a night of restless sleep and exhaustion the following morning, he knew he needed to pen a letter to the Governor of New Jersey.

*Princeton, May 24. 1781*

*Sir:*

*My long and steady attendance in Congress for sixteen months past, makes it necessary for a relaxation of my mind and restoration of my health that I retire for some time at least, and if agreeable to the Legislature, I wish it may be to the end of my present Delegation, and that my resignation may be accepted, which this is intended to solicit.*

*By my absence there will be but two members remaining, and they mean to attend only one at a time. This in the course of a few days will deprive this state of a representation unless an appointing of one or more members speedily takes place. I continue of the same opinion as heretofore those three members are preferable to five, provided such can be found who will devote their time to that service. Few constitutions can bear such constant attendance. Some relaxation is necessary.*

*With all due regard and esteem, I have the honour to be, Sir, your obedient and humble servant,*

*Abra. Clark**

Abra was granted a leave of absence. He returned briefly to Philadelphia to finalize his work and turn over leadership to the new delegate chosen by New Jersey. While there he continued to work as hard as he had always worked.

Upon retiring back to home, Abra had to learn how to relax. At first he spent much of his first weeks home sleeping. Sarah hushed the children so Abra could rest, and she brought food to his bedside so he could save his strength. Letters would

*actual letter

arrive, but Sarah would put them aside until Abra awakened. She had a table put into their small bedroom so Abra could sit and write undisturbed by the rest of the household activities. Sarah smiled a lot. She thought she had forgotten how to do that. She was so very pleased that Abra was home and there to talk with each evening. She had nearly forgotten the pleasure and company of a husband in her bed. Each night she would blow out the candle on the work table when Abra would fall asleep, and she would finish her housework, then quietly crawl into the bed and curl up next to her husband. At first he was so exhausted, he never even awakened. Then as he regained his strength, he would pull Sarah into his arms and sleep with his arms surrounding her. For the first time in years Sarah allowed herself to relax and sleep deeply and soundly. Abra slowly regained his strength.

When Abra learned that Thomas Jefferson was nearly captured in early June when seven members of the Virginia legislature were captured, he was alarmed and all the stresses he had felt while in Philadelphia returned. Jefferson was now serving as Governor of Virginia, and the British were well aware that he was the writer of the venomous document which had begun the war. Abra had nightmarish dreams that night as his thoughts revolved around potential capture of himself and his family. His dreams were filled with visions of the torture of Thomas, the capture of Stockton, the killing of Hannah Caldwell, and all the other nightmarish events that had filled his mind over the past five years. Sarah awoke when Abra was thrashing about in his sleep, and she calmly awakened him. Abra jerked away and was feverish to the touch. Sarah cradled his head in her arms and sang a quiet hymn as Abra fell asleep again in her arms. This is what he must have been doing in Philadelphia, she thought. Silent tears fell down her face as she thought about Abra and how he had braved through these nightmares on his own while away from her. Her heart swelled knowing her husband was facing his own mental torture, and sacrificing his own health. She remembered back to the taunts Abra had faced at the start of this war when people of the town challenged him as to what sacrifices he would have to make since he owned so little land. Sarah thought that of all the people she knew, Abra was the bravest man for fighting for what he believed in. She fell asleep still holding Abra's head in her arms.

Throughout the summer, Abra continued to regain his strength. The few men who were still living in town would come to the Clark house and discuss the latest news. Abra typically would receive posts from friends of Congress or the New Jersey legislature, so he remained apprised of the various battles and victories. In August when the British hanged Colonel Isaac Hayne in Charleston, they thought it would be a warning to the Patriots to surrender. Instead, it further angered the Americans and strengthened their conviction to win the war. By late August word arrived that Washington had moved both the American and French troops to fight together and march into the South to take back control of those states. Meanwhile the French naval fleet fought the British fleet on Chesapeake Bay. Cornwallis was left without any support, and as a result he was facing a strong and committed Continental Army. By October Washington had conducted a siege upon Yorktown and won. On October 17 Cornwallis surrendered his army to the Americans.

When Abra heard this news he jumped up and swung Sarah in the air. "Now this is what we needed! This is the kind of victory that will finally end this war!"

Sarah laughed and slapped Abra's shoulders. "Abraham Clark! You put me down this instance! You are supposed to be recuperating and saving your strength, not swinging me about like I was a child's rag doll!"

Abra put Sarah down and took her face between his hands and kissed her firmly on the lips. "Mrs. Clark. We are watching history! All this work, all this time, all these sacrifices so many have made is finally paying off. I can feel it in my bones. This victory is exactly what we needed. You wait and see. Every man worth his salt will rally to the cause and see that the dream we dared to believe in will be a reality." Abra once again picked Sarah up and swung her around. Abra laughed from deep within his soul, and Sarah joined him while she falsely protested being swung about. The children came into the room and they, too, laughed and jumped around, although they weren't quite certain what they were celebrating. The Clark house was filled with happiness, perhaps the first time in over five years!

The happiness was quickly quieted. It was late in November when word came to Abra through a mutual friend that Reverend James Caldwell had been killed by an American sentry. Abra was dumbstruck. "By an American? How can that be?"

The messenger said, "It was James Morgan. Morgan reported that the Reverend refused to have a package he was carrying inspected."

"That makes no sense," said Abra. "James has been nothing but supportive of the American efforts. He would not elicit confrontation when matters of security were at hand."

"Agreed. Witnesses said the Reverend didn't even have a package in his hands. There are those who are saying Morgan took a bribe from the British to kill Caldwell. Others think the bribe came from Loyalists."

"This war is tearing apart everyone. I cannot believe someone would take such a bribe. James was as fine a man as there could be. With Hannah killed, now their children are left orphaned. What is to become of them?"

"Don't know. Heard that some of the families that have been helping with the little ones since Hannah's death are going to keep the children"

"I just cannot believe this. James, gone? How many more

friends, fathers, sons have to perish before this war comes to an end?" Abra took Sarah in his arms and held tight. Both were silently praying for their own sons' safe return, and praying that James and Hannah Caldwell had not died in vain.

Abra and Sarah attended the service for James. He was laid to rest next to his wife outside what was the church he had served so well in Elizabethtown, New Jersey. Abra spoke at the service and shared memories of James' humor, his wit, his dedication. "He was a rebel priest," said Abra, and those in the small congregation nodded and chuckled at the remembrances of his sermons which were filled with support for independence. "God needed a soldier on his side," said Abra. "I'm just glad we had the opportunity to follow his lead during his time here on earth."

Meanwhile word came to Abra that Congress had elected unanimously John Hanson as the first President of the Confederation. Abra had not been in Philadelphia for the signing of the Articles of Confederation, nor had he been there for the election of Hanson, although he knew he would have cast an affirmative vote. He had taken a rest, but he was beginning to feel restless. Sarah looked at her husband and said, "Abra. You need to go back to Congress. It's time." Abra looked at his wife and knew she could read into his heart.

# Chapter 19
## *1782*

**The rest at home was refreshing** and renewing, although Abra acknowledged that he never felt as strong as he once had. The chest pains had subsided, and he was finally sleeping through the night. The New Jersey legislature was anxious for Abra to return to Philadelphia as they respected his dedication and keen persistence to attendance. Abra said his goodbyes to Sarah, and once more traveled the familiar path to Philadelphia.

Abra was told of the hanging of James Morgan on January 29th in Westfield, New Jersey, for the murder of Reverend James Caldwell. Murder. Abra's emotions were strained as he saw Morgan as a traitor to their cause, however the British viewed Abra and the rest of Congress and all the American troops as traitors, and traitors were punished by death. Abra thought that hearing of Morgan's death would grant him satisfaction and closure, however it didn't. It just seemed so pointless that a man would take a bribe to kill. Killing in war was justified, but taking bribes to kill someone on your own side was unconscionable. Abra was glad that Sarah was able to help their neighbors in the care of the Caldwell children, although they felt that until the war was over, it was best that the Caldwell children not stay on the Clark farm. Abra could not bear the thought that Loyalists might injure the Caldwell children in retaliation to Abra's work in seeking freedom from Britain.

Although most of the states felt the surrender of Cornwallis at Yorktown was the end of the war, it was far from true. Battles still continued, especially in South Carolina. The Americans attempted to take back Charleston, however British troops remained firm. Marion's Brigade attempted several attacks, but were thwarted by the British. Foraging raids by the British were continually attacked by Marion's Brigade, however in-fighting among the officers, lack of ammunition, and disorganization disrupted the Colonial cause. In March, after yet another failed attempt to capture the British, Francis Marion wrote, "My brigade is composed of citizens, enough of whose blood has already been shed. If ordered to attack, I shall obey; but with my consent, not another life shall be lost on the eve of their departure." Marion had served as a respected strategist who had rallied his men into victory after victory, however by this point, Marion was falling ill due to the swamp fever which plagued so many of the men who fought in the South, and the long years of battle were wearing all the soldier's thin. When Congress received word of the failed battles, which were really no more than attacks on foraging raids, sadness overcame them. They knew this war had to come to an end, and relying on the last major battle ending with Cornwallis' surrender, they knew it was time to begin the work of formally ending this war.

In late March Congress received word that Lt. General Henry Clinton had been replaced by Major General Guy Carleton as the British Commander-in-chief in America. Abra and others of Congress debated why the British would be changing administration when peace seemed near. Some felt that the British knew the Americans were weary of battle and with a new commander-in-chief, new strategies could be considered in a last ditch effort to turn the tide of this war. Others felt Clinton did not want the distinction of losing such an important war credited to his name.

In April of 1782, the preliminary peace negotiations began in Paris. The commissioners of the peace treaty were John Jay, John Adams, Benjamin Franklin, Henry Laurens, and William Temple Franklin. It seemed even the British were weary of this war. On May 23, 1782, Sir Guy Carleton ordered British troops to evacuate Savannah and the province of Georgia. At first when the notice arrived, the Royal Council in Savannah expressed "astonishment" at the order. Astonished or not, General Clarke ordered his troops to pack up and move their regimental baggage out of Savannah. While the British were moving their supplies out of Savannah, General Anthony

Wayne attacked. Loyalist sent a flag of truce to Wayne, however Wayne sent notice that any Loyalist who chose to enlist in the Georgia Continental Infantry for two years or the duration of the war would be spared. Wayne called for a formal removal of the British and the turning of the keys to Savannah over to Lt. Colonel James Jackson, in recognition of his loyal service to the cause. July 11 the British filed out of Savannah, led by Brigadier General Alured Clarke. Sixty large boats were loaded with British soldiers, Loyalist militia and the King's Negroes. They set sail for the West Indies. Another boat sailed for St. Augustine on July 21$^{st}$ with the Indians who had served the British, and on the 23rd the Hessians sailed for New York.

When news was carried to Congress about the evacuation of Savannah, all felt this was an acknowledgement by the British of the end of the war. Celebrations and hearty congratulations were heard everywhere, and as various posts arrived describing the evacuation, crowds of delegates gathered to list and compare stories.

Meanwhile word came that General Nathanael Greene was fearful that the British who evacuated from Savannah would move into Charleston. Greene ordered Wayne's troops to march to Charleston as soon as possible. On July 25$^{th}$ Lieutenant Colonel James Jackson's troops and the British marines battled at Delegal's Plantation in Georgia. A message from General Anthony Wayne reported that the British sailed from Tybee with his "motley crew of regulars, Indians and Tories" and had arrived on Skidaway Island in Georgia. Wayne wrote, "*The duty we have done in Georgia is more difficult than that imposed upon the children of Israel. They had only to make bricks without straw, but we have had provision, forage and almost every other apparatus of war to procure without money, boats, bridges, etc. to build without materials except those taken from the stump; and what was more difficult than all, to make Whigs out of Tories...*"

Again, the delegates assured themselves that the Americans had done the impossible. Britain had long been considered the greatest army of the world, and they, the struggling, and rag-tag colonists, had faced them and had won. The delegates were certain that the end of the war was within grasp. Abra felt relief as he knew his sons would be free once the war was declared to be at an end. He had learned that Aaron had escaped his prison; however Thomas and Andrew's progress remained unknown to him. Abra had not heard any communications from them or about them for over a year. He prayed nightly that they were still alive, and he hoped that he would soon see them. When Congress received news that young John Laurens had been ambushed and killed in South Carolina, it brought back all the fears that those serving in Congress were traitors to the British. Young Laurens was the son of the first President of Congress. Delegates mourned the loss of this brave young man who had so much promise, and felt empathy toward their friend and colleague at the loss of his son. That night Abra's dreams were filled once again with nightmarish dreams of his sons on the prison ship Jersey. He awoke and took refuge with his Bible, seeking reassurance that all would be well.

The ongoing issues with the Indian tribes as allies to the British were frustrating for Congress. The Wyandot, Ottawa, Ojibwa, Shawnee, Mingo, and Delaware had joined British forces and had battled against Daniel Boone and the Kentucky militia on August 19th. George Rogers Clark then led the Kentucky militia against the British into the Ohio territory. Congress feared that involving the western territory could potentially lessen their effectiveness in fighting the British in the states. It seemed Congress was continually faced with more distractions which would eventually become major issues. They knew that the Indian question would need to be addressed at some point. There was also the issue of the territory militias and whether they would need to be compensated for their war efforts. Abra knew they were having difficulty getting the thirteen states to pay their war debts and the problem of paying their troops was nearly insurmountable, let alone how they would deal with the territory militias.

On September 10th, Congress brought the matter of Robert Aitken's production of a complete Bible for a vote. It had been well over a year since the issue had been brought to

Congressional attention and the committee finalized their choice. Not only did the Congressional Resolution adopt Aitken's proposal, but they provided the financial support necessary for the printing. Congress recorded that they, "highly approve the pious and laudable undertaking of Mr. Aitken."

"It may seem like a small thing," said Abra to a group of fellow delegates sitting at dinner that evening, "yet it is a thing of great importance for our men. My Bible has been my rock and foundation during the past years away from family and home. I could only hope that my sons would find similar comfort in having a Bible as their companion during their times of solitude." Although the typesetting began immediately, the process would take a lot of time to complete. It was the hope of Congress that the finished product would be ready for their troops by the following year.

By October the French troops were departing for home. American troops began arriving at New Windsor Catonment, in New York, for the winter encampment. The encampment transformed meadows and forests into a camp of almost 600 log huts where 7000 troops, and 500 women and children stayed. The high ranking officers were quartered in private homes and Washington stayed at Jonathan Hasbrouck's house in Newburgh. Although conditions were far better than ever before experienced, the camp was filled with negative talk about the progress of the Paris peace talks, and the inability of Congress to resolve the issue of back pay for the troops. Washington feared that if these issues were not quickly resolved, their whole fight for Independence would be for nothing.

John Hanson had been serving as the first President of the Confederation for a year. Prior to him Samuel Huntington had served four months as President; then Thomas McKean served for less than four months. Neither left any job description or protocols for Hanson. As such, Hanson relied on Congressional delegates to help him determine where his attention was needed. The biggest issue he faced was the paying of troops for which he did not readily have a solution. There were often threats against Congress by soldiers who demanded their pay, and threatened that they would dethrone Hanson and put George Washington on the throne. There were many members of Congress who abandoned their roles in fear of their lives. Fortunately, Hanson and other delegates, like Abra, stayed and held the government together. As the war was coming to an end, it was Hanson who demanded foreign troops to leave American soil. Hanson created the Great Seal of the United States which would be used by all American Presidents on any official documents. He was also able to establish the first Treasury Department, the first Secretary of War and the first Foreign Affairs Department. He served until November 3, 1782 and Abra felt that he had done an exceptional job, despite the early threats and dissatisfaction by soldiers and citizens, and the lack of support from those delegates who deserted their posts.

In one of his final acts as President, Hanson pushed for the passage of a day of Thanksgiving. It seemed that there needed to be some sort of celebration which would draw the new United States together. The war was won, but the common people were left feeling disassociated with each other and this new government. The majority of people had suffered financial losses during the war. Many had lost family members. Friends and neighbors had become enemies. Each state had been a government unto itself ruled by a British appointed governor, and now each state was to be part of a bigger government which most people couldn't understand. Hanson knew a time of healing was needed, and Thanksgiving Day would afford people the opportunity to look at what this newfound freedom would afford them. The Proclamation read:

"IT being the indispensable duty of all Nations, not only to offer up their supplications to ALMIGHTY GOD, the giver of all good, for his gracious assistance in a time of distress, but also in a solemn and public manner to give him praise for his goodness in general, and especially for great and signal interpositions of his providence in their behalf: Therefore the United States in Congress assembled, taking into their consideration the many instances of divine goodness to these States, in the course of the important conflict in which they have been so long engaged; the present happy and promising state of public affairs; and the events of the war, in the course of the year now drawing to a close; particularly the harmony of the public Councils, which is so necessary to the success of the public cause; the perfect union and good understanding which has hitherto subsisted between them and their Allies, notwithstanding the artful and unwearied attempts of the common enemy to divide them; the success of the arms of the United States, and those of their Allies, and the acknowledgment of their independence by another European power, whose friendship and commerce must be of great and lasting advantage to these States:——Do hereby recommend to the inhabitants of these States in general, to observe, and request the several States to interpose their authority in appointing and commanding the observation of THURSDAY the twenty-eight day of NOVEMBER next, as a day of solemn THANKSGIVING to GOD for all his mercies: and they do further recommend to all ranks, to testify to their gratitude to GOD for his goodness, by a cheerful obedience of his laws, and by promoting, each in his station, and by his influence, the practice of true and undefiled religion, which is the great foundation of public prosperity and national happiness."

It was signed on the 11th of October. Abra considered the positive effects such a proclamation would have for the common citizens who had been facing losses and the stresses of war. It was good business to remind Americans that they had allies helping them, and there had been successes in the war, and pointing out that the various public councils were in harmony. Abra chuckled to himself. Perhaps they were not necessarily in harmony, but he was certainly working as hard as he could to make them harmonious. Abra felt Hanson had done a good job, considering the lack of support he had received throughout his administration. At the end of Hanson's term, Elias Boudinot would serve as President of the Confederation. Abra knew they would have to reevaluate this Presidency role and term of office, but that would be part of the Constitution, of which they were already writing preliminary drafts.

By December 14 the British troops left Charleston. This was the last British outpost, although the British still occupied New York City, and the evacuation certainly meant the formal end to the war was finally near. The signing of the initial articles of peace with France and Spain were close at hand, which the colonists knew meant peace for America would follow. The British were still occupying New York, however they knew that they were unable to control the North, and they had been unable to defeat the South. The British citizens were no longer in strong support of the cost, both financially and in lives, of this war. Washington knew that he had to keep the troops together as they were most susceptible to British attack. The British were still fighting the French, Dutch and Spanish in the West Indies, so they had not totally recalled their troops. Keeping the American Army intact until a treaty was signed was Washington's challenge.

As messengers arrived at the Pennsylvania State House and relayed information of the British troop evacuations to the various delegates, all were assured that the war was soon to be over, and that the former colonies of Great Britain would indeed be free. The delegates who had boisterously celebrated each and every battle won were now solemn in their receiving this news. The emotions ran deep among these men who had sacrificed so much in order to see this day arrive. They took this news quietly and returned privately to their rooms. When Abra learned that the war would soon come to an end, he too left the hall and returned to his meager room where he fell to his knees and prayed. Silent tears fell down his cheeks as he reflected upon the many losses, the many sacrifices, and the many stresses so many had faced. Abra thought about the men who had signed the Declaration of Independence with him. Most were no longer serving the government. Abra was one of the few who had remained with Congress through most of the years since 1776. The work needing to be done was just beginning. He knew that the delegates would now have the very real task of putting their new government into action and Abra feared the Articles of Confederation were not strong enough to maintain unity among all the states.

# Chapter 20
## *1783*

**On February 3 of 1783** Great Britain recognized the United States as independent. The following day Great Britain declared they would stop hostilities. It was a time of great satisfaction, yet total confusion as the individual states wanted answers to how government would work. 1783 began with dissatisfaction among many of the civilians and soldiers throughout the thirteen colonies. Many were not happy with the way the new government was beginning. Soldiers were unhappy because they wanted their wages, and wanted to disband and return to their families and homes. Congress was fearful that if the soldiers were not kept under control by Washington there could easily be a military coup by other countries, or even England. Washington was ever mindful of the difficulties Congress had in getting the new government organized, and he used his influence on the men to keep them in training and ready to face any attempted military takeover.

Abra was still serving in Philadelphia. He continued to be admired by many of the delegates because of his punctuality and integrity. He was quick to direct delegates back into the important tasks at hand. Everyone knew that Abra would hold all accountable to protecting the common man and any proposed legislation would have to pass his exacting standards. Abra was both admired and disdained for his attitude that politicians were public servants and that making speeches and having speeches published in local newspapers was simply showboating and was intolerable. Abra was known for his firm commitment to Congress and ability to ignore peer pressure for the absurd. Such an example was his stand on wearing the traditional wigs which member of Congress wore. Abra had refused to wear the wigs early on when he first came to Congress. Most delegates gladly wore their wigs as a sign of their position in government. Abra had no time to devote to the silly notion of wearing a wig and spending hours with the greasing of the hair with pomatum, curling it with a hot iron and rolling it in paper, then blowing a mixture of starch and plaster of Paris onto it go give it the white look. What nonsense, Abra thought, and told anyone who questioned his unwillingness to comply with the style what he thought about it. Abra always cited George Washington's wearing of his own natural hair, although he did attempt to give it the style of the powdered wigs. "But by wearing a wig you needn't spend time caring for your own hair," argued one of the delegates who had chided Abra's decision to not wear a wig to Congress.

"The time spent on such nonsense is something I can ill afford," stated Abra in a firm and non-yielding voice. "I would rather spend such time writing letters to my family, or further protecting our freedom from outsiders." That was the end of pressuring Abra to conform to the accepted style. Of all the signers, Abra had the least fortune. Most of the other signers were large land owners and came from families of wealth. Abra never felt inferior as he felt he best represented the common man who he wanted to protect. His not wearing an exterior sign of wealth and power was one more way he felt he would remind other delegates that they should remember the common man.

By April 15th, the preliminary articles of peace ending the war were ratified. The Hessians of Germany had been a strong force in helping the British. 17,313 Hessians returned to their homelands. There were however over 12,500 Hessians who did not return home to Germany. Around 7,700 of these had died in the war. After being presented with propaganda initiated by Ben Franklin that every Hessian who deserted would receive 50 acres of land, 5,000 Hessians decided to stay in the states or in Canada. Abra thought Franklin was a genius in his ability to manipulate the Hessians through the various propaganda strategies he used. Land was certainly not an issue as there was much open land, as well as land taken from Loyalists, and land within the territories. As Abra pondered this he realized that the bulk of immigration to this country had been from England

and now to populate the United States, there would need to be more people of different nationalities joining them in order to settle the country. The Hessians, Germans, Swedes, Dutch and other ethnic groups were already the first major influx of immigrants. Abra knew that the United States was already looking at expansion to the western territories. In 1783 the United States had an area of approximately 800,000 square miles, much of it rich arable land. As new immigrants would arrive, they would want land, and the government would want settlers to travel west to settle. The Congress had not yet fully developed a government which would ensure all thirteen states were joined as one country, and already they were looking at western land acquisition and all the issues this would encounter. Many of the Loyalists had received land grants in Canada on July 16th, so Abra knew their population would change as many former countrymen would seek Canadian land rather than stay among the now legal traitors to England.

Congress moved to Nassau Hall in Princeton, New Jersey on June 30, 1783 and remained there until November 4th. Congress had moved because they feared mutiny by the 400 soldiers of the Pennsylvania line which moved onto the State House in Philadelphia where Congress had been meeting. The troops had gone unpaid for several years of the war. Nassau Hall was the largest building of any college in the United States, so it would serve a useful purpose in housing Congress as they regrouped and attempted their restructuring. The

Pennsylvania government's refusal to provide security for Congress as it worked in Philadelphia was the main reason for the move to Princeton. For Abra, the move meant that he could see family more often, although his work continually drove him into late hours. The business of financial security for the newfound government was constantly being threatened, especially when Congress was continually approached asking for compensation for everything involved in the war.

It was on September 3, that the Revolutionary War had formally ended with the signing of the Treaty of Paris. On November 2nd at Rocky Hill, New Jersey, George Washington gave his Farewell to the Army speech, and disbanded the army. On November 3, Thomas Mifflin became the third President of the Confederation. On November 25th the last of the British troops and ships left the United States' soil. Washington was able to retire to his plantation at Mount Vernon after saying farewell to his officers on December 4th. Not long afterward it was reported that King George of England declared that George Washington was the "greatest man in the world." What a compliment, thought Abra, that King George would recognize what Washington had done to defeat the greatest military force in the world. Perhaps this was the first international recognition the new United States needed to begin their work in building their reputation. As King George's words were shared throughout the states, it did much to provide a feeling of pride in their newfound country.

Abra was disappointed that Congress had taken so long to approve the printing of the proposed Aitken Bibles. As 1783 was coming to a close the long awaited Bibles were finally ready for distribution, however not until the army was disbanding. George Washington was so happy with the Bibles he stated that "It would have pleased me well if Congress had been pleased to make such an important present to the brave fellows who have done so much for the security of their country's rights and establishments." 10,000 copies of the Aitkin Bible were distributed throughout the states, and quickly dubbed the "Bible of the Revolution."

Those who admired Abra did so because he was not pretentious. Abra was known to not present long-winded, self-promoting speeches in or out of Congress. A newspaper article printed in New Jersey spoke of Abra's attitude. It was titled, "A Thought for Today" and it quoted 2 Samuel 23:3: "He that ruleth over men must be just." Abra had responded and was quoted as saying, "Oppose tyranny in all its strides. Guard against every step depriving us of Constitutional liberty." When the newspaper was published, Abra's admirers smiled and said that summed up Abra's attitude. Tyranny of all kinds, whether it was governmental, military, or want of personal gain, took away from the end goal of Americans which was freedom and liberty. Abra could tolerate no one who sought advancement because of the war and the new government.

Unfortunately, there were many who saw the new government and freedom as an opportunity to advance their own careers and causes. To them, Abra's attitude was unacceptable, and Abra was viewed as an obstacle to their being paid for their war sacrifices and expenses. Abra felt strongly that he and his wife, Sarah, and his boys and his family had all sacrificed during the war years. Abra had chosen to serve in the Congress, and as such, had sacrificed financial and personal gain. What he found was that as soon as the war was closing, many came forward to demand personal payment for the roles they had played in the revolution. It surprised Abra to see which men stood forward waiting to be compensated for their sacrifices and service during the war.

Congress was presented with a resolution to compute pay on behalf of all officers of the army based on the sacrifices they had made during the war. Abra was known throughout Congress as a strict economist and he knew that the treasury was impoverished. Abra vehemently opposed such an idea as he felt that officers and legislators alike had sacrificed out of the desire to gain independence. The common man had no say, other than to fight the war created by those in power. Many of the common men had lost everything in this war. "All of us have sacrificed. Perhaps more than anyone else, the common man has sacrificed. He had nothing to start, and what little he did have went without care the duration of time spent serving this cause. Many men are returning home to find nothing there, and yet they do not stand before this Congress asking for compensation for their losses. Many Congressmen here sacrificed. I sacrificed the protection of my family by my continued work in the Congress, which I did willingly. I sacrificed property which was destroyed during battles. Three of my sons were taken prisoner during this war. I have lost many nights sleep to the concerns in my heart and mind in seeking a successful conclusion to this war. Yet I would find it unconscionable to ask to be repaid for such losses. At what price would we set for such sacrifices? If we allow such compensation we do so at the expense of this country and our earned freedom. I ask the proposal be withdrawn and officers shall receive no additional compensation above their wage. If we allow such a resolution we risk bankruptcy of a government we are just trying to begin. Let us not allow our own personal greed to overcome our common sense. Instead let us view the successful end to this war and our newfound freedom as our compensation."

Lively discussions were held about the resolution. Those who opposed Abra's stance immediately set to work in guaranteeing Abra would not be in Congress any longer. One of his friends said quietly, "Let it go, Abra. It is not important enough to hold fast to this idea. There are those who want you out of Congress because of your convictions."

Abra refused to step down and shared his belief that the new nation was for the common man. To bankrupt it before it could even begin was not acceptable. At every opportunity he would voice his firm conviction that it was the Congress's duty to protect the common man by saving the new nation from insurmountable war debt. There was a strong infrastructure who wanted to subdue Abra's opinions, and they worked to discredit his reputation. To Abra's dismay, he learned he had lost his seat in Congress in 1784; however he immediately obtained a seat in the New Jersey Legislature.

# Chapter 21
## *1784-1786*

**Congress had moved** to the Maryland State House in Annapolis, Maryland on November 26th, 1783. Although Abra was not a part of Congress, he continually received letters asking his opinion and advice from those who respected his work. On January 14, 1784 Congress ratified the Treaty of Paris, and the war was officially over. In the Treaty Britain recognized the colonies as free and sovereign states; established boundaries between the United States and British North America; granted fishing rights by Americans off the coast of Newfoundland and the Gulf of Saint Lawrence; recognized that debts were to be paid to creditors on either side; provision of restitution by the United States to Loyalists; prevented future confiscations of Loyalist property; prisoners of war were to be released and British property and slaves of the British were to be left unmolested; gave both the United States and Great Britain access to the Mississippi River; territories captured by Americans prior to the treaty would be returned without compensation. Although the treaty was signed and ratified, not everything was moving in the direction dictated by the treaty. Congress immediately had to work on settling the dictates of the treaty and communicating with Great Britain about issues they needed to complete. The lack of communication would make the final ratification and compliance difficult.

As 1784 started, Abra began working in the New Jersey legislature. He quickly learned of the many issues New Jersey was facing. The new nation's capital moved from Princeton NJ in 1783 to Trenton NJ in 1784 so Abra was always well apprised of what Congress was discussing. However, since Congress moved from Philadelphia to New York in 1784, Abra felt a sense of relief as he was able to spend more time at home for the first time in years. His political enemies may have prevented him a role in Congress, but working in the state legislature allowed Abra time with family.

Abra's sons survived the war. Aaron had been released in a prisoner exchange, and both Thomas and Andrew were able to escape the Jersey. Thomas, although severely weakened by his treatment on the prison ship, immediately returned to Elizabethtown to be reunited with his wife and son. Andrew, however, was bitter about the war and his father's inactivity in securing their freedom from the prison ship. Andrew returned to see his mother, but had very few words to say to his father. Andrew's youthful appearance and outgoing personality had changed to a quiet man who avoided looking his father in the eye. Andrew was thin and pale and his face was angular, so unlike the face Abra remembered. Abra was hurt. Quietly one evening, Andrew left the Clark farm and left no information as to his plans.

When Abra realized Andrew had left, he immediately sought Thomas' insight. "Thomas, have you spoken with Andrew at any length?"

Thomas answered, "Father, give him time. The war changes a man, and life on the Jersey was indescribable. Andrew was bitter that you had not acted on our behalf to help us escape that hell hole."

"Thomas, you know I could not do that. The letter they forced you to write demanded I renege on signing the Declaration. To do that would be treason to the very cause of the Revolution. I also could not ask Congress to act on my behalf. Other fathers had sons who were fighting this war and they had no one to speak on their behalf. I could not take advantage of my position. As it was, Congress found out and demanded Washington put an end to your torture. For that I was grateful, but I could not ask for further influence."

"I know that, Father. But Andrew faced many demons on that ship. He knew I was being tortured, but he did not let anyone know he, too, was your son. It was Andrew who persuaded other prisoners to push bread crumbs through the key hole that I might have some food. Andrew told me later that he felt he had betrayed me and acted cowardly by not identifying himself as a Clark."

"For God's sake. Had he identified himself it would have been suicide. You and Aaron were older and had trained as officers. Andrew was nineteen when he mustered, but had not faced any difficulty in his life." Abra lowered his head. "I prayed every night for my sons' safe return. I cannot even imagine the horrors you faced on that ship."

"Although I faced the torment of the British officers and starvation, I believe Andrew saw and lived the day to day horrors. Every day they had to dump bodies off the ship, or were ordered to bury them in shallow graves along the shore. Men were sick with dysentery and human waste filled the air with rancid stench which was unbearable. Andrew was always a sensitive young man, and I think the nightmares of the Jersey will continue to haunt him for some time. Food that was sent by our government to feed the prisoners onboard was taken by the British and distributed to their troops. Andrew had to load food shipped for American prisoners and exchange it for the rotting food of the British camps. He also had to help bury the dead, or dump bodies only to watch them float in the shallows."

Abra said quietly, "I prayed every night for your safe return."

Thomas responded, "Father, I have to admit that I often prayed that I might die rather than live through another day onboard that ship. Many of the men did so. No human being should suffer as we did. I had a wife and child which would give me hope and reason to survive. Andrew only had his nightmares."

"Do you have any notion where he was headed when he left here?" asked Abra.

"I believe he wants to travel to western New York. It is still wilderness there and I believe he wants to give himself time to think and rid himself of the war memories."

Abra was saddened to think of his son leaving for the wilderness, but knew that he was a young man of nearly twenty-five, not the young boy he remembered before the war began. This war had taken away so much from so many, yet Abra was thankful that he did not have to bury a son. About 25,000 Americans had died in the war; about 7,000 of those died in battles, and about 25,000 were wounded. Yet there were survivors of the war who would carry the wounds of the war mentally and emotionally for the rest of their lives. Abra was saddened that one of his sons was one of the mentally and emotionally scarred.

Upon returning to the state legislature Abra quickly learned that Thomas Jefferson had proposed that Congress form a committee to consider dividing the western territories into states. Abra and his colleagues felt this was an excellent idea as it would build the new country's size and strength and keep military coups from claiming western areas. Jefferson also proposed that by 1800 they abolish slavery. This issue, however, did not receive the same positive response. Abra and others discussed the fact that nearly every large landowner had slaves. Many of the indentured servants had gone off to fight in the war and buying into slavery had been the only option to maintain the homestead. Even Abra had a mother and two sons as slaves to help Sarah in his absence. Although Abra was not against freeing the slaves, he believed that convincing the Southern states it was a good idea would be difficult as the majority of the plantations were operated using large slave populations. Abra also argued that many slaves had fought in the war on both sides. British took slaves of the Patriots and had them fight against the Americans, and many slaves asked to fight and in 1776 Washington allowed them to fight. The 1st Rhode Island Regiment held 250 former slaves and freedmen, and The Bucks of America was an all Negro unit in Massachusetts led by Samuel Middleton who was the only Negro commissioned officer in the Continental Army. Abra felt that the Negroes had done an honorable job in fighting the British, and as such should gain their freedom.

As it turned out, Jefferson's proposal about abolishing slavery lost. Abra knew that tensions ran deep on this topic as Jefferson had proposed freedom for slaves in the Declaration, and that section had been omitted in the final copy because of the raging debates and fear that the actual document would never reach a final consensus unless that hot topic was eliminated. Abra knew that the topic was hotly contested on both sides and this issue could become the fodder for further unrest between the states. They had just earned their freedom. They could ill afford to already find reason to disrupt the peace.

Abra fully intended to free his slaves, however currently they were useful on the Clark farm as Sarah was still running things herself. Now that Thomas had returned from war, he would take his family and move to their own home. Sarah and Abra treated their Negroes well, but without help on the farm, Sarah would be helpless. Abra had written in his will that should Sarah outlive him, their slaves would be freed upon her death. Should Sarah die before him, Abra planned on freeing them immediately. Such thoughts saddened Abra as he knew that in order to continue working as he had done throughout the war; he had to rely on an institution which he despised. Certainly there had to come a time when all people would live equally in this country He had used indentured servants on the farm for years, just as other New Jersey farmers had done. It was when he left for Congress that Abra bought the woman and two boys to work on the farm. He remembered Sarah being angered that he had done this. He also remembered Tillie's face when she and her two boys were delivered in the wagon. She held onto her boys fearful that they would be torn from her. Sarah quickly eased her fears and Tillie bowed before Abra and said, "Thank you Masta for not separating me from my boys." Abra had paused and looked at the woman and said, "You are not to call me Master." Tillie was confused. "You will not be mistreated here. You will be working for Mrs. Clark and the boys will be working on the farm. You will be provided food, clothing and shelter. You will not be mistreated here, nor will you be separated from your boys." Tillie's dark face showed the streaks of tears down her cheeks. "I promise you that you will be treated fairly here. All I ask is that you help Mrs. Clark with the children, chores, cooking and gardening. Your boys will not be mistreated on this farm. They will work the farm with my son, Andrew."

Tillie and her boys easily adapted to the ease of the Clark farm. Sarah grew comfortable with Tillie who always had a story to share about any event. If someone had a toothache, Tillie had a story to tell of a toothache that made Sarah and the children laugh until their sides ached. If a tool was misplaced, Tillie would tell a story of a farm tool that had been borrowed, lent out, stolen, and then sold again to the original owner. No matter what the incident, Tillie had a story to go with it. Sarah enjoyed her company and work ethic. Tillie made life on the Clark farm a little more bearable when Abra was away. It was Sarah who had demanded that Abra write in his will that Tillie and the boys be given freedom one day. Abra sighed. He wished circumstances were different that Tillie were only a good friend, or even a hired woman, not a slave. Sadly, the reality was that if she were free she could easily be sold back into slavery in the South. In a sense she was protected on the Clark farm although the whole institution of slavery was still distasteful to Abra.

Abra was always proposing legislation which would guarantee fairness to all people. It became obvious in 1784 that many lawyers were creating such a backlog of court time that only those of wealth could afford to be represented in court. The more time a lawyer spent in court, the more he charged his client. Those without, especially after the costs of war, could not afford to be represented in court. Abra saw this as an issue of inequity and proposed a very controversial bill called, "An Act for Regulating & Shortening the Proceedings in the Courts of Law." Abra told his friends, "If it succeeds it will tear off the ruffles from the lawyers' wrists." The bill passed and it quickly became known as "Clark's Law," which made legal assistance more accessible to the general public. The law was a guarantee that all people could be represented in court, not just those with large purses. Later the law was revised and replaced with a new code of conduct expected to be followed for all trials.

In February, 1785, Abra heard the news that John Adams was being sent to England as an ambassador. Although England had refused to send an ambassador to the United States, they felt there was a need to address issues which became apparent after the war and needed attention. Abra was most concerned about the pre-war debts owed to British creditors and now that they were separated, how would debt collection occur? Another fear the United States had was that England had a number of forts along the Canadian border, and Congress was fearful that England had not dismantled these forts which made it appear they were looking for an opportunity to strike again. If lasting peace was to remain, the forts would need to be abandoned. The British were concerned with how the United States was treating the Loyalists. Many had their land and property had been taken during the war, and England felt this was unjust. Abra and other legislatures pondered how John Adams would fare as an ambassador when it was evident that England was making no attempt at building "peace and harmony," as stated in the Treaty of Paris, with the new United States, but were building a case of how unjust the United States was in treating its citizens.

In November, 1784, Richard Henry Lee became the sixth President of the Confederacy, taking office after Thomas Mifflin had served. The Articles of Confederation only had one branch of government, the legislature. The members of the legislature were elected annually and the person elected by Congress as President of Congress was the leader until the next election. The President had no executive powers. Abra continued to watch closely the progress of Congress. By November, 1785 John Hancock would be named President, however Hancock's health caused him to not attend Congress. In his absence, David Ramsay served, then Nathaniel Gorham. Gorham was then elected in November of 1786.

The United States was quickly expanding. Congress passed the Land Ordinance of 1785 in May, dividing the Northwest Territories into townships of six miles square. Each township had 36 lots of 640 acres each. A lot sold for $640. Abra's farm was 300 acres, so when his sons talked about the size of the western lots, and the cost, they found the idea of relocating very appealing. There was much discussion about how affordable the lots would be for those who had the money and the notion of moving. Throughout New Jersey, many who had lost so much from the war considered moving. Many of the local farms had everything burned during the war. Abra had been lucky that his house had not been burned, although his crops and outbuildings had been destroyed. Others lost everything. Not only were local families wanting a fresh start, they wanted to leave behind the memories of the war and how it tore apart families and friends. Abra pondered how his family had changed during the war. He had at least enjoyed raising Aaron and Thomas, and even Andrew, but the younger children saw very little of their father as he was constantly off to work in Congress or the state legislature. Now his children were talking of moving far away to take advantage of the land grants the government was offering. Abra knew this was a good decision, but he missed the life he thought he would have with Sarah, watching his children and grandchildren grow. Abra's work typically interfered with such wonderings and he would be abruptly pulled back into his reality of work.

Abra wrote a pamphlet titled "The True Policy of New Jersey, Defined." In it he identified issues on trade, money printing and money lending. The pamphlet was meant to establish a clear understanding of the paper money bill being considered by the New Jersey legislature. It was Abra who sponsored a bill in the New Jersey Assembly supporting the printing of paper money which was issued against land owned by the state. The printed money would be lent by loan offices that would put their land up as security. The paper money would be legal tender which would be used rather than the typical gold and silver coins used in the past. Abra spent hours writing letters to delegates from New Jersey in Congress to support the idea stabilizing the Continental finances. New Jersey had suffered so much in the war as many battles were fought in their state, and the troops had been housed in their state.

Abra felt that New Jersey should not pay any further war debts until other states agreed to a five percent levy to pay for their share of the war debts accrued by Congress. New Jersey was a state which faced financial difficulties due to its location. They lacked businesses and western lands to use as resources which other states had. Because they had no trade, they had to rely on citizens of New Jersey paying higher taxes to meet the debts the state had made during the war, and the expenses they now faced with the new government. While Abra was thrilled they had rid themselves of the oppression of Great Britain, they were now overwhelmed with debts to the government, and on loans from larger and more prosperous states. Abra told fellow citizens "to face up to our new "crisis." Beware that we may have knocked off the shackles of British tyranny but we could now suffer ourselves to be duped into as bad a situation by artful interested designing men." Abra felt the larger states looked at New Jersey as a place to sell all of their goods, thus making to make their fortunes greater.

Abra promoted his plan as a way to rejuvenate the New Jersey economy by encouraging New Jersey residents to spend their money within the state and avoid imports from other states which might be considered "vanities," or unnecessary purchases. Too many in New Jersey were trying to keep up appearances with the grandeur seen in the homes of the wealthy in other states. The lack of money in New Jersey had left many men without work as they could not afford the tools of their trade. The establishment of paper money would allow these men to set up their industries, allowing them to profit, as well as the state through the taxes from the products.

The topic became a national issue when much of Abra's commentary from his pamphlet was copied into a publication titled "Political Intelligencer," in 1786. A letter submitted to the publication had anonymously been written urging Clark to "prescribe a large dose of industry and frugality as a cure for the economic woes of New Jersey." When Abra read these words he immediately reacted, stating that, "I have already done it according to my capacity and proposed ways and means for the application to be made, and also to put a stop in some measure to our buying foreign luxuries. I am confident that it is the true policy of New Jersey and as such have considered it and I expect you may soon see it in print."

New Jersey was ripe with foreclosures. Many had borrowed money to purchase their land and homesteads, and then the greedy lenders had forced immediate repayment, thereby forcing the borrower to sell his property at less than its value. Typically the very same creditors purchased back the property, thereby twice gaining profit. Abra knew that creditors were often from wealthier states like New York and Pennsylvania. He viewed them as "foreigners", no less dangerous than what Great Britain had been to New Jersey. It was only the promise of paper money which Abra saw as a means to correct the impoverished state New Jersey had found itself in after the war.

Abra knew the best way to see action taken was to encourage a grass roots campaign for change. He published the addresses of the New Jersey delegates in Congress. He said, "Use humble petitioning only, and no doubt you may be heard. If not your only hope is in the next election of representatives." The plan worked. Over ten thousand New Jersey citizens sent in letters before the February session began in the New Jersey legislature. Two out of three writers supported paper money. Abra's guidance of having citizens take on letter writing campaigns waged a positive change in the government's decisions.

The legislature defeated the proposal, but Abra kept the channels open by urging newspaper campaigns informing the New Jersey public about the benefits of paper money. When letters appeared supporting the idea of selecting new representatives, a change of heart was soon seen. A special session was held in May and the bill passed by one vote. Abra smiled. "The common man *does* have a say. It is his vote!" said Abra to his colleagues.

Abra was selected in September, 1786, to be a delegate at the Annapolis Convention in Maryland. Abra considered it to be a huge honor to be selected for such weighty work. Twelve delegates from five states arrived for a "Meeting of Commissioners to Remedy Defects of the Federal Government." Five other states had appointed commissioners who had not arrived in time for the meeting, and three states had done nothing in appointing commissioners. Their main work was to examine commercial trade, especially in the Chesapeake Bay area. It was evident that the Articles of Confederation were limited in their effectiveness, and trade between the thirteen colonies was problematic. The commissioners agreed there were not enough states represented to actually make any strong proposal, however they did produce a report for Congress asking them to form another convention in Philadelphia in 1787. The mission of the Philadelphia Convention was to look at the problems in their government. Abra was convinced if they could develop better trade between the states, the economic problems they were facing could be greatly diminished. Abra's disappointment in the poor attendance was obvious, but he left feeling that they had done an important job in outlining what needed to be addressed the following year.

In 1786 Abra found himself intervening on behalf of debtors after the war. The debtors owed large sums of money to a small group of creditors who demanded immediate repayment. Thus, many were facing foreclosures or loss of property as they did not have the funds immediately after the war to repay their debts. Abra sponsored a bill to allow paper money to be used for a limited time rather than silver or gold to repay debts. The paper money would be issued based on property owned. This became a huge political contest between Abra and the wealthy creditors. Abra argued that the debtors were honest and wanted to repay their debts, but to demand silver and gold payment would bankrupt those who had the least ability to afford such a loss. Abra argued that the Revolution had been fought to protect all people. The bill was finally passed, and Abra was then known as the "Father of paper money" throughout the state, and eventually even in Congress. Again, Abra made political enemies each time he challenged the wealthy who had become greedy. Despite his political enemies, Abra remained firmly fixed in his belief that the needs and rights of the common man needed to be protected. One of his friends said, ""But for every man you make an enemy, you will increase your friends by multitudes.

Our local farmers have never had a champion for their rights, Abra. You appear to be that man!" Abra felt this was his duty in serving his state.

During his remaining years in the New Jersey legislature, he worked on promoting manufacturing and trading centers within their state in order to increase their financial standing. The new government was hard pressed to collect taxes to pay for the war, so it was Abra's desire to get New Jersey financially stable so they would have the ability to pay their war debt. One fall evening when Abra was home, his sons Aaron and Thomas came to visit. Talk during dinner had been of the post war economic depression Americans were facing. There was a need for tax revenue to pay for the costs of war and setting up a new government, yet many could not afford it. There was a shortage of money and many farms were foreclosing. Abra said, "We got word that Congress has been trying to deal with the money problems we are facing. Coins are being minted like they do in Spain. There will be a $10 gold piece, a $1 silver piece, a tenth of a dollar coin in silver and copper pennies."

Aaron said, "We needed some kind of currency that everyone uses. There are still those using pre-war currency. Many stored all their currency before the war, and now it isn't worth the paper it was printed on."

Abra nodded. "People are getting angry about this. Everyone is suing everyone else for debts, and to go to court it costs too much money. That's why I proposed the legislation I did in the legislature."

"It didn't matter much in Massachusetts. Daniel Shays, a veteran of the war, went bankrupt and lost his farm. He had served this country as a captain, comes home to find that he can't pay taxes or live like a free man. He led a mob to the courthouse and kept them from doing business there. Same thing happened in New Hampshire. They all want government to print paper money that can be circulated to help the common man" said Thomas.

"True. Shays nearly faced treason for standing up with his mob against 600 militiamen who were guarding the Massachusetts Supreme Court. Can't blame him. He did what we asked. He fought. He sacrificed. And now he has nothing and stands to lose the little he's got left" Abra said. "I guess all these bankruptcies and protests have finally made an impression in Congress. They created a US Mint. I'd imagine we should be seeing some changes economically in this country. It can't come soon enough."

During his three years serving the New Jersey legislature, Abra's family blossomed. Thomas had two more sons: Abraham who was born in 1785, and David, born in 1787. The Clark farm was often filled with family. Aaron and his wife Susanna, and their two little ones, Winans and Elizabeth would come to visit whenever Abra was home from the legislature. Thomas and Elizabeth and their three sons lived nearby so they were often visiting the Clark farm. Hannah and her husband, Melyn Miller were reunited after the war and they settled on a farm near the Miller homestead. Sarah married Clarkson Edgar soon after the war ended, and she was expecting her first child. Abraham Jr. was married to Hannah Perkins, and they had taken a parcel of the Clark farm to manage. Only little Abigail was left in Sarah's care when Abra would leave to work in the legislature. When the entire family got together, Tillie would be in her glory cooking alongside Sarah and sharing yet another of her stories about curious children. The Clark farm was filled with laughter and happiness, except for the obvious absence of Andrew. Abra would look at his growing family and smile with pride that peace had finally come to this nation and he only hoped that every family had the kind of happiness he had in his heart. It was the first time that he recalled actually enjoying his family since the early years of his marriage.

# Chapter 22
# *1787-1788 The Constitution*

**The New Jersey legislature** knew that Abra's political style was forceful when supporting the causes he felt affected New Jersey. Abra had been blackballed from Congress several years by those who felt he didn't stand on the popular issues the aristocrats and wealthy felt they deserved. By 1787 even those who had been against him realized that they now needed Abra to fight for the rights of all men. New Jersey stood to be ecumenically destroyed by the wealthier and larger neighbors despite there being more common men than wealthy citizens. Abra was a protector of their rights. There was also the issue of inequality between the states. In recognition that Abra could best serve all of the United States, and protect the rights of New Jersey, Abra was once again called upon to be a delegate in Congress. Congress was now meeting in New York at City Hall, so once again Abra was packing and on the road. At least this time Thomas and Aaron were living near enough to Sarah that he felt confident she would be fine in his absence.

As always, Sarah saw Abra off and told him that she continued to be proud of the sacrifices he made for his country. Abra thought about this on the long trip to New York. Without Sarah at home, he would never have been able to do what he had done. She was indeed a remarkable woman.

Since Abra had been involved in the Declaration of Independence, and in the Articles of Confederation, it seemed only common sense to the New Jersey legislation that Abra needed to be involved in the important work Congress was now facing in New York. Their fear for New Jersey was that because of their size, they would not have the kind of equal representation they had fought to have during the war against England.

It was already apparent that the Articles of Confederation were inadequate and the threat of the newly formed government falling apart before it ever got started was evident to those involved. George Washington was unhappy with the Articles. Fighting the war was a sacrifice for everyone and unless there was a solid government established, the new United States would become individual countries, and they would be ripe for military coups from within, and eventually from outside the country. Once again Congress would be called upon to better organize the new government of the United States.

Delegates from twelve states (Rhode Island did not send delegates) met from May 25 to September 17 at the Philadelphia Convention with "The sole and express purpose to revise the Articles of Confederation." Congress would then need to approve and ratify the out coming legislation, and the states would need to ratify the proposal. Washington attended the Constitutional Convention in Philadelphia. He was unanimously elected as president of the convention. As such he worked to facilitate the delegates in their efforts. Abra and other delegates in Congress considered George Washington the best choice to run the country, however they knew that he would demand a document that would solidify and protect all the states and citizens. Abra knew his role in organizing the Constitution was essential. The Constitution would be the means to guarantee the protection of the rights of the common man. Abra felt this was his mission.

In May, Abra was also named to the Philadelphia Convention. It had been Abra's suggestion that another convention meet because of the poor attendance at the Annapolis Convention. It was in the Philadelphia Convention that the Constitution would be written. Abra was to be one of two replacements in the four man New Jersey delegation to Philadelphia.

This choice was met with disappointment in Congress. "I hear that Clark is a chosen to be a member of the Convention," Nathan Dane of Massachusetts said. "If he goes to the Philadelphia Convention I think we cannot expect New Jersey, at present, to attend Congress very steadily." Everyone knew that if Abra went to Philadelphia he would be committed and attend all of the meetings. However, the new member of Congress would likely not be as committed as Abra, and the delegate's absence would affect New Jersey's representation.

Abra seldom felt overwhelmed in any decision he made while working in the legislature, however he was torn between working on the Constitution at the Philadelphia Convention, or remaining in Congress. A setback in his health finally made the decision for him. Abra felt that he needed to remain in New York rather than traveling between the two cities and trying to be productive in both arenas. Abra explained to his friends, "To be on both Congress and the Philadelphia Convention serves neither well. My overextension would be unfair to Congress, especially in view of the financial issues we are presently facing. The incompatibility in the two appointments is evident, thus, I chose to work in Congress, and not in Philadelphia." Abra sadly sent his regrets to the New Jersey legislature recruiting delegates to the Philadelphia Convention.

Richard Henry Lee also denied the appointment to the Philadelphia Convention as he felt those attending the convention would send their vote to Congress which was meeting in New York on issues based upon their work and opinions in Philadelphia. Abra agreed with Lee. It would not be fair to vote in Congress on issues he had not been present to hear debate upon.

In Abra's place, the son of his good friend, Elias Dayton, was selected to represent New Jersey. Abra was pleased with this choice as he felt Jonathan Dayton had a good head on his shoulders and his involvement in politics was well suited. He had confidence that Jonathan would further endorse what he had proposed at the Annapolis Convention. It was well known that James Madison and delegates of Virginia had drafted the idea which became known as the Virginia Plan. In it there was a proposal that was known as the Large State Plan. In this plan both houses of the legislature would be determined based by population, thus protecting the power and interests of the larger states. Such a plan was not in accordance to what Abra felt was good for the smaller states, nor for the poorer states. Their interests and needs could easily be negated by those states with more power. Thus the New Jersey Plan was conceived. Abra was firmly convinced that Dayton and the other representatives would see the logistics of the New Jersey Plan he so strongly advocated. In William Paterson's New Jersey Plan, or Small State Plan, as it was being called in the Convention, the Articles would grant additional powers to Congress and the Congress would have equal representation from each state.

Abra noted that many of the delegates at the Convention had a wide variety of political views. There were many arguments which ensued, mostly about the number of representatives each state would be allowed to have. Abra strongly opposed the Virginia Plan, which was well known prior to the start of the Convention. Within Congress members debated just as hotly as those at the Convention debated. Abra rose and addressed the delegation, "My dear sirs. The Virginia Plan sounds fair to states which have large populations. My state of New Jersey is land-bound and of small population, however my state fought dearly for our Independence, and to not have equal representation merely because of our size lessens our importance. Did we not suffer greatly throughout the war? Were not there many battles fought within our state? Did we not pay our full share of war debt? How then can our voice be discounted strictly because of population. I say no, Sir, to the proposed Virginia Plan. I stand by the New Jersey Plan which says each state would have the same number of representatives. After all, each state would then be equal and have equal voice."

At the Convention, the same debate raged. Abra was disappointed when he learned that Dayton had not taken the stand Abra had anticipated. New Jersey delegates William Paterson and David Brearly opposed the Virginia Plan for a national government. Both were verbal and strong in their persuasion of other small states in joining them in opposition to the Virginia Plan. However, Paterson and Brearly were unable to persuade Dayton to join them in supporting the plan which would strengthen the small state's say in governmental power, while having both an executive and judiciary check and balance.

The main difference in the New Jersey plan was that there would only be one unicameral house which would have the same number of representatives from each state. Paterson hotly announced that he would never support the Virginia Plan, and he would work to have New Jersey deny its ratification. As the Convention continued their work on the proposed Constitution, elements of the New Jersey plan were used, most importantly in the design of Congress which would have equal state representation.

George Washington listened and guided the men into compromise. It was Roger Sherman of Connecticut who finally proposed a two-house legislature. There would be a Senate which would have equal numbers of representatives from each state, and there would be a House of Representatives, which would have one representative for each 30,000 citizens in the state. After several days of debate, it was agreed to have the two house legislature plan, and it became known as the Great Compromise. Gouverneur Morris of New York agreed to hand-write the 4,300 word document in its final form.

The Constitution provided for a national government which would make and enforce laws, and collect taxes. This Federal system of government would provide two governments: the state government and the national government. The upper house of the legislature, the Senate, would have equal representation with two senators from each state. The lower house of the legislature, the House of Representatives, would be based on population. All four of the New Jersey delegates signed the revisions and the Constitution, and became known as Federalists. The Constitutional Convention had met for a four month period. On September 17, 1787 the delegates were to sign the Constitution. There were 55 delegates, however only 35 delegates were actually present and involved in the writing of the Constitution.

When word arrived that the Constitution had been signed, at first Abra was angered. "I found their choices not such as I had wished and expected," said Abra when he heard the outcome of the Philadelphia Convention. However, the compromise in the representation in Congress appeased him, and he knew that in order for the work of Congress to move forward, they needed to regulate the issues of finance throughout all the states.

Even though Abra had reservations, when the finished document was voted upon, he pushed for the ratification, "notwithstanding its imperfections," Abra said. Abra was quick to write to his friends and sons that, "I cheerfully gave my assistance" in getting the Constitution ratified in New Jersey, and limited any negative commentary. New Jersey was well known for their political opposition, yet the ratification of the Constitution went smoothly with little interference or debate, despite the loss of the New Jersey plan focus.

It was Abra who stood before Congress on December 18, 1787 to announce that New Jersey was now the third state to ratify the Constitution. While Congress wanted all thirteen states to ratify, they knew that with New Jersey's acceptance, it was time to consider how to put this new government into effect. Abra made a motion that a committee be formed to determine how the Constitution would be put into operation. "Gentlemen, I understand we need a form of government, and certainly this document puts into place a well-conceived plan; however my misgivings are that we must remember to continually protect the common man lest we repeat the mistakes of Europe where the common man is oppressed. I strongly urge this contingency to consider a list of amendments be considered to guarantee such oppression does not occur." Immediately discussion broke out among the delegates. Abra looked around the room to identify those who agreed with him. James Madison was nodding his head slowly and did not participate in the sidebar discussions on his colleagues. Abra knew in Madison he could trust changes would be made. Although Abra was against ratification of the Constitution prior to the amendments being written, he realized that the main document needed to be ratified before amendments which would protect the common man could be added. The constant drain of give and take was beginning to take its toll on Abra. He slowly took his seat and maintained eye contact with Madison who continued to slowly nod his head and tap his finger on the table.

As the various states continually debated about ratification Abra continued to worry about the potential misuse of power by a central government. His concern continued to be for the common man and as he told others, "I perceive that some parts of this new Constitution can bear too hard upon the liberties of the people" he told Madison as they shared a dinner and discussed what modifications would need to be made to the Constitution. Madison was already penning ideas and Abra was one of several men who met with him to share their ideas for potential amendments.

The ratification became final June 21, 1788 with nine of the thirteen states having signed. Melancton Smith, who had been very vocal against the Constitution, declared that New York may ratify the Constitution "on condition that amendments would be made." Abra immediately took interest, as this, too, was his concern.

There was a huge celebration in the streets of New York at their finally ratifying the Constitution and Congress cancelled their session. With the free time allotted to Abra, he sat and wrote a letter to Thomas Sinnickson, admitting his disfavor with the Constitution.

*New York, 23 July*

*My Dear Sir,*

*As to my sentiments respecting the new system of government, although you do not ask my opinions, yet, as I find by your letter it will be acceptable, I think it not amiss to give them. They have at no time been concealed. I never liked the system in all its parts. I considered it from the first, more a consolidated government than a federal, a government too expensive, and unnecessarily oppressive in its operation; creating a judiciary undefined and unbounded.*

*With all these imperfections about it, I nevertheless wished it to go to the States from Congress just as it did, without any censure or commendation, hoping that in case of a general adoption, the wisdom of the States would soon amend it in the exceptionable parts.*

*Strong fears however remained upon my mind until I found the custom of recommending amendments with the adoptions began to prevail. This set my mind at ease. It became clear in my opinion from the oppositions, and the general concurrence in proposing amendments, that the present plan must undergo some alterations to make it more agreeable to the minds of the great numbers who dislike it in its present form. The Amendments I wish are not numerous. Many proposed by the different conventions appear of but little consequence, yet some are important and must be acceded to if ever the government sits easy.*

*From this state of the matter, wishing amendments, as I do, you will readily conclude I anxiously wish every state may come into the adoption in order to affect a measure with me so desirable; in which case, from the general current of amendments proposed, we shall retain all the important parts in which New Jersey is interested.*

*To your query about our paper money, I dare not venture*

*a conjecture what effect the new government will have upon it. I suppose, however, no interference will be had in that or any law now in force so far as respects citizens of the same State. In Continental affairs and between Citizens of different States I Suppose the case will be otherwise. Our paper probably will not then be received in the Treasury of the United States or in our State by citizens of another State, in which cases it will cease to be a legal tender.*

*As to the Arrears of Taxes payable to the Continental Receiver, I believe our paper will readily be received. The difficulty of obtaining money from the exhausted state of our finances makes our money, notwithstanding the loss sustained upon it, eagerly sought after. I know public creditors are anxious to obtain orders on our loan officers when they can hear he hath any of our paper on hand. Large orders have been given upon him which the holders accepted in expectation of receiving paper only. As to specie they know at present none is expected.*

*If any remedy is applied to our paper money it must come through our legislature. I believe it would have a good effect if the interest and such of the principle as may be paid in was destroyed, and the amount of the interest raised by taxes.*

*It is said the Speaker is about calling our legislature on account of the Adoption of the New Constitution; this is altogether unnecessary as the New Congress will not be convened before February. The situation of several States require such a distant time; the usual time of meeting in October will be soon enough to make the necessary provision for appointing officers etc. We have been some time in suspense about the event of the New Constitution in this State; the accounts of last evening were that the Convention had adjourned to a future day. If that is the case they mean at next meeting to adopt it. Before I seal this I may likely hear whether the above report is true or not.*

*P.S. I cannot find that the account of the Conventions adjourning is supported by any good authority.*

*I am your humble servant,*

*Abra Clark**

When Abra completed the letter he felt a sense of catharsis in that he had finally vocalized a plan of action. He would immediately set to work with Madison and others to get amendments added to the Constitution once all states had ratified it. Abra felt the New Jersey Constitution had provided for all officials of government to remain dependent upon the people who had elected them and communication was encouraged. He feared that with the Constitution, government legislators would not be as tied to the people. Senate would be elected by the state legislatures, not by the people. Their six year term would guarantee they did

*actual letter

not need to interact with the electorate. He also feared that in the House, larger states would have more representatives, thus more power. Abra did not like the use of an electoral college to elect the executive. Abra was quite vocal with his colleagues about his reservations with the judiciary as their power did not appear to be specifically defined. Yet, Abra was quick to admit, the Constitution was far more in line with a Republican government than the Articles had been. In the end, Abra agreed that the Congress, as described in the Constitution, would have the power to solve the financial woes states like New Jersey faced. For that, Abra said, the shortcoming of the Constitution was compatible.

Several of Abra's colleagues were astonished that Abra was still disappointed in the outcome. "How could you not support this document? You were one of the greatest supporters when it came to representation, and you agreed that you were satisfied with the two house system through the Great Compromise. Aren't you pleased with the end result?" asked a fellow delegate.

"I agree that the two house system is certainly a fair compromise, and I whole heartedly support it."

"Then why are you still so concerned about the Constitution?"

"I cannot agree about the way it is written. There are opportunities for the common man to be overshadowed by those more powerful. This document gives us a great governmental structure, however it needs bylaws or additions which spell out for all the protections and rights guaranteed to the common man," said Abra.

Several nearby delegates overhead this discussion and looked at each other with raised eyebrows. "So, Clark is still trying to upset the applecart," said one. "It will not sit well when word is shared that Mr. Clark was against the Constitution."

"He didn't say he was against the Constitution," said the other. "Just that he has concerns for protecting the commoner."

"Ah, protection against whom? Us? Those who have land and wealth? Is it Mr. Clark's desire to make them our equals so they can be handed everything we have?" The other delegate looked back at Abra, then at his companion. He knew that it would not take long before Abraham Clark's name was circulated in a prejudicial manner.

Not knowing that there were peers who were already plotting his downfall, Abra began to research amendments which could be added to the Constitution. Abra planned to begin correspondence with James Madison who had been instrumental in the writing of the Constitution, yet a strong critic of the Constitution without guarantees of individual rights. Abra pressed Madison to consider such amendments in order to protect the common man, those who needed protection against big government and those with the wealth and power to manipulate those without equal resources.

# Chapter 23
## *1789*

**In late 1788**, prices of food and products in the states finally stabilized for the first time since the war had begun. Abra felt great relief as this would begin the economic recovery New Jersey and the rest of the country needed. As 1788 came to a close, Congress was still operating under the Articles of Confederation. Upon the start of 1789, Congress would follow the new Constitution. As Congress was closing for the year, there was excited expectation of how well the new government would work. Abra, too, was excited, and he was running for election in the First Congress under the new Constitutional design.

Abra had made political enemies. Disgruntled creditors from the war, lawyers and former army officers worked hard to block Abra's election to the First Congress in 1789. As ammunition they spread rumors that Abra was against the Constitution and was Anti-Federalist. They also rumored that Abra was not even a candidate and wasn't really running for office. With manipulated election strategies, which included early poll closing, especially in districts where Abra had strong support, Abra lost the election and his opposition won. For the first time in his political career, Abra was in the minority in the elections of New Jersey. Abra was stunned and disappointed.

Despite his loss for a seat in Congress, Abra was quickly appointed a commissioner to settle the financial accounts of the state of New Jersey with the United States. Abra accepted this post, knowing he would run again for the Second Congress the following year. Abra's days were filled with research, meetings, and paperwork. Abra gladly did this work as he felt the records needed to be accurately organized and all accountings made in an honest and forthright manner.

Across the United States everyone awaited word as to who would be their leader. Everyone agreed it should be George Washington. His leadership throughout the war and throughout the aftermath was unquestionable. Although Washington was certainly a man of great ambition, he at first declined the position feeling it would be self-serving. Washington, although recognized as a supreme military leader and compassionate citizen, was indeed, a modest man. He was approached by nearly all the delegates about becoming the leader of the United States. When many stated they wanted to title him, "King George," Washington firmly declined stating that they had fought many years to rid themselves of one King George, and they certainly did not need to replace him with another. Instead he suggested the title of "Mr. President." Congress quickly determined they would call him President.

As 1789 began, Abra followed closely the first election. Ballots were cast on February 4th, and the final count was to be done on April 6th. Abra learned that Congress had difficulty in getting started in their work as so many of the members had difficulty making arrangements in traveling to New York City and securing housing. Finally on March 4th the First Congress under the Constitution opened for business; however it was not until April 1 that they had enough members for a quorum. In the meantime the House of Representative began their work. It was exciting times for those who followed politics. Everyone wanted to be certain that the Constitution was being followed, and the new government structure would work. On April 6th, the ballots were counted and George Washington was voted President, and John Adams Vice President. Washington had received 100% of the Electoral College votes. Once advised of his selection, George Washington left Mount Vernon for New York City.

Abra insisted that Sarah join him in traveling to New York City for the April 30th swearing in of George Washington as the first President of the United States. At first Sarah objected, but Abra was adamant. "Sarah, all these years you stood by my side and supported my work in the New Jersey Legislature and in Congress. You handled all the farm issues on your own. We have heroes who fought for our independence, but you held down our home, just as other women did across the country. You faced the same terrors I faced in worrying about our boys. You would wait anxiously for news of the war so that you could direct your prayers for the right cause. You need to be by my side to witness the product of our work. George Washington did an excellent job as our General, and I am certain he will guide this country into stability with a firm and fair hand. He has only been a name to you. I want you to witness this magnanimous man and see the fruits of our labors." Sarah was touched that Abra insisted on her traveling with him. She immediately set out to borrow a ball gown and accessories as Sarah was a frugal woman and had none of these at her own disposal. With trunks packed, the Clarks headed to New York City.

Abra and Sarah positioned themselves so they could view the swearing in ceremony. Washington was 57 and stood tall and proud as he was sworn in on the balcony of the Federal Hall. Cheers could be heard throughout streets as Washington answered his swearing in with, "So help me God." He then kissed the Bible as an affirmation that God's hand had helped him to this point, and that God would help him guide the country to success. Abra glanced at his wife and saw her wiping a tear from her cheek. "Oh, Abra. So many nights I would kiss my Bible after praying for your safety and the safety of our children. What a wonderful man Mr. Washington is in showing the public his religious convictions." Fireworks exploded and Sarah and Abra enjoyed the sights and sounds of New York celebrating. George Washington left the balcony to give his short acceptance speech to Congress.

Abra and Sarah stayed for the first inaugural ball on May 7th. As a signer of the Declaration, Abra was invited to the ball, and Sarah was thrilled at the prospect of meeting Mrs. Washington. "After all, she too stood by throughout the war while her husband fought on the front lines," said Sarah. As Abra and Sarah went through the receiving line, Abra addressed Washington with the title he believed people were using. "Congratulations and best wishes, Your Excellency."

"My dear Mr. Clark. We fought too long to break the binds of European royal courts. I am just a citizen who was chosen to lead. I'd prefer to be called 'Mr. President.'"

Abra laughed. "Mr. President, you continue to amaze me. Let me introduce you to my wife, Mrs. Clark." When Washington turned his attention to Sarah, Sarah blushed as she bowed in front of the President who took her hand and kissed it.

"Oh, Mr. President. I had hoped that I would meet your wife this evening. Is she here?" said Sarah. The President told Abra and Sarah that she had stayed behind at Mount Vernon to take care of business there before traveling for the inauguration, but had not arrived yet in New York.

Abra said, "She must be an incredible woman to have safeguarded your plantation and support you throughout the war."

"Indeed. Just as Mrs. Clark stood by your side as you took on the very dangerous work of declaring our need to break from the tyranny of Great Britain. Many a great man was able to achieve great things when he had a great woman standing at his side."

The ball was wonderful. Abra made certain Sarah was at his side and introduced her to many of the men he had worked with since 1776. When Sarah was whisked away to visit with some of the wives, Abra visited with many of his former Congressional colleagues. As the evening progressed, the Assembly Rooms were filled with dancing couples. The President managed to dance with several of the New York society ladies. He danced two cotillions and a minuet, and Sarah commented on how graceful he was on the dance floor. "I know you said he was a strong General in the war and he led his men honorably, but I would never have expected him to be such an accomplished dancer and have such ease in talking to all of these people. Look, Abra. The ladies told me that those men are French and Spanish dignitaries who came for the festivities. Oh, Abra. I am so disappointed that Mrs. Washington did not arrive in time for this occasion. I would so like to have met her."

Abra responded, "Sarah, I should think she is much like you!" Abra kissed his wife's hand and led her to the dance floor in a quiet corner. Sarah was not accustomed to formal dancing in such a public setting, but she did enjoy a minuet with her husband. Sarah's face beamed and Abra looked at her lovingly and thought that he had never seen her look more radiant. Sarah looked into Abra's eyes and felt love and pride well within her. Her lip began to quiver and Abra abruptly grasped her hand. "Sarah, is something wrong?"

"No, Abra. Everything is right. I am so very proud of you and I am most proud of your part in making this country independent." Sarah and Abra continued to enjoy their evening together, and watching the new President as he walked with dignity and grace to each small grouping of people. It was a night Sarah would never forget.

After returning to New Jersey, Abra went back to work on the New Jersey finances. He followed Congress' motion and first tax laws. They voted on an 8.5 percent protective tax on thirty items, however quickly charged a lower tax on American shipments. By the end of July Congress had passed the Tonnage Act which placed a fifty cent per ton tax on foreign ships entering United States ports, and thirty cents on American built for foreign owned ships, and six cents per ton on American ships. Abra knew people did not like taxes; however this was a way to guarantee that the United States would be able to afford their new government, and it would encourage more American trade and less reliance on foreign trade. The tax made good economic sense.

Abra continued to watch with great interest the work of Congress. Abra was always interested in matters of finance.

When he learned that Congress had voted a salary of $25,000 a year for the President, the figure seemed unbelievable. Washington declined the salary as he was already wealthy. He stated that he wanted to be viewed as a public servant. At first, everyone was thrilled; however Congress quickly realized that if they did not give a salary for this position, only the wealthy would seek to lead the country. When presented with this, Washington agreed and accepted the salary. Abra was impressed with the foresight of Congress in this issue.

The Elizabethtown men would often find their way to the Clark farm and Abra would often sit on the front porch, or around the kitchen table and talk about politics. Nearly every New Jersey family had lost relations in the war, or had been hit by economic strain because of the damages to their farms. Often the men would get together to rebuild a barn or house which had been lost during the war. New Jersey was especially hard hit. Abra's sons Thomas and young Abraham would join in the conversations. Thomas had returned from war with a distinctive change. He walked with a limp and often would move stiffly like a man filled with arthritis. His coloring was always ashen and his face was lined from the frown lines he always wore. Despite his changed appearance since the war, he remained an active advocate for the democracy he had fought to obtain. Abra would sit and look at his son and feel the pride he had in his son who had given so much. "I'm telling you, the men would follow Washington anywhere. If he said things would get better, you couldn't help but believe they would. Many men said they would have high-tailed it home, but a visit from Washington high atop his horse as he moved up and down the lines would inspire any man to keep fighting." Thomas stopped and began coughing. Abra was concerned that his son could no longer carry on a conversation without being stopped by fits of coughing. Elizabeth quietly walked by with a cup of water which Thomas took from her hand. She stood behind his chair and stroked his back waiting for him to finish his drink.

"Perhaps we should get home, Thomas. The night air is chilly and I have a full day tomorrow," said Elizabeth, who was already beginning to show her pregnancy. It wouldn't be long before she was unable to leave the farm. The worry in her eyes as she looked into Thomas' eyes was evident. Abra knew that Elizabeth had been handling most of the work at their farm because Thomas' health was not good. He smiled at Elizabeth as she bent to help her husband rise from the chair. Thomas said his goodbyes to the men in the kitchen and struggled to pull his coat up his arms. Sarah had already gathered Jonathan and little Abraham and was buttoning their coats. Thomas and Elizabeth gathered the children and led them out to the wagon and pulled blankets over them. Sarah carried out several pies and some fresh eggs she had gathered that evening to send home with Thomas. Thomas again fell into a coughing fit as he helped Elizabeth into the wagon. By the time Thomas got into the wagon, the two boys were already asleep. “Fresh air always gets to them,” laughed Elizabeth.

“Cover up as well,” said Sarah. “This evening spring air can give quite a chill.” As the wagon pulled away Sarah and Abra stood watching it disappear into the darkness. The sound of yet another coughing fit could be heard in the night air. “I’m worried, Abra. Thomas does not look well.”

“I know. I thought he had improved after the war, but it seems this last bout of illness has set him back. His lungs do not sound good at all. I mentioned to him tonight that he needs to send for the doctor to look him over. He laughed it off and said it would pass once the sun stayed out longer.”

Sarah shook her head and looked to the sky. “I certainly hope he regains his strength. We will have to send more help out to the farm to help with the planting. The boys are too little and Elizabeth will deliver late spring so she won’t be able to do much.”

“I’m certain Thomas will turn the corner. He always does,” said Abra as they returned to the kitchen and their guests.

Abra was very content in his work in the New Jersey legislature. His stays away from home were limited and he was able to be home much more than when he had been in Congress. His happiness, however, was brought to an abrupt end when his son, Abraham, arrived at their door late one afternoon. “Father, it’s Thomas. He died this afternoon. Elizabeth asked me to fetch you and Mother. I already stopped at Aaron's and told him. He said he would follow me here shortly."

Thomas was only 37. Once the war was over, Thomas had remained weak because of his treatment on the prison ship, Jersey. The recent bout with pneumonia had left Thomas too week to recover. His lungs were not strong enough to endure the deep coughing fits he suffered over the past months. When Sarah heard the news she dropped to a chair and sobbed. Abra cradled Sarah in his arms, and thought of how difficult it must have been when their daughter had died during the war and he was not there to support her. Sarah quickly composed herself and wiped her eyes with her kerchief, and withdrew to the kitchen to gather supplies to take to Elizabeth. As Aaron's horse galloped up the lane, and Abraham and Abra left the house to meet with Aaron. The three talked of arrangements.

"We'll bury him next to Cavalier and little Abraham in the family plot next to the church," said Abra. "Your mother will want to gather together food and go to his house to comfort Elizabeth and the boys. Elizabeth has to be exhausted with the newborn. Jonathan can watch after the younger boys while we help Elizabeth with the body."

Abra went into the house and Sarah was already in the kitchen preparing to bake for the funeral. She was dictating a list to Abigail of supplies needed in town. Tillie was at Sarah's side reassuring her that Thomas had already met his Maker and all would be well for Miss Elizabeth and the boys.

"Abra, go ahead with the boys. Susanna will fetch me and the food and we will meet you at Thomas' house," said Sarah. Abra looked at her face which was set as if she commanded herself not to cry. How Abra admired her strength. She was the strongest woman he knew. So many of the women of Elizabethtown had faced losses, yet moved forward, never letting their grief rip them apart. For the first time Abra found himself considering how easy it was to escape to work in the government, or even to fight on the front lines. Remaining behind and having to watch the women folk clean up after the war was worse than waiting for reports from the battle lines.

Abra and Aaron stopped by the tinsmith to have the coffin plate made. "What should we put on it?" asked Aaron.

"Thomas Clark, son, brother, husband, father. 1753-1789. Age 37 Revolutionary War Captain," said Abra. "Thomas was not materialistic, and I think this will be suitable. I have already lost three children in this life. Little Cavalier, Abraham Jr. and Elizabeth. I also don't know the whereabouts of Andrew so I am uncertain if he is alive or has passed on. I never anticipated burying another child of mine," said Abra with a sigh.

After the tinsmith, they stopped at the cabinet maker and loaded a coffin onto it. By the time they got to Thomas' farm, Elizabeth had already bathed and dressed the body. Her face was strained and tear streaked. Jonathan had taken little Abraham out in the yard to keep him busy, and a neighbor was caring for little David as Elizabeth took care of her husband. A number of women were already in the kitchen quietly cooking and baking an assortment of pies and food and speaking in hushed voices. Abra and Aaron arrived and several men who were sitting outside picked up the coffin and carried it inside the house. It was Aaron and several of the men who lifted Thomas's body and placed it respectfully into the coffin. Abra looked at the face of his son and all the recently forgotten terrors that had held him captive during the war returned. He said a silent prayer, and then left the room to walk in the open air. He needed to be alone with his thoughts and his memories.

The following day Thomas' coffin was placed on the wagon and taken to the church which had been rebuilt. A small procession followed to the church. Abra remembered his old friend James Caldwell and his wife who had both lost their lives during the war. Abra was now a trustee of the church and he was certain James would have been proud of how quickly the people of Elizabethtown had worked together to rebuild their church, especially since so many had lost so much during the war. The tinsmith arrived and nailed the coffin plate to the lid of the coffin. Sarah and the family gathered around the coffin for a last look at Thomas. Elizabeth reached in and straightened his jacket. Sarah softly brushed his hair from his forehead. Abra patted Thomas' hands which had been neatly placed on his abdomen. The family stepped away and the lid was nailed into place. The mourners joined the family in the little church and a service was held in Thomas' memory. It was Abra who stood to share stories of Thomas's life. He included the tales of Thomas' upbringing, his marriage to Elizabeth, and the pride he had in his three sons who had fought in the Revolution. He then shared the stories that Thomas had told Abra after the war.

"My son, Thomas, was named after his grandfather, a man who I admired and loved. My son was the same kind of man. Thomas immediately sought officer training as soon as it became known that war with England was eminent. He was commissioned First Lieutenant, March 1, 1776 and then became First Lieutenant. As an officer he commanded detachments of his company stationed in Woodbridge from July to November, 1776; was at the Battle of Trenton, Dec. 26, 1776; at the Battle of Princeton, Jan. 3, 1777, where he succeeded Captain Neil, who fell. We all heard the story of how the Redcoats were holed up in Nassau Hall and young Alexander Hamilton was ordered to fire a six pound shot at the enemy. The cannonball went through the window and hit a portrait of King George II in the head, completely decapitating it. Thomas congratulated young Hamilton on his cheeky aim. Thomas' men praised him for his humor in an otherwise difficult time when the war was on our own New Jersey ground. Thomas later became Captain of Artillery in the Continental Army, Feb. 1, 1777, and was at the Battles of Brandywine, Germantown and Monmouth. He served as Captain of his own Company of Artillery in the Continental Army. He was then transferred to Whaleboat Service as leadership was needed in the naval battles happening at that time. Now, my son was an excellent horseman," said Abra. "He would travel up and down this entire countryside during his youth, and that proved a valuable trait as he was quickly called upon to be a scout for General Washington when it was told that Thomas was an excellent rider and he knew the countryside. Thomas' horse was rather persnickety, and no one else could handle him but Thomas. Thomas was taken prisoner while he was off scouting and accused of being a spy by the British. He was imprisoned and his friendly personality had him talking to the officer in charge of the prisoners. This man told Thomas that he was to be shot after a trial, and since this young man had taken a shine to Thomas, he helped create a plot for Thomas' escape. Because no one could handle Thomas' horse but him, Thomas was made to take care of all the horses by taking them daily to the Raritan River for water. The officer told Thomas to let his horse move away from him, and then he would distract the others while Thomas went to fetch the horse. Now the distraction did not last long and other British soldiers tried to pursue Thomas, but his horse was much faster. They opened fire on Thomas but only his head and the horse's head were sticking out of the water, so they weren't much of a target. Once they landed on the opposite shore, Thomas rode off to freedom.

"Now the second time Thomas was captured he was not so lucky. He was taken prisoner on the British ship, Jersey, which was just off Staten Island. When it was discovered that Thomas was my son, he was placed into the dungeon of the ship and tortured and starved. My other son, Andrew, was also on that ship, but his identify was not learned by the British. Andrew encouraged other prisoners to push bread through the keyhole so Thomas would have small portions of food. Thomas was made to write letters asking those of us in Congress to renege on our traitorous acts and become Tories. When General Washington was told about the treatment Thomas was getting, he quickly planned retaliation as gentlemen were not to behave so crassly, even in war. He threatened like treatment of a British officer, and soon the torture stopped.

"Thomas and Andrew were able to slip off the ship one night and swim to shore. The two split up and Thomas, who had been suffering ill health on the ship, decided he needed to return to Elizabeth. When the British discovered he was gone, they went in pursuit of him and traveled to our farm where Elizabeth was staying during the war. Thomas was hidden in the garret, and although the British searched the house against Sarah and Elizabeth's protests, they did not find him. Thomas stayed on with Elizabeth and his young son, Jonathan, until his health became stronger, and he left again to serve until the war was officially over even though his wife and his mother protested that he was not strong enough to go back to war. Thomas felt strongly that he needed to see the war come to a successful end.

"When Thomas returned home he was appointed Commissioner of Essex County and has done a fine job there, adjusting payrolls and settling issues of debt due the Militia and Troops who have been raised for the defense of the Frontiers of the State.

"Family and Country were Thomas's passions. A father could not be prouder of a son as I am of Thomas." Abra lowered his eyes, drew in a deep breath, and slowly took his seat. He held Sarah's hand as the reverend closed the funeral ceremony. Abra and Sarah followed after their son's coffin and watched as it was lowered into the family plot. Abra looked around the cemetery and there were many graves of boys and men who had fought in the Revolution. His son was at rest among these other heroes.

The sadness that Abra felt at the death of his son was compounded when Aaron announced that he was going to take advantage of securing some of the frontier land promised to Revolutionary War soldiers, and planned on moving into western Pennsylvania.

"Father, New Jersey holds too many bad memories of the war. I truly feel like my family needs a fresh start and I want to take advantage of the free land being offered by the government to soldiers," said Aaron.

"Your leaving will sadden your mother, however I completely understand, Aaron. Your family is young and this is an opportunity for you to make a real life for yourself. I understand how you feel about all the losses here. It is hard to look around without remembering how things were before this war scarred the face of our countryside. The cemetery by the church is a constant reminder of the price this family has paid. I know this is the best choice for you, but it will be difficult to see you leave," said Abra.

That evening Abra broke the news of Aaron's plan to Sarah. She sat with her sewing in her lap and made the motions of working on it, but Abra knew her heart was breaking. After she was able to compose herself she said, "At least we have Elizabeth and her boys to care for here. It saddens me so much to know those little boys will not remember their father. At least we can offer them a home and stability."

It was only a month later that Elizabeth announced that she was also going to travel and take the boys with her after Aaron and his family was settled. "Who will see you out there," asked Abra, for he did not feel Jonathan was old enough to protect his mother in travel.

"I will go with Jonas' family. They are related to my mother. He will watch over us as we follow after Aaron." Sarah bit her lip and found an excuse to enter the house to get something. Elizabeth started to follow her, but Abra stopped her.

"Let her be for a moment. She will take this hard. She

has come to love you like a daughter, and she had visions of watching your boys grow into young men. Sarah is the strongest woman I know and she will be all right. She just needs a few minutes alone to gather herself," said Abra.

Sarah knew that she would miss Aaron's children, and Thomas's children, but she also knew that the memories of the war held many victims. Sarah had confided in Abra her thoughts. "Thomas' illness was due mostly because of the fever he took while on the prison ship. He was never the same after that. Andrew came back angry. Thomas came back ill. And Aaron came back wanting to move away from the memories of war."

Abra looked at his wife and knew she was right. There was little they could do to dissuade them from leaving. Abra thought of the short burst of happiness he had felt after the war ended. It was momentary, but he knew that in dark days he would always treasure those times. If this was affecting him, he could only imagine how this was all weighing on Sarah. He looked at Sarah and saw her shoulders squared as she went about her work and her face was firmly fixed. Her strength gave all of the family courage.

Work with the New Jersey legislature kept Abra busy, but Abra wished he could be part of this first Congress as they put the wheels of government into motion. By the end of July Congress had already organized various departments of government like that which dealt with Foreign Affairs, Postmaster, and Treasury. By September Congress had put together the judicial branch as set up by the Federal Judiciary Act. Abra marveled at the plan to have federal cases start in a district court, then circuit court, then Supreme Court. Congress had done an excellent job in organizing the court system, which was of prime interest to Abra as he felt the common man needed to have a guaranteed means of appealing decisions if they were unfair.

What Abra was most interested in, however, was Congress' submission of twelve constitutional amendments. Abra had been very vocal on this matter, and had written numerous letters to James Madison, who had worked on the Constitution. Abra felt that the Constitution as it was originally written did not provide safeguards for the common man. Abra had pushed for the ratification of the Constitution knowing that once it was ratified, the states would begin to identify the problems and demand amendments. At first he was fearful that there would be no proposed amendments, however various states began to propose changes. "The wisdom of the states will soon seek to amend it in the exceptionable parts. The present plan must undergo some alterations to make it more agreeable to the minds of the great numbers who dislike it in its present form," said Abra. He was right. He urged Madison to draft amendments to protect the common man from the potential oppressiveness of government. Many had already voiced amendments protecting freedom of religion, speech and assembly. What Abra wanted were protections for the common man so things he had heard of during the war would not happen again. In New Jersey, many poor farmers were forced to quarter troops during the war, which they could ill afford to do. Abra did not want to see people suffer cruel and inhumane punishment. He had also fought long and hard against court cases taking too long to come to trial, and their protection to due process in the courts with a non-biased jury. He wanted this protection in the amendments. Abra still wanted to protect smaller states in the House of Representatives, and he wished for amendments which would allow for more representation in the House. Abra had also wanted to limit the amount of salary members of Congress could grant themselves. Abra knew that this issue was one of the reasons his political enemies had manipulated the election to keep him out, yet Abra stood firm in his conviction that governmental leaders should not take advantage of the poor through increasing their own salaries. These were among the amendments Abra asked James Madison to consider.

Abra's mind was put at ease when he learned that James Madison did take his advice and proposed twelve constitutional amendments on September 25th. Abra felt his efforts were justified by the proposed amendments. Now the difficult part would follow, getting all the states to ratify the proposed amendments. Abra knew his political enemies would not want to see the House Representatives amendment and the salary issue become law. Abra hoped that he would be elected the following term to return to Congress where he knew he would be committed to getting the twelve proposed amendments ratified.

During 1790 Abra continued to work on the finance committee. He continued to be included in communications as to the progress of Congress. When he learned that Ben Franklin died in April, it was too late to attend the funeral. When Abra heard that there had been over 20,000 mourners, it did not surprise him. "20,000 people, Abra? How could that be?" asked Sarah.

"He was a man of so many talents," said Abra. "He was one of the founding fathers of this country, and a man who used his wit and humor to calm men when tempers were at their worse. He never stopped. He could be listening to a most detailed report, yet be working on a drawing of something he invented, or factoring a computation for a financial argument. He was a printer, a writer, a diplomat, and a musician. There were few like him. He was an extraordinary man! I was very blessed to have known him. I will always admire the work he did in keeping those of us in Congress on course."

"At least he lived a long life," said Sarah. "I should think that at 84 he had a very satisfying life."

"I'd imagine if he lived another twenty years he'd have continued living a remarkable life," said Abra sadly thinking to himself that it was unlikely he would ever meet anyone like Franklin again.

As the year came to a close, Abra campaigned to be a member of the House of Representatives, and this time he won.

# Chapter 24
## *1791-1794*

**Sarah said her goodbyes** to Abra as he left Elizabethtown for Philadelphia. Abra would be a member of the House of Representatives as of March, 1791. His political enemies had kept him out of the first Congress; however it was known that Abra was a fair and just man who maintained his values and beliefs. Abra was excited to be part of the forming of the new government. The main work of the House was the ratification of the amendments to the Constitution. Abra's stand on the twelve proposed amendments was clear to everyone.

Abra had communicated at length with James Madison throughout his absence from Philadelphia about the need for such amendments and fully supported Madison's proposal. Two of the amendments, however, continued to cause major debates in both the Upper and Lower Houses of Congress. The number of representatives in the House continued to be a sore spot for Abra as he felt smaller states would have less influence and this could cause legislation to be favored for larger states.

The other issue of an amendment against Congress voting raises for themselves also met disfavor. Abra spent much of his time in meetings trying to push for the ratification of all twelve amendments, however in the end, only ten were accepted. Most of the work done in 1791 was on the ratification of the Bill of Rights, as the amendments were being called. These ten were ratified on December 15th of 1791 and Abra was relieved that the rights of the people had been protected. New Jersey was the first state to ratify the amendments because of Abra's support.

Abra felt his work had been justified as the Bill of Rights would protect the common man from big government and the potential of the country becoming one ruled by aristocrats. Of all the men who had been involved in the Declaration of Independence, and the writing of the Constitution, and the creation of the Bill of Rights, it was Abra who best represented the common man. He did not come from a family of wealth. He did not take on the pretentiousness many of the men did as they became part of the government. Abra had not sacrificed his ethics or his values throughout his tenure in government. As such, he had made enemies throughout the years, but as men looked at Abra's service, even his enemies had to agree that they knew where Abra stood on any given issue. He was never to be bribed or persuaded on any issue. His commitment to the ordinary citizen stood solid.

After a brief visit home during the holiday season, Abra

returned again to Philadelphia. President Washington had addressed Congress last year in a formal summation, or state of the union. When President Washington addressed Congress on January 8th 1792 for the Second Congress, he outlined some of the successes the United States had accomplished. The financial progress included the successful First Bank of the United States. There was also the excise tax which was placed on distilled alcohol. The government had also secured another loan from Holland to establish itself. Washington also discussed the foreign and domestic debt issues. Government issued bonds that had been sold in order to help pay for the debts of the Revolutionary War and Washington was pleased, as was Abra. All these financial decisions were necessary in order to keep the business of government and unification strong.

Among the issues which Washington felt needed attention was the rising problem with the numerous Indian tribes in the new territories. Although they had tried peaceful treaties, there had been incidents of broken treaties and the government issued retaliatory action. Security in the western frontier was of utmost importance as settling of land and development of this land was a way to guarantee financial stability for the country. States were also to not acquire land from Indians without federal approval through the US Trade and Intercourse Act. Abra was especially worried about the Indian business as Aaron was now on land where Indians often frequented. Also, the last Abra had heard of Andrew, he was moving among Indians in western New York. Abra had no real contact with Indians as they had last been in New Jersey before he was born, so he was uncertain how this government would deal with them as a people. Abra's only real involvement with Indians had been during the war when he followed the reports of the various tribes helping the British.

The final announcement was that President Washington was developing a District of Columbia, which would eventually become the capitol of the country. A sense of pride was felt by everyone when they learned of Washington's plans. The District of Columbia would be a well planned and executed city where government buildings, memorials, and public parks would be established in a manner that would build pride and confidence among all citizens.

The 1790 census report was returned to Congress and the results were very informative. They learned that there were 3,929,214 Americans, with Virginia having the largest population with 691,727. 19% of the population was African Americans, and of those 90% lived in the Southern states. Native Americans were not counted however it was believed that there were eighty tribes with 150,000 people. The average birth rate of a white family was eight children born. The average age of white Americans was sixteen years. The largest American city was Philadelphia with 42,000 persons, New York with 33,000, Boston with 18,000, Charleston with

16,000 and Baltimore with 13,000. Most Americans were involved in agricultural pursuits. It was also discovered that the center of population was approximately 23 miles west of Baltimore, Maryland, which made it reasonable that the capitol of the country be located here.

1792 was an exciting year for Abra as he watched the work they had done on the Constitution taking form. Although he was happy with the way the government was forming, he felt tired and found he needed more rest. Abra had noticed the change when Thomas had died, yet he pushed himself forward to continue his work. He reasoned to himself that the stresses at home were far worse during the war when the safety of his wife and children was unknown to him and was a constant state of worry for him. Now his family was grown, Sarah was safe at home, and he was no longer looking over his shoulder in fear of retaliation from the British, yet Abra knew he was not feeling as energetic as he had before.

1792 brought many exciting additions to the government and to the country. The United States Post Office was established in February, the United States Mint in April, the United States Military Draft in May, and the New York Stock Exchange was established in May.

Abra continued to serve on finance committees, as that was his expertise. The government had proposed a manner of using force to implement tax collection. It was Abra who worked tirelessly to block this strategy. "We must remember that the average American does not have the resources to pay taxes which are levied by those moneyed men who are very industrious in creating laws and systems which place the burden of financing government on those who can least afford it. If we do not break this cycle of 'lords and tenants' which our ancestors used to their advantage and to the disadvantage of those who came to this country for a fresh start, we will see an unchecked spiral of economic hardship. To not break this cycle would leave the average American to lose their political freedom to wealthier ones who controlled their economic destiny. We fought a war to rid ourselves of that mentality. Let us not revisit it. Let us not perpetuate both government and aristocracy," Abra said rather forcefully in the committee meetings designed to finance government. Abra, although not typical of the representatives who came to Congress, was respected for his never changing stand of equality for those he felt he represented. In the end, Abra's dogged passion persuaded others to change their tactics.

By October, the U.S. Executive Mansion was begun in the new District of Columbia, being built by freemasons. It was to become the home of the President of the country. Abra's interest in serving the government continued and he was once again elected to the House for a second two year term.

In November, George Washington was once again elected as President of the United States. Although he had resisted a second term, he again agreed in an effort to guarantee that political parties would not divide the foundation which had been established. Although Washington did not believe in political parties, nor ever joined one, he was considered a Federalist, and as such he believed that there needed to be a strong central government. While Abra approved of Washington as a president, he was a Republican as he continued to support the individual rights of the common man.

Abra returned to the House of Representatives in 1793 to face an issue which made him question his own values. John Davis, a runaway slave had been kidnapped from Pennsylvania by three Virginians. The case was brought to the attention of Congress as Pennsylvania's governor, Thomas Mifflin, wanted to extradite the three men who had kidnapped Davis. Beverly Randolf, Virginia's governor, had refused. Congress then had to debate the issue of compliance of interstate laws. The issue of slavery was solidly wrapped into this debate, and the states which supported slavery were vocal and demanding the passage of a Fugitive Slave Act whereas runaway slaves would be returned to their rightful owners. All four New Jersey Congressmen, Alias Boundinot, Jonathan Dayton, Aaron Kitchell, and Abra, were against slavery and protectors of free Blacks. Although Jonathan Dayton had proposed legislation to protect free Blacks, his proposal did not pass. In the end, all four New Jersey Congressmen voted for the Fugitive Slave Act as it gave recognition of state's property rights, including slaves who were considered property.

Abra struggled with this legislation, as he saw the potential for abuse in the future. He also struggled with the equality of man and the fact that slavery went against equality. Yet, he had three slaves. When he was home he talked with Sarah about their slaves.

"You know that I feel hypocritical in my supporting the Fugitive Slave Act. I must admit I see problems with the legislation as it stands. I am always announcing my belief that all people need to be treated equally, yet I have three slaves."

"Abra, you certainly have never mistreated Tillie or her sons. In fact, Tillie says it was her luckiest day when they landed on our farm," said Sarah.

"Lucky. How is knowing you are owned by another human being lucky," said Abra.

"You have treated Tillie and the boys fairly. You never treated them like property. You've given them a portion of land to farm and to sell their produce for their own profit," reminded Sarah.

"And I have it in my will to release them once you pass away. It had only been my intention to give you the help you needed while I was away," said Abra.

"We have talked of this before, Abra. Look at the number of New Jersey farmers who have slaves. Most are good men, but we have heard tell of some who abuse their people."

"Sarah, I succumbed to the social habits when I bought Tillie and her boys. It was a way to give you help in my absence during the war, and even now when I am away. I also have a problem with this legislation which I did, indeed, vote for. Yes, we need to allow each state to have its own laws, despite our not agreeing with them. Big government tells everyone what they can and cannot do, and I am against that kind of government. I voted for it because it allows each state to have their own laws, even if I don't agree with them. Yet, with this legislation, I am predicting there can be those who would abuse the free Negroes. Let's say Tillie is free and she moves to Pennsylvania where there is no slavery. What if someone gathers her up and sells her back into slavery under the guise of returning a fugitive slave? What if she is split from her boys, and they are abused?"

"I would not want that to happen, Abra. Yet I understand how you feel about Tillie and the idea that you 'own' her and her sons. I don't think of her as a slave."

"Thinking or not, it is so. I am a hypocrite to say it is acceptable to own Tillie because it suits my needs. Yet, now I am fearful that we have created the means for lawless men to take advantage of those Negroes who are free. Add to this problem that if a slave is a fugitive, they are considered that for life, and if they have children, their children can never be considered free. There is something drastically wrong with this institution." Abra continued to fret over these issues, knowing there would be no easy answer.

Abra found that his work in the House was very rewarding

as things were happening at an alarmingly fast rate. It was exciting to be part of the decision making process and to witness the many changes occurring. One of the highlights of 1793 was when George Washington officiated at the cornerstone-setting of the U. S. Capitol. The ceremony featured many Masonic rites, and those gathered were thrilled that the new capital of the country was taking shape both legally and physically.

All was not happy, however. 1793 was to turn into a year which potentially could destroy the country. The French Revolution had begun, and Great Britain joined the coalition against France. The United States was trading with both England and France, and had declared neutrality in the matter. When the Royal Navy seized American ships, Americans reacted by demanding war with Great Britain. Washington knew that entering into another war had the potential to destroy the United States. He immediately sought a plan to put an end to the English aggression. Abra had it in mind to present legislation, however his health began to be an issue.

The spring of 1793 was very wet, and many mosquitoes bred in Philadelphia. In August, a group of refugees from Haiti arrived, and many were sick. Within the next several months an epidemic arose in Philadelphia, which was the largest city in the United States. The fever began to spread, and the symptoms were recognized by everyone. On September 7th, government had to be shut down because of the epidemic. Many came down with the strange disease called Yellow Fever, including Abra.

As Abra left Philadelphia and was traveling home, he began burning with fever. He was unable to keep food down and when he vomited, a black color was seen. Sarah quickly sent for the doctor, and Abra was quarantined in the house. The doctor had Sarah give Abra cool baths. She fed him watered soup and bites of bread. The doctor reassured Sarah that Abra's skin had not yellowed, so she was hopeful he would recuperate. He did, however Abra was left very weak. As the year ended, Abra slowly regained some of his strength, but never completely. As 1794 approached, Abra told Sarah that it was necessary for him to return to Philadelphia. He was fearful that another war with Great Britain would result unless Congress was able to stop it. Reluctantly, Sarah packed Abra's belongings and watched him as he left after promising he would take frequent rests and eat regular and healthy meals. She prayed he would regain his strength.

When Abra returned to the House in March, they began making up for time lost due to the epidemic. Many did not return to Philadelphia. Whole families had left the city; however President Washington was in the city and working hard to restore confidence in the city and the government. Although Abra returned ready for the work that needed to be done, physically he was weak and tired yet he did not let this hinder his determination.

The emotions of the country were obvious and Congress was faced with immediately handling the problem with Great Britain. On March 27th, Jonathan Dayton made a motion to sequester all debts due to British subjects in order to pay back Americans who had trade lost by the seizing of their ships and cargo by Great Britain. Abra, who typically refrained from political debate interruptions, stood up. "Gentlemen. With respect to Mr. Dayton, I put forth on the floor the resolution that we suspend, for a time, all commercial regulations and prohibit all trade with Great Britain until they made full compensation to our citizens for the injuries received from British armed vessels and until the western posts should be delivered up." Debates then followed on both propositions brought forth from the New Jersey Congressmen.

President Washington wanted to send an envoy to Great Britain, and asked Alexander Hamilton to do this. Hamilton asked for someone else to go, and John Jay was selected on April 16th to adjust the difficulties between the two countries. Abra's proposal then became the subject of debate. Those against said that because Jay was to try to build a treaty with England, Abra's proposal would be an obstacle as the language was menacing and would be received with indignation. Jay would be there to negotiate and language such as what Clark had suggested would limit Jay's ability to negotiate.

Those for the proposal stated that it was within the duty of the legislature to regulate commerce. Abra's resolution was voted upon and passed the House by a majority. However on the 28th of April it was defeated in the Senate by one vote, that of Vice President John Adams. John Jay did leave to negotiate a treaty with Great Britain in order to avert a possible war.

Congress adjourned on June 9, 1794, and Abra, exhausted and weak, retired from public life.

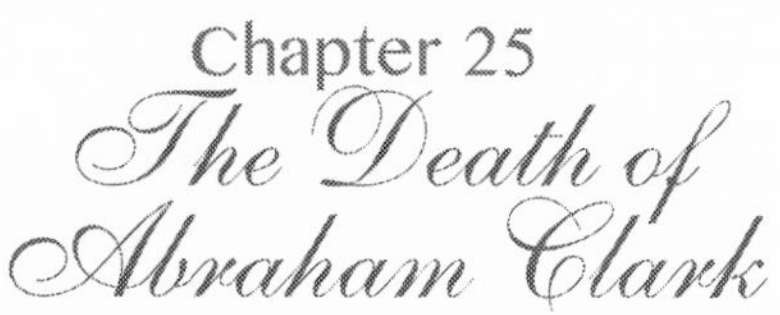

# Chapter 25
# The Death of Abraham Clark

**A tired and weak Abraham Clark** returned to Elizabethtown at the end of June, 1794. When he arrived he caught Sarah unawares. She was in the kitchen rolling out pie dough and one of her grandchildren was pushing her fingers into the dough. Sarah looked up, saw Abra standing in the doorway and dropped her rolling pin and ran to the doorway.

"Did you do it?" she asked.

"Yes. I put in my resignation, although Sarah, I have such mixed emotions about it."

Sarah stood by his side and reassured him that he had served his country well. It was time for others to pick up the hard work at hand. "Abra, you have made certain that the foundation of our government has rights guaranteed to all men. You need to be proud of the role you have played."

"Sarah, there is still so much more to do. Yes, the Bill of Rights certainly protects those who cannot protect themselves, but there is still such inequity in this nation. Just look at slavery. I am part of that problem."

"Abraham Clark. We have discussed this before. If you are indeed this upset, then let's put an end to our ownership."

"I understand that slavery is part of our society. That does not make it right. I have fought all these years against inequities among the white population. Who needs protection more than these slaves? The Fugitive Slave Act will further jeopardize the slave population. Should they be given freedom, there will be those who will take advantage of the Fugitive Slave Act and capture those who already have their freedom, and resell them in states which will accept such trade. How is that free? I've written in my will that Tillie and her boys will eventually have their freedom. I should be heartless to think that their future might be that they would be resold under this Act and placed in a position where they would never have hope."

"Abra, you cannot solve all problems. It is time for others to take up the cause. You can still write your letters, just as you did for the amendments you wanted added to the Constitution. Your influence certainly made a difference there. Madison took your ideas and placed them into his proposed amendments. You can fight this fight, but at home, and through letters. Besides, Mr. Clark, I have not had the pleasure of your company for very long throughout our lives together. You have always been off surveying, or legislating.

Perhaps it is time for you to be retired, and oversee this farm." Sarah wrapped her arms around Abra's shoulders.

Abra faced Sarah and looked into her eyes. "Mrs. Clark, you are right. It is time to retire. There is still much work to be done, but I cannot justify keeping my position in the House and not being in attendance."

Sarah slid her arm through his and walked with him to sit in one of the kitchen chairs. The grandchild looked at Abra and cried. "She doesn't know you, Abra," said Sarah. Sarah scooped the child into her arms and bounced her while the little girl held tightly around the neck, her lower lip pouting and her eyes looking suspiciously at Abra. Sarah sat across from her husband and looked into his face. He looked older than when she saw him last. His eyes were tired and his shoulders were drawn forward. "Abra, it was time. You have worn yourself out with all the work you have done."

"Perhaps you are right. Perhaps it is time I put in my time as husband, father, grandfather, and farmer," chuckled Abra. "Would you be offended if I just went off to take a short nap" asked Abra.

"Certainly not," said Sarah. She walked with Abra and helped him pull off his boots and she pulled back the quilt on the bed. Abra lowered his head to the pillows and took a deep breath.

"Just a short nap, Sarah. It was a long ride today." His eyes were closed and his breathing was soon regular and deep.

Sarah stepped out of the room, and summoned the little girl who was peaking in at the strange man.

When Abra awoke it was early afternoon. He came to the kitchen and he could see Sarah outside in the small garden. Tillie was with her and the two were planting something. Abra sat and watched the two for a few minutes, then poured himself a glass of water and cut himself a slice of bread from the loaf under the cloth.

Sarah looked toward the house and she could see Abra sitting at the table. She quickly wiped her hands and came into the house. "How are you feeling? You slept all day."

"Should have wakened me," said Abra.

"No, you needed your rest. It will do you good. Are you up for walking around the farm a bit?" asked Sarah.

"Certainly. I need to adjust to my new lifestyle, and now is as good a time as any," laughed Abra.

The two walked around the property. Abra stopped often to stretch and look up into the sky. "You'd better wear a hat, Abra. You are not used to standing outdoors and the sun will certainly burn you," said Sarah.

"You're right," said Abra. "I think I've spent the majority of my life at a desk, or at a table but mostly indoors. I don't think I've been outside this much since the days I did surveying work," he laughed. "I think it actually feels rather good."

The two talked about the farm, the crops, the church, and the neighbors. They talked about the children and letters which Sarah had received from Aaron. "You know Elizabeth took the oldest, Jonathan, to Maryland to live with relatives out there. She left young Abraham and David with Aaron on the farm in Pennsylvania. They've been there since 1790. I'm rather surprised that she hasn't come to get the children, although I think Aaron has done well with the boys. Poor David didn't even know his father," said Sarah as her eyes welled as they typically did when she spoke of Thomas.

"I noticed we need a new bridge put in over the creek. I think I am going to get that taken care of soon," said Abra as he wanted to get himself focused on the farm and making himself useful.

"No hurry," said Sarah. "However it would be wonderful to have that done as it would save a considerable amount of time when traveling north."

The two spent hours talking, and that evening several local men came to visit. Abra was now sixty nine years old. When the men began talking politics, his face lit and he became quite animated. Sarah knew that he would continue to miss Philadelphia, but she was happy he was home at last. She studied his face and posture and thought that the yellow fever had left him a bit frailer, but his face was still lively, as was his voice when he talked.

Summer passed quietly on the Clark farm, and Abra, who was not accustomed to being home during the summer months, found that he enjoyed his routine. It was now

September, and it was a hot Indian summer day. Abra had spent the day working in the vegetable garden, and chopping a bit of wood for Sarah's fire. When his cousin and his wife arrived, Susan decided to take the wagon home after visiting with Sarah. Abra promised to take William home after dinner. Abra and William talked about the bridge Abra had built which was about to be completed. The two decided to inspect the work, and got into a wagon and drove to the northern part of the farm. Abra complained that he felt clammy and was thirsty and he should have taken a bucket of water out with them to the bridge. The hired hands had finished the bridge, and Abra wanted to finish the railing leading to the bridge. The two men worked for about an hour and Abra began to feel nauseous. "Abra, you all right?" asked William.

"Yes. I just think I have gotten overheated," said Abra as he wiped his brow with the back of his hand. "I think I need to give it a rest today. I'll drive you home, and then get back to my place. I am really not feeling too well."

"Abra, if you aren't feeling well, I'll just ride back to your place and borrow one of your horses to ride back home."

"No, no. We are already half way to your place anyway. It's really no trouble. I just think I overdid it today," said Abra, again wiping his brow.

The two climbed into the wagon and Abra took the reins and headed the wagon toward his cousin's home. William talked about family, the church, and the dryness of the soil on the farm, but Abra only responded to about half of what was said. Once they got to William's farm, William jumped off the wagon and invited Abra in for some dinner. "Maybe you just need to eat something, Abra. That'll shake it off."

"No. I'll take a bit of water, but I think it best that I just head on home." William gathered a ladle of water from the pump and Abra drank it, but he swallowed too fast and his stomach turned.

"I think I'd better just head on home right now," said Abra. "Tell the wife we will get together for dinner soon." Abra waved goodbye and pulled the reins to turn the horse back in the direction of the Clark farm. The entire time the feeling of nausea was strong, and his skin felt clammy to the touch. About a quarter mile from the Clark farm, Abra's body seized and he slumped in the wagon. When he came to, he slowly picked up the reigns and managed to get the horse to continue the path home. By the time Abra pulled into the yard in front of the Clark house, he could barely hold himself up. His head was spinning and his muscles ached. Sarah came out of the house and knew immediately that Abra was ill. She helped him off the wagon and walked him into the house and to the bed. Abra collapsed immediately onto the bed and Sarah ran to fetch cloths and a basin of water. She dipped the cloths into the water and soothed the cloths onto Abra's face, temples and neck. "Abra. How long has this been going on?" she asked. Abra shook his head with a slight motion and closed his eyes.

William and Susan came to the door and called in to Sarah. Sarah told them to come to the bedroom. "What's wrong? William told me Abra was not feeling well, and we got so worried we packed up and followed back here," said Susan.

"I think maybe he's had heatstroke," said Sarah. "William, can you fetch the doctor?"

William left immediately and Susan stayed to help Sarah in any way she could. Sarah called Abra's name quietly, but he did not respond. She continued to wipe his skin with the cool cloths, and tried to awaken him to drink some water, but Abra did not respond. Before William arrived back with the doctor, Abra took his last breath. Sarah sat quietly at his side, holding his hand and silently weeping. Susan entered the room and recognized that Abra had passed and she placed her hands on Sarah's shoulders. "I'm so sorry, Sarah."

"I had him so little to myself," said Sarah. "I only had him a couple of months to myself without planning his next trip to government. I just think he wore himself out. All the years of worrying about us, worrying about the war, worrying about this country. I just think all that worrying took away his strength."

"Had he come directly home instead of insisting on driving William home, he could have gotten out of the sun and cooled his body down," said Susan. "He was a good man, Sarah."

"The best," said Sarah. She stood and leaned over the bed and kissed Abra's forehead. "The best," she said again as she openly wept.

Sarah sent letters to Aaron and to Thomas' wife, Elizabeth, knowing that they would not arrive in time for the funeral. She handled business just as she had all the years Abra had been off in government. The funeral service was held in their church, and the small Presbyterian Church was filled to capacity.

The eulogy was given by his son, Abraham, who outlined the many roles Abra had played in his life. "Abraham Clark, my father, started as a surveyor, then country lawyer, often taking food or trade for his services. He was a pious man, and believed strongly in his faith, and was a trustee of the church. My father had written us when the war began saying, 'Our fates are in the hands of An Almighty God, to whom I can with pleasure confide my own; he can save us, or destroy us; his Councils are fixed and cannot be disappointed, and all his designs will be Accomplished.' His words reflect his deep commitment the God, and to the work he chose to do for this country. When he was called to serve his country, he did so willingly, and set his name to the Declaration of Independence which made him a traitor to Great Britain, but a hero to those who were now enjoying the benefits of a new country and government. Abra had served in the state legislature and in Congress, sacrificing the comforts of family and home in order to serve the greater good of the people of this country. Never once did he use his position to his advantage, even when his own sons were imprisoned during the war. He told those who pressed him to use his office to manipulate a favorable outcome for his sons that others had children in the war, and their parents had no recourse to improve their position, so he could not do that. My father had been instrumental in guaranteeing the newly written Constitution contained a bill of rights which protected the common man, something he valued as being one of the most important contributions he has made on this earth. Throughout his years of service, Abraham Clark never took on the airs of the affluent, but identified with the common man. He was not ambitious of personal wealth or gain. He had argued fearlessly on issues which would benefit Americans and protect them from those who used their affluence to oppress others. Above all, Abraham Clark was known for his passion for liberty and equality. I will miss my father, as will my siblings and our families. I know that my mother will never fill the void of his loss. I also know that this country will miss his calm and dedicated service which helped make us a free and independent nation."

As Abraham took his seat next to his mother, he enfolded Sarah in his arms, and she looked into his face and smiled with tear streaked face.

Abra was buried next to his sons, Cavalier and Thomas, and daughter Elizabeth. Not far away was the grave of his father and uncle, and of his good friend, Reverend Caldwell. "He is now among those who he loved in this life and had gone before him," said Sarah as she touched the coffin plate before the coffin was lowered into the ground. Abra's children, Abigail, Abraham, Hannah and Sarah were able to be at the service, and offered their mother the support she needed to let Abra go.

The obituary posted in the New Jersey Journal on September 17, 1794, was proudly read to the family as they gathered after the funeral was over. Sarah read aloud the words printed:

*On Monday last, very suddenly, the Hon. Abraham Clark, Esq. member from this State, to the Congress of the United States, in the 69th year of his age. In the death of Mr. Clark, his Family has sustained an irretrievable loss, and the state is deprived of a useful citizen, who, for forty years past, has been employed in the most honorable and confidential trusts, which he ever charged with the disinterestedness, ability, and indefatigable industry, that rebounded much to his popularity; indeed it may be said of him, that he was a person from his youth, with whom the amor patriae piedonerated every other consideration. It could not be expected that such a character would pass unnoticed by the jaundiced eye of envy and faction, which was really the café' with the deceased, but his conduct was so unequivocally upright, that the unvenomed shafts of envy could never remove him from the confidence of the people, or shake his popularity.*

*Mr. Clark was a man of sound judgment, lively wit, and*

*very satirical; in the exercise of which he made sometimes enemies.—As a Christian, he was uniform and consistent, adorning that religion that he had early made a profession of, by acts of charity and benevolence.*

Sarah sighed as she read the words. She studied the print for a moment more, then dropped the newspaper and looked around the table at her family gathered there. “Abra certainly made his share of enemies while fighting for the rights of those who could not defend themselves. I truly believe that if he is to be remembered, it will be for his fair mindedness in protecting all men, and his non-ending love for our country. I will miss him.” Sarah looked across the table at her children and her grandchildren gathered there. “I would expect each of you to honor Abra and live your lives in a manner which would make him proud.” Even the youngest of the grandchildren looked at Sarah and nodded his head in understanding.

For months after the funeral, Sarah received numerous letters from the many people who Abra touched with his loyal and dedicated patriotism. Even the President wrote Sarah a kind letter stating that Abra was indeed one of the dedicated and valued founders of this great country.

Years later a marble slab was erected on the place where Abra was buried. The following inscription sums up the life of Abraham Clark.

## A Founder For All

Firm and decided as a patriot,
Zealous and faithful as a friend to the public,
He loved his country,
And adhered to her cause
In the darkest hours of her struggles
Against oppression.

# Acknowledgments

Family has always been important to me. I became interested in genealogy from the time I was in high school, and I had penned out a simplistic family tree focusing only on my grandparents, aunts, uncles and cousins. It was not until I became a parent that I began to search for more family ties, looking back into past generations. My mother had always told us that our great, great, etc. grandfather, Abraham Clark, had signed the Declaration of Independence. I had great pride in that story; however I never had the family tree or documentation to make that a meaningful family connection. It wasn't until I began using the Internet that I discovered I could find more genealogical information. My cousin, Dennis Clark, had already organized much of the family tree and had sparked my interest in doing even more research. What I found was a tangled web of name changes and inconsistencies, as well as many dead ends as I tried to make sense of the involved Clark family tree. What I learned was that Abraham Clark had many children, but only a few families can actually trace back directly to him as few of his children had children of their own.

Whether I can ever prove the missing links between myself and Abraham Clark is yet unknown. I have a gut feeling that I may never find what I seek. However, Abraham Clark is certainly in my blood because I have learned so much about him and respect the things that he did in his lifetime. We all know the major players of the Revolutionary War. We learned their names and the names of so many of the battles. But, there is so much more. Heroes, like Abraham Clark, will help us color our historical roots for more than mere names, dates and places read in our history books. Abraham Clark's life has fascinated me. I have found similarities in our lives and values. If these traits can be passed down from one generation to another, then I am certain I have inherited some of those very same qualities that Abraham possessed.

Despite my uncertainty in being able to directly prove lineage, this experience has helped me in sharing family stories with all my extended family. This book will be a testament to my maternal family, as well as to all Americans. Abraham Clark may or may not be my great, great, etc. grandfather, but I am proud to say he is certainly my American Forefather!

I thank my husband, Michael, for his support in my investigations and discoveries, and his growing interest in our family genealogies. To my children, Mike and Mark, this book is a gift of love so they will honor their roots. To my cousin,

Dennis Clark, I thank you for inspiring me to further search our family roots. To John Gurnish, colleague and historical expert, I thank you for your dedicated editing of this novel. To Sarah Hamlin, thank you for your careful and thorough proofreading and enthusiastic feedback. To former student and now consultant, Dale Pease, I thank you for your artwork and technology and networking support.

# About the Author

Barb Baltrinic is a Kent State University M.Ed. graduate; a 35 year classroom teacher in the Akron Public Schools, and presently a full-time liaison for The University of Akron. She is a National Board Certified Teacher; has spoken at many state and national conferences; 17 published articles in educational magazines; national, state and local education award winner. She is the wife of Michael Baltrinic, a former teacher, and mother to two grown sons, Mike and Mark.

# Historical Background

Thomas Clarke and his wife, Elizabeth Gosslinge Clark, lived in Bradford and Brohme, respectively, in Suffolk County, England in the early 1600's. The gentle, rolling hills and farms were home to them. Their son, Richard married Ann Winston of Belton, England, in 1639, and they too farmed.

Their son, Richard Clarke II, decided to relocate, first to the Barbados in 1634, and then immigrate to Southold, Long Island, New York in 1651. He met and married Elizabeth Moore of Salem, Massachusetts. Richard had been a shipbuilder, but decided to return to his roots of farming. The young family left New York for the quiet of Elizabethtown, New Jersey in 1678. They bought a large tract of property on the Upper Easter Road, about halfway between Rahway and Elizabethtown. The vegetables they raised were sold in Elizabethtown. Elizabeth and Richard had seven sons and a daughter. The children all adapted well to the quiet New Jersey farm area. The boys, (Thomas, Richard, John, Joshua, Samuel, Ephriam and Benjamin) and daughter (Elizabeth) made Elizabethtown their home and settled in the area when each became of age.

Richard and Elizabeth's oldest son, Thomas, became a yeoman, a man who owned his own small farm, and he took great pride in farming it. Thomas married Hannah Norris and the young couple had four sons: Thomas Jr., Abraham, Daniel and James.

It was Thomas Jr. who really enjoyed the life of farming. He obtained a small piece of land and then married, Hannah Winans and began his own family. The couple loved their lives as small farmers. Because of Thomas' reputation of fairness among the Elizabethtown area, Thomas was called upon to be an alderman. Thomas Jr. and Hannah only had one child, a son, who was born on the Elizabethtown, New Jersey farm. He was named after Thomas' brother, who Thomas greatly admired. Abraham was a captain in the military, and represented a fine example of political leadership in Thomas' mind. His son, born on February 15, 1726, was named Abraham Clark. Young Abraham couldn't have had better mentors than his uncle and his father. His uncle was a well-known military man who was well respected among the people of Elizabethtown. His father, Thomas, was known not only as a farmer, but as a local magistrate.

Little did Thomas know that the skirmishes and political unrests which were reaching concern in 1765 would bring about a change not only in the colonies, but a change for his son, Abraham Clark. Both Thomas and his brother Abraham died on the same day, September 11, 1765, and they were buried next to one another in the small Rahway Cemetery. Neither Thomas nor Hannah would live to see the difference their son, Abraham, would make in the world. In the fall of 1765 it became evident that trouble was brewing between England and the colonies.

Made in the USA
Charleston, SC
27 September 2013